TIME PLAGUE

Kim Megahee

The Kimmer Group

GAINESVILLE, GEORGIA

Mark,

Hope you enjoy it!

Martha says it's my best work!

Cheers,

K

The Kimmer Group, LLC
Gainesville, GA 30506
info@AuthorKimMegahee.com

Publisher's Note: This is a work of fiction. Names, characters, places, and incidents are a product of the author's imagination. Locales and public names are sometimes used for atmospheric purposes. Any resemblance to actual people, living or dead, or to businesses, companies, events, institutions, or locales is completely coincidental.

Book Layout © 2017 BookDesignTemplates.com

Time Plague/ Kim Megahee. -- 1st ed.
ISBN 978-1-7340190-6-3

Cover Design By
Aleaca / 99Designs.com
Vesna Tišma

Cast of Characters

Character	Role
638	An Operative from the year 2086
Dr. Robert Astalos	The inventor/discoverer of time travel.
Dr. Robby Astalos	Younger self of Robert Astalos.
Addison Crumpton	Wanda Taylor's VP.
Lt. Ed Cutty	New member of the HERO Team.
Avery Detweiler	President Taylor's Chief of Staff.
Gen. Mike Drake	Retired US Army Ranger General. Drake is the liaison between the HERO Team and the President of the United States
Detective Trevor George	Civilian on the HERO Team. Formerly a cold case detective with the Atlanta Police Department.
President-Elect Wade Harrison	Winner of the 2036 election.
Lt. Karen Hatcher	HERO Team Member.
HERO	An acronym. "Historical Event Research Organization."
Lt. Daisy Lagunas	New member of the HERO Team.
Senator James C. Lodge	Leads the HERO Team's Congressional oversight committee.
Megan McAllister	McKnight's live-in girlfriend.
Janie McKnight	Marc McKnight's sister.

Character	Role
Col. John McKnight	Marc McKnight's father; Assassinated in 2012 in Paris
Maj. Marc McKnight	The operational lead of the HERO Team.
Maj. Rachel Patterson	Renegade U.S. Army Ranger Major; held McKnight's job in the year 2086; captured by Marc McKnight and incarcerated in 2036
Dr. Pritchard	Expert in infectious diseases at the CDC in Atlanta
#3 / Laura Rand	Senior advisor to President in 2086
David Ritter	Senior agent in the Washington D.C. Office of the FBI.
Arthur Smalls	A CIA Agent
Maj. Sheila Souther	Commanding officer of the Iceberg Detention Center.
#4 / Oliver Stagne	Senior diplomat in the State Department in 2086.
President Wanda Taylor	President of the United States
Sarah Tyler	Captain Tyler's wife.
Capt. Winston Tyler III	The Executive Officer and Mission Planner for the HERO Team
Lt. Mitch Wheeler	HERO Team Member.
Dr. Kathy Wu	Civilian. Mission Planner for the HERO Team.

CHAPTER ONE

Sunday, December 22nd, 2086 - 2:00 PM, Manassas Battlefield Park, Manassas, Virginia

Major Marc McKnight landed in the open field as planned. It was cold and looked like snow.

He stood and turned in a circle for his 360 scan. He hoped he would see signs of activity, any hint of human life.

As far as he could tell, there was no one left alive on the planet.

Except for his team. Lieutenant Hatcher stood ten feet from him. She was executing her 360 scan. When she finished, he glanced at her and their eyes met. In Hatcher's eyes he saw no fear, but he did see despair and disappointment.

"You were correct, sir," she said.

McKnight grunted.

God, I hate being right about stuff like this.

Hatcher was his best warrior, but there was no need for fighting here. So far, they saw no one. Not at Telegraph Road. And not here.

"Let's get out of the way, Lieutenant. Tyler and Wheeler will return any time now."

They gathered up the gear and samples they brought with them from Telegraph Road and moved twenty yards north of the landing position.

The mission was successful. They did their job. He remembered the familiar saying: "The operation was a success, but the patient died."

I don't think this is what the President had in mind.

He looked skyward and took a deep breath. Despite the threatening snow clouds, the sky never looked so clear and the air never smelled so fresh. He saw a few flakes and frowned.

I need to send a status message, but I need Tyler and Wheeler's reports.

"Major?"

"Yes, Hatcher?"

She looked around. "This looks like what I expected nuclear winter would look like."

"Yes, I thought of that. But it can't be, right? There should be radiation readings or something."

"Yes, sir. But it's eerie. Surreal."

Two time bubbles appeared, emitting brilliant light. McKnight almost hoped it wasn't his men. He wanted to find someone — anyone — alive in this year.

Two figures were jumping in, one in each bubble. After a moment, the glare from the bubbles subsided enough for him to be certain it was his team members.

At least they're safe.

The two bubbles bulged and disappeared, leaving the two men kneeling on the grass. They gathered their gear, some jars and boxes, and strode over to McKnight and Hatcher.

"I assume you found the same thing we did?" McKnight said to Tyler.

Captain Winston Churchill Tyler III was McKnight's executive officer. On this mission, Tyler's assignment was to hook up with people he met on a previous mission and learn from them how the history change in 1986 affected the year 2086.

"If you mean nobody alive, sir," he said. "You're correct. Not a soul."

"Report."

"Yes, sir. I found the farmhouse we stayed in, sir. Nobody's been there for a while. I didn't find anyone. I found this, though." He held up a bag.

"What is it?"

"Human remains, sir." Tyler left the words hanging.

McKnight waited for him to continue. In the silence, snow began to fall in big, heavy flakes.

"Not any of our people, sir. I found a bicycle and rode it into town. No moving cars, no stores open, and these remains. They're all dried out — no telling how long ago they died. Years, maybe. I thought they might help us understand what happened."

"Good, Captain. Lieutenant Hatcher and I collected some, too."

McKnight turned to Wheeler.

Lieutenants Karen Hatcher and Mitch Wheeler were the time travel specialists. McKnight thought of the two as a unit. They were close friends from their days as cadets at the North Georgia Military Academy.

Despite his name, Wheeler was Hispanic, born and raised in Detroit. Hatcher was a city girl from Atlanta. Both were accomplished soldiers in their own right and accepted the assignment to McKnight's team for the science and the adventure.

"Lieutenant, report."

"Yes, sir. As planned, I jumped into D.C. to check out the international communications center and the government offices. I even went into the White House. Nobody, sir. No security, no guards, nothing. I found one body, but some animal got to it and ripped it to shreds."

"Was that the cause of death?"

"No, sir, I don't think so. Probably a scavenger searching for something edible. The body was mostly dust when the beast found it."

"What about communications?"

"No wireless access anywhere I went. My phone didn't pick up any carrier or signal at all. Everything appears to be down."

"That's what we discovered," McKnight said. "And?"

"I found a comm port in one building. There was no signal on the line. I tried a couple of computers, but there was no power."

"What about the comm center?"

"There was no electricity, but I found a gas generator with some fuel and cranked it up. I got one of the newest shortwave radios up and running and tried to get someone to respond."

"And?"

Wheeler sighed. "If there's anyone out there, sir, they aren't listening to the radio. There was no one broadcasting anywhere that I could find. I heard transient noise I assumed was geological or seismic, but that was it."

McKnight considered this.

"Conclusion?" he asked.

Wheeler smiled without mirth. "We're the only people alive on the whole damned planet, sir."

McKnight grunted and made eye contact with the three officers before him.

"Hatcher and I found the same thing at Telegraph Road. The time Engines are there, but they have about an inch of dust on them. We found the digital history backup disks and brought them with us. We also have human remains, soil samples, and air samples."

Hatcher nodded and said, "No signs of life at all. No one has been in our office for at least ten years."

"Okay," McKnight said. "We have what we came for. It's time to return home to 2036. Any recommendations?"

"Only one, sir," Tyler said. "I think we should invoke Andromeda protocol."

The others nodded.

"I agree," McKnight said. "If a bug caused this, we can't risk taking it back with us to Telegraph Road. I'll send the message."

He glanced around. The snow was sticking to the ground, and it was snowing harder now.

"In the meantime, let's get out of the wind and the snow." He pointed to a small grove of trees. "Let's hunker down under those trees."

They picked up their gear and samples and carried them to the trees. McKnight pulled out his phone, brought up the beacon comm app, and started typing.

> <<< Kathy, we have completed the mission. No casualties or injuries. Request you invoke Andromeda Protocol. Please ACK. >>>

He clicked the Send key, and the message traveled to his time beacon, then across the years to the time Engine in the lab in 2036.

After thirty seconds, a message came back to him.

> <<< Understood. ACK Andromeda Protocol. I will coord with CDC. Stand by. >>>

McKnight read the message to the team.

"Let's get close together," he said. "We don't know how much room they have at the CDC landing room, but I don't expect it to be as big as our lab. Pull all your samples and gear close to you so that nothing gets left here."

McKnight didn't need to say it. He knew all three officers had jumped dozens of times, but he felt he should say something. They needed to know he was in command, no matter what happened.

I hope they're not as scared as I am.

He checked to ensure his own samples and gear were near enough for the time bubble to include them.

His phone pinged. He pulled it out and read the message aloud.

> <<< You are go for Andromeda. Jump in 30 secs. GL. Kathy >>>

"Thirty seconds, team. Stand by," McKnight said.

"Yes, sir," they said in unison.

McKnight knelt, and the others followed his lead.

He felt the hair rise on his arm.

Static electricity. The initial sign of a jump.

"Here we go."

Four separate and discrete time bubbles formed around them, then they resolved into one bigger bubble. Inside, the windstorm began. McKnight felt like he was inside a tornado. The furiously spinning white, sparkling light whipped his clothing about.

He glanced at Hatcher. Her raven ponytail was first spinning around, then flaring out. After two seconds, the spinning light inside the bubble grew so brilliant he had to close his eyes.

Then he felt his body lurch backward, and he was falling through a field of shooting stars.

After a moment, he felt concrete under his feet and fell backward.

Dammit! I wasn't leaning forward enough.

He jumped to his feet, hoping the others didn't notice.

Snowflakes caught in the time bubble spun and danced their way to the floor. McKnight looked at the others, noting that everyone survived the jump. Tyler was fumbling around in his satchel.

Looking for his nausea meds. He always gets sick from the jump.

"Everyone okay?" he asked.

Hatcher and Wheeler nodded, and busied themselves with confirming that all their gear and samples made the jump.

"I will be in a minute," Tyler said, and poured the anti-nausea medication into his mouth.

The room where they landed was about thirty feet by thirty feet, with a twelve-foot ceiling.

"Guess we didn't have to worry about the room," Hatcher said.

"No kidding," Wheeler said. "We could get up a game of flag football in here."

"Don't start just yet," McKnight said. "We're going to be busy for a while."

He found the comm station on the wall next to the door. Before he could push a button, the display lit up. It showed a black woman in surgical dress, her dreadlocks gathered into a single mass of hair down her back. Behind her glasses were two brown eyes that sparkled with intelligent excitement. Her image grew larger as she approached her camera.

Her voice blared through a loudspeaker. "Major McKnight, can you hear me?"

McKnight pressed the talk button. "Yes, I can."

"I'm Doctor Pritchard. I'll be your interface. You need anything, ask for me with the red call button. Are you and your team okay? Is anyone injured or anything? Has everyone we expected arrived?"

McKnight pressed the talk button again. "Yes, ma'am. We are all A-okay. No injuries. We're all here."

"Very good," she said. "We will process you in a few minutes. Doctor Wu is on the line and wants to talk to you."

"Patch her through, Doctor. And thanks."

Pritchard's face disappeared, and Kathy Wu's face replaced it. Kathy was the team's civilian mission planner and sometimes operated the time Engine during a mission.

"Major, are — alright? — Anyone injured? What is your—?"

"Kathy, your transmission is breaking up. We are all okay, no injuries. We asked for the protocol to make sure we didn't…"

He stopped. Kathy was looking at the controls for her display and shaking her head.

She can't hear me.

Kathy's image disappeared, and Pritchard's face reappeared.

The loudspeaker boomed. "Can you hear me, Major?"

"Yes, I can." McKnight fought the urge to yell and match Pritchard's volume in the room. "We had a poor connection."

"Yes, I know. I have another call for you. It's from the White House."

McKnight glanced at his teammates. Wheeler and Hatcher raised their eyebrows. Tyler shrugged.

He turned back to Pritchard. "Well, by all means, Doctor, put the call through."

Pritchard's face vanished and the brown face every American knew replaced it. Wanda Taylor, the President of the United States. Her familiar voice came in through the loudspeaker.

"Okay, thanks... Major McKnight, this is Wanda Taylor. Are you there? Can you hear me?"

McKnight drew in a deep breath. "Yes, Madam President. I can hear you."

Taylor moved away from the camera and allowed McKnight to see the others in the room. He recognized General Drake, the executive sponsor for the team and its projects. He also recognized Wade Harrison, the President-elect of the United States. Taylor's successor.

Taylor turned to Drake. "General? Want to take it from here?"

"Yes, Ma'am. Major McKnight, please report. What did you find and why are we on Andromeda Protocol?"

McKnight shook his head. "Things aren't right, sir. We jumped to Manassas, Virginia, in 2086 and worked our way into downtown D.C.—"

"And?" Drake said.

"We gathered some air samples and some soil samples. We even brought back some plant samples."

"What about the people? Who did you talk to? How did they act?"

"Sir, we didn't find anyone. No one at all."

"No one would talk to you? Is that what you're saying?"

"No, sir. I mean, there's nobody there. We found some human bones, but we didn't find anyone alive. Not one person. We didn't detect any radio or TEV broadcasts. No drivers on the road, no vehicles of any kind. We're afraid some biological agent got out of containment or maybe was released on purpose. That's why I invoked Andromeda, sir. I didn't want to bring something back with us. It might be dissipated by now, but we'd rather be safe than sorry."

Drake frowned. "Thank you, Major," he said. "Stand by for orders."

"Yes, sir."

Drake turned toward the President. Her face was as pale as her dark skin would allow.

"Something we did?" she said. "Did I cause this?"

McKnight saw Drake reach back toward the camera, and the call ended.

He turned to face his team.

"Wow," Wheeler said. "I'm glad I'm not in *that* briefing."

"We have enough problems of our own," McKnight said. "Let's get Doctor Pritchard back on the line and find out if we're ever going to get out of this nice but boring room."

Saturday, December 6, 2036 - HERO Team Lab, Alexandria, Virginia

SIXTEEN DAYS EARLIER

McKnight, Tyler, and Wheeler fell through the field of stars they always saw while time traveling.

The team accomplished their mission in 2086. They rescued McKnight's girlfriend, Megan McAllister, and as a bonus, they captured Oliver Stagne, the man who planned her kidnapping.

When they landed in the HERO Lab, McKnight felt the familiar tug. They fell backwards on the Engine platform.

Two MPs approached and hauled Stagne up and away from them and dragged him away from the time Engine. They pulled his hands behind his back and secured them with nylon restraints.

Stagne ordered at least ten murders in McKnight's time. He pulled the strings that orchestrated time travel missions from 2086 to change the course of history and allow a takeover of the United States government.

Not anymore.

McKnight rose and watched the MPs lead Stagne from the lab. His anger at the man drained away, replaced by relief when he saw Megan standing there, safe again.

He turned and helped Tyler to his feet.

Tyler was his roommate at West Point. They were unlikely friends because of their differences. McKnight was from Oregon and introverted, Tyler was from Georgia and outgoing. McKnight was dark from his grandmother's American Indian blood in his veins, Tyler was fair-skinned from the Irish blood that permeated his family tree.

Their passion for excellence and patriotism drew them together. The two men found a perfect vehicle for their passion - the US Army Rangers. They worked together on several missions, and Tyler was his first choice for his executive officer on this, the HERO Team.

"Nice work, X.O.," McKnight said.

Tyler grinned. "All in a day's work, sir."

McKnight and Tyler pulled Lieutenant Wheeler to his feet.

Despite his name, Wheeler was Hispanic, but born and raised in Detroit. He and Hatcher received their officer training at the Ranger School at the University of North Georgia. McKnight brought the two onto the team for their expertise in physics and exemplary combat records.

Wheeler pointed over McKnight's shoulder.

"Sir, I think your girlfriend would like to talk to you."

McKnight turned as Megan rushed into his arms. Tyler and Wheeler fist-bumped and walked away as he embraced her.

I got her back. She's safe. I took her for granted and almost lost her.

He smiled at Megan through tears that threatened to flow.

"I'm so sorry, Marc," she said. "How could I have been so stupid? They met me at the hospital and told me you were back, but you were injured. When we got to the car, they threw a sack over my head."

"Don't be sorry," he said, and pulled her closer. "It wasn't your fault. If I had shared more with you, you'd have known better. My fault, my responsibility. I'm sorry. I promise to keep you in the loop as much as I can, from now on."

She stood on her tiptoes and pulled his face down to hers. "I knew you would come for me, no matter what."

"I'm just glad you're okay. I couldn't forgive myself if they'd hurt you because of me."

She buried her face in his chest and he closed his eyes, thankful for the moment.

After a few seconds, he opened his eyes. *What about Hatcher and Rachel?*

Hatcher had returned from the future moments before he did, bringing Megan and Rachel Patterson with her. He wanted to reassure himself that Hatcher was okay and Rachel didn't escape.

He needn't have worried. They were nearby in the lab's break area. Rachel was still unconscious from a single blow to the face, dealt by Hatcher.

I need to wrap up the mission.

He pulled away from Megan. "Honey, I've got to tie up some loose ends…"

She nodded and touched his cheek with her hand. "I'll go wait in your office. I really don't want to know what happens next."

"Right," he said. "I'll probably finish the work in a half hour, and then we can go home."

"Okay." She kissed his cheek, turned, and left the lab.

He shifted his attention back to Hatcher and Rachel.

Rachel Patterson was an Army Ranger major in 2086 and ran Stagne's time travel operations. Rachel was dangerous and unpredictable. McKnight spent the last six months of his life trying to stop her, and he was glad she was finally in custody.

Rachel held him prisoner for a short time in 2086, and her instability showed through when she interviewed him.

Stagne drew her into his coup plans early in her military career. At the same time, she became infatuated with the Ranger 'legend' that was Marc McKnight. Rachel's interest in McKnight was diametrically opposed to Stagne's ambitions for her, which created conflicting emotions and goals in her mind.

McKnight was confused by Rachel's obsession with him. She put him up on a pedestal for a service record he hadn't lived through yet. When he was around her, she alternately begged him to run away with her, and threatened to kill him. McKnight was certain she needed psychiatric care.

Hatcher made eye contact with him.

He pointed at Rachel. "Make sure Kathy deactivates her time beacon so she can't jump out."

Hatcher nodded, gave him a thumbs-up, then turned back to Rachel.

Some people referred to Lieutenants Hatcher and Wheeler as "the twins", because of how they interacted. Sometimes McKnight was sure they could read each other's thoughts.

While Wheeler was from Detroit, Hatcher grew up in Atlanta. He was a prankster and clown, and she was serious and introverted. She was tall with jet black, shoulder length hair pulled back in a ponytail. The freckles on her nose and her light complexion completed the impression she was the girl next door.

That image faded as McKnight got to know her.

Hatcher was the best hand-to-hand fighter McKnight knew. He was the only person in the regiment who beat her in a Physical Training match. But he only did it once.

Relieved that Rachel was under control, he focused on the third prize — two 2086 vintage time Engines. The devices were in Rachel's lab when they arrived to rescue Megan. Getting two advanced technology time Engines was a bonus, and would allow the HERO Team to skip decades of technology research. The next step would be to reverse-engineer the technology and incorporate it into their own Engines.

McKnight looked for the two time Engines. He found them on the western side of the lab. Doctor Astalos, their chief scientist and the inventor of time travel, hovered over them.

McKnight chuckled to himself. *The man is 107 years old, and he's grinning and jumping around like a kid on Christmas morning. I'll bet he can't wait to dive into those Engines.*

But the real benefit for taking the machines was that Stagne's people couldn't launch a rescue mission. Or at least, not right away.

A familiar bass voice interrupted his thoughts.

General Drake!

Drake was a war hero from the Mideast wars in the early 21st century. He was a legend in the Rangers, and the entire regiment called him "The Dragon" for his performance in Afghanistan as a young officer. He came out of retirement at the President's request to be the liaison between the HERO Team and the Executive Branch.

McKnight took the assignment on this team because of his interview with Drake. He remembered thinking he would follow General Drake anywhere, and he still felt that way.

Drake was talking to a conference call display and looked very unhappy. McKnight saw President Taylor on the display.

What's that about?

McKnight felt a presence at his side.

"What's going on, sir?" Tyler said. "The General looks pissed."

"Yes, Captain, I believe you're right."

"What do you think it is?"

"Beats me. Based on his expression, I doubt we'll like the outcome." McKnight turned to his long-time friend and smiled. "Forget it for now. Let's go home and let the politicians and generals worry about what's next."

"No problem here, sir. I haven't seen my wife in a week. But one more question for you."

"Sure."

Tyler pointed at Rachel. "What do you think they'll do with her and Stagne?"

"They'll take them out of circulation."

"Kill them, sir?"

McKnight shook his head. "No, I don't think so. Not that our government isn't capable of it, but they may need them later. These two understand the 2086 revolution better than anyone. We dealt them a massive blow today, but it's not over yet."

"So, they'll put them on ice somewhere?"

"Yes. Even the President won't know where they are. Plausible deniability, you know. But someone will, so we don't lose what they know."

"Gitmo, maybe?"

"Maybe," McKnight said, "but certainly out of sight. They've just become ex-people."

General Drake continued to talk with the President through the conference display. To McKnight, Drake appeared agitated and angry.

Tyler gestured at Drake. "I'd love to be a fly on the wall for that discussion."

Drake stopped talking and listened to the President, but he still frowned and folded his arms across his chest.

"Me, too," McKnight said. "But not tonight." He slapped his friend on the back. "C'mon, Winnie, let's get out of here. Tell your much-better-half wife I said hello."

"Ditto," Tyler said. "Oh, wait. I forgot. *I* have a beautiful wife… and *you* don't. *You*, my friend, just have a beautiful girlfriend that needs a ring on her finger."

"What?"

"Jeez, Marc, come on. What are you waiting for? Do I need to hit you between the eyes with a two-by-four? I think I have one at the apartment. Wait here, I'll go get it."

Tyler didn't move. He stood there, grinning at his friend.

McKnight stood in silence for a moment, then he spoke. "I've been coming around to that idea. I'm just not sure I'm there yet."

"Are you kidding me? I've seen the way she looks at you and, more importantly, I've seen the way you look at her. Remember how it felt when Stagne kidnapped her? You were ready to move Heaven and Earth to get her back."

McKnight stood still. *Are my feelings that obvious to everyone around me?*

"It's time, man," Tyler said. "Ask my cousin to marry you. You know in your heart it's the right thing to do. *And* it's the right time."

"You know I'm not good at making important decisions quickly."

Tyler laughed out loud. "You make important decisions all the time. This isn't deliberation. It's fear. What are you afraid of?"

McKnight paused, then said, "Nobody knows me as well as you, Winnie."

"That's what friends are for, Marc. To tell us the truth, when we need to hear it."

He's right. It's time.

Drake ended his call and approached them. "Am I interrupting anything, Gentlemen?"

"No, sir," McKnight said.

"No, sir," Tyler said. "I was just advising the Major on how he's procrastinating about marrying the best woman he ever met, with the possible exception of my grandmother."

Drake looked at McKnight. "Well, I can't speak to that, but I don't see any downside if you love her. And it looks to me like you do."

"Yes, sir."

Drake's expression softened. "Do what you have to do, Marc. Don't let me influence you."

He glanced at Tyler and then back at McKnight. "Okay, get out of here, you two. Get here early Monday. We have work to do."

CHAPTER THREE

<u>Sunday, December 7, 2036 - 6:35 AM - McKnight Apartment, Alexandria, Virginia</u>

McKnight opened his eyes and blinked in confusion. Then he relaxed.

My apartment. I'm home.

He rolled over and saw Megan sleeping next to him. Careful not to disturb her, he slid off the bed and stepped into the bathroom. He started the shower, stripped off his tee shirt and athletic shorts, and slipped past the curtain into the tub. He let the water massage his body as his mind shook off the fog of sleep.

Megan has put up with a lot from me these last few months.

He poured liquid soap into a washcloth and rubbed it into a thick lather. As he washed himself, he thought of how much she meant to him. His sense of relief at her rescue was amplified by the memory of the dread he felt before the mission.

It's time for me to commit to her. She deserves it, and it's overdue.

McKnight rinsed off the soap, dried himself, and got dressed.

The next most important thing intruded on his thoughts.

Coffee.

He tiptoed through the bedroom to the kitchen. Megan was still sound asleep.

He made coffee and sat at the kitchen table, his hands curled around the cup.

Tyler was right. It's time I made her an honest woman.

He smiled at the antiquated attitude reflected by his friend's words.

It's a good thing she didn't hear Tyler say that. She'd have kicked his butt.

He smiled again and wondered what date she would like to set.

Soon, maybe? Before New Year's?

McKnight shook his head.

Idiot. Weddings take time to plan. She'll want plenty of time to set everything up.

He rolled his eyes.

Clearly, *I'm not good at this stuff. I need to tell her how I feel and let her drive it. Whatever she wants is what we'll do. I want it to be special for her.*

He finished his coffee and tiptoed back into the bedroom. Megan hadn't moved since he got up.

She must be exhausted from everything that happened the last couple of days.

He laid on the bed beside her and watched her sleep. She was lying on her side facing him with the upper leg drawn up even with her waist.

He marveled at the beauty of the woman beside him. Her strawberry blonde hair spread across her pillow and obscured part of her face. The lack of makeup allowed her freckles to show more than usual. He loved those freckles and couldn't understand why she didn't.

He looked at the shape of her hip and thigh under the sheets and felt desire awaken in his core, then fade into wonder and awe that such a beautiful creature would choose him without promise or commitment.

It was then that he decided. He wanted nothing more than to be with this woman for the rest of his life.

He smiled. He reached out and ran a finger down her shoulder and arm, then to her waist, her hip and her thigh down to her knee.

"Hey, you," she mumbled.

He looked at her face and saw one impossibly blue eye open and watching him. The ends of her mouth turned up in a sleepy smile.

"Hey," he said, and plunged into deep water. "I love you, Megan."

"Me, too," she mumbled, her eyes blinking sleepily.

"You deserve better than me, but I want to make a commitment to you."

Her eyes closed. "Good," she said.

"I want to formalize our relationship," he said. "I think we should get married."

Her eyes blinked open, then closed again.

She rolled away from him. "That's fine, dear," she whispered.

McKnight almost laughed out loud.

Maybe I should have waited until she was awake.

He slipped off the bed and walked back into the kitchen. He made another cup of coffee and stared out the window. The sun was rising in the east and it was going to be a nice day.

He pulled on a jacket and stepped out onto the apartment's tiny deck. Megan had outfitted it with a couple of fabric chairs, a small table, and a gas grill. He sat and cradled his coffee in both hands.

I'm really not good at this relationship stuff. I'll try again later.

His mind wandered to work plans and priorities.

He heard the door to the apartment open behind him. He looked back over his shoulder and saw Megan standing there, shivering in her housecoat. Her hair was tousled and covered half her face.

"Marc McKnight, did you just propose to me when I was less than half awake?"

He paused, not sure what to say.

"Well, maybe. What if I said yes? What would you say?"

"I'd say your timing sucks," she said, and went back inside.

McKnight sighed and looked at his watch. *It's only seven in the morning and I've already screwed up royally. What else can go wrong today?*

He considered getting more coffee, but he realized he didn't want any and set the coffee mug down on the table.

The door behind him opened again. Megan came out and sat in his lap. She wrapped her arms around his neck and kissed him.

After the kiss, their eyes met, and she was smiling.

"Yes, I'll marry you, in case there was ever any doubt."

He kissed her again and said, "I'm sorry my timing wasn't better. I didn't even think about timing. I finally stopped being afraid and couldn't wait to tell you. Do you understand what I'm saying?"

"I do," she said, and playfully tapped his nose with her forefinger. "I know you better than you *think* I do, *Mister* Major McKnight. Maybe better than you know yourself."

McKnight chuckled.

I guess I didn't screw it up beyond repair.

"The only thing is," she said, "I wish I had a more romantic story to tell my mom and my friends. You know, the whole princess thing."

McKnight rolled his eyes in self-disgust. "I didn't think about that. I'm sorry."

She smiled at him. "It's okay. Everyone's proposal story should be different. That's what makes it interesting."

"If that's the only problem, we can fix that."

"Huh?"

"I'm serious. Let's go ring shopping and then out for a romantic dinner tonight. We'll go someplace nice and I'll propose again and you can tell *that* story."

She smiled. "That's sweet, but it's unnecessary."

"I know," he said, "but it's an occasion worthy of celebration. Let's celebrate tonight — just the two of us, before we tell anyone else."

She pushed back from him and looked him in the eye. "You're serious, aren't you?"

"You bet I am. You're precious to me and I want you to have something special to remember it by. Let's do it."

"Okay," she said, then laughed. "You talked me into it. You and me — ring shopping, dinner, conversation, and dancing."

McKnight chuckled. "I don't think I mentioned anything about dancing…"

Megan threw back her head and laughed. "I don't know why I thought I could slip that past you. Okay. Dinner and conversation." She pushed back and wagged her finger in his face. "But don't you tell anyone — nobody — until I tell Mom and Gramma. They'll be offended if they aren't the first to hear about it."

"Okay. I love you, Megan," he said and kissed her before she could respond.

When the kiss ended, she got off his lap and said, "Come on, let me make you some breakfast."

"Oh, my gosh," he said. "A yes and breakfast, too? I could get used to this marriage stuff."

She wagged her finger in his face and said, "Don't."

He laughed again.

Her expression turned serious, and she said, "I just remembered. In all the excitement, I forgot to tell you."

"What?"

"Janie called you a couple of days ago."

"Janie who?"

"Janie, who?" she said. "Your sister, Janie. You know, the actress?"

Janie? I wonder what's up. She almost never calls.

"What did she say?"

"Not much. She said y'all hadn't talked in a while and she wanted to catch up."

"Okay, I'll call her." He looked at his watch. "It's too early to call now. Theatre people keep different hours than us normal folks."

"So I've heard. Give a performance, party until dawn, then sleep to noon and do it again. They suffer so much." She grinned at him.

"Yes, but I remember the hours she put in practicing her piano and singing lessons. That's when I realized my baby sister was no longer a kid, but a responsible person with a mission in life. Yeah, I'm proud of my little sister."

Megan wrapped her arms around him. "Yes, I can tell. You're right. She's worked hard to get where she is."

She untangled herself from his arms and pushed him toward the kitchen. "Go sit down and I'll get started on breakfast. You can call her afterwards."

McKnight sat and watched her move about the kitchen.

I'm so lucky.

He waited until afternoon to call Janie.

When she answered, he apologized for not replying sooner and asked how her show was going.

"Oh, Marc, I'm so glad to hear from you. Yes, everything's going fine. And how are you and Megan doing?"

"We're great," he said. He almost told her about the engagement before he remembered his promise not to mention it yet. "Better than good," he said.

"That's great," Janie said.

"And you?"

"Well, great, I guess. The show opened here on Broadway three weeks ago, and there are no signs of it closing soon. Some people are throwing around the 'H' word."

"The 'H' word?"

"Hit. The word 'Hit'. Sales are good and it looks like we may have a long run."

"That's outstanding, Janie. I know you've been working hard to make it happen. I'm very excited for you."

"Well, it's too early to tell, but we're hopeful. And I got a call from another producer who's considering me for another show. He wants to open right after this one closes."

"Wow!" he said. "But you wouldn't leave if this one was a hit, right?"

"Maybe. It depends on a lot of things. The point is, I have options. In the theatre business, that's a nice thing to have."

"Amen. That's great."

"Yes, it is," she said. "Anyway, I called you the other day because I was feeling down."

"Down? About what?"

"Well, I was thinking about Dad."

Dad. It's been almost twenty-five years now.

"Yes, I know," he said. "It was so long ago, it's more like a dream now."

"That's what I was thinking, Marc. I miss him, but…"

"But what?"

"I forgot what he looked like for a few minutes. I had to think hard to remember him."

"Jeez, Janie, don't beat yourself up. You were only five years old. Give yourself a break."

"Yes, I know all that intellectually, but emotionally I'm worried."

"About what?"

"About forgetting him altogether. I don't remember the day they told us about his death… Do you?"

He did. The memories flooded back.

Third grade. Smith Elementary School. They called me out of class and said, "bring your books." I went to the school office where Mom was waiting for me in the principal's office. He left the room so she could tell me in private that my father was dead. Then we went home.

"I remember, but it seems like such a long time ago."

"Does it still hurt, Marc?"

"Yes, but it doesn't hurt like it used to. I guess our subconscious mind allows other things to dull the pain and loss. Though I do think I've been slow to develop close relationships because of it. You know, the fear of letting someone get too close to you?"

"Yes, I agree. I thought maybe it's why neither of us has married, or found the right person yet. You're thirty-three and I'm thirty. Most of our friends are already married."

McKnight winced. Now he didn't want to tell Janie the good news.

"Well, I don't think it's anything to worry about," he said. "It'll happen when it's supposed to happen."

"I guess you're right. Did you ever wish you could go back and prevent it? In your job, I mean?"

How could she understand it was one of the great disappointments of his life? An Iranian terrorist assassinated their father in Paris in 2012. McKnight spent hours studying the details after he became an officer. Today, they knew most of the details. And he was a time traveler with the ability to change the past, but bound by law and honor not to change it.

"Of course I have," he said. "I used to think about how I would prevent it if I had the chance. But it's not permitted."

"I know," she said. "I'm just working through my emotions here. It's just that, well, since Mom passed, I've thought a lot about Dad and how much she missed him as she got older."

"Yeah, I understand. I wish there was something I could do, but I can't. We have to let it go. If there's anything I've learned from this job, it's that history is sacred and changing it has consequences beyond the obvious. For every positive change you might create, there's always negative consequences that make you wish you hadn't done it. It's better to leave things as they are."

McKnight heard her sniff and her voice was a little shaky. "Yes, I know. I'm just letting my emotions run away with me. You know how dramatic we theatre folks are. I feel better now. Talking to you always helps me cope."

"Good. No worries, Sis."

"I'll let you go," she said. "I have lunch scheduled with the cast and I need to get ready. Thanks for listening to me."

"It's okay, Janie. Call me whenever you need to talk. I'm here for you."

"Thanks, Marc. I love you, goodbye."

"Love you, too, Sis. Call me anytime."

CHAPTER FOUR

Monday, December 8, 2036 - 09:55 AM - Large Conference Room, Telegraph Road, Alexandria, Virginia

McKnight entered the conference room early. Drake called for a briefing, which implied a mission for the team. Why else would he call them together first thing on a Monday morning?

Kathy and Trevor were already in the room when he arrived.

"Good morning," he said.

"Good morning," they replied in unison.

Doctor Kathy Wu was one of the three civilian members of the team.

When they formed the team two years ago, one requirement was for at least one non-military member of the team, and Kathy was General Drake's choice for several reasons. Among them were her deep background in planning and analysis and an eidetic memory. Her ability to work with troublesome people was not the least of her talents.

Trevor George was the second civilian. He came on board after assisting with the team's first mission. The mission centered on a cold case murder in Atlanta in 1984. Trevor was a cold case detective with the Atlanta Police Department and the case was in his backlog. Drake was so impressed with Trevor, he offered him a position on the team.

Trevor was attracted to the job, but even more attracted to Kathy, and so became part of the team. Since then, he's gotten involved with the time Engine operation and mission planning.

Kathy and Trevor lived together now in Alexandria.

"Do you know what this is all about?" Kathy asked.

"No," McKnight said. "I'm sure we'll know a lot more in a few minutes."

The rest of the team filed into the room.

They reserved the head of the table for the General since he was presenting. McKnight sat next to the presenter's seat. Tyler, Hatcher, and Wheeler sat in a row next to him. Kathy and Trevor sat on the opposite side, leaving a space next to the presenter for Doctor Astalos, the third civilian on the team. Doctor Astalos spent time each week tutoring Wheeler, Hatcher, Kathy, and Trevor on the time Engine. He always said he was getting old and needed to pass on what he knew, but it was clear to McKnight that Astalos loved to teach and work with curious people.

The General was never late, and today was true to form. He entered the room at 10:00 AM.

"Ten-HUT!" McKnight said, and the soldiers leaped to attention. Out of respect, the civilians rose as well.

"As you were," Drake said, and placed a folder on the table. Everyone waited for him to sit, then followed suit.

He glanced at the faces around the table and nodded.

"First, I'd like Doctor Astalos to bring us up to date on the state of time travel technology. Doctor Astalos, do you have any updates on our capabilities?"

Astalos brought himself to his feet.

"Robert," Drake said. "Please feel free to report sitting down."

Astalos shook his head. "No, General. When I can't conform to the team's traditions, it's time to retire."

"Very well," Drake said. "Please proceed."

"Thank you, Mike. In short, there's no change. We can time jump to any period that is a multiple of twenty-five years from a starting time and place, including the zero multiple. All we need is a vector for the destination. That window of opportunity extends about seven days on either side of the exact anniversary, so the window of travel is limited to about fourteen days centered on that anniversary."

"Thanks, Robert. Next, I—"

"Sir, there's one more thing. I have new technology in the works to save us time and energy, but it's not quite completed, so I'll brief everyone when it's ready."

"Very good, sir. We look forward to that," Drake said, and then gestured toward Kathy and Tyler.

"Doctor Wu and Captain Tyler, you're the official planners for the team and I apologize for not involving you in advance in this new mission. I wanted to talk to everyone and give the official and unofficial word on it to everyone at the same time. I want to get everything out on the table before we start."

There were nods around the table.

Drake pushed the overhead interface cable into the output port of his phone and turned his chair around to face the monitor screen on the wall behind him. The display lit up and showed a picture of an elderly man.

"Does anyone not know who this man is?" he asked.

McKnight knew exactly who it was.

George Kosar. Seventy-five years old. Hedge fund guru and billionaire. Instigator of revolutions. Funder of radical left factions. The purse behind Antifa and dozens of violent political disruption groups around the world.

The team's last mission was to prevent Kosar's grandsons from turning the US government from a republic to a theocratic dictatorship in 2086. That last mission removed Oliver Stagne and Rachel Patterson from the Kosar Movement, but they didn't yet know if the mission crippled the coup effort.

"He might be the evillest man that ever lived," Kathy said. There were more nods around the table.

"Are we planning to take further action to stop the Movement in 2086?" McKnight asked.

"No, we're not." Drake looked around the room. "Other thoughts? Ideas?"

No one else spoke.

"Okay. As usual, all this is classified. Understood?" He glanced at the expectant faces around the room. There was no dissent.

He turned back toward the screen and thumbed his phone to change the slide. A picture of President Wanda Taylor appeared on the screen. Her attractive brown face shone with confidence and cordiality.

"Okay, well, here it is. The President has declared the individuals Oliver Stagne, Rachel Patterson, and George Kosar as clear and present dangers to the security of the United States. As such, she has instructed the Joint Chiefs of Staff..."

Drake turned around to face the team. "And us... to take such actions as required to remove the threat posed by these three individuals."

"What does that mean?" Kathy asked. "Does she want them killed?"

All eyes focused on the General.

"No, she wants them removed to where they can no longer impact society."

"What does *that* mean?" Kathy asked.

"Well, we already have Rachel and Stagne in custody," McKnight said. "It's okay with me if they spend the rest of their life behind bars somewhere. Is that the idea?"

"I believe that is already in progress," Drake said.

"Sir, are they going to Gitmo?" Tyler asked.

"I don't know where they are right now, and I'll bet the President doesn't either." Drake shifted in his chair. "Those two have committed at least ten murders and they're going down for that."

"Will there be a trial?" Trevor asked.

"Probably not," Drake said.

Trevor opened his mouth to speak, but Drake held up his hand.

"I know, Trevor. Consider this. There is no precedent for trying someone for crimes committed in another time, or a person who goes to the past and commits a crime. It's outside our legal experience. Such a trial might take years, and they could get off the hook on a technicality. The President isn't willing to chance it."

Drake looked at McKnight. "Would you be okay with releasing them and sending them back to their time?"

McKnight sighed. "No, sir. That wouldn't be my first choice. No."

Drake pointed at Hatcher. "How about you, Lieutenant? Would you be in favor of letting them go?"

McKnight didn't have to guess how Hatcher would answer. Rachel kidnapped her, tortured her, and brainwashed her to kill her commanding officer.

"No, sir, I wouldn't," Hatcher said.

Drake nodded at her. "Nor would I. It isn't legal, but I'm at peace with it."

"Sir," Trevor said. "What about George Kosar?"

Drake smiled at Trevor. "And now we come to the point of this meeting — what to do about George Kosar."

He cleared his throat and continued. "It's clear that the future Movement is his brainchild and his revenge on the United States for, well, for existing. He's been a thorn in the side of every President for the last forty years. His global network and his influence reaches into dozens of governments including our own, and he's committed to bringing down our republic."

"Why haven't we arrested him?" Kathy asked.

"Because he hasn't broken any American laws with which the DOJ can make a case. Intelligence reveals that he funds all kinds of plots and political machinations, but it's all done through shadow companies and layers of money laundering. There isn't any legal justification for it. A lot of moral justification, I'm sure, but no legal justification. The DOJ can't touch him at this point. By the time we could pin him down for something, he'd die of old age."

"But that's not what the President wants, is it, sir?" Tyler asked.

Drake looked at Tyler, but said nothing.

Tyler continued. "That's why the President is looking to us. She doesn't want to arrest him. She wants to erase him."

"What?" Kathy said.

"Go on, Captain," Drake said.

Tyler looked at McKnight, who nodded.

"Well, it seems to me," Tyler said, "that if you go back twenty-five years and take him out, you erase a lot of the damage he has done. We might pick an exact time when his influence begins, but it's moot because our technology limits our access to times that are a multiple of twenty-five years from the present. That would be around December 2011 if we traveled today. If I remember correctly, he was already pretty influential by then."

Tyler paused. "So the mission would be to take him out back in 2011?"

"Correct," Drake said. "Except for the year."

Tyler's eyes widened. "Further back? That would be... like 1986?"

"Is that what this is about?" Kathy said. The look on her face approached fury. "We're going to take out a person for things they haven't done yet?"

Drake leaned back in his chair. "That's it. The President has issued an executive order for a mission by us and the Navy to abduct George Kosar in the year 1986. We are to bring him back to our time, and keep him alive, but separated from all outside communication."

"I can't believe this," Kathy said.

She pushed back from the conference table. "It's inhumane. This is contrary to human decency and certainly a civil rights violation."

She stood. "I'm sorry, General Drake, but I can't be part of this. I'll submit my resignation from the team and have it on your desk today." She looked at Trevor.

After a moment, he nodded and said, "I'm afraid I have to agree with Kathy. As much as we love this team and y'all, we can't do this. I'm with her."

Trevor stood and left the room with Kathy.

Doctor Astalos pushed back from the table.

"I understand where they are coming from," he said. "But if I've learned anything in all my years, it's that sometimes there are hard things that must be done." He stood. "I'll be back," he said, and left the room.

Drake looked at the soldiers left in the room. "Well? Anyone else?"

The team exchanged glances and looked at McKnight.

"Sir, permission to speak freely?" he asked.

"Yes, Major. Go ahead."

"Thank you, sir. It's clear to me we're talking about removing a business executive with fifty years of work. Putting aside what he's tried to do to our country, we're talking about a man who's created thousands of jobs and movements. He's one of the driving forces behind several global initiatives, like the Open Society Foundation, for example. My point is this man has affected thousands. Removing him from history will cause millions of history changes. We might not even recognize the world that'll result from him disappearing. No offense intended to the President, sir, but this is a dumb-assed and dangerous idea."

"Hear, hear," Tyler said. The others nodded.

Drake smiled.

"Well, if it helps any, I agree with you. It *is* a stupid idea. And dangerous. I spent the weekend trying to rally political influencers to talk her out of it. The politicians are afraid to say anything and the command officers would love to see Kosar gone, however short-sighted that idea is. The short story is she's determined to do it. Kosar has tweaked our collective noses so many times over the past forty years that she feels compelled to do something. Her second term as President is over in a month, so she sees no political downside, even if the public finds out about it. And half of the public would think she did the right thing."

The officers looked at each other.

"Look," Drake said. "I could refuse like Kathy and Trevor did. So could all of you. But then, they'd just find someone else less qualified than us to run the mission. I see it this way. The mission will be successful, but the results will be catastrophic. We will have to fix it, and I'd much rather have this team be the people who fix it than someone they pull in from elsewhere. Does that make sense to you?"

"I'm in," McKnight said. "Because I agree. It'll be a disaster, but I'd rather our team fix it than someone else. Our experience with the technology makes us the best choice."

He turned to the team.

"I think General Drake will agree that anyone who wants to be on the sidelines for this one can do that without fear. In fact, I want to minimize our involvement as much as we can."

McKnight looked back at Drake, who nodded.

"Okay, we'll meet back here at 2:00 PM to plan the mission. Sir, did you want to add anything else?"

"Yes, I do," Drake said. "The earliest we can leave is December nineteenth. They're setting up a place for Kosar and the other two, but it won't be ready until then. In the meantime, I plan to continue to lobby the President to change her mind. With any luck, this meeting and the planning will all be a waste of time. That's all."

"Thank you, sir," McKnight said. To the team, he added, "Dismissed."

The team stood to leave, but Drake touched McKnight's arm. "Hang around for a minute, Marc."

The other officers filed out of the room.

"There's something else we need to organize, Marc," he said. "After the mission — if it happens — we'll need to assess the impact by traveling to the future to see what's what. We'll bring on a couple more resources because we'll need more manpower. So be ready for that."

"Yes, sir."

"Thanks for being positive about this. God help us. I think this is ill-advised from the get-go, and I just hope we don't bring about Armageddon in the process… I'll see you at 2:00 PM."

CHAPTER FIVE

<u>Sunday, December 8th, 2086 - 12:00 PM - Washington, D.C.</u>

They exist. They aren't a myth or a legend. The government dismisses them as bogey-men and -women, but they exist all the same.

It started out as an experiment in cloning. Governments called cloning immoral and borderline legal until they declared it illegal in 2050.

But it never stopped. It just went underground.

Governments act and respond for political and financial reasons. The United States responded like other powerful nations. Their leadership condemned cloning and passed laws forbidding the practice, but allowed it to continue in secrecy.

Cloning provided a force of clandestine resources to carry out special projects for the party in power. Politicians and others called on these resources when they needed something done beneath the public radar.

If you're wealthy and have government connections, you can enlist their services. If your rivals and opponents believe you have sufficient clout to hire these resources, they respect and fear you.

In the United States, the Operations Management Team trained and managed the clones and called them Operatives. The average man on the street has heard of them, but most citizens dismiss them as rumors and hearsay. But the threat that 'an Operative will come for you' is enough to scare any dissident.

The experiment started in 2030 with the idea that the Team could clone a powerful warrior and turn the result into a lethal asset. The Operations Management Team searched far and wide for the DNA of one thousand warriors who lived between the years of 1750 and 2035. Most were military officers and law enforcement personnel with stellar records, but the DNA of selected criminals also found its way into the databank of samples.

They trained each clone from an early age to be efficient and fierce fighters. They taught them to be experts at improvisation and adaptation. All clones studied electronics, digital computing, and mechanics to increase their effectiveness.

The Operations Management Team endeavored to train all emotions and morals out of the clones. They wanted assets who would do the bidding of the state without question, whether it was a secret seduction or the wholesale slaughter of innocents.

More than anything else, they taught the Operatives that their mission was sacrosanct. It mattered to them more than their own life. Whatever patrons contracted them to do, they did it with all their might, knowledge, and ingenuity.

Trained Operatives enjoy complete autonomy within their mission. They answer to no one.

Operatives keep to themselves, and none reveal their identity to anyone other than their patron. They never take credit for their missions, nor is their involvement ever admitted by anyone.

No Operative has a name. When an Operative requires a name for a project, they use common names. All have a number and it is all they need.

Their reputation, successes, and abilities are associated with their number, and the people who engage them know which numbers represent the skills they want.

Sunday, December 8, 2086 - 1:55 PM - A Law Enforcement Center - Washington, DC

The Operative walked into the Law Enforcement Center at 935 Pennsylvania Avenue. She wore a black skin-tight jumpsuit that made her appear taller than her 5'10'' height, and her slim athletic figure enhanced the effect. She carried a black backpack.

She approached the security desk.

"May I help you, ma'am?" he said.

"Yes, I was summoned to appear." Her level contralto voice flowed like honey.

The guard picked up the clipboard with the appointment schedule. "Yes, and your name is…?"

"I'm 638," she said.

"Oh," he said. "Just one moment, please. Sorry for not recognizing you. I have an envelope for you."

He handed her a manila envelope and waited attentively.

She turned it over and noted that someone printed '638' on it. She opened it in front of him. Inside was an access card to the building and a business card with nothing but a room number on it.

She waved it at the guard. "Where is this room?"

The guard leaned forward and peered at the number. "B34," he said aloud. "That would be in the basement. Do you need an escort?"

"No," she said. "I'll find it."

"Do you have any more questions? Is there anything else I can do for you?" he said.

The man resembled nothing so much as an aged dog hoping to please his master.

"No."

She turned and walked to the last elevator on the right. It wasn't her first time in this building, but she had never been to this room. She entered the elevator and turned to face the door. A man dashed down the hall to her elevator, but didn't enter when he saw her. He shook his head and smiled.

Her skin was a healthy pink and, even at forty-two years of age, she had freckles across her nose. She wore no makeup, but was attractive regardless. She wore her blue-black hair pulled back in a ponytail, held in place by a simple black band. Lean and muscular at

135 pounds, her stern expression topped off an overall appearance that discouraged questions.

638 noted the lack of traffic in the basement hallway. She found room B34 and stopped outside the door.

She visualized her donor's image.

Give me your strength.

She took a deep breath and entered the room.

There was an audible click when the door closed behind her.

Locked! This is no ordinary assignment.

The room contained two metal tables, two chairs, and a large mirror on one wall.

One table and the two chairs stood in the center of the room. She noticed metal loops on the table and on the chairs.

It's an interrogation room.

The other table was smaller and pushed against the wall underneath the mirror. There was an envelope and several items on it.

She strode to the space between the large table and the mirror, then stood at attention.

"638 reporting as ordered," she said.

When there was no response for ten seconds, she nodded and stared at the mirror. As trained, she waited without moving.

After two minutes, a female voice floated into the room.

"Sit down, 638."

The Operative executed a parade turn and walked around the table. She allowed the backpack to slip off her shoulder and she set it next to the chair. As trained, she sat at attention on the edge of the chair, her hands in her lap.

"I am Number Three," the voice said.

Number Three is a woman. Consistent with my briefing at Operations Center.

She filed the voice away for future use. She would know it if she heard it again.

"638, Have you been told anything about your current benefactor?"

Everything.

"Nothing, ma'am. I'm told to report here and all I know is what you've told me."

"638, what do you remember about your early training?"

What do I remember? Nothing I want to talk about. And I know how to stop this line of questioning.

"Nothing, ma'am. I remember nothing before I was eighteen. Is there something you need to know about it? I can try to find out if you like?"

"No, 638. No. I was just curious. You are older than most Operatives, are you not?"

"I have not kept track, Number Three. I suppose I'm older than most."

"Yes. And how old are you?"

"The records say I am forty-two."

"And they tell me you have survived this long because you are the very best."

"Thank you, Number Three."

"Don't thank me, 638. I have a new assignment for you. Are you fit? Are you ready to take on an assignment?"

"I am, as always, Ma'am. I cannot yet afford to retire."

"If you are successful in this assignment, your reward and payment will allow retirement. If you want it."

The Operative said nothing.

After a pause, Number Three said, "Do you know who Oliver Stagne is?"

The Operative hesitated.

Is?

"Oliver Stagne was a special assistant to the President of the United States," she said. "But I heard he died earlier this year. Is that not true? The report of his death in a traffic accident was short and void of details."

"Hmm. That was a cover story. Do you know who Rachel Patterson is?"

"Yes. She is the lead of the FTS, the Federal Time Services team. She's an Army Major, I believe. In the 75th Regiment."

"That is correct," the voice said. "She and Stagne were working on a project for me and an armed force from the past kidnapped them. The attackers also took the two time Engines assigned to Major Patterson. Their leader was Major Marc McKnight. Do you know the name?"

"Are you referring to the time travel hero from the 2030s, ma'am? Yes, of course I do. Every child learns about him during their training."

"Not every child's history lesson is accurate, 638."

The Operative frowned.

"The victors write history, 638. Major McKnight's motives and history were darker than most people know."

The Operative shifted in her chair. "Why weren't they pursued? I mean, Major Patterson ran the government's time travel team." she asked.

"As I mentioned, Major McKnight took her time Engines when he kidnapped her. But we have the software backups and travel logs for her machines. The technicians are recovering the software from the backups and installing it on new Engines, even as we speak."

"Excuse me, Number Three," she said. "But what can I do to help?"

There was a pause. The Operative wondered what was happening on the other side of the mirror in front of her.

After ten seconds, Number Three spoke again. "I want you to find Mr. Stagne and Major Patterson. Then bring Major Patterson back to me."

"Major Patterson," the Operative said. "But not Mr. Stagne?"

"No. As he was careless enough to be kidnapped, he can stay where he is. But Major Patterson is a different matter. I need her help in some pending negotiations. That's all you need to know."

"And where shall I start?" the Operative asked.

"We believe Major Patterson was taken to 2036."

"2036?" The Operative frowned again. "As in the *year* 2036?"

"Yes," Number Three said.

"I'm not trained in time travel."

"You are a problem solver, a fixer. You're one of our best. I'm sure you will figure it out."

"Yes, Number Three. When shall I start?"

"Now. Immediately. Go to the table at the window."

The Operative rose, picked up her backpack, and approached the table.

"There, you'll find a dossier that contains information about Major McKnight — work address, home address, known associates and teammates, friends, family, romantic interests, etc."

"Yes, ma'am."

"Major Patterson had a GPS beacon in her right forearm, but we believe McKnight has deactivated it. But like many essential personnel, we injected her with location markers. Even if they detect the markers, they cannot easily remove them from her blood without killing her. Do you see the GPS locator on the table? It's standard issue for our time travelers. We programmed it to track Major Patterson once you arrive in 2036. When you land there, engage the locator and it will tell you where she is."

"Yes, ma'am."

"In the dossier, you'll find ID cards and currency cards. The red bag contains small carat diamonds worth three million dollars. These and your standard tech pack should be enough to allow you to move about at will in 2036."

"Yes, ma'am. What is the other technology here?"

"It's a personal shield. It will render you nearly invisible."

"Nearly? What does that mean?"

Number Three didn't speak for a minute.

She put me on hold. She had to ask someone.

"638?"

"Yes, ma'am?"

"The technology deflects light. If someone is not looking directly at you, they may not see you. If they look directly at you, they will see a shimmer or distortion of light. They can't identify you, but they will know something is there."

"I see," the Operative said. "Will the shield stop a blade or a bullet?"

"No."

"Will it stop any projectile thrown at the user?"

"No, it's a stealth device only."

"I understand. Any side effects from use?"

Another long pause.

"I don't know from personal experience, 638. But I've heard the shield produces nausea after use. You may wish to experiment with it before using it on the mission."

"Thank you, I will. Where do I go to arrange travel?"

"In the dossier, you'll also find an address and an appointment time. The appointment should be a couple of days from now. That will allow you time to make whatever arrangements required for an extended leave."

"Yes, ma'am," she said.

"I see you have on one of the new mission suits."

"I do."

"How does it work?"

"Simple. When disengaged, it appears as you see it now — a black leather jumpsuit. When engaged, it reflects the surrounding colors. It is very effective in the outdoors as camouflage. Not so much in the city. It's powered by a small radioactive isotope and should have enough power to operate for ten years."

"I see."

"Pardon me, Number Three," the Operative said. "You said something about an extended leave. How long do you expect it will take to find her?"

"I don't know."

"I see."

"638?"

"Yes?"

"Do not come back without Rachel Patterson. Do you understand?"

"Yes, Number Three."

"Good. As I said, there will be a significant reward for you when you complete your mission — more than any other you have undertaken. You're dismissed."

The Operative heard a faint pop after the voice.

The microphone is off. End of Interview.

She stuffed the items from the table into her backpack and walked to the door. She stopped in front of it and heard a click.

The meeting went well.

She opened the door and walked down the hall toward the elevator.

Monday, December 8, 2036 - 2:00 PM; Conference Room at Telegraph Road, Alexandria, Virginia

When McKnight returned to the conference room at two o'clock, the entire HERO Team was there, including Astalos, Kathy, and Trevor. Astalos and Trevor were upbeat, even cheerful. Kathy was stone-faced.

McKnight waved at her. "Hi, I'm glad you're here."

Kathy glanced at him, and a small smile stole across her face. "I'm still looking for some assurances, but I'm not angry anymore."

"About what?"

"Let's wait until General Drake gets here and I'll ask him my questions."

"Ask me about what?" Drake said from the doorway.

"Ten-HUT!" McKnight said.

The soldiers stood and snapped to attention. The civilians rose as well.

Drake saluted them. "As you were."

Once everyone settled, he spoke. "This is the planning meeting for this mission, but if there are questions before we begin…?"

"I'd like to clarify a few things," Kathy said.

"Very well. You have the floor, Kathy, and by the way, I'm glad you and Trevor are back."

"Thank you, sir. I want to apologize for walking out earlier without getting all the information. I failed to do my duty as a mission planner because I lost my temper."

She glanced at the faces around the table.

"For that, I'm sorry. I still don't like the project. It's a disaster with millions of change points that could cause unforeseen history changes. We might not even recognize our own time, let alone the future."

"Yes, I agree," Drake said.

"So," she said, glancing at Astalos, "Doctor Astalos told me you were opposed to the kidnapping, too."

"That's true. I don't want to, but if we refuse to do it, they'll just get someone else less qualified to do it."

"That's why we came back. Trevor and I, we don't think it's a good idea. But if they give it to someone else, they won't have the experience to fix it. If things get screwed up, we need the most experienced resources on the job, and that's us. So we're back."

"That's great, Kathy. We appreciate that. Now I have to ask the obvious question before we proceed. Will you give me your best effort to make the mission successful, even though you oppose it?"

Kathy looked at Trevor. They both nodded.

"Yes, sir, we will," Trevor said. "We believe in questioning and dissenting, but we have to stick together to find our way to the other side of this."

"Yes," Kathy said. "And as long as you're still trying to get it canceled, we know we've done all we can to do the right thing."

"Good. Thank you," Drake said. "But what if I can't get it canceled? President Taylor is a strong person, and she believes she's doing the right thing. She'll listen to Doctor Astalos and me, but she may not see it our way. What then?"

Kathy and Trevor glanced at each other.

"We're in all the way," she said. "We think it's a bad idea, but we'll do our best to make it the right idea."

"I agree," Trevor said.

"Very well. Major McKnight, would you like to run the planning session?"

"If you don't mind, sir," Tyler said. "I think I can save us all a lot of time."

Drake chuckled. "Well, by all means, Captain Tyler. You have the floor."

"Thank you, sir," he said, and leaned back in his chair. "Here's what I've been thinking. Our involvement should be minor. We don't have these skills — kidnapping, I mean. I see us as facilitators. Let the Navy do the kidnapping. Our job should be to get them there and get them back safely. That's all."

"I like it," McKnight said. "What do you have in mind?"

"Simple. The SEALS come here and I brief them on the beacons, then we go to 1986. They grab Kosar and sedate him. I get everyone back here in one piece. The SEALS take the prisoner and go their merry way. No big deal, no muss, no fuss."

"It minimizes our exposure if it all goes south," Hatcher said. "I volunteer to be on point."

"Too late," Tyler said. "I've already volunteered."

"I didn't hear you say that, sir, and if I may speak freely... it's a minor operation and you should delegate it to a lower level officer."

"In that case," Wheeler said, "it should be me. You've always said you're more important than me, Hatcher."

"Shut up, Wheeler. I did no such thing, I—"

"Okay, you two," McKnight said, unable to suppress a smile. "I get it. You'd all like to go. It's Tyler's plan. He goes."

"Yes, sir," Wheeler and Hatcher said together.

McKnight turned to Drake. "Sounds like a good plan to me, sir."

"I agree and approve," Drake said. "Captain Tyler, the mission date will be December nineteen. Will you please write up the plan and send it to me by tomorrow morning? I'm sure there'll be no problems with it."

"Yes, sir."

McKnight turned to Kathy. "We'll need a follow-up mission. Here in this time, and in the future. We'll need to determine if we've screwed up everything and created new dangers and problems we have to fix. My thought is that it'll change the present; maybe significantly. It's my hope the mission creates as many problems as it solves, and we can make a case for reversing the change."

"I can plan that," she said. "Who will be on the team?"

"You decide. My thought is we'll have an enormous amount of stuff to look at, so it'll require all four of the military team members. I hope Doctor Astalos has his time frequency tracker all optimized and ready to go."

"Oh, it'll be ready," Astalos said. "I'm thinking I will need a dampener to tone down the amount of change. It'll be ready by the nineteenth."

"Good," Drake said. "Unless Major McKnight has anything else, we're all done here."

"No, sir, nothing else. Ten-HUT!"

Everyone rose, and the officers saluted Drake. He left the room.

"Okay, people," McKnight said. "We have work to do, so let's get to it. Dismissed."

Sunday, December 8th, 2086 - 2:46 PM - Washington, D.C.

The Operative walked through the slums that surrounded downtown D.C.. Like many other American cities, time and reduced responsibility policies had taken their toll.

She could have taken a cab or another ride app service, but she preferred walking for the physical act of it. She could think while she walked, and she readied her mind for the study required to prepare for her new mission.

The price for her exercise was the odorous and somewhat dangerous route she took from her patron's place of business.

It was only a matter of time before someone accosted her on the route. It happened before and would happen again.

The man stepped out of an alley and directly into her path. She stopped and assessed the danger level. The man was four inches taller than her, and she estimated his weight at 250 pounds.

"Pardon me, ma'am," he said. "But could you spare fifty bucks for a poor starving veteran?"

She stood in front of him with her hands on her hips.

"No, I can't," she said. "Please step aside. I have no time for this."

She stepped to the right, but he sidestepped to remain in front of her.

"I'm sorry you don't have any money on your person. That tight jumpsuit looks really sexy on you, and I can tell there's no room for a wallet. But maybe if you checked in your backpack, you might save this poor soul from starving today."

638 noted his shabby, dirty clothes and ample belly. "I doubt you'll starve today. I have somewhere to be and you're keeping me from it. You're creating a dangerous situation for yourself. Please step aside."

She tried to go past him on the other side, but he stepped again in front of her.

The man laughed. "Now, is that any way to treat a veteran? Of course, if you have no money, you could still help me out." He pointed to the alley. "Why don't we slip into my office and we can have a little fun? The lack of food isn't my only hunger." A hint of menace came over his expression and he leaned forward. "You won't be sorry, I promise you that."

The Operative sighed. "Very well, have it your way. For the record, I'm already sorry." She visualized the image of her donor, took a step backward, and waited.

The look of menace turned to anger. "Sorry?" he said. "For what?"

Another man appeared at his side. "Bill, for Chrissakes, are you stupid?"

Bill tore his eyes away from her and looked at his friend. "What?"

The other man pulled on his sleeve and stood on his tiptoes to speak into his ear. "Can't you tell she's an Operative?"

The big man laughed. "Mike, you are such a gullible ass. Operatives aren't real. They're just made up ideas to scare people like you."

"Bill, I'm not joking. I know a guy who stopped a woman here before. He tried to rob her, and she beat him to death."

Bill glanced back at 638 and laughed, then looked back at Mike. "You think this little witch can take me? I don't believe it." He turned back to her. "You don't think you can kill me, do you, honey?"

"Of course not," she said. "I don't have that much time."

Bill did a double take and stepped toward her.

Mike clawed at his sleeve and said, "Bill, don't take the bait. Let her go. I have some good weed here. Let's do that instead."

Bill shook his head. "So I heard Operatives have their number tattooed on their wrist. If you're an Operative, let me see it."

"I didn't say I was an Operative, and I really must be on my way. Please move."

"Enough of this," he said. He pushed Mike away and swung a massive arm at her.

She ducked and sidestepped to avoid the blow. She grabbed his arm and pulled it to increase his momentum, then used her hip to take him off balance and flipped him to the pavement.

She turned to Mike to confirm he wasn't a threat. He held his hands up in defense and stepped backward.

Bill jumped to his feet and bellowed a cry of anger. He charged the Operative, and she killed his forward momentum with a hard kick to his upper chest. She spun and struck his knee with her heel with sufficient force to break it. The big man went down on both knees and screamed in pain.

She landed in ready position and launched another kick. The ball of her foot struck him square on the nose, shattering the cartilage there. Bill went down and didn't move.

She landed in ready position, then relaxed when it was clear the threat no longer existed.

She looked at Mike. He stood back in the alley with his hands up, palms out. His face was a mask of fear.

She turned to walk away, then stopped. She stared at Mike until he raised his eyes to meet hers.

"Your friend should have listened to you. Tell them at the emergency room he has a broken knee and a concussion at least, maybe a broken rib, too. And he might have a brain injury."

Mike's voice trembled as he responded. "Okay," he said.

She glanced at her watch as she walked away. The encounter with Bill cost her five minutes she could have spent studying or working out.

Next time I won't waste so much time trying to avoid complications. Better to just dive in and get it over with.

CHAPTER SEVEN

Thursday, December 11, 2036 - 1:38 AM - Cameron Park, Alexandria, Virginia

It was a cold, moonless night in Cameron Park. Snow was threatening.

A deer pawed the dead lawn, searching for a tuft of edible grass. It raised its head and sniffed the air, then ran down the hill toward the watercourse of Cameron Run.

Static electricity filled the air, and a brilliant white silhouette appeared. It lit up the entire lawn, but no one was there to see it.

The light faded, leaving the Operative there, kneeling. She pulled her phone from her backpack and typed a status message for Number Three.

<<< 638: Arrived in 2036. Mission started. >>>

She selected her time beacon as the destination and pressed the 'Send' key. The message was received by the beacon and forwarded to her time Engine in 2086.

Her phone pinged, and she checked the text messages.

<<< 003: ACK >>>

She got the message.

The Operative engaged her mission suit. It would reflect the night sky and the snowy terrain, reducing the ability for others to see her as she passed. She slipped her phone back in her backpack and drew out a compass. After she determined which way was East, she looked in that direction, and nodded. She stood and slung the backpack over her shoulder.

Now to find shelter for the night.

She started walking east at a pace of four miles per hour. The last known destination for Major Patterson was five miles away. She would find a wooded area and camp for the night. Tomorrow, she would begin her search.

Thursday, December 11th, 2036 - 11:00 AM - Kingstowne Towne Centre, Alexandria, Virginia

The Operative sat on a bench outside the Chipotle Mexican Grill and pulled the GPS locator and wireless hub from her backpack.

First things first. Test out what I was told.

Before jumping to 2036, they trained her on the mission data in her implant. She wondered if the implant was as innocuous as described. The purpose of the implant was to have a copy of the mission data. If she screwed up and changed the time continuum, the people who sent her could figure out what she changed. A byproduct of the mission data was the ability to level herself and remember why she was there if someone else caused a history change.

She activated the app on her phone and swept it across her thigh. The mission app captured and displayed the data on her phone. She saw the list of all previous missions and their reports, but she was only interested in her own mission. Satisfied she could access what she expected, she ended the app and set her phone down.

She turned on the wireless hub and set it to 'Analyze Protocol'. For the next few minutes, it would search for wireless networks, learn the period's wireless protocol, and establish itself as a wireless hotspot. Thereafter, she could use it to access the current internet.

The device dinged faster than she expected. The protocol was like that of 2086, and now the browser on her phone connected. She nodded and picked up the GPS locator.

She confirmed they set the programming to Major Patterson's serial number and pressed the 'Find' button.

It will be Washington D.C. or Guantanamo Bay in Cuba.

Her research led her to believe these were the most likely locations for McKnight to hide Major Patterson.

A location displayed on the locator.

Well, that doesn't look familiar.

The coordinates didn't match the GPS coordinates of D.C. or of Guantanamo. She transferred the coordinates to her phone and searched the internet for them.

The Operative smiled at the results. The coordinates were near Rachel, Nevada. She chuckled at the coincidence.

Rachel Patterson is being held in Rachel, Nevada.

She calculated the distance to the location. It was over 2400 miles.

I'll have to fly there.

She outlined the steps to get there and started checking them off. She found a diamond trader in the shopping center and sold five stones for $4000. Next was a booking to Las Vegas on United Airlines and a Jeep for transportation. The earliest she could travel would be the next day in the afternoon.

She booked a local room and searched for transportation options. Thirty minutes later, her Uber driver dropped her off at the Hyatt Hotel in Old Town Alexandria.

The Operative would spend the night there, then travel tomorrow to Las Vegas and Rachel, Nevada. While at the hotel, she checked out the options on the GPS Locator. She found some additional settings that would be useful.

Friday, December 12th, 2036 - 3:30 PM - United Airlines Flight 2304

The Operative took an Uber ride from the hotel to Ronald Reagan Airport. She arrived just in time to hurry along the jetway to her flight. Her first-class ticket put her in the front of the aircraft.

She had traveled by air before. But in the past, it was always on military aircraft. Once, she traveled in the second seat on a fighter jet. Her flight today was almost too comfortable by comparison.

She looked around at the other first-class passengers. Some were asleep. Some typed into their laptops. One woman read a paperback book.

She found one man staring at her. When their eyes met, he winked at her.

Ignoring him, she looked out the window at the countryside 30,000 feet beneath her. She felt as if she was stationary and the world was flowing slowly past her. She leaned her head against the side of the bulkhead and allowed herself to relax. After a few minutes, she slept.

She woke when she felt the need for a biological break. The man met her eyes as she rose and walked back to the lavatory. It was cramped, but she'd used worse facilities.

When she opened the door to exit the lavatory, the man was there, blocking the passageway.

He smiled. "I'm a charter member of the mile-high club. Want to join?"

She didn't know what he meant, but she guessed he was suggesting sex. He was not unattractive, but...

Not the time. Not the place.

She smiled, poked her head out of the lavatory, and looked both ways.

When she met his eyes again, she whispered, "Not now. After the flight." She winked, pushed past him, and walked back to her seat.

She spent the rest of the flight sleeping. When the wheels touched the runway in Las Vegas, the jolt awakened her. She blinked a few times to orient herself and checked the time.

11:30 PST.

The man was sitting across the aisle, whispering with the woman in the seat next to him.

Good. Maybe he can be her *problem.*

But when she disembarked, he fell in step with her. She had hoped he had lost interest, but he was waiting for her.

"Where would you like to go?" he said.

I have no time for this.

She glanced around and pointed. "There. Come on."

She walked to the women's lounge on the concourse. At the entrance, she turned to him and said, "Let me make sure no one's inside. Wait for my signal."

She entered the lounge. Except for a woman touching up her makeup at the mirror, there was no one in the room. She noted the toilet stalls and a sofa on the left, then approached the woman.

"Excuse me," she said, with a European accent. "There is a man following me. I came in here, but I'm afraid. I think he will come in here after me. Could you please help me and find a police officer?"

The woman stopped what she was doing and turned to her. "Oh, my gosh! Are you all right?"

"I am now, but I'm afraid he means to hurt me. I think he has a gun."

The woman put her hand to her throat. "How terrible! I'll go report him. Do you want to come with me?"

The Operative smiled. "How nice of you to offer, but I couldn't let you put yourself in danger. I'll be all right if you hurry."

The woman stuffed her cosmetics into her purse. "I'll go right now. Good luck." She turned and ran toward the door.

The Operative followed her. When she reached the entrance, the man looked confused, staring off to the right. She looked in that direction and saw the woman hurrying away.

She visualized her donor's image.

"Quickly," she said to the man, beckoning with her hand. "We don't have much time."

He pointed at the retreating woman. "What was that all about?" he said.

"I ran her off. Come, hurry! Give me your coat."

He took it off and handed it to her. She threw it on the sofa and opened the door to a toilet stall. "Hurry!" she said.

He came toward her and she pushed him past her into the stall, caressing his chest and his face. She ripped his shirt open and kissed his chest. He wrapped his arms around her. She reached down to his crotch and massaged him through his clothes.

"Push your pants down! Hurry!" She brushed her breasts against his chest. "Umm…"

He released her and tugged at his belt buckle. Awkwardly, he pushed his pants and underwear down to his knees.

"Mm, that's how I like it," she said. She reached down, cupped his testicles, and gripped his penis.

The man groaned with pleasure.

She tightened her grip on his testicles and yanked up with all her strength. The man gasped. She struck him on the nose with the heel of her hand and drove the nasal cartilage out of position. With his head tilted back, she struck him in the throat. She heard something crack. He fell backwards onto the toilet seat, unconscious.

She turned and left the stall, picked up his overcoat, and stepped out of the lounge. She could hear a commotion ahead in the terminal. Donning his overcoat, she walked with her head down.

Five seconds later, an airport security officer flew by her at a dead run. Trailing several feet behind him was the woman from the lounge. The Operative kept walking.

She picked up her backpack at baggage claim and caught the rental car shuttle to get her Jeep.

Fifteen minutes later, she was on her way to her hotel.

I'll need to pick up some more hiking gear before I head up to Rachel. Just in case I need additional props for cover.

She looked forward to a good night's sleep to prepare for what promised to be a challenging day.

CHAPTER EIGHT

Saturday, December 13th, 2036 - 02:30 AM - US Highway 93, Nevada

She drove north on US Highway 93 on her way to Area 51. Her original plan was to sleep in Las Vegas overnight and drive up in the morning. After some deliberation, she skipped the hotel and started the drive. After all, the sooner she got there, the sooner she could accomplish her mission.

She needed camping gear and found a sporting goods store on edge of the desert. Only in Las Vegas would you find an outdoor sports store that was open all night.

It may have been a mistake. Area 51 was 120 miles from Las Vegas - up Interstate 15, turn left onto US Highway 93, and left again onto Nevada Highway 375, also known as the Extraterrestrial Highway.

Not a complicated drive, but she didn't count on the fatigue factor. The terrain was flat, and the road was long and straight. The lack of scenery in the dark didn't help.

At first, the novelty of driving a car kept her awake. She hadn't driven a vehicle in... how long? But once she got it moving, there was little to challenge her, and she grew bored.

Now sleep kept stealing over her and she would jerk awake, realizing she had been asleep while driving 70 miles per hour.

Not smart. Time for a break.

She stopped alongside the road. She set her phone to allow her ten minutes. From training, she knew a power nap would give her an hour of alert time if she limited the nap to ten minutes. If she napped longer, only hours of sleep would restore alertness.

She closed her eyes. Her last conscious thought was about the man on the plane. She didn't feel remorse. She guessed she would find Rachel and return to the future long before the authorities traced her here.

The earliest things she remembered were the barracks and the Aunts and Uncles who trained them. She must have been four years old.

Everyone had a number, not a name. Girls had even numbers; boys had odd numbers. She never knew why.

Every day they learned about fighting and obedience. If you refused to fight or to obey, an Aunt or Uncle took you off somewhere and no one saw you again in the camp. Perhaps they took them to another camp?

638 was always tall for her age, and she was the best fighter in the camp. It came naturally to her. She remained humble and learned new things from every boy or girl she fought.

At night, they learned about things from the computer screens. Things like biology, science, physics, tactics… To 638, this was more fun than fighting.

As they got older, the boys and girls acted differently around one another. Then an Uncle caught a boy and girl together, after hours, naked behind a shower room. They admitted they discovered a new type of play.

The Uncles and Aunts didn't forbid it. But the next day, they pitted the boy and girl against each other in combat. The two danced around like they were sparring, but no blows landed. The Uncles and Aunts grew angry and demanded they take their combat seriously, but they persisted in half-hearted exchanges of swings and misses.

Then an Uncle stood, drew a weapon, and killed them both. It wasn't the first death 638 had seen. Months before, they shot a boy for stealing from his bunk mates. 638 didn't understand what they did wrong. She listened closely while the Uncle expressed regret and explained how the two forgot their mission — to become perfect warriors for the United States.

The Uncles and Aunts didn't discourage sexual activity, but they penalized you if you didn't take your mission seriously. Whenever a boy and girl played at sex together, the Uncles and Aunts somehow found out and forced them to fight each other the next day.

Playing with a boy always meant a beating from the boy the next day. No girl wanted to experience that more than once. Soon, the girls grasped the danger and refused to play.

638 was the exception. She bloomed early. She was pretty and the subject of fantasy for many of the boys. But they knew acting on that fantasy might result in a beating from her, and none of them wanted to be humiliated in front of the other boys.

You must not lose sight of your mission, the Aunts and Uncles said.

638 understood. We are Operatives of the United States. Nothing is more important than our mission.

She felt the phone vibrate when the ten-minute timer went off. It was time to continue the journey. She started the car and pulled out onto the highway again. She had another hour of driving to do.

Fatigue was setting in again when she saw the first sign. It said Area 51 was a restricted area and not open to the public.

Now that she was near her destination, she forgot about sleep. She stopped and looked again at the Nevada roadmap.

Area 51 was at 4500 feet in altitude and she wanted to get above it to observe the entire facility. With her locator, she calculated where she was and looked around for the mountain she picked earlier. It was south of Area 51 and about 7000 feet in altitude. She drove up a dirt road to 6000 feet and carried her camping gear up the rest of the way on foot.

And so she found herself on a mountaintop in the desert at 6:50 AM and two miles from Area 51. It was cold at that altitude, and she shivered.

She remembered reading that people in 2036 thought there were aliens held captive at Area 51. Fifty years later, she hadn't heard about or seen an alien, so she assumed it wasn't true.

She set up the tent, but didn't risk any light.

No sense attracting unwanted attention.

She wrapped herself in a blanket and stood, looking down at Area 51. There were only a few lights there.

She studied the buildings with her binoculars. In the low light of stars, the buildings all looked alike. There was nothing to show which one might house Rachel. It could even be underground.

Out of long habit and caution, she looked back down the road she traveled from Las Vegas. She guessed she had three days before the police tracked her from the airport to this location through the car's tracking device.

Now that she was here, she took another reading on Rachel's position. The facility below her stretched across twenty degrees of her compass, and she wanted to know exactly where to look for Rachel. She pulled up her position on the map and oriented it where the camp was straight ahead.

She checked the locator for Rachel's position, but the vector didn't point at the facility at all.

Damn it. I must be tired.

She checked her calculations again and got the same result. She stood and let the blanket slide off her shoulders. Pointed north from her current location, the locator showed the vector and the distance.

She's not in Area 51.

The Operative copied the vector and the distance and calculated a new location for Rachel. About fifty miles to the north. She copied the location to her phone.

When I was in D.C. and saw the location, I assumed it was Area 51. A stupid mistake.

She raised her binoculars and looked in the vector's direction.

There's another place out here somewhere. A place more secret than Area 51.

She was tempted to slip inside the tent and sleep, but her curiosity and anger at herself for jumping to conclusions wouldn't permit it. After packing up the tent, she collected her gear and hiked down the mountain to her Jeep.

She would resume her search for Rachel north of her current location. About fifty miles north.

Saturday, December 12th, 2036, 8:05 AM - Extraterrestrial Highway near Rachel, Nevada

The sun rose over the mountains in the East as the Operative hurried to the location north of Area 51.

She set her locator to detect the direction of Rachel Patterson's signal. It read as straight ahead on the highway. She kept her speed just under the speed limit. The last thing she needed was an encounter with a Nevada state trooper.

As she approached the town of Rachel, she almost missed it. A few buildings on the left. She noted the only hotel in town — the A'le'inn — the name being a poor pun on the word "alien".

She estimated the signal originated twenty miles north of town. When she crossed the fifteen mile threshold, she raised the locator and pointed it down the road. The vector skewed to the right. She held it there, glancing at the readout every few seconds.

The vector drifted right, away from the road. When the vector's movement was perceptible, she slowed the vehicle. As she approached a valley between two hills, the vector swung hard to the right and disappeared.

She hit the brakes and stopped. She turned in her seat, pointed the locator behind her, and re-acquired the vector.

I passed it.

She laid the locator on the seat and drove in reverse until she lined up with the valley between the hills.

There! A dirt road. I missed it.

She parked the Jeep and got out. Fifty feet down the road was a dirty red and white striped sign that read "ROAD CLOSED".

She walked to the sign and leaned against it, peering down the dirt road as it disappeared around a bend in the hills.

The base of the two signposts caught her attention. She expected the posts to be stuck in concrete. But that isn't what she saw. They hinged the posts at ground level and the metal was shiny.

This sign lies down for access to the road.

She looked at the sign again. The dirt she saw formed a pattern. A tire tread pattern.

There's something down that road and someone visited recently.

Alarm bells went off in her head.

Why isn't this place guarded?

Her brain caught up with her senses.

Who says it isn't?

She wanted to get closer, but it wasn't an option during the day.

I'll come back when it's dark.

She walked back to her Jeep and drove it further north on the highway. If anyone observed her, she hoped she looked like a hiker searching for a new place to explore.

After she traveled ten miles, she turned around and headed back for Rachel. She would rent a room, get some sleep, and return to recon the area after dark.

At the A'le'Inn, she booked a room. Once inside, she slid the lock into place and looked around. The room was dingy and dusty, and it needed painting. An old bed with squeaky springs and a vanity sat against the far wall. An ancient wardrobe and a rickety desk sat against the left wall.

She set her backpack on the bed and removed her laptop and the locator. She turned on the locator and checked again for Rachel's beacon. Rachel Patterson was somewhere north of her current location.

Tomorrow, she would get close enough to pinpoint Rachel's precise location.

CHAPTER NINE

Saturday, December 12th, 2036 - 10:26 PM PST - The A'Le'Inn hotel, Rachel Nevada

The Operative left her hotel room and looked north and south along the Extraterrestrial Highway. There was no traffic. Southward, there was a bar and grill with three vehicles out front. She could hear music and laughter coming from the place.

Saturday night in the big city.

She got in the jeep and sped north on the highway.

She passed the dirt road between the two hills and went another four miles before shutting off the vehicle's lights and coasting to a stop. A large patch of scrub brush grew to her right. It wouldn't hide her vehicle from people who were searching, but they wouldn't see it if they weren't looking. She pulled the Jeep in behind the brush.

She tightened the straps of her backpack and jogged across the desert to the back side of the northern hill. When she was halfway to the hill, she pulled out her binoculars.

Let's see what we have here.

She raised them to her eyes. No movement on or behind the hill caught her eye.

She switched the binoculars to infrared mode. The volume of laser light on the hill startled her.

Whatever this place is, they want to keep people out.

She needed to be on top of the hill to see the big picture, the facility between the hills. There were only two lasers on the back of the hill. These pointed down the slope rather than across the slope.

She hiked to within 300 feet of the two lasers and looked through the infrared lens again. She stood between, but out of range of the two beams. A clear path up the hill lay ahead. As she moved the binoculars away from her eyes, she detected movement. She looked again. The lasers moved. Now they converged in the middle of the slope.

The Operative shook her head.

Not bad. If you don't have enough lasers to cover the slope, you change the configuration so they move around at intervals.

She studied the lasers' movement to catch and analyze the pattern. She was impatient, but not foolish. Even if it took a couple of nights, she would figure it out.

Careful to prevent its light giving her position away, she pulled out her phone and started the notes app. She guessed at the time the laser switched position and noted an "x1" for the first crisscross position. After ten minutes, the lights switched back to the previous position.

Let's assume the interval is ten minutes.

She recorded the change and watched for the next one.

After three hours, she understood the pattern. She would have a ten-minute corridor up the hill in thirty minutes. After that corridor closed, the lasers would cross and uncross for ten minutes, covering the hill. If she was below the crisscross point when the random crosses began, the lasers would detect her movement. If she could get past the crisscross point in that ten-minute corridor, she'd be behind the lasers and safe.

She looked up the hill. Could she get past the crisscross point before the lasers started their random crosses?

Probably. It will be a sprint up the hill with all my gear.

There was no option. She had to try. She crept to the edge of the lasers' range at the foot of the hill. From her backpack, she pulled a bottle of pills and swallowed one. The drug would hyper-oxygenate her blood and increase her endurance.

At two minutes before the corridor opened, she rearranged the items in her backpack to balance and distribute the weight as low as possible. Then she pulled the backpack onto her shoulders and cinched it as tightly as she dared without restricting her breathing. The weight would throw her off balance if it shifted around.

She kneeled in a sprinter's starting pose. At the instant she expected, the lasers shifted and the open corridor appeared. She launched herself forward, sprinting flat out between the two lights and up the hill.

At the four-minute mark, her legs complained from the effort. They pumped like pile drivers. She pushed out all thoughts of exertion and pain, and focused on the point she had to reach. She didn't dare look at her watch because it would slow her down.

I'm close! I have to be close!

She tripped over something and fell on her face. She scrambled to her feet and started running again. Her legs reflected light. The lasers had found her. She dropped to the ground.

Her fall down the slope delayed her enough for the laser crisscross to catch her. She struggled to get her breath under control and listened. In the distance, she heard a klaxon blaring.

This place will be crawling with people in no time.

She scrambled to her feet and ran to the summit of the hill. From there, she could hear men whispering and running.

No place to hide.

She engaged the mission suit. It would help, but it wouldn't be enough at close range. She glanced around her. Could she bury herself enough to hide?

No.

Could she fight?

Yes, but would it make a difference?

No.

She closed her eyes and relaxed her mind. The answer flashed in her brain.

The personal shield!

She tore open her backpack, pulled out the shield, and closed the backpack. She dug a shallow hole in the sand and hid it. She strapped on the personal shield and activated it. She remembered the instructions — "If you're still and they don't look right at you, they won't see you." She curled into a ball.

She hoped the instructions were true.

Within ten seconds, a squad of men swarmed the top of the hill. They were in full battle dress and armed. The Operative went into shallow breathing mode. She could keep it up for thirty minutes before her blood oxygen got too low and she would pass out and start breathing at a normal rate.

The squad leader directed his men to search the hill, while he stood on the top.

A night scope covered his right eye. She made out the words 'US Army' printed on his breast pocket. With amazement, she realized the personal shield must also defeat heat sensors.

The squad leader paced back and forth on the hill. Once, he walked within a foot of the Operative's nose. If he were alone, she would have taken him out. But it was too risky with his squad all around her.

After fifteen minutes, the squad leader ordered his men off the hill, took one last look around, and followed them down the slope.

The Operative didn't move. If she were in his shoes, she would leave someone hidden on the hill for thirty minutes after they left, just in case.

She did the quick calculation in her head. *Thirty minutes is 1800 seconds.* She started counting the seconds. She would wait 2700 seconds before moving.

Her body ached from inaction. She needed to move.

At the 1800 second mark, a man rose from the scrub brush near her. He stood, looked around, then started down the hill. She wanted to follow him, but knew she shouldn't.

Discipline.

She remained still and let the stress bleed away.

At the 2100 second mark, a woman stood up. She was only five meters from the Operative. She laid still as the woman looked around, then started down the hill to follow her comrade.

638 gave the woman thirty seconds to clear the top of the hill. Then she moved. She crawled over to the edge and confirmed she was still walking down the slope.

She deactivated the shield, shrugged it off her shoulders, and vomited into the sand next to her. She crawled back to where she hid the backpack and pulled it out of the sand. It took a second to shake off the excess sand and pull out the binoculars.

She crawled to the edge of the hilltop and focused the glasses on the woman. Her teammate waited for her two-thirds of the way down. They stopped moving.

Why?

Then the reason was apparent. The glow of two cigarettes levitated in the dark.

The two were smoking before going back to... where? In the still of the night, she heard them talking, but they were too far away to understand their words. She widened the lens so she could see around them. Then she tightened the lens and focused on the sand at their feet. There were dozens of cigarette butts at their feet.

A smoking break place?

She scanned the area for low buildings or something to suggest a structure.

From where?

The two soldiers threw down their cigarettes and picked up their equipment. One of them reached down and pulled up a metal panel. It was an access door. They disappeared into the sand and the panel closed behind them.

Underground. They're underground.

Now it made sense.

She checked the time. It was time for the next corridor between the lasers. She stuffed her gear back into the backpack and started down the hill toward the crisscross point. Once the corridor opened, it should be easier to get down the hill.

She was wary of the place where she tripped and fell. She didn't want to trip again on her way down. Then she saw it and understood. She had tripped over a low profile air vent.

The corridor opened, and she ran down the hill. She made it to the bottom and beyond before the random laser crisscross started. She disengaged the mission suit, jogged to her Jeep, and drove back to her hotel room. Once inside, she showered to wash off the desert. It was nearly 6:00 AM. She laid down on the squeaky bed and fell asleep.

She first learned of her donor when she was eight years old. Her teacher took the class to a separate part of the camp. It thrilled 638 and the other children to go where they had never been. This building contained hallways of life-size photos of men and women on the wall.

638 marveled at the pictures as she passed them. One particular picture captivated her attention. It depicted a tall, stately woman wearing a uniform and standing at attention. She had long black hair and a slim, athletic body. Her expression was one of happiness and confidence. 638 thought she must be the most beautiful woman in the world. She reached out to touch the picture.

The teacher appeared beside her. "Do you know who she is?"

"No," 638 said, withdrawing her hand. "Is she a great warrior? She's beautiful."

"She is your donor. She is the reason you are here."

"My donor? What does that mean?"

"The doctors took a sample of her cells and used them to create you. You will look exactly like her when you mature."

"I will?" The idea thrilled 638.

"What is her name?" The teacher asked.

"I don't know."

"And you never will. Memorize what she looks like."

638 stared long and hard at the image. She committed everything in the picture to memory — the long black hair, the curves of her body, the strength in her face and posture.

"Do you have it?" the teacher asked.

"Yes."

"Good, now close your eyes and visualize her. Don't open your eyes until I tell you."

638 complied.

"Now, go over every detail of her face and body in your mind."

After a full minute, the teacher spoke again.

"Do you see her?"

"Yes."

"Open your eyes and look at her picture. Find what you visualized incorrectly, and correct it."

638 did as requested.

"Very good," the teacher said. "Never forget who you came from. It is an honor to be her clone. She is one of only a thousand to donate cells. You must dedicate your life to living up to her high standards — to become the best Operative you can. Make her proud of your work here."

"I won't forget. I'll make her proud."

"Use her image as a symbol to give yourself strength. Visualize her image again and again when you need strength."

"Yes, ma'am, I will."

The Operative awoke before 8:00 AM to noises outside her room. A peek through the window showed two kids trying to corner a jackrabbit in the yard. As she watched, the creature dashed this way and that, finally escaping and hopping toward the desert and freedom.

Relieved that she wasn't in danger, she went back to thinking about the mission. She had one option.

I'll get in and find Rachel. She's there and I'm going to get her out.

CHAPTER TEN

McKnight sat at his desk, working on the verification mission.

Planning this mission was an enormous challenge. When the SEALS snatch Kosar, a massive wave of changes will sweep across history. Putting aside his political meddling, the man developed a financial empire that involved hundreds of organizations. Each organization hired people, so the changes would affect those lives.

Wu couldn't estimate the number of changes. She said the number of variables was too large to even attempt the estimate. McKnight agreed with her.

He shook his head.

Snatching Kosar will be a disaster.

He agreed with Kathy's opinion that they should have a second mission ready to go — a mission to return Kosar to his life in the year 1986. At his suggestion, Kathy jumped at the chance to create the plan, even though General Drake hadn't authorized it yet.

He turned and put his feet on the credenza. He picked up the wall remote and clicked the "Transparent" button. The wall turned clear, giving him a full view of the woods behind the building and the sky above them.

All I need is a starting point.

He closed his eyes and folded his hands behind his head.

What would be the most important thing to check?

A few ideas came to him.

We should start with the government. Who's President? Are there power challenges or threats in the world?

After a few minutes, he spun his chair around and set to work at his computer. All he needed was a strawman plan to start with.

Create a rough document and get input from Tyler and Kathy. It's a lot easier to fix a plan than to write one from scratch.

There was a knock at his door.

"Come," he said.

The door opened, and Hatcher stuck her head in. "Got a second, Major?"

"I do. Come in, Lieutenant."

"Actually, sir, I need you to come to the lab. The General is asking for you."

McKnight stood, went through the door, and joined Hatcher in the hallway.

"That's weird. He usually tells me when he's coming by. What does he sound like?"

"Uh, himself, sir."

They walked side by side down the hall toward the lab.

"I mean…" McKnight said. "Oh, never mind."

They reached the lab door and Hatcher held her access disc against the lock. It clicked, and the doors slid apart. They stepped into the lab.

Against the far wall stood General Drake, with Tyler and Wheeler at parade rest in front of him. To the left, Tyler's wife Sarah and Wheeler's wife Lisa stood. With them were Hatcher's parents, General Connie Hatcher and Colonel Richard Hatcher. Doctor Astalos, Kathy Wu, and Trevor George stood together behind General Drake.

Kathy waved and walked over to McKnight. "Hello, Handsome."

Before McKnight could respond, Kathy punched him on the bicep of his left arm. He winced at the pain. "What was that for?"

"That's for not telling me you and Megan were engaged. Serves you right."

"How did you find out?"

"Megan told me."

A familiar voice came from behind him. "You come here often, soldier?"

McKnight whirled to find Megan standing there. The others laughed, and Hatcher and Kathy walked across to stand with Wheeler and Tyler at parade rest.

Megan slipped her arm inside his and pulled him toward the others.

"What are you doing here?" he asked. "What's going on?"

Her eyes twinkled. "Why don't you ask General Drake?" She walked with him to where Tyler was standing, pulled her arm from his, and stepped away.

"Now that we're all here..." the General said, then smiled. "Major, please fall in with the others."

McKnight formed up with the others and came to parade rest.

"Congratulations, sir," Hatcher said out of the corner of her mouth.

"Ditto, sir," Wheeler said.

Drake came to attention and said, "Ten-HUT!"

The four officers snapped to attention.

"I've waited a long time for this team to be recognized for their service to our country," Drake said. "And today is the day."

Trevor appeared, carrying a table with four small boxes on it. He placed it next to Drake.

Drake selected a box and said, "Major McKnight, please step forward."

McKnight stepped forward and came back to attention.

"Major, I won't make a long speech about your accomplishments here because it would bore you and everyone here already knows most of it. You're being promoted to Lieutenant Colonel." He handed McKnight the box and said, "Your Silver Leaves, sir." He stepped back and saluted McKnight, then extended his hand.

McKnight shook it and said, "I don't know what to say, sir."

"Say thank you, Colonel."

McKnight stammered out his thanks.

Drake picked up another box and stepped sideways. "Captain Tyler, please step forward."

Tyler stepped forward and came to attention again.

"You're promoted to Major. *Colonel* McKnight tells me you're the best X.O. on the planet. He's been pushing this for quite a while." Drake handed the box to Tyler and said, "Your Oak Leaves, sir." Then he stepped back and saluted Tyler, who returned a crisp salute.

Drake extended his hand, and Tyler shook it. "Thank you, sir."

"You deserve it, Major Tyler."

Drake sidestepped again and picked up the two remaining boxes.

"Lieutenants Hatcher and Wheeler, please step forward."

Hatcher and Wheeler moved forward in perfect unison and came to attention.

"You two have shown exceptional courage and determination in a unique job. I look forward to meeting the young officers you two train in the future. You're being promoted to Captain. We are bringing on two junior officers to expand the team so we can take on more projects. Here are your Bars."

Drake handed the boxes to them, stepped back and saluted. Wheeler beamed and Hatcher was stoic as usual. They snapped off salutes and shook the General's hand.

Drake stepped back in front of the team. He looked back and forth between their faces.

"It's been my pleasure to mentor this team, and we've come a long way together. Now the times are changing and we must change with them. The HERO Team is being expanded. We will split it into two command units and both will report to me. I offered the second command position to Major Tyler, and he has accepted. This second command unit will focus on a special project as its first assignment. Major Tyler will work alone initially in a planning mode. When the time comes, Major Tyler will get more resources to fill out his team and execute the project."

"I'm not at liberty to speak here about Major Tyler's mission, but he will update other members of the team as needed and permitted. There is one more change. Robert Astalos will continue in his role here with Colonel McKnight's team, and Robby Astalos will go along with Major Tyler. We will manufacture two new time Engines for use by Major Tyler's team."

"And now, I invite your families to come forward and help you with your new insignias," Drake said. "Dismissed."

He waved the families over to join them.

Megan stepped in front of McKnight. She reached up behind his neck and pulled him down so she could kiss his cheek. Her smile was dazzling. "I'm so proud of you, Marc. You've worked so hard."

McKnight handed Megan the box and repositioned himself so he could see the others getting their insignias pinned to their collars.

Sarah Tyler had been their friend long before she and Tyler married. Her bright red hair and blue eyes stood out in a crowd. As Sarah pinned Tyler's Oak Leaves onto his collar, he caught McKnight's eye and smiled. Then he looked back at Sarah.

I wonder what the new project is?

McKnight made a mental note to ask Tyler about it.

Lisa Wheeler pinned Wheeler's bar onto his collar. She hugged him and he kissed her. Then he stuck his right arm out toward Hatcher. Without even looking, the two friends fist-bumped each other.

Hatcher stood at attention, and her parents together pinned the Bars on her blouse. Stone-faced as she could be, McKnight could see a hint of pride and satisfaction.

Hatcher always claimed she didn't feel pressured by her parents. McKnight imagined what it would be like to have two senior officers for parents. He believed she got pressure from them, but it was a fraction of the pressure she put on herself.

"What are you thinking about, Marc?" Megan asked.

He scanned the officers from his command again and smiled in satisfaction. "Just enjoying the moment."

Trevor appeared in front of him and offered a shot glass of dark brown liquid. "We need some traditions for the unit. I think a Kentucky whiskey toast is just the thing."

McKnight chuckled and took the glass. "Well, I believe you're right."

Trevor moved to the center of the room and raised his glass. "To the HERO Team!"

In unison, the entire group shouted, "The HERO Team!"

CHAPTER ELEVEN

Monday, December 15th, 2036 - 6:32 PM - Telegraph Road, Alexandria, Virginia

McKnight and Megan watched the others celebrate their promotions.

He noticed that Drake and Tyler moved over to the time Engines and were talking with Doctor Astalos.

I wonder what that's all about?

"Megan?" he said.

"Yes?"

He pointed at Drake and Tyler. "I'm going over to see what they're talking about."

Her eyes followed his glance across the room, then settled back on his face.

"Abandoned again, am I?" she said.

McKnight opened his mouth to speak, but nothing came out.

"I'm *kidding*," she said, and patted his cheek. "I want to talk with Sarah and Lisa about some wedding ideas I have. Go on, play soldier. See if I care." Her eyes sparkled as she shooed him toward the other officers.

As he approached them, Drake looked up and said, "Marc, I'm glad you're here. I want to talk to you and Winnie about the new organization. Why don't you two get a drink and meet me at the outside conference room? I'll join you as soon as I finish with Robert here."

"Yes, go ahead," Astalos said. "I think I have something new you'll like."

Tyler and McKnight glanced at each other, nodded, and went back to the break area. Trevor had set up a temporary bar there. He wore an apron and a floppy straw hat and played up his role as bartender. Both officers opted for a Blue Moon.

Refreshments in hand, they walked out the loading dock door to the outside conference room. Despite the name, it wasn't a room at all. It was a picnic table where the team gathered during the warmer seasons.

By this time, the sun had gone down, and they expected a chilly discussion.

Reaching the area, they realized someone had the foresight to set up a gas space heater next to the table and lanterns in the oak tree beside it. The heater was going full blast, and the area was comfortable despite the time of year.

"Well," McKnight said. "Congratulations on your promotion. I was afraid senior command might be blind and promote some asshole with connections. It's good to hear the system worked for a change."

Tyler chuckled. "The General tells me you've been pushing on it for a while. Thanks, and congratulations back to you. Considerably overdue by my way of thinking."

"Thanks, and you're welcome. Drake understands the promotion game. He's put you in a position where we both have similar responsibilities. It makes it easier for him to say you should have the same rank. I feel another promotion coming for you pretty soon."

"Well, I thought of that. I hope I'm ready."

"You are."

"Thanks, Marc. Hey, remember back at the Point when we used to sit and drink beer and talk about what we'd do when we became generals?"

McKnight laughed. "Yeah. We were plebes, and we thought we had all the answers."

"Right. Blissfully ignorant."

Drake came out of the building and approached them. "Am I interrupting anything?"

McKnight and Tyler jumped to attention. "No, sir," McKnight said.

"As you were, gentlemen," Drake said. "Marc, I want to give you some insight into Winnie's new assignment."

"Yes, sir."

The General sat at the picnic table and motioned them to join him. They sat together across from him. Drake folded his hands together on the table and looked at McKnight.

"We've been working on an assignment for you to bring about some real changes to our government. It's no secret that partisan infighting in Congress has made it impossible for them to get anything done. I'm talking about the George Washington project, Marc. Bringing Washington to our time to explain to Congress what the Founding Fathers intended in the Constitution. It was President Taylor's idea and I think it's a great idea, but we have to be very careful not to screw up history while we're there."

"Yes, sir. I've been thinking about this and it brings a big question to mind. The ideal time to talk to him would be after his two terms as President. That's 1797. Based on our 25-year limitation, we won't be able to travel to that time for another ten years. We could jump today to 1812, but Washington will be dead for twelve years then."

"That's right, Marc," Drake said.

"If we go today, we're a couple of months before the Constitutional Congress and they haven't written the document yet. How is he going to explain what the Founding Fathers intended?"

"That's a brilliant question," Drake said. "In fact, I asked the same question. I'm glad you have that perspective."

"Yes, sir."

"Here's what President Taylor told me. There's a danger that this infighting and corruption of the legislative process will escalate into a shooting war. With the current situation, there's no telling what will happen. It could mean revolution, which carries a big price tag in terms of lives lost. It might also mean the end of this bright light American provides for the rest of the world. She believes Washington will contribute enough to change that flow and put us back on course."

"I don't follow that, sir. How could he know the future?"

"He won't, of course. History tells us Washington was in touch with many of the thought leaders back then. Hamilton, Jefferson, Jay, Madison, and the rest. They're already talking about the shortcomings of the Articles of Confederation that were implemented after the War for Independence. He won't know the results of the Convention of course, but he's familiar with all the arguments."

"I see. So he'll have familiarity with the issues, but not the result."

"Correct," Drake said. "Given his context, he'll have good input after you show him what they came up with."

"You mean, give him a copy of the Constitution they haven't written yet? Wouldn't that risk changing history?"

Drake shrugged. "Maybe, but we won't allow him to take a copy back to his time. On the other hand, Washington would return to 1787 with a sense of certainty that they can work the differences out."

Tyler spoke up. "Permission to speak freely, sir?"

"Of course."

"It still sounds pretty risky to me."

"Yes, it does," Drake said. "But the President believes the risk is greater if we do nothing. I talked with President-Elect Harrison about it as well. The President briefed him on the situation, and he agrees with her. We need to draw both sides of Congress back toward each other. Senator Lodge thinks it's worth a try as well, though he's skeptical that it'll make a difference."

McKnight considered this. "Okay. Thanks for the explanation, sir. It's a little scary, but I understand it now."

Drake looked back and forth between the two officers.

"Now, I need to ask you two something," he said. "Can you two commit to doing everything you can to accomplish the spirit of the mission? If not, we need to know now."

McKnight looked at Tyler, then spoke. "I can, sir. I'll do my best to make it happen."

"Me, too, sir," Tyler said. "If it can be done, we'll do it."

"Good," Drake said. "Back to the reason for this discussion. Major Tyler's project supports that mission. Here's what we've learned. No doubt you two are familiar with Francis Marion?"

"Of course," McKnight said. "He's considered one of the first Army Rangers. He and his raiders used tactics against the British that were unheard of. New and brilliant."

"Correct. And where did he learn those tactics?" Drake asked.

McKnight paused. "From the Indians. Radical tactics for that period in history. Soaking off attacks. Ambushes. Stay away from direct confrontation with the enemy. Target the officers. Attack and run away."

"Correct," Tyler added. "The British hated it. They considered it barbaric. They preferred the more civilized approach of lining two armies up forty yards apart and slaughtering each other."

"Correct," Drake said. "The colonials couldn't fight that way. The British Army was better trained and outnumbered them. They had to innovate or lose. They almost lost anyway, but they somehow pulled it out. Thank God. And now we come to the point."

Drake pulled his phone from his pocket and tapped on it. "I want to make sure I give you exact information about this." He pulled a pair of reading glasses from his blouse pocket and set them on his nose.

McKnight and Tyler glanced at one another. Neither had ever seen Drake with reading glasses.

"Some additional information has surfaced in Marion County in South Carolina. It's two diaries. One of them belonged to a clerk in Captain Marion's unit. The other diary belonged to a corporal. The two diaries describe concurrent events and line up with each other."

Drake let his words sink in.

"In the clerk's diary, we found a receipt, paid to a contractor for tactical and strategic training in early 1762."

"So what's unusual about that?" McKnight asked. "Don't they have a lot of documentation about Marion's unit?"

"Some," Drake agreed, "but most of it came from the Revolutionary War. Remember, in 1762 they were fighting the French and Indian War, where the colonists lined up with the British. They called Marion the Swamp Fox, but he didn't get that name until the Revolutionary War. But I'm digressing a little. We have little from the 1760s, and what we have is valuable. Like this receipt, for example."

Drake handed his phone to McKnight. Displayed on the screen was a picture of a handwritten receipt. The service rendered by the contractor was 'Training in the arte of Indian Combat tactics'. McKnight handed it to Tyler and looked back at the General.

Drake was grinning.

"Excuse me, sir, but what's so funny?" McKnight asked.

"Son of a bitch," Tyler muttered.

McKnight turned to him. "What?"

"Look at the contractor's name and signature, Marc." Tyler handed the phone back to him.

McKnight squinted at the image on the phone and used his fingers to enlarge the image. It was blurry, but the name of the contractor was clear.

Winston Churchill Tyler III.

McKnight looked at Tyler. "Is that your signature?"

Tyler nodded. "Sure looks like it."

McKnight turned back to Drake. "So we think Tyler taught Marion and his men modern-day strategic and tactical methods? Hand-to-hand combat?"

Drake shrugged again. "We don't know everything. But it's clear Tyler was there. The corporal was a poet and author, and his diary contained an excellent description of the contractor and it matches Major Tyler."

"So he has to be there to play that role?" McKnight turned back to Tyler. "What do you know about the Indian strategies and tactics?"

"Some, but I'm not sure that's what we taught them. I would tell them it came from the Indians. What else could I say? But some say the Indians provided the tactics, and Marion and his raiders adapted them to their needs. And they passed those tactics on to other units, who passed it to others. It may very well be that our mission trained them on modern tactics, which helped them win the war. How's *that* for a time paradox?"

"All that aside," Drake said, "we know Tyler was there, and they paid him to teach them how to fight. And if Tyler's name gets to General Washington, it'll add credibility for you when you contact him."

"Wow," McKnight said. "That's incredible. But we could make it work."

Drake nodded. "So Major Tyler will travel back to work with Marion and his raiders. He'll be taking with him two junior officers he will train on time travel and eighteen century culture and battle tactics. They'll be there about six months and make history."

Drake stood, and McKnight and Tyler followed his lead.

"And with that," he said. "I'll leave you two to consider the importance of your assignments. We're all counting on you. The fate of our fight for independence just might rest on your shoulders, Major Tyler."

He turned to McKnight.

"And the persistence of our form of government may depend on you, Colonel. Good night, gentlemen."

Drake turned and walked back toward the building and the continuing celebration inside.

CHAPTER TWELVE

Wednesday, December 17th, 2036 - 4:00 PM EST - McKnight's office, Telegraph Road, Alexandria, Virginia

McKnight sat in his office, thinking about the coming changes to the team.

Wheeler found a pair of lieutenants that looked promising after reading two dozen resumes. He was coming by at 4:00 PM to review the selection.

Someone knocked on the door. It was Wheeler, right on time.

"Still have time for a review, sir?" he asked.

"Sure. Come in."

Wheeler stepped into the room, came to attention and saluted.

"As you were, Captain. Sit down," McKnight said, and pointed to a chair.

Wheeler sat and laid his portfolio on the desk for McKnight.

"Here they are, sir."

"Tell me about them."

"Yes, sir." Wheeler picked up the first page, glanced at it, and handed it to McKnight.

"Here's the first one, sir. Lieutenant Daisy Lagunas. El Paso, Texas. Mixed Caucasian and Mexican heritage. Five foot six, brown hair and eyes. Fluent in English, French and Spanish. Marksmanship medals, degree in physics, skilled at making and disarming bombs. High marks in weapons, especially handguns, and strategic thinking."

"Sounds impressive. What's she like? Would she fit in with the team?"

Wheeler hesitated a little longer than McKnight liked. "Is there something wrong, Captain?"

"Oh, no, sir. I was just trying to choose the right words. She's a little shy, maybe because of her mixed heritage. Like me."

"You're not shy."

"No, sir, but it took a while, and I grew up in South Detroit. Lots of kids of all kinds there. But it's not the same in South Texas. If you're mixed, some Texans don't like you and neither do some Mexicans. Once you prove yourself, nobody thinks about it anymore. I'll get her to open up. And Hatcher would be an outstanding role model for her."

McKnight shook his head. "I'm not running a home for misfits."

"Oh, no, sir. Quite the contrary. She's smart, an excellent shot, and has experience in firefights at close range. She'll be fine, sir. My thoughts were about helping her out of her shell. She can do the job, no question."

McKnight looked at Wheeler for a moment.

"Okay, she's approved. Who's the second candidate?"

"I think you're gonna like him, Colonel." He glanced at the page, and handed it to McKnight.

"Lieutenant Edward Cutty. Six foot two, 220 pounds, sandy hair, brown eyes. He's a big boy, sir. Looks like Superman's kid. I get the impression his family is wealthy, and he's well-traveled, but he doesn't talk much about it. He speaks passable French, but picked up a lot of Arabic in the Mideast. He's humble but confident, Outgoing. Degree in Business Management and Computer Science. High marks in hand-to-hand combat, sharpshooter medal. Served as a sniper in the Mideast."

"Well, that could be handy. I hope we never have to use that skill."

"Yes, sir. I agree. But there's no substitute for it when you need it. I think he'll make a good planner and someone for Kathy to bounce things off."

"Okay. They look pretty good to me. Set them up an interview with Kathy for next week. Anything else?"

"No, sir," Wheeler said as he rose from his chair. He saluted McKnight, picked up the portfolio and left the room.

Okay. Check that off the list.

Friday, December 19th, 2036 - 9:45 AM EST - Telegraph Road, Alexandria, Virginia

McKnight stood with Trevor and Kathy at the time Engine console. They were waiting for Tyler and the Navy SEALS to show up for their mission to 1986 to kidnap George Kosar.

"I didn't know our country did kidnappings," Kathy said.

"It's pretty rare," McKnight said. "I've never heard of a kidnap mission, but I guess we have them. I've known about a few assassination missions. Those are pretty rare, too. Usually we don't, because then someone we don't know takes over. Then we have to figure out who they are and what they're capable of. Better the Devil you know, right?"

Trevor nodded. "Kathy's a SEAL groupie."

"Oh, puh-lease," she said, and socked Trevor on the arm. "I am *not.*"

"Just wait until they get here. We might have to hold her back." Trevor reached for her, and she pulled away.

"Don't touch me," she said, then flashed a grin at him.

"Are we using the old Engine or one of the new ones you captured?" Trevor asked.

"The old ones," McKnight said. "Doctor Astalos is still checking out the new ones. He says no one uses them until he tests them out."

The loading dock door opened and in walked Tyler with three men. All four wore period costumes, which were shabby-chic for Hungary during that time.

Despite their efforts to appear ordinary, the SEALS radiated power and their clothes couldn't mask their fitness and size. They carried several pieces of communications gear on a stretcher.

Tyler waved at McKnight, and the men took position on the time Engine platform.

"Aren't they going to introduce us?" Kathy asked.

"No, that's exactly what they will not do," McKnight said. "They're trying to maintain a low profile. That's hard to do if we have introductions all around."

"See what I mean?" Trevor said. When Kathy shot him a reprimanding glance, he turned and busied himself with the time Engine.

The SEALS kneeled on the Engine platform.

Tyler stepped over to the console. "Do we have beacons for everyone?"

"We do," Kathy said. "Here they are." She handed Tyler four beacons on chains.

"Thanks, Kathy. We'll be ready to go in just a second." He handed the beacons out, one to each of the SEALS and one for himself.

"Okay, men," he said. "Just like we practiced."

The three SEALS nodded and stared at the floor.

"Very good. Don't forget to keep your entire body inside the bubble, or you'll be sorry."

Two of the SEALS exchanged a look of uncertainty, bordering on panic.

"Kathy, we are ready to go at your convenience."

"I copy. Trevor, can you assist me, please?"

"Yes, ma'am," he said, and stepped behind the console.

"All right, gentlemen," Kathy said. "Target location is the shore of Lake Balaton, Hungary. Target time is 04:00 PM local time on December nineteenth, 1986. Are you ready?"

Tyler and the SEALS nodded.

"Travelers acknowledge Ready... Engine powered and ready to go. On my mark... five... four... three... two... one... Go."

Trevor pulled the trigger. The hum from the Engine rose in pitch and volume. Static electricity filled the air. A brilliant globe of spinning light formed around them. Their hair whipped around in random directions as if there was a hurricane inside the globe.

"I love this part," Trevor said.

McKnight glanced at him and suppressed a grin.

The hum grew louder, and the pitch rose until it was so high it was barely perceptible. Then it bulged and went out with a loud crack, and they vanished.

The room seemed darker now by comparison.

Trevor smiled. "That just never gets old."

"Yes, I know," Kathy said. "You say that every time."

"I do." He glanced at Kathy and laughed.

"How long do we expect them to be gone?" McKnight asked.

"A couple of hours," Kathy said. "We learned Kosar regularly went boating with his two sons in the afternoons. The team will go to the shore and wait for Kosar to land. I'm sure it'll be no problem. He'll have three SEALS there to take him, and it's supposed to be him and his sons. And they're little kids."

"Good. I'm going to my office to get some work done. I'll be back at 11:00. If they return before then, please let me know."

"Sure thing, Colonel," Kathy said, and executed a short curtsy.

McKnight resisted the urge to laugh. He loved Kathy's irreverent sense of humor. She never showed it in formal situations, but it was always there in the everyday operations. He presumed it was her way of diffusing tension.

He headed for his office.

Friday, December 19th, 2036 - 11:05 AM EST - Telegraph Road, Alexandria, Virginia

McKnight returned to the lab. Kathy and Trevor were still there. "How's it going," he asked. "Any word?"

"Just their arrival message," Kathy said. "Nothing out of the ordinary so far."

"Good. That's what I like to hear. When do we expect them back?"

"Any time now, I guess. The timing of the mission depended on when Kosar and his boys returned to the beach. The longer they took, the longer the mission would take."

They didn't have to wait long. Less than five minutes passed before the hair on McKnight's arms stood up. "Here they come."

"Yup," Kathy said.

The time bubble appeared, and brilliant light filled the lab. Tiny light particles furiously spun inside the bubble.

McKnight saw silhouettes in the bubble. He identified Tyler and the SEALS. Another man lay on the stretcher.

The globe bulged out and dissipated, leaving the men on the platform. They stood, and the SEALS gathered around Tyler.

"Thanks, Major," the tallest one said. "We appreciated the training and the support. Couldn't have done it without you." They shook his hand.

"That was great," one man exclaimed. "I'd love to do it again."

The other SEALS glanced at each other, and one said, "You're an idiot."

"You didn't like it?" the first man asked.

The other two burst out laughing.

"It was okay," the tallest one said. "Except for the beginning and the end."

"And the middle part," the other said.

Then they laughed. The tallest one said, "Okay, let's go put this guy on ice."

The SEALS carried the stretcher and their gear out the loading dock door.

Tyler watched them leave, then walked over to the Engine console.

"How was it?" McKnight asked. Kathy moved over and slipped her arm into his.

McKnight chuckled. *She really is a SEALS groupie.*

He glanced around for Trevor and found him in the lab break area. Trevor grinned at him and waved.

"It was… uneventful," Tyler said. "Very professional. I thought they were napping, but when the time came, they snapped into action without a word to each other. They just talked to him. You could see in his eyes he knew he couldn't escape."

"Good," McKnight said. "What was Kosar like?"

Tyler shrugged. "He was just a young man in his early thirties. It's hard to believe he's the man who's caused our leadership so many problems over the years. Of course, he's just a poor, small business owner. He hasn't begun his career in stocks and futures yet."

"Hmm," McKnight said.

"He was calm. He must be guilty of something, though. First, he asked the SEALS if they were the Russians. When Roscoe said no, he asked if they were the Americans. He seemed relieved when Roscoe said yes."

"No kidding. Where are they taking him? Did they say?"

"No, they didn't."

"What do you think? Gitmo, maybe?"

"Maybe," Tyler said. "They mentioned a place called the Iceberg. And you heard Roscoe say they were putting him on ice."

"I thought they were going to kill him," Kathy said. "That would be a bad idea."

"No, they're not," he said. "If they were going to, they'd have done it right away. These guys are really efficient. Besides, we might need to take him back if everything goes crazy, right? I think they'll take him someplace safe where they can get to him fast if they need to."

"I guess we don't need to know," McKnight said.

"Yeah, and I don't want to know," Tyler said. "I say good riddance and let's get on with our next mission."

"Not yet. We still need to see what changes we created by snatching Kosar."

"Yup. What's the best way to do that?"

"There's the mission in three days."

"Three days?" Tyler said. "I thought we would go sooner."

"I thought so, too. But it takes a while for changes to filter their way through the years. After we confirm there isn't a huge number of changes—"

"Are you kidding?" Kathy said, pointing at McKnight. "... If there isn't a huge number of changes? I don't believe that for a second."

"Correction," McKnight said. "If there isn't a huge number of changes in our time, we still need to go to the future — to 2086 — and see if the revolution he caused is still on, or if his removal takes all the steam out of it."

"I have an idea," Trevor said. "The last time we had a case where we suspected a history change, we got Doctor Astalos to check his Time Frequency analyzer."

"Not a bad idea," Kathy said. "What do you think, Marc? Are you in?"

"I am. Winnie, how about you?"

"Thanks, but no thanks. I still feel a little ill from the trip. I think I'll pass."

"Fine," McKnight said. "Trevor? Kathy? Let's go see Doctor Astalos."

CHAPTER THIRTEEN

Friday, December 19th, 2036 - 11:45 AM EST, Doctor Astalos' office, Telegraph Road, Alexandria, Virginia

Trevor, Kathy, and McKnight made their way to Doctor Astalos' office. His door was closed.

"He might not be here," McKnight said.

"No, I saw him earlier," Kathy said.

McKnight knocked. There was no answer.

He knocked again.

They heard a muffled grunt. McKnight looked at the others, then pushed open the door.

Astalos was looking at code on his computer. His head jerked up as they entered.

"Sorry, Doc," McKnight said. "I think we may have caught you at a bad time. Shall we come back later?"

"Too late," he said. "I'm already disturbed." He looked at his watch, then at his clock on the wall.

The old man smiled at them. "It's good you did. I've been working on code for three hours straight. I need to get up and stretch. What can I help you with?"

Trevor spoke first. "Doctor Astalos, when we chased a murder case a few months ago, do you remember you confirmed the murder was an illegal history change by looking at your Time Frequency analyzer?"

"Yes, of course I remember."

"Since we just completed the mission to kidnap George Kosar, we wondered if you could check it to see if there are any serious changes to history as a result?"

Astalos rolled his eyes. "I'm embarrassed I didn't think of it myself. Of course we can."

He rose and walked to the server on the north wall of his office and pulled out the terminal pad. He pressed a few keys and a three-dimensional holograph display appeared above the server. It was a graph with the time on the horizontal axis and a volume counter on the vertical axis. The horizontal axis scrolled slowly from right to left as seconds ticked by.

"As you can see, I've updated the analyzer to show the passage of time, rather than be a time snapshot."

"Okay, so what are we looking for, sir?" McKnight asked. "I missed the lesson you gave these two about what the analyzer does."

"Sure," Astalos said, and leaned back against the edge of his desk. "Time has a frequency, like a musical tone. It stays constant as long as no changes to history occur. Changes to history cause the frequency to have disruptions or spikes. To make it easier to see the spikes, I've tuned the frequency out so we only see the history changes. Changes will create vertical spikes on the graph. From our point of view, a flat line along the horizontal axis is good."

"You're saying we want a flat line," McKnight said. "A flat line equals no history impact."

Astalos touched his finger to his nose and pointed at McKnight. "You got it."

"Let's check on what happened with the event today." Astalos swiped his hand from left to right to turn time back to 1986.

McKnight glimpsed several spikes as the graph flew by. "Doc, what were those spikes back there?" he asked.

"Your previous missions."

"But I thought we fixed everything that happened. How can there still be changes?"

"There are always changes when you travel. Most of them are minor, like when you breathe air that otherwise would not be breathed. You make footprints on soft ground that weren't there before. You brought atomic particles back with you that should still be in the past."

McKnight, Trevor, and Kathy glanced at each other.

Astalos chuckled. "Don't let it bother you. Most are too small to have an effect, and nature compensates. Therefore, the time frequency has spikes, but they settle down and disappear when they no longer matter."

"What does that mean?" McKnight said.

"Well, here's an example. You travel back and create footprints in the desert. That creates spikes in the time frequency. But then a wind comes and fills your footprints with sand. That calms the frequency, because nature covered your tracks. The wind blew that day, no matter what you did. Tracks or no tracks *before* the wind, there are *no* tracks *after* the wind, either way. Make sense?"

"Yes, thanks. Please continue, Doc."

Astalos swiped left to right a few times and the year 1986 came into view. He halted the motion of the graph and looked at December 1986.

"Okay, I see some spikes here." He put his hands into the holograph and drew them apart to stretch out the graph and magnify the portion around December nineteenth.

There was a slight grouping of spikes on the horizontal line. Astalos pointed to the leftmost spike. "Okay, there's your kidnapping. It doesn't look like much effect yet."

He scrolled forward ten years to 1996. The frequency line went back down.

"Does that mean there's no effect?" McKnight asked. "How can that be? The man created a massive fortune, and now that won't happen. Why don't we see that?"

"You're not considering how a history change flows through time. We believe time is folded, based on the evidence. That's why we can only visit times that are twenty-five years or a multiple thereof from the exact present. But the impact of a history change rolls forward through time like a wave."

"How long does it take for a change to manifest in the present?" Kathy said.

"It depends on how long ago it happened and how big it is. From what we've observed, minor changes settle down and don't matter in the long term, so they disappear and the frequency settles back down. If it doesn't settle down, it's a fast wave and comes to the future faster. If it's a big change, the wave moves slower because of all the physical changes."

"I see," she said. "So what about this change?"

"Well, if it doesn't get any bigger, it should be here by tonight. But if it does, it'll slow down. If that's the case, it'll have a more serious impact — it will change a lot more stuff."

"That's my bet," Kathy said. She looked at Trevor, then McKnight. "I still think this'll blow up in our faces. Marc, I've got the correction mission already planned. You could go tonight and return Mr. Kosar to his own time."

"Well, we'll cross that bridge when we come to it." He turned to Astalos. "Thanks, Doc. Let us know if the impact grows."

"Of course, Marc, I..."

"What?"

Astalos stared at the graph. It had moved to 1997.

"I think I saw a small uptick, just now." He expanded the graph again, focusing in on early 1997. "Yes, see? There's a small upward movement. Not much, but a little. I'll monitor it and let you know if it gets bigger."

Thanks, Doc, McKnight said. "We'll let you get back to your coding."

"Good," Astalos said. "You're going to love what I'm working on. It's going to save you lots of time and energy."

"I'm all for that, Doc. Thanks." He motioned for Kathy and Trevor to follow him out the door.

Out in the hall, he spoke to them in a low voice. "Kathy, I think you're on the right track. I'm not questioning my orders, but I'll talk to the General for putting Kosar back and finding another solution. I think this one will have all kinds of flaws. Just have your plan ready for implementation."

"You bet, sir." She threw him a salute and beamed at him.

CHAPTER FOURTEEN

Friday, December 19th, 2036 - 10:10 AM PST - Outside the Iceberg Detention Facility, Rachel, Nevada

The Operative crouched next to the access panel on the hill. She pulled the locator from her satchel and checked again for Rachel. The device showed she was within a hundred horizontal meters of Rachel. She looked around, then checked the altitude. According to the device, Rachel was one hundred meters below her.

She's still here, and underground. I need to get in and assess the playing field.

After three days of observing the patrols, she found a penetration opportunity. It was a narrow gap, but it was a chance and she would take advantage of it.

They ran patrols every day, but she could approach the access panel at night and wait with the shield activated. She thought she was getting used to the shield. It still made her ill, but she could tolerate it longer. A headache came with it, but she could deal with that.

One patrol always took a smoke break before starting their walk around the hill. The hole in security was narrow. Most patrols came up through the access panel and secured it immediately. But one trio of soldiers came up, lit cigarettes, and then closed the panel. The gap in vigilance was less than ten seconds, but it might be enough. If she was quick enough and wore the personal shield, she could jump through the panel before they finished lighting cigarettes and returned to close it. She could widen the gap with a distraction in the opposite direction. It should work.

She made two previous attempts to breach the facility. On both occasions, a different team came out of the panel and closed it.

But her opportunity came. Crouching five feet uphill from the panel, she heard familiar sounds from inside.

A patrol is coming out. I hope the shield works just as well in the full light of day.

She activated the shield and picked up the rock she selected. As the first hint of nausea surfaced, she told herself it was only for a few moments.

The panel opened, and she scanned the faces of the men in the patrol. The first man out was familiar. Two more men followed him out as he lit his cigarette.

The Operative moved to the panel and was about to jump in when a fourth man came out.

They've increased the patrol size.

She stepped back one step from the panel opening. When no one else came out, she took the plunge. She threw the rock over the men's heads. When it landed beyond them, they turned away at the sound. She visualized her donor's image, slipped past the fourth man, and descended the stairs into the facility.

It was hard to see. After the bright light of the desert in daylight, the artificial light was dim.

She reached the bottom of the metal staircase and hid beneath it.

Did they hear me? Did anyone follow me down?

Above her, the access panel closed and the darkness increased. She waited a full minute for her heart to stop pounding and her eyes to adjust to the dimness.

When she could see better, she ventured out from under the staircase. The little light she perceived came from a single bulb in the high ceiling. She was in a closed room with a single door.

Almost like a security mantrap.

Am I trapped?

Had she underestimated the security of the facility? Had she defeated the outside defense, only to be snared by a mantrap inside?

It didn't make sense. The facility was in the middle of nowhere, and only someone in top physical shape could get up the hill past the security lasers. More security was likely unnecessary.

If it's a mantrap, there should be lights everywhere and someone should be challenging me by now. And where did all those men come from when I triggered the lasers? There must be a guardhouse near here.

She walked to the door and turned the knob. It wasn't locked. She opened it a crack and peeked through. A lighted hallway was on the other side. She closed it and leaned against the wall to think.

No door locks. It can't be a security feature. The staircase is isolated so light from the facility doesn't get out when the panel is opened at night.

She opened the door again, peeked, then slipped through.

She could hear people talking. The voices came from a room on the left. Again thankful for the shield, she tiptoed to the door and peered around the corner. Inside were soldiers playing cards, reading and using computers.

This is the guardhouse. This is where the troops came from the other night. I need to be prepared to sneak back by if I leave this way.

She walked away from the door and began her reconnaissance.

She passed an office and saw a clipboard hanging on the wall next to the door. After looking both ways, she took the clipboard.

Carrying this will create the illusion that I belong here and I am working on something.

Her head pounded, and her stomach was up in her throat. She needed to turn off the shield.

As she crept along, she noticed the hall was a tunnel. It was a perfect tube about thirty feet in diameter. They flattened the bottom out to make walking easier.

A medium-sized truck could drive through here. It's bigger than I expected.

At an intersection, she found a map on the wall. The facility looked like a giant 'X' with three levels. She peered down both turns to ensure no one was coming. She took a picture of the map for reference.

On this top level was a motor pool where the vehicles and main entrance were located. The commandant's office and other administrative offices were here, too. A gymnasium was on this level, along with a bar, a movie theatre, and a recreation hall.

The troop barracks and medical facilities were on the second level. Twenty detention cells populated the bottom level. On the map, the cells looked huge.

The gymnasium was fifty meters from her, down the cross corridor. She headed that way.

It was too early for much gym traffic. In the women's locker room, there was only one soldier there. The Operative watched as the woman stripped off her clothes, slipped into gym shorts and t-shirt, closed her locker, and left the room.

This was better than the Operative hoped. She expected to break into several lockers to find clothes that fit well enough to appear natural. This soldier was about her size.

She defeated the lock on the woman's locker and took an Army Combat Uniform and the soldier's ID card. She guessed the soldier would work out for thirty minutes to an hour, shower, then spent about thirty minutes looking for the card before she reported it. That should be enough time to recon the facility.

She walked into the toilet area, turned off the shield, and vomited into the toilet. Then she pulled the combat uniform on over her mission suit. She attached the ID card and checked herself in the mirror. She bore little resemblance to the owner of the ID card, but it would suffice as long as no one challenged her.

It'll have to do for now.

The next order of business was to find Rachel.

I'll start with the detention level. That seems obvious.

She checked the map again for the elevators and staircases. The security around the elevators was likely to be tighter. She chose the staircase.

Inside the staircase, she checked the locator again. Rachel was less than twenty meters away horizontally and fifty meters vertically.

She's right below me.

The Operative sighed. Soon she would have to use the shield again. That meant more nausea and more headache.

CHAPTER FIFTEEN

Friday, December 19th, 2036 - 1:16 PM, Robert Astalos' Office, Telegraph Road, Alexandria, Virginia

Robert Astalos was relaxing by a lake in upstate New York, a fishing pole in his hand. He heard chirping. At first, he couldn't discern where the sound was coming from. His tackle box, maybe?

No.

He checked his pockets. Phone?

No. What the devil?

He twitched and woke up.

He had fallen asleep at his desk while studying a screenful of computer code.

What a dream! Fishing and then chirping...?

I still hear chirping.

He looked at the items on his desk. It was his phone. He picked it up.

A notification blinked at him from the display.

> <<< *Analyzer Threshold Met... Sending results to email.* >>>

He checked the time.

Only a couple of hours!

He called up the email app on his desktop and waited for new mail to arrive from the server.

There it is.

The analyzer sent the message at 1:10 PM. He opened it. The history changes from the Kosar kidnapping had reached the threshold he set to trigger an alert message.

He yawned as he accessed the Time Frequency Analyzer app he designed and looked at the data.

Is this true? What the hell?

He rechecked the time. Less than ten minutes from the notification and the changes had already doubled.

Wow.

He selected the texting app and entered Marc's and Kathy's numbers into it. General Drake was at the facility today, so he added his number to the address line. He paused for a second to compose the message, then typed:

<<< *Mike/Marc/Kathy, Time Frequency Analyzer shows significant changes from the Kosar kidnapping in the last few minutes. I expect it to increase fast. Please join me in my office if you can at 1:30 PM for a briefing. — RA* >>>

Astalos waited for a response.

McKnight responded, followed by Kathy. Both acknowledged they were on their way to his office.

Friday, December 19th, 2036 - 1:30 PM, Robert Astalos' office; Telegraph Road, Alexandria, Virginia

After talking to Doctor Astalos, McKnight decided to lead the briefing for General Drake.

At 1:30 PM, Drake arrived to meet with McKnight, Robert Astalos, Kathy Wu, and Tyler.

The meeting began with the Time Frequency Analyzer. McKnight spoke while Astalos worked the Analyzer display.

"As you can see," McKnight said, "the changes to history started in 1986, when the SEALS pulled Kosar out of history. The changes were minor and nothing much happened until 1997, when Kosar's sons were 19 and 20. At that point, the boys got involved with Kosar's brothers in the arms business. In our previous history — the one with

George Kosar in it — the boys worked for their father doing promotion. George didn't get interested in anarchy until he amassed a fortune. But in our current history, they missed their father's guidance and went into the arms trade."

"From that point on, the changes to history escalate. Most of the impact is in Europe, the Mideast, and Asia. The validated impact to the US is small, but…" McKnight pointed to Tyler and Kathy, "We believe the potential impact is off the scale."

"Noted. Okay," Drake said. "What's different?"

"Before we get into that, sir, one last word on the change wave. It's slowed down. That's not good news because it means history's frequency is not settling down. Instead of compensating for the change we made, it's skewing away from the original track. According to Doctor Astalos, the wave has reached the year 2044. We've planned a mission to go to 2086 in three days. The wave will reach that time by then."

"Okay. What's the good news, bad news story here?"

"Yes, sir. First, the absence of George Kosar means there's less capital available for anarchy in the United States. More on that later. The Kosar brothers' chief customers are Iran and ISIS."

"ISIS?" Drake said. "Weren't they wiped out during the Trump Presidency?"

"Yes, sir, but they resurfaced under the next administration, which was friendlier toward Iran. They aren't widespread, but they dominate the small area they occupy in western Iraq. It's bad news, but not immediately threatening to the US."

"Okay. Who do they get their weapons from?"

"Good segue, General," McKnight said. "They get them from the Russians and the Chinese Communist Party."

Drake shook his head. "That's not good. I would expect the Russians, but CCP's presence in central Europe is troubling. Do the Russians know CCP is there?"

McKnight shrugged. "We don't have any indications either way. I find it hard to believe they don't, but it's possible."

Drake grunted. "Okay. What else?"

"In the western hemisphere, Homeland Security is aware that factions in Argentina and a nasty group in Oregon have made overtures to the Kosar brothers, looking for support in both cash and weapons."

"Can the Kosar brothers support either group's agenda enough to make a difference in the results?"

"We think so, sir. The brothers haven't agreed to any deal yet. At least not that we know of. But it bears watching. The group in Argentina is sending agents into the US through our Mexican border. When they get in, they try to inflame Hispanic populations with identity politics methods. The group in Oregon is a remnant of Antifa, which was active in the 2020s. It's important to note George Kosar supported both these organizations in our original history. At least this item is trending back toward our previous history."

"So snatching Kosar didn't make any difference?" Drake said.

"I wouldn't go that far, sir, but it's trending that way here in the United States."

"I see. Okay, what else?"

"The next one worries me the most," McKnight said. "There are still some Iranian-supported Islamic cells in the US, and Homeland Security suspects at least one cell of radicalizing scientists and workers at the Center for Disease Control."

"I see why you worry about that one, Colonel," Drake said. "What do we know?"

"Just some observations, sir. Homeland Security saw one man associated with the Atlanta cell at a local club with a female scientist from the CDC."

"But it could just be recreation for the jihadis, right?"

"It could, but I don't believe so in this case. Do you remember we had ten murders this summer that we attributed to Rachel Patterson and her radicals in 2086?"

"Yes. She and her people used time travel and murder to shape the political positions of our Congress. Is there any relationship here?"

"Yes, sir. All ten murders were close to the same M.O., but one was distinct from the others. That one murder had no political implication we could find. When I was Rachel's reluctant guest in 2086, I asked her about this. She pointed out that she ordered nine political murders, not ten. I never learned which of the ten it was, but in that one case, the victim was a scientist in the CDC. The *same* scientist that was seen with the Jihadi at a local club."

"I see your logic. That *is* suspicious."

"Yes, sir. If it is possible, I'd like to have Rachel questioned about this. I'm pretty sure Rachel killed her or had her killed. We now believe she killed the woman to prevent her from giving the Iranians a deadly pathogen. Rachel can kill people without remorse, but *not* without a motive. We need to understand this and the only way to do that is to interview her."

Drake nodded. "Agreed. I'll arrange it with the President. Let's go there this evening. Can we do a non-time jump there, Robert?"

"Absolutely, Mike," Astalos said. "Give me twenty minutes and the precise location where she is and I'll have things ready."

"Good," Drake said, "and I'll arrange a welcoming committee for Colonel McKnight." He glanced at his watch. "What else?"

"Actually, sir," McKnight said, "I'd like to send Captain Hatcher to talk to Rachel. With me, she'll be flirtatious and dance around the subject. But Hatcher knows her better than anyone, and Rachel is afraid of her. Hatcher will get more out of her."

"Okay. Welcoming committee for Captain Hatcher. What else?"

"Two more things, sir," McKnight said. "I know your time is short. I want to point out that, as we all know, the Iranians have been trying to get a nuclear weapon for years and, through the Kosar brothers, they now have two sources — the Russians and the Chinese Communist Party. Both want to increase their influence in the Mideast and providing WMDs to the Iranians is a simple way to do that."

"Understood. Thanks. And the last item?"

McKnight pointed at Kathy. "I want Kathy to speak to this subject. With her background in politics, she understands this better than me. Kathy?"

McKnight stepped aside as Kathy stood.

"Thank you, General Drake, for giving me a few minutes to share my thoughts. You already know I was against the idea of snatching George Kosar. We kidnapped him earlier today, so we still have a six day window to jump to the date of the kidnapping. We should put him back."

"That's the President's decision, Kathy."

"Yes, sir, I know. But she listens to you. General, I don't need to tell you about the leadership of Iran. They belong to that sect of Islam that believes they're called to bring about Armageddon. We know, if they get a viral pathogen or a nuclear weapon, they *will* use it on Israel. They hate us for supporting Israel and interfering with their jihad, so the US is their second most desirable target. They think it's their purpose to bring about the end of the world, and they don't care if it's a bomb or a biological weapon. And I believe their goal is now more likely because we snatched George Kosar. We should put him back and end this timeline. We've made history changes before, but always to put things back to the original timeline. Changing history on purpose and checking the results is not the way to go. There's always the chance we'll screw things up so bad we can't fix them. I understand why President Taylor wants George Kosar out of the picture, but this approach is too dangerous."

Drake smiled at her. "And I agree with you, Kathy. I'm briefing the President in a couple of hours. I want you to come with me. With the information Colonel McKnight provided and your perspective, we have our best chance to convince her to stop and put Kosar back. I'll send a car to your apartment at… 4:30 PM? Will that work?"

"I'll make it work, sir, and thanks for the opportunity to make my case."

"It's our case, Kathy, but I'm happy to let you make it."

Drake turned to McKnight and Astalos. "Gentlemen, I'll arrange the visit to the Iceberg for Captain Hatcher. Call me when she's ready."

"The Iceberg, sir?"

"Yes, that's where they're keeping Stagne and Rachel, and George Kosar is on his way there. It's an underground facility in the Nevada desert. It was built as a bio-warfare lab, but the Army converted it to a max security prison. Captain Hatcher can interview Rachel there and find out what she's willing to tell us."

CHAPTER SIXTEEN

Friday, December 19th, 2036 - 12:46 PM PST - The Iceberg Detention Facility, Rachel, Nevada

The Operative descended the stairs to the bottom level. She opened the door a crack and peeked through. She saw people twenty meters down the hall.

The clipboard will come in handy.

She looked at her watch. The owner of the ID card she stole must have reported it by now.

Stay sharp! Don't get noticed.

She walked down the tunnel toward the people, trying to look like she belonged there.

The first person she passed was guarding a cell. She nodded at the guard and stole a look at the name above the door.

301 - Oliver Stagne.

Her heart leaped. I must be close. She continued down the corridor and found a second guarded cell.

303 - Rachel Patterson.

Her excitement grew as she continued down the tunnel. She reached the tunnel crossroads and turned left. After going twenty meters, she looked back to confirm she was alone. Satisfied, she stopped and leaned against the sloping wall.

She checked the locator again. Rachel was at the same vertical level and back down the corridor about eighty meters.

It appears she's in her cell. I've accomplished the first part of my mission.

She closed her eyes and checked off what she would have to do.

Subdue the guard.

Figure out how to open the door.

Convince Rachel she should come along.

Time-jump out.

Do I take her out now or come back later?

She checked her watch. Time was getting short before the security team realized there was an intrusion in progress.

There was another cell in front of her. The sign above the door read: *311 - George Kosar.*

The cell was open, and there was no guard. She walked to the entrance. There was a schedule posted next to the door and she scanned it. It was a cell preparation checklist: all the tasks required to get a cell ready for a new occupant.

This Kosar guy arrives at 3:30 PM today. She glanced at her watch. Plenty of time.

It occurred to her it would be useful to know what the inside of a cell looked like. Rachel's cell should be similar, if not identical.

On her tiptoes, she dashed back to the crossroads and confirmed no one was coming her way.

Then she noticed the cameras. She chastised herself for not seeing them earlier. It wasn't like her to miss a detail like that.

Could something be impeding my judgement? Watch your posture. Act like you belong here.

She leaned against the wall and studied the clipboard for a few moments, trying to look like she was working. Then she went back to the cell. The door resembled a bank vault.

She stood in the doorway while she put on the shield. If she was lucky, the doorway would be a blind spot between cameras in the hall and cameras in the cell. She didn't want to get trapped inside the cell when someone arrived.

She took a deep breath and entered the room.

The cell was brightly lit. It was large — about forty by forty feet. It contained a toilet area, a bed, a furniture pit group, a desk, a large

TEV screen, and a kitchen. It even had an exercise area with a universal, a treadmill, and a state-of-the-art stationary bike.

The light switch by the door was complex. It had several modes to it. Someone set it to the sunlight option. Other options were nighttime, artificial light, rainy day, and twilight. She switched between the settings. The authenticity of the lighting impressed her.

The inmate will never leave this room. It provides every amenity except freedom.

She paused to consider the implications.

There will be no opportunity to grab Rachel in transit from one place to another. I have to break into her cell to get her out.

It occurred to the Operative she had been in the Iceberg for too long. Her chances of being detected and captured were going up by the minute.

Her head was hurting, and a wave of nausea swept across her. She left the cell and walked back down to the crossroads and turned left, away from Rachel and Stagne's cells. The community bathroom of that hall was fifteen meters down.

She slipped inside, entered a stall, and pulled off the shield. She vomited into the toilet and fell to her knees and heaved until she felt drained and dehydrated.

What if using that thing has permanent effects? It can't be good.

The room spun, and she hallucinated. She saw disease and panic. Riots and burning buildings. A frightening populace. Soldiers controlling crowds.

A plague...

She saw Number Three ordering her to isolate herself. She saw a cabin in the mountains. There was no map or sign, but she knew she was near Estes Park in Colorado. She had never been there.

There's been a plague. Everyone is dead.

She could see the coming civil war in the United States. And her mind's eye showed her again how they commissioned her to come to the past and liberate Rachel Patterson.

Her conscious mind told her the two memories were inconsistent.

Training kicked in. She pulled out her phone, scanned her implant, and pulled out the mission statement. She skimmed it, and she understood.

There's been a change in history. I'm seeing both pasts and the new one will soon take over. They sent me to a cabin in Colorado to avoid dying.

She used the locator to check on Rachel. The device behaved oddly. It flashed Rachel's location, then it showed it couldn't find her. The display flashed between these two messages, then stuck on the latter.

<<< Subject Not Found >>>

What?

The klaxon startled her when it erupted in sound. A loudspeaker crackled and a disembodied voice said, "Intrusion alert. Intrusion alert. All personnel report to their duty stations. Point of intrusion is cell 303. Security to the intrusion point."

Rachel's cell!

She reluctantly donned the shield again and ran to the door of the bathroom.

Three soldiers in full battle dress ran by her. She followed them down the hall toward cell 303.

When they arrived at the cell, she noticed Rachel's name was no longer printed on the sign above it. A glance at Cell 301 told her Stagne was gone, too.

She looked for the common bathroom on this wing. It was thirty meters back up the tunnel. Using the locator would have to wait until this situation resolved itself.

Several guards were standing around the cell entrance, and one female soldier was speaking through the intercom to the interior of the cell.

"I'm sure the Major will decide that, ma'am," the guard said. "Please lie on the floor in front of the door with your arms and legs spread out. Do not resist when we enter the cell."

A thin voice came out through the intercom. "Understood. I'll comply."

"Thank you, ma'am."

From the elevators came a pair of officers, a woman and a man. The woman was a major, and the man was a lieutenant.

The guard at the console turned to face the major and saluted.

"What's going on, Sergeant?" she asked.

"The intruder is inside, ma'am. Female. She claims to be a friendly. She mentioned your name."

The major paused for a moment. "Okay," she said. "Crack it open. Stay safe, everyone. Don't take any unnecessary risks. Go now."

"Yes, ma'am. Team Charlie. Go now."

The door cracked open, and the armed team entered the cell. After ten seconds, the Operative heard the team pronouncing the room all clear.

The major pushed her way through the soldiers outside the cell and entered. Her lieutenant followed her. A soldier pushed the door closed.

The nausea rolled up into her throat. With an effort, she pushed it down. She moved to maximize her view into the room when the door opened again.

CHAPTER SEVENTEEN

Friday, December 19th, 2036 - 4:13 PM EST, Telegraph Road, Alexandria, Virginia

Hatcher arrived at the Telegraph Road office and walked into the lab.

Doctor Astalos was waiting for her. Wheeler was also there, programming the jump. As she approached the time Engine, Wheeler waved at her.

She nodded, and he went back to his jump configuration. The Engine hummed under his fingers.

"Hello, there, Captain Hatcher," Astalos said. "All set to jump?"

"As ready as I ever am."

"Good. It sure beats taking a flight to Nevada."

"That, it does. Wheeler, how's it going?"

"Great," Wheeler said. "I wish I was going with you. I'd like to hear what Major Patterson has to say for herself."

"I know where you're coming from. All things considered, I'd rather it was you instead of me. But the Colonel is hoping she'll be more candid with me in private."

"Yeah, he's probably right."

"Do you know who you're meeting there?" he asked.

"Yes. It's Major Souther. She was at the Academy with the Colonel and Major Tyler. Let's get going. Do you have a beacon for me?"

"Yes, ma'am," he said, and handed a beacon and chain to Hatcher.

"Thanks." She slipped the chain over her head and knelt on the Engine platform.

"Good luck, Captain Hatcher," Astalos said. "Mitch will do the honors today. This is a non-time jump. We're sending you to the Iceberg Detention Center in Nevada without a time component. It's 4:15 PM here in Virginia and you will land in Nevada at 1:15 PM Pacific Time. Mitch?"

"Thank you, Doctor." To Hatcher, he said, "We're already gone through most of the checklist. Do you acknowledge possession of your beacon?"

"I do," she said.

"Traveler acknowledges receipt of beacon." He held up the Engine trigger, flipped up the trigger guard, and said, "Initiating travel in five... four... three... two... one... mark!"

Wheeler pressed the trigger and the Engine hum rose in pitch and volume. The time bubble formed around Hatcher and the windstorm started. She felt the spinning air tugging at her clothes. She tied her raven hair back into a ponytail, but it still stung her cheeks as the bubble's tornadic winds blew it around her face.

The sound and light escalated until brilliant light filled the room. Hatcher closed her eyes.

The bubble bulged, and she fell through the familiar field of stars.

Soon, she perceived a dim room around her. The walls appeared to be made of stainless steel. Indoor/outdoor carpet covered the floor.

The time bubble bulged, and she fought off the backward pull. She stood and looked around.

A tall, attractive blonde officer stood ten feet away. The oak leaves on her collar identified her as a major.

Major Souther.

The officer smiled and approached her.

Hatcher came to attention and saluted. The Major returned the salute.

Colonel McKnight briefed her on Souther. The comely woman in front of her was a friend from the Academy. She was a year behind

McKnight in school and lived across the hall. The Colonel said she was smart and efficient.

"Major Souther?" Hatcher asked.

"Yes, Captain Hatcher," she said. "It's a pleasure to meet you."

"Colonel McKnight sends his regards. He said it surprised him to see you here. He said to tell you, and I quote, 'Last I heard, she was shooting up targets with new weaponry. This duty seems inappropriate, somehow.'"

"*Colonel* McKnight?" Souther said. "Moving up in the world. I hadn't heard. So he briefed you on me? What did he say?"

"He said you were friends at the Academy, ma'am."

Souther stared at Hatcher for a moment. "Yeah? I can see he trained you well. Okay, tell the Colonel that I'd rather be shooting up targets with excessive firepower, but they needed me here. My commanding officer set up this place and needed an officer to run it, so I volunteered to help until they could find someone. Hopefully, I'll be back on the shooting range within a month."

"I understand," Hatcher said with a smile. "I'll tell him. I'm sure he'll be glad to hear it."

"Yes, please do. Colonel McKnight and I are old friends, but he probably told you that. Anyway, I see you're here to see Major Patterson. I'm presuming you'd like to get to it?"

"Yes, ma'am, I would. By the way, I didn't get a briefing on this place. Can you tell me anything about it?"

"Yes, Captain. When the Secretary called to say you were coming, he gave me permission to share with your team. I can give you the abbreviated tour on the way to the Major's suite." She gestured to the right, and said, "This way."

They walked down the hall.

"Suite?" Hatcher asked.

"That's what we call them. Security features were already on each of the labs. They have vault doors and a security system for going in and out. It was pretty obvious that they would be ideal for long-term cells. They're big — about forty by forty feet. We have twenty of them."

"Impressive, ma'am."

"Yup. And you didn't get a brief because it doesn't officially exist. It was originally a biological warfare lab. When that work was absorbed by CDC, the facility was no longer needed."

"I see."

"Right now, we're 212 feet below ground. We have three levels and we're on the lowest one. That's where the suites and the monitoring station are. We have our own positive pressure air system, we're hermetically sealed, and the place has its own personal self-destruct system in case a bug gets out of containment. "

"Wow."

"Yes, ma'am. We're self-contained and can hunker down for three months without having to open the doors. We even have enough compressed air in storage to last a month."

Hatcher looked around as they walked. The hallway was a steel tube with the bottom flattened for traffic. There was a drop ceiling above with bright recessed light. It felt more like a hospital than a germ warfare installation.

"We have labs, a mess hall and kitchen, a barracks, TV and Rec room, an armory, locker rooms, gym, workout room and plenty of storage, electrical, and nuclear power closets," Souther said. "Altogether, we have about 200,000 square feet of usable space."

"That's amazing," Hatcher said. "What's the staff requirement?"

"Project plans called for a major to command, a medical captain, two lieutenants, and thirty enlisted personnel. The doctor, one lieutenant, and six enlisted staff support the guests. The other lieutenant and enlisted personnel are on protection detail."

"How did this place come to be? I mean, the Iceberg? Why did they repurpose it?"

"Good question. I've been here since it started… about two months ago. You should have seen it when I got here. The bio people shut it down tight. We had to bring all the systems and equipment back online. To answer your question, my understanding is the Colonel and your team created the need."

"We did?"

"Yes, I believe so. Our government is looking for a facility to replace Gitmo. There are always people out there who want to harm the United States, and their civil rights are going to be violated to keep them contained." Souther shrugged. "They're too dangerous to release, so we have to put them somewhere."

"People like Rachel Patterson?" Hatcher asked.

"Yes," Souther said. "While Gitmo has been useful, it's still a place that costs political capital every year."

"I think I'm understanding why they call it the Iceberg. Because they want to 'put someone on ice', if you will."

"Yes. They don't want to kill them, but they don't want them out walking around and causing trouble, either. For that purpose..." She waved her arms at the facility. "This place is perfect."

"How many prisoners are kept here?"

"As of now? Just two."

"Rachel Patterson and Oliver Stagne?"

"Yes. And my understanding is that a guy named George Kosar is on his way here, too."

"What are the arrangements for Mr. Kosar?"

"He'll still be in shock, I think. He arrives in a couple of hours. They told us he'll be unconscious, and he thinks it's 1986. We won't tell him it isn't. He'll be one frustrated puppy. He'll want to know why he's here and I can't answer that question. We'll stream old network television into his cell and provide him with any books he wants to read. He'll also get all the movies and food he can consume."

"Sounds boring. I feel sorry for him."

"Me, too. Do you know why he's coming here?"

She doesn't know? Ah, yes, the change wave passed through this time already. Before we snatched him, everyone knew about Kosar the globalist.

"It's a long story, but believe me, he deserves to be here. But I have a feeling we'll pull him out soon."

"Okay. Can I ask why?"

"No. Sorry."

"No, no problem."

Change the subject.

"What do you think of Major Patterson and Mr. Stagne?"

"Stagne? Not much. He's lost it. Completely out of touch. He must have been a big deal before, so he orders my people around like they're his people. I don't think he's dangerous at this point."

"What about Rachel?" Hatcher asked.

"She's hard to read. Clearly intelligent, and I'm told she's an Army Ranger officer from the future. She seems more like a suck-up to me."

"What do you mean?"

"She's very polite and eager to curry favor. Charming, too. She acts like she wants to be best friends forever, right? My orders and instincts tell me not to believe anything she says. I feel like she's sucking up so she can get special treatment and privileges."

Hatcher laughed. "I guess that's true. She can be that way."

"Now that I think about it," Souther said, "She's mentioned a man who did her wrong. From the description, she might have been describing Colonel McKnight. Is that a possibility?"

The Colonel was right. She's quick.

"Maybe. There's not always a close relationship between what's true and what she thinks."

"Okay. I get that." She paused. "She arrived here with a nasty cut across her nose. Is your team responsible for that, too?"

"You bet. I gave it to her myself. I popped her to get control of a situation, and I'd do it again in a heartbeat. Believe me, she had it coming."

"Understood. Then I'm led to understand you see her differently? Not a suck-up?"

"Well, yes, she *is* a suck-up, but I do see her differently. It's likely she's planning her escape already, and sucking up to get information about the place. She's not playing with a full deck at least part of the time."

"Is that your professional opinion, Captain?"

Hatcher chuckled.

The Colonel told me she would question everything.

"No, just personal experience." She looked at the ceiling and paused.

If I don't convince her of Rachel's capability, I'm putting her in danger.

"I'll tell you this. Maybe it'll give you some perspective. She tried to kill me once. Her people captured me and kept me bound up like a turkey in a supermarket. Her actions ranged from kissing me to programming me to kill Colonel McKnight — all within minutes. I watched her kill a man because she didn't like him, and she didn't even blink. She's capable of murder and wouldn't hesitate to kill either of us if she thought it was to her advantage."

When Hatcher looked back at her, Souther was searching her face. "I'm presuming the programming didn't take?"

"No, ma'am, it didn't. We're past that now. My point is, don't underestimate Major Patterson."

After a moment, Souther said, "Okay, Captain. I get the message. I'll be careful."

She pointed to the left, and they turned down another passageway.

"One more thing, Captain?" Souther said.

"Yes, ma'am?"

"When she arrived, we gave her a thorough physical. I got the results this morning."

"And?"

"And she has a malignant tumor in her abdomen. Cancer."

"How bad?"

"Bad enough. It's treatable, and she should live if she gets treatment, which of course we'll provide."

"I see. Does she know?"

"I planned to tell her today. But I'm holding off until you have your little talk with her. Is that all right with you?"

Hatcher nodded. "Yes, ma'am. I want her sharp and focused on me. You can tell her afterward. Or I can tell her."

Souther shook her head. "No, I've got it. I'll have all the charts and X-rays for her."

"Okay. Thanks, Major."

"No problem. Ah, here we are. We're pretty close to her cell now," she said. "Off the record...?"

"Yes, ma'am?"

"What's the Colonel's status now? We used to go out together, but orders separated us before anything real developed. Is he in a relationship?"

She's interested in the Colonel. I can save both of them some embarrassment if I share a little personal detail.

"He's about to get married," she said. "He met one of Tyler's cousins about eighteen months ago. They've been together ever since. Her name is Megan. And you? What can I tell him about you?"

"Ha," she said. "Still kicking around. Bummer that he's taken, but I'm glad for him. Lucky girl."

"If I were candid, I'd say the Colonel believes he's the one who's lucky."

"Ah, then she really *is* lucky."

Hatcher looked at Souther and received a smile.

They approached a steel vault door with an armed corporal in front. He snapped to attention when they approached.

"Ah, here we are," she said. "At ease, Corporal."

Souther touched a switch on the comm panel and spoke.

"Major Patterson?"

After a moment, Hatcher heard Rachel's melodious voice through the speaker.

"Yes, Major, I'm here. Where else would I be?"

Souther gave Hatcher a knowing glance.

"You have a visitor. Are you presentable?"

"Yes. Who is it?"

Souther looked at Hatcher, who shook her head.

"It's an officer from the HERO Team."

There was a pause. "I'll see him. Give me a moment, please."

She thinks it's the Colonel. Boy, is she going to be pissed.

Thirty seconds passed and then Rachel responded. "Thank you, Major. He can come in now."

Souther beckoned Hatcher over to the comm console and pointed to a red button. "If you need anything, press the red button on the comm station. I'll be right here. Shall we record your conversation?"

"No, it's not necessary."

"Okay," Souther said, as she opened the vault door. "Good luck, Captain Hatcher."

Hatcher saluted Souther and stepped through the door.

CHAPTER EIGHTEEN

Saturday, December 19th, 2036 - 1:30 PM PST, Iceberg Detention Center, Rachel, Nevada

At the sight of Hatcher, Rachel's expression turned from interest to disdain.

She was standing by the door as Hatcher entered, wearing a beige prison jumpsuit. A white bandage covered the bridge of her nose. Both eye sockets were greenish-purple from the injury, but showing signs of healing. She turned on her heel and strode to the other side of the room.

Not happy to see me.

Hatcher looked around the room. It was furnished like an upscale high-rise apartment, except that everything was in one room. There was a sleeping area with a bed, a sofa, love seat and easy chair, along with a kitchen, and a large screen TEV. Some exercise equipment and a Peleton stood in another corner. A bathtub and toilet sat discreetly behind potted plants.

All the luxuries of home.

"Hello, Karen," Rachel said. She gestured with a grand sweep of her hand. "Welcome to my apartment. I apologize for not offering you a drink. There doesn't appear to be any in the place, and I haven't been out to the grocery."

Hatcher nodded.

"I'd have dressed more appropriately to receive a caller, but all my wardrobe is identical to this. Shall we sit down?" She moved to the couch and patted the place beside her.

Hatcher sat across from Rachel in the easy chair.

"You don't look as bad as you think," she said, and tried to smile at Rachel. "Other than that, are you being treated well?"

Rachel shrugged and leaned back on the sofa, extending her arms to rest on the back cushions. "Well, I suppose so. I'm still alive. Dare I hope that I'll soon be getting out of here?"

I shouldn't give hope, but I don't want to dash the little hope she has.

"I don't know, Rachel. There are those who wanted you dead, but we talked them out of it."

"How kind of you."

"It wasn't easy, I can tell you that."

"Is a lawyer out of the question?"

"Yes, I'm afraid it is. But that might change."

"And what would make that happen? If I cooperate with you?"

"That would be a nice thing to say on your behalf, but I don't think it would carry much weight."

"I see."

Hatcher leaned forward in the chair, her elbows on her knees, her hands clasped together.

"Do you mind if I ask you a few questions?"

Rachel laughed out loud.

"Of course, you can, darling. And I might even consider answering them." She extended her hands toward her as if she expected an embrace. "I told Marc there would be a time when he needed me, and he didn't even have the courage to come here himself."

"Yes, you did tell him that. And I guess you were right."

"If I answer your questions, will you get me out of here?"

Hatcher paused.

"It's not up to me," she said.

"Poppycock! If you told them you needed my help, they'd let me out."

"If it was up to me, you wouldn't get out. You've already shown me what you're capable of."

Rachel glared at Hatcher for a moment.

"No get out of jail free card, no answers," she said.

Hatcher wanted to say something to convince her, but the look on Rachel's face made it clear there was nothing she could say.

"That's it, then," she said. "I'll just get out of your hair."

She stood and walked over to the comm console, but turned back to Rachel before she touched it.

"I'll ask the commander to let you have your uniform back. You earned your Oak Leaves and should dress as an officer." She gestured toward the ceiling. "Even in here."

She turned back to the console.

"What would your first question have been?" Rachel asked.

Hatcher turned back toward her. "It doesn't matter, does it? If you're not planning to respond…"

"Karen, Karen," she said, and waved her back over to the furniture group. "You know I'm starving for intelligent conversation, and the staff here says as little as possible to me. Come sit, and maybe we can talk some."

Hatcher made a show of reluctance, but returned to the easy chair and sat.

Rachel waited for her to speak.

"The tenth death in 2036," Hatcher said. "Can you tell me about it?"

"Ah, he remembered!" Rachel said and beamed. "He thought we killed ten people for political reasons, and I told him only nine. So he *was* paying attention."

"The tenth was different from the others. There was no politician at the scene, and they identified the victim. She was the target."

"Excellent," she said. "And do you remember what she did for a living?"

"Yes. She was a microbiologist at the CDC, specializing in lethal diseases. In short, a biological warfare expert."

"True. What do you want to know?"

"Why was she killed, and what is the connection to the other murders?"

"Wow, that's a lot to ask. So you weren't able to establish a connection between the other nine and this one? The answer is very simple."

"Really?" *The FBI searched and searched for the connection. How could it be easy?*

"Really," Rachel said. "Oh, Karen, you should see your face. You're making it harder than it is. It's simple. There *is* no connection. What else do you know about her?"

Hatcher fidgeted in her seat. *No connection.* "But you... or your team... killed her. Correct?"

"Oh, yes. And with excellent reason. I repeat, what else do you know about her?"

"We know Iranian jihadis were sniffing around the CDC, looking for opportunities to hook up with and seduce employees. This is something we perceived as dangerous."

Rachel nodded. "As did we." She leaned back on the sofa again. "Eventually, she met and succumbed to the romantic advances of a young jihadi... He was a handsome devil. His intent was to radicalize her, to bring her under his control. Love is a powerful lever, wouldn't you agree?"

Hatcher nodded.

I think I see where this is going.

"She turns a bug vial over to him," Rachel said. "It's a nasty one. The CDC never found a cure or antidote. He passed it over to his handlers, who intended to use it in 2086."

"On Israel?"

"It didn't matter. The Iranians enhanced the bug so it couldn't be stopped. But yes, they would have used it against Israel first."

"You couldn't stop the series of events..."

"You know the restrictions as well as I do, Captain. I could only access time in twenty-five-year slices. I traveled to 2061 and searched for a way to slow them down. Between 2036 and 2061, they radicalized her, she handed over the bug, and they went underground. I couldn't find any trace of them. It was only a matter of time before they trotted it out and went to work."

"You couldn't find them or her. It was too late to stop it?"

"Correct, Karen. The Israelis were closing in on them. We feared their use of the bug was imminent, so we took the only action we could. We traveled back to 2036, and took her out before she got involved with the jihadi. That closed down the entire chain of events. Her death was a sacrifice for the greater good. To be honest, I regretted it, but I was doing my job and I believe I saved the world from a devastating plague."

"Too bad you couldn't have killed the jihadi instead," Hatcher said.

Rachel nodded again. "We considered that. Another might have taken his place and succeeded. Besides, she was the one with the dangerous access and an unstable emotional state. It was inevitable."

"I see your logic," Hatcher said. "How about a related question? How did you find out about her?"

"Joey told me about her."

"Joey? Joey Kosar? George Kosar's grandson?"

"Yes, Joey had his own intelligence operation. He told me about lots of things. Political assassinations. An economic war in Europe. All kinds of stuff."

Hatcher studied her boots. *This gets scarier by the minute. What else could happen?* "What else can you tell me that Joey said."

"Joey?" Rachel said. "Joey, who?"

Hatcher jerked her head up to look at Rachel.

She's glowing. The time wave is affecting her.

She stood and stepped toward Rachel.

Rachel stared at her.

"You're glowing," Hatcher said, unable to articulate what she feared.

Rachel looked at her hands and held them up before her face. They were transparent. When she looked back at Hatcher, terror was in her eyes. The aura surrounded her and intensified.

Rachel's body became transparent, and she disappeared.

She doesn't exist on this timeline! Something happened to her.

The lights in the cell went out. The room was pitch black.

She stood and tried to remember the exact direction of the comm console.

Flashing red lights came on in the cell and a klaxon sounded.

A loudspeaker overhead called for attention.

"Intrusion alert. Intrusion alert. All personnel report to their duty stations. Point of intrusion is cell 303. Security to the intrusion point."

After a five second pause, the message repeated. The lights continued to flash.

In the oscillating light, Hatcher could see the room's configuration change. The furniture disappeared, and a single table and chair appeared in its place. She made her way to the comm console and pressed the attention key to contact Souther or the guard outside. No one responded.

Am I the intruder?

She pressed the signal button. A female voice answered.

"Caller, state your name. Who am I talking to?"

"Operator, this is Captain Karen Hatcher, US Army. Please tell Major Souther I'm on the line."

"She's on her way to your location, ma'am. Are you armed?"

"No, I'm not. And I'm not a danger to the facility."

"I'm sure the Major will decide that, ma'am. Please lie on the floor with your arms and legs spread. Do not resist."

"Understood," she said. "I'll comply."

"Thank you, ma'am."

Hatcher shook her head. *What a mess! And now we don't have Rachel.*

For a moment, she considered clicking her beacon and jumping out. But she needed to talk to Souther. The team would come back here to retrieve Kosar and return him to 1986.

I'd better prepare for anything.

She hid her beacon. There was a high probability they wouldn't recognize it for what it was, but it was incongruous with her combat uniform, and that might create interest in it. She took it off and slipped it into the side of her boot. Then she laid spreadeagled on the floor next to the door. After two minutes, the loudspeaker spoke again.

"Breach of door is imminent. Do not resist. Do not move."

Hatcher tried to relax. Don't show any sign of aggression. Be subservient.

With a click, the round door swung open.

Hatcher saw the business end of a semi-automatic rifle appear, followed by an MP in full battle dress. Two more MPs followed her into the room. They dragged Hatcher to her feet, bound her arms and hands behind her back and sat her in the chair.

"Clear," one MP shouted. Hatcher heard it repeated from outside the door.

Major Souther walked in the door, followed by a lieutenant. She approached Hatcher.

"Who are you?" she said. "And how the hell did you get in here?"

"I'm a member of the HERO Team. You know my commanding officer, Colonel Marc McKnight."

"Name-dropping won't help you here, soldier. Who are you and what are you doing here?"

"I'm Captain Karen Hatcher and I work with Colonel Marc McKnight and Major Winston Tyler, both of whom you know. I came here an hour ago, met you, and you brought me to this cell to interview Major Rachel Patterson."

"Major who?" Souther said.

"Rachel Patterson, ma'am," Hatcher said. "Look, I know this is confusing, but history has been altered and we're now on a new timeline. You don't remember me, ma'am, but it's true. Call Colonel

McKnight and ask him. He'll tell you what's going on."

"I don't remember that. And there are no prisoners in this room. How did you get in here?"

"Yes, I know you don't remember me, but please listen to me. A change in history has created a shift in this timeline, causing much to be different. The prisoner was in this room. Something changed in the timeline and she disappeared."

Hatcher tried to stand up, but the soldiers slammed her back down in the chair.

Souther put her hand out. "No need for that. I know a Marc McKnight. Except he's a major, not a colonel." She stepped closer. "Cut her loose."

A soldier produced a knife, hesitated, then cut the ties binding her.

Hatcher rubbed her arms and hands to restart circulation.

"I'm leaving you here in this cell, Captain, while I contact Colonel McKnight."

Souther turned to her lieutenant. "Get this room set up for long-term occupancy. By the book."

"Thank you, Major," Hatcher said. "I'm sure Colonel McKnight will clear this up for you right away."

"I'm counting on it, Captain. If he doesn't vouch for you, you'll spend a lot of your time here. In fact, *all* of your time."

"He will, ma'am, I promise you."

"Are you sure about this, Major?" the lieutenant asked. "Shouldn't we just drop her off at the stockade?"

"No, I'm not sure, Lieutenant," she said. "But it's my decision."

She turned back to Hatcher. "The only reason you aren't on your way to the stockade is because I know the Colonel and what work he does. You sit tight, Captain. I'll be back to see you."

"And you can trust me, ma'am. I'll wait here for your decision."

"I'm sure you will," Souther said.

Hatcher sat down at the table. Souther and her team retreated from the cell, leaving her alone.

I could use my beacon and jump out now, but that might make things worse. We need to be on good terms with these folks.

She decided to sit tight and make herself at home.

Come on, Colonel. Get me out of this jam.

CHAPTER NINETEEN

Friday, December 19th, 2036 - 1:55 PM PST - The Iceberg Detention Facility, Rachel, Nevada

With her shield set on maximum, the Operative waited outside Rachel's cell. The nausea threatened to overcome her senses, but she couldn't take a chance on missing something. Her head throbbed from the shield exposure.

Could someone have time-jumped into Rachel's cell and taken her out?

It was a possibility.

Patience.

The door opened again.

She saw a woman sitting at a table inside the door, but only for an instant. The major and her lieutenant blocked her view as they exited the cell and closed the door behind them. But she saw her for long enough.

She was stunned.

"I don't want anyone talking to her without my permission," the major said. "And get Colonel McKnight on the phone right now."

"Yes, ma'am," the lieutenant said.

The Operative almost missed the reference to McKnight. She filed it away and focused all her consciousness on the woman in the cell.

She looked like me! How in the world?

As quietly as she could, she moved back down the corridor to the common bathroom. Once inside, she shed the shield, closed herself in a stall, and vomited. The room reeled, and she fought to keep her balance.

After a minute, the headache and nausea subsided, and she could think again. She stood and leaned against the stall wall to steady herself.

Was that me?

She shook her head.

The woman was younger by fifteen to twenty years. I don't remember being here before. It couldn't have been me.

Could it be another Operative? Another clone?

She had never heard of donor material used to create more than one clone. It was possible, she reasoned, but she didn't remember reading or hearing about it.

Another Operative? What does that mean? Could Number Three have grown impatient and sent another Operative?

She had only been in 2036 for eight days. It didn't make sense. She felt sure Number Three would have contacted her before expending the resources to send another Operative.

She ran out of options. The only other possibility must be the truth. To her knowledge, no Operative was ever allowed to meet their donor. The DNA that made her — her essence — came from the woman in the cell. They were the same person.

What is she doing here?

She stood up and straightened her combat uniform, checking to ensure she hadn't soiled it with her vomit. She looked into the bowl as she flushed the toilet.

Blood!

Something was wrong. It might be an esophageal abrasion from the vomiting, but she suspected it was something worse.

It must be the shield.

Use of the device had a cost. She couldn't tell how bad it was, but she was sure it would get worse every time she used it.

But it would be worse to get caught here.

She experienced a moment of panic, then training took over. She closed her eyes and slowed her breathing. After a minute, she could think again.

I accomplished the first part of my mission, but Rachel is not here. Whether she jumped out or disappeared because of the history change, the bottom line is, she isn't here. Until I locate her again, there's nothing I can do here.

She picked up the shield. She had to use it at least one more time — to get out of the Iceberg. After that, never again. She would go back to the access panel, don the shield, and get outside. Once she escaped this place, she'd decide what to do next.

The Operative left the bathroom and turned away from Rachel's cell. She ascended the stairs at the end of the tunnel to the first level. Now, she was thirty meters from the panel stairwell door, but she didn't dare try to open it. It would have an alarm, and she didn't know the procedure for opening and closing it. She would wait for the next patrol.

There was a bulletin board on the wall around the corner from the guard shack. While she waited, she busied herself looking at the bureaucracy documents pinned to the board.

She didn't have long to wait. She heard noises around the corner and checked. A patrol of three came out of the shack and prepared to enter the stairwell. They did a gear check and opened the door. She donned the shield, activated it, and slipped through the door behind them.

The patrol started up the stairs, and she followed them as closely as she dared. When the panel opened and the troopers passed through it, she hurried to get close and tailgated them out.

It was twilight outside.

The troopers began their patrol, and the Operative climbed to the top of the hill. She confirmed they were not coming her way, then deactivated and stripped off the shield. She felt wretched and needed to rest. Stripping off the combat uniform, she engaged her mission suit.

I wish the mission suit worked as well as the shield.

She waited until it was dark, then donned her night vision glasses, checked the pattern of the laser security system, and waited for the security window to open. When it did, she sprinted down the hill.

It consumed almost all her strength. She collapsed at the bottom and crawled beneath a scrub bush. Sleep beckoned and this time she responded.

When she awoke, the temperature had dropped. She shivered and stumbled back to the Jeep.

My stamina is shot. I need rest.

She pulled out the locator and searched again for Rachel Patterson. After a minute of scanning, she shut off the device. Rachel's signal was no longer there. She could have time jumped out. If not, then either her location markers were destroyed — which implied she was dead — or she wasn't where the locator could sense her. None of these scenarios were good news. Without more information, she could not continue the mission.

I've failed. For the first time, I've failed.

She struck the steering wheel with both fists. Tears of frustration and anger came to her eyes. She wiped them away and closed her eyes.

No, don't give up yet. Ask for guidance. Number Three may know something I don't.

She drew out her phone and typed a status message for Number Three. She proof-read it, then sent it to the beacon for transmittal.

> *<<< 638: Rachel GPS locator markers no longer detected. Last known position was in an underground bunker protected by military security force, but she is no longer there. Please advise. >>>*

After waiting five minutes and not receiving a reply, she started the Jeep and returned to the hotel. Number Three's reply would reach her there.

Friday, December 19th, 2036 - 6:49 PM PST - The A'le'in Motel, Rachel, Nevada

When she reached the hotel, she took a shower to wash off the dirt and stress. She checked her phone for messages. There was no response from Number Three.

Rachel's not here, and Number Three is unresponsive.

It was failure, and she hated it. Never had she failed to complete a mission. This was an unfamiliar experience for the Operative. She didn't know how to process the concept of failure.

She sat on the bed and stared at the opposite wall.

There's no other option. I'll return to 2086.

She didn't know what else to do.

She packed her gear, moved it to the center of the room, and pressed the beacon switch underneath the skin of her left forearm. She waited for the shimmering aura that preceded time travel, but it didn't come as fast as she expected.

Maybe it takes longer to activate when you're traveling back to the origin?

She faced the truth after a minute of waiting. The time Engine was not responding. She was not going home yet.

It crossed her mind she might be stranded here in the past forever.

Not productive. Focus on the problem.

She used deep breathing to settle her mind, then began the logical task of working through the problem.

Either the beacon has malfunctioned, or the time Engine is not running.

She had never heard of either possibility happening.

Maybe the Engine lost power somehow?

It was unthinkable, but it drew her mind back to her once vague memory of a cabin in Colorado. The memory was clearer now.

A plague started in the Middle East. Operations Management sent me to the cabin. 'Don't talk or interact with anyone' they said.

She used her phone to scan her beacon again for the mission records. There was no mention of any plague.

So history changed in 2086 after I left. That's why there's no response. No one's listening.

She pushed all the negative thoughts away and focused on the mission. She heard Number Three's voice in her memory. 'Find Rachel Patterson and don't come back without her.'

"Now's the time to think." She would sleep and then decide.

The Operative laid on the bed and closed her eyes. She felt a tinge of nausea just beneath the surface. She opened her eyes and saw the shield on the floor next to her gear.

What have you done to me?

CHAPTER TWENTY

Friday, December 19th, 2036 - 3:15 PM PST - The Iceberg Detention Center, Rachel, Nevada

Hatcher sat at the table and waited. She hoped it wouldn't be long before the Colonel got her out of this cell.

Almost as if she wished it into existence, the door opened and Major Souther entered.

"Well, Captain," Souther said, "It appears you are who you say you are. I just got off the phone with Colonel McKnight. He says you're one of his best."

"Thank you, Major. I'm glad he caught up with you."

"No, I called him. We're old friends, and it was a good excuse to talk to him. He said you jumped in earlier to interview one of our guests here, though I can't remember a damn thing about it. How long have you been here today?"

"A couple of hours, ma'am."

Souther sat across the table from Hatcher.

"So what just happened, Captain? How come I don't remember you?"

"Did the Colonel share with you what our team does?"

"I already knew. Colonel McKnight and I were at the Academy together and have followed each other's career since then."

"Good," Hatcher said. "That saves time. The timeline you live in changed. You had a guest because of a timeline. A change occurred to that timeline in the past and caused it to skew in a different direction. It's complicated, but after the change, your guest was never here. There are usually a few residual memories, but they fade quickly, depending on how much exposure you had with the guest. The longer the exposure, the longer the memories persist."

"I see. The colonel's explanation seemed familiar, but I couldn't quite see it in my mind."

"Yes, ma'am, that's the nature of fading memories. Anyway, I need to get back to work. May I leave now?"

"Oh! Yes, of course, Captain. But one more question, if I may?"

"Yes, ma'am?"

"Colonel McKnight said you have a beacon? Something you could have used to jump out of here. Does it not work down here in the Iceberg?"

"Yes, it does."

"Oh. Why didn't you just jump out?"

Hatcher nodded. "Major, I didn't want to leave you with questions unanswered. I think we'll need to come back in the near future. You have another guest here named Kosar, right?"

"He's not here yet, but he'll be here soon. What about him?"

"Without going into too much detail, let me just say I'm sure we'll need to come back for him pretty soon. I'd like to ask you if it would be okay for us to jump in and out at will?"

Souther shook her head. "No, it wouldn't. I'm responsible for everything that happens here. No one goes in and especially out without me knowing about it. Sorry."

"I understand. I'd feel the same way. How about if we coordinate with you in advance each time?"

"I'm not opposed to it, but let me call Colonel McKnight and we'll work out a procedure around it. This place is my responsibility and I have to know and understand what's going on."

"Yes, ma'am. Thanks for being flexible." Hatcher looked at her watch. "I need to be going. Our team will take new action soon, and I'd like to be a part of it."

Souther nodded. "No problem, Captain. Someday, you'll need to explain to me how a time machine can act like a teleportation device."

The two officers stood.

"I'd be happy to share it with you, Major," Hatcher said, "when we have more time."

"Over beer," Souther said. She smiled for the first time.

Hatcher grinned. "That's my preferred method, Major."

She stepped away from the table. "I need space here," she said. "Don't get close to the sphere when it forms."

Hatcher pulled her beacon from her boot, squeezed it, and a time bubble formed around her. Souther moved toward the door.

The air inside the bubble spun, sending Hatcher's ponytail flying in all directions. Hatcher could see Souther outside the bubble, shielding her eyes from the glare of the white light emanating from the sphere. She knelt to keep her balance. The brilliant globe bulged, and she fell through the familiar field of stars.

Friday, December 19th, 2036 - 6:20 PM EST - Telegraph Road Lab, Alexandria, Virginia

McKnight watched as Hatcher landed on the Engine platform in the lab. As always, she kept her feet beneath her during the jump. When the bubble dissipated, she strode over to him and saluted.

"As you were, Captain. Report."

"Yes, sir," Hatcher said. "I landed in the Iceberg. Major Souther met me there. We walked to Major Patterson's cell. I talked to her. She admitted the tenth death was unrelated to the other nine murders in our previous case. She said she did it to prevent the scientist from hooking up with a terrorist and giving him access to a dangerous plague."

"Unrelated, eh? Well, that ties up that loose end. Then what?"

"I asked her how she knew about the scientist. She said Joey told me before she disappeared. She acknowledged she was referring to Joey Kosar."

"I think I see the timeline now. Since George Kosar went missing, his kids went in different directions and so did his grandkids. Joey never met Rachel in New York, so she never heard of him, let alone the scientist. The jihadi seduced the scientist, she gave the bug to Iran, and they used it, bringing about a world plague."

"The logic works, sir," she said. "But it seems crazy to me to unleash a plague if you can't control it."

"Agreed, but that's the world. When we go to 2086 to check the effects of snatching Kosar, I bet we'll find desolation. That's what happens when we can't talk a politician out of a stupid move. President Taylor has done good things, but she screwed the pooch on this one."

"Yes, sir. I learned something else, too."

"What was that?"

"I don't know if it applies now, but Major Souther told me Rachel has cancer."

"Cancer? What kind?"

"She didn't say, sir. She mentioned it while briefing me about Rachel's condition before I interviewed her. Rachel doesn't know yet."

"I see." McKnight considered this new fact and shrugged. "Okay. For now, it doesn't matter. Make sure it's in your report."

"Yes, sir."

"We need to get prepared to jump to the future as soon as possible. We need to see what damage we did by snatching Kosar. Kathy was right. Snatching him was a really bad idea."

"Yes, sir."

"Get with Wheeler," McKnight said. "Let's get ready to check out the consequences. I'll update General Drake while you and Wheeler start on mission implementation. See Kathy, she's the planner on point. And we'll need to take Mr. Kosar back to 1986. She's already working on that mission."

"Oh," Hatcher said. "That reminds me. I talked to Major Souther about us jumping into the Iceberg to pick up Mr. Kosar. She said she would call you to work out a procedure. She doesn't want us jumping in and out without her knowing about it."

"Good thinking. Yeah, I don't blame her. I'd want the same thing. Okay. Find Wheeler and let's get things rolling."

"Yes, sir," Hatcher said. She saluted him, executed a perfect parade turn, and headed for the office she shared with Wheeler.

Saturday, December 20th, 2036 - 6:30 AM PST - the A'le'inn Hotel, Rachel, Nevada

The Operative saw the sun's rays filtering through a dingy window. The sleep helped; she felt less ill. She rose to the side of the bed.

She shook her head. Her next step still seemed unclear.

She stood and stretched, then looked out the window.

Oh, no.

A Las Vegas police car stood outside.

They tracked me here.

She expected them to show up here a few days before, but they didn't, and she forgot about them.

Just when she needed to sit here and think, they showed up. Now she'd have to run.

She activated the mission suit, grabbed her gear, the combat uniform she wore, and her backpack, and walked out of the room. She glanced left, saw an officer there, and turned right. She bumped into another officer and lost her grip on everything. Her gear and backpack hit the floor with a thud.

The man was six inches taller than her. He looked confused by the reflections off her suit as she approached, but smiled as she ran into him and grabbed her by the shoulders. She slammed the heel of her right hand into his nose, followed by a jab with her left to his Adam's apple.

The man staggered backward, but didn't go down. Instead, he dropped to one knee and pulled at the pistol at his side. She threw herself at him, spinning so her back was toward him. She slammed into his chest and grabbed his gun hand with both hands. He grunted under the impact. She threw her head backward and struck his bleeding nose again. Then she pointed his gun at his partner and fired it, striking the man in the neck.

She untangled herself from the first officer. Despite his pain, he groped at her, trying to grab her.

She stepped back and drove the heel of her left foot into his face.

The entire encounter took less than four seconds.

One, maybe two, casualties.

She picked up her gear, backpack, and clothes and ran to her Jeep. She cranked it and popped the clutch to launch herself onto the road, going north.

Where to, now?

She considered it. No good options. She chose the desert. At least they'd have to look harder to find her.

She drove ten miles at top speed, then got off the road and drove another fifteen miles, the Jeep skidding around in the sand.

When she stopped, she covered the Jeep with bracken and crawled under it to find the LoJack device. She disconnected it from the engine, disabled it, and threw it as far as she could.

Using the combat uniform, she built shade next to the Jeep and slipped under it. She should be safe for long enough to figure out the next step.

I should rest.

She closed her eyes and tried to relax. Unbidden, she saw the woman from the cell in her mind's eye.

Was she really my donor? Why was she there and Rachel gone?

More questions came and went. She catalogued each thought for review and then shut them down.

Don't waste energy and time when you don't have enough information.

She cleared her mind and fell asleep.

439 was her only friend. When did she first meet her? She couldn't remember. 439 had always been there, right next to her.

638 loved her spirit. Her sparkling eyes, her brilliant glowing blonde hair, and her wonder at everything. She noticed things 638 did not, and 638 envied her for her perception and observation skills.

638 thought about enduring all the daily exercises while her body used them to get stronger. But during exercise, 439 marveled at the sky and the trees on the distant mountains.

638 knew 439 was weak. She wasn't as tall or as slim as 638, but her shape was pleasant.

Boys noticed her, too. But 439 wouldn't play with the boys. She knew she didn't have the strength to survive in combat.

When boys hung around 439, 638 would get her away from them before anything could happen.

638 hid her friendship with 439 from others. Friendship was something the Aunts and Uncles discouraged. Empathy and friendship were signs of weakness. It was a common cause of mission failure; they said. Better not make friends in the camp. Operatives don't need close friends — they need resources they could trust.

CHAPTER TWENTY-ONE

<u>Saturday, December 20th, 2036 - 10:46 PM PST - Nevada Desert near Rachel</u>

It was after 10:00 PM when the Operative awoke. She still felt ill from the personal shield, but the sleep helped restore her energy.

She shivered, then pulled down the uniform she used for shade and slipped it on.

She looked up. The night sky was filled with visible stars. She relaxed her mind and took in the spectacle. It was easy to have peace here.

She pulled the locator out of her pack and checked it again.

Still no Rachel. I wonder if I can program this thing?

She searched the capabilities of the locator and found the programmable section. She created a test loop to check for Rachel's beacon every four hours. Each attempt to find Rachel would create a log entry she could check. The locator would chirp if it found her signal.

She didn't try to jump back to 2086 again. Her memory of a plague was proof enough she couldn't go home.

With every use, the shield took strength from her. She feared it was doing her serious harm and considered discarding it, but it was a powerful tool she might yet need.

What do I do now?

Her objective was no longer no longer attainable. Number Three ordered her not to come home without Rachel. But Rachel no longer existed — at least not in this time.

The Operative decided she should go back to 2086 and regroup.

Her scheduler sent her to a cabin in Colorado to avoid the plague. If her scheduler expected the plague, wouldn't Number Three know about the plague and quarantine herself?

She's still alive somewhere. What if I go back and find her? I could be a valuable asset to her in the new world, the world after the plague.

Her beacon didn't work. She couldn't use the Federal Time Services machines in 2086. She went over the possibilities again.

Engine down.

Engine destroyed.

Engine not watching for her beacon.

Beacon broken.

Beacon signal insufficient to reach the 2086 Engines.

No one there.

Every option presented an obstacle. Worse, she couldn't address the problems. She was alone in this time.

Be creative.

She closed her eyes and relaxed. There must be a way.

The solution came in a flash.

There are time Engines in this time. Why can't I use one of those to go home?

McKnight and his team controlled the machines in Washington. If she could get there, she could force someone to send her back to 2086. Once back in 2086, she could search for Number Three.

McKnight and his people might know why she couldn't find Rachel.

Another reason to go to Washington.

But the trip was not possible. It took all her strength to overcome the police officers at the hotel. She was too weak. And she couldn't take a plane; they'd be watching for her.

I'll have to drive there.

It would take three days. Would she have enough strength left when she got there? And how would she cope with any law enforcement she might meet?

Getting a good night's sleep would help, but her health and capabilities were declining.

What am I thinking? Check the obvious.

She reached inside her pack and withdrew the medical kit. There were standard issue drugs in the kit that might help. If she took them, she'd be down for two days to let them work.

She stood and scanned the horizon. She could see the lights of a small town in the distance.

I'm too vulnerable here. Too exposed.

She wanted to leave for Washington, but it was the wrong thing to do.

Tomorrow, I'll find a place to hide and sleep for a couple of days. Then, I'll have the strength to travel to Washington.

Sunday, December 21st, 2036 - 7:16 AM PST - Desert near Rachel, Nevada

The Operative awoke at first light. The desert heated up, and the sun had crested the mountains in the east. The metal on her Jeep clicked as it expanded.

She assessed how she felt.

Better, but not good enough.

The shield damaged her body somehow, and she needed to heal. She needed an isolated place where she could take the restorative drug and rest while it did its work.

She stood and searched the horizon. In the distance to the west, she thought she saw movement.

Is it a vehicle?

She couldn't tell, but she felt exposed. If they were serious about finding her, she was too close to where they might look. She packed everything, stowed it in the back of the Jeep, and looked back toward the west. She didn't see vehicles, but there was dust rising to the west.

The sun's rays bouncing off a distant windshield was all it took to convince her she wasn't deep enough in the desert. She jumped in the Jeep and drove slowly toward the east, hoping to generate as little dust cloud as possible.

Camping out in the open was not an option, and she needed warmth. She couldn't build a fire without telling everyone within twenty miles where she was.

She headed for the mountains, where she expected to find both shelter and a hiding place.

After an hour, she reached the foothills. She explored two box canyons with no luck before she found one that met her needs. The mouth of the canyon faced north, but the canyon itself curled around to the east. A tiny stream trickled down the middle of the canyon.

She tried to drive into the canyon, but it was too narrow to venture very far. She parked the Jeep just east of the canyon's mouth and covered it with bracken and scrub brush. Then she hiked into the canyon. In her weakened state, it was hard-going, but about a hundred yards into the gulch she found a shallow cave in the wall.

She explored the cave. It extended thirty feet into the wall. She confirmed no animals or snakes were in the cave, then built a fire and set up a barrier to discourage any that might come along. She rested, then hiked back to the Jeep to get the rest of her gear.

Carrying everything back to the cave exhausted her energy.

After resting again, she used the combat uniform, some food tins, and a spare blanket to create a small tower that would topple over if anything or anybody crossed the cave threshold.

She needed to make one more trip to the mouth of the canyon and cursed herself for not thinking of it earlier. There was no reception inside the canyon. She walked out to the Jeep and tuned her phone to the police band. There was chatter about still looking, but nothing sounded like someone was on her trail.

She checked the log file of the locator for a sign of Rachel, just in case.

No luck.

She walked back to the cave and stretched out on a blanket. She drew the med kit out of her pack and opened the emergency regenerative drug pack.

Unbidden, a memory floated up to her consciousness. An enemy pursued her on an assignment and shot her with a small caliber weapon. She was in hiding and took the drug as a last resort. She was certain the drug saved her life.

She smiled without mirth. She hoped the age of the pack wasn't past the 'use before' date. Satisfied it was okay, she gave herself a shot and fixed a light meal.

She wasn't hungry, but her body would need fuel to heal and rebuild. After she ate, she laid on the blanket and fell asleep.

638 walked by the Uncle and Aunt barracks on the way to dinner. She heard them talking inside the building.

She didn't care what they were talking about, but there was something in their voices that captured her attention. Maybe it was the urgency with which they spoke. Or maybe it was the topic, which she didn't understand.

One phrase stuck with her. "Cull out the weak."

What did that mean? The Aunts and Uncles always talked about how bad it was to be weak. So "culling" must be something that gets rid of weakness.

638 was all in for banishing weakness — her friend 439 would welcome help to eliminate her weakness. Wouldn't that be a good thing? Then 638 wouldn't have to look after and protect 439.

638 didn't worry about being "culled". She was strong. She didn't give it a second thought.

CHAPTER TWENTY-TWO

<u>Sunday, December 22nd, 2036 - 2:45 PM, Oval Office of the White House, Washington, D.C.</u>

President Wanda Taylor sat in the Oval Office with General Mike Drake, Chief of Staff Avery Detweiler, and President-Elect Wade Harrison. Together, they monitored the mission to 2086. They received a report from Kathy Wu. She advised the team made it back from 2086, but requested to come back to the CDC isolation room in Atlanta.

Drake knew this was a bad sign.

McKnight invoked Andromeda protocol. He's concerned about contamination.

The White House communications officer established a connection to the mission team in CDC and notified President Taylor that Colonel McKnight was on the line.

"Okay, thanks… Colonel McKnight, this is Wanda Taylor. Are you there? Can you hear me?"

McKnight's voice sounded hollow through the speaker. "Yes, Madam President. I can hear you."

The video came alive, and they saw McKnight and his team standing in a room, surrounded by jars and boxes.

"General Drake?" President Taylor said. "Want to take it from here?"

"Yes, ma'am. Colonel McKnight, please report. I'm here with the President. What did you find? Why are we on Andromeda protocol?"

McKnight's image on the screen looked haggard, and he shook his head.

"Things aren't right, sir. We jumped to Manassas, Virginia in 2086, and worked our way into downtown D.C."

"And?"

"We gathered some air samples and some soil samples. We even brought back plant samples."

"What about the people? Who did you talk to? How did they act?"

"Sir, we didn't find anyone. No one at all."

"No one would talk to you?" Drake asked. "Is that what you're saying?"

"No, sir. I mean, there's nobody here. We found some human remains. But we haven't found anyone alive. Not one person. We can't detect any radio or TEV broadcasts. No drivers on the roads, nothing. That's why I invoked Andromeda, sir. If a bug or virus did this, I didn't want to bring it back with us. It may be a false alarm, but we'd rather be safe than sorry."

"Thank you, Colonel. Stand by for orders."

"Yes, sir."

Drake turned to look at the President. Her face was as pale as her dark skin would allow.

"Something we did?" Taylor said, her voice little more than a croak. "Did I cause this?"

"I don't know, Madam President," Drake said. "But we'll find out."

The President shivered.

"Avery, get her some water." Drake said. "She doesn't look well."

"What? Oh, sure thing, General." Detweiler dashed to the coffee service and poured ice water in a glass. He handed it to the President.

Drake turned to President-Elect Harrison. "Wade, we need to go back and prevent Kosar's kidnapping." He glanced at his watch. "We took him three days ago. There's time to go back and scrub the mission."

"I agree," Harrison said. "But I'm not the President yet. I don't have any official standing."

"Oh, right," Drake said. He turned back to the President. "Madam President? Are you okay?"

She took a sip of water and stared at the wall above Drake's head. "Yes," she said.

I don't think she is. She's not focused.

"Avery?" she said. "What's the population of the earth?"

"Ma'am?"

"The planet, Avery. What is the population of this planet?"

"Right around eight billion, Madam President."

Taylor's eyes refocused on Drake. "Is it fair to say the population would be ten billion by 2086?"

"Yes, ma'am," Drake said, "but we can fix it. We can send someone back to stop Kosar's kidnapping before it even happens. We can prevent it."

Taylor's eyes glazed over. "I'll go down in history as the President who killed ten billion people."

"No, ma'am," Drake said. "We still have time to—"

"I killed ten billion people."

She looked at Drake. Her eyes showed terror, anguish, and regret all at once. Then her expression changed. Her face went blank, and she stared over Drake's shoulder. She dropped the water glass.

Drake caught her as she fell sideways.

"Get the doctor in here!" Detweiler yelled into the intercom. "And find Vice President Crumpton."

Drake and Harrison lifted the President and laid her on the sofa.

"What do you think, General?" Harrison said. "Stroke?"

"Maybe. Whatever it is, she's out of action," Drake said, as he checked her pulse. "And we need an executive order for authorization to reverse the Kosar kidnapping."

"Well, just do what you need to do."

"Wade, as you just pointed out, you're not the President for another twenty-nine days. It's up to Vice President Crumpton."

The doctor came in with a nurse and kicked them out of the Oval Office.

Once outside in the reception area, Detweiler rejoined Harrison and Drake.

"I found the Vice President. He's on Air Force Two, on his way to Paris. They've turned the plane around and he'll be back here in two hours."

"Good," Drake said.

Harrison stared at the door to the Oval Office. "I hope she'll be okay."

"Me, too," Drake said. "I guess we'll have to wait for Vice President Crumpton to get out an executive order."

"Don't be too optimistic," Detweiler said. "Addison Crumpton has never been a fan of the time travel projects. I've heard him say he'd shut it down if he could."

"Surely he wouldn't stop us from fixing a history change?" Drake said.

"Yeah, why wouldn't he allow that?" Harrison said.

Detweiler shrugged. "I don't know, but Addison Crumpton is his own man. He'll decide for himself what to do. I'm just saying he isn't a fan of time travel projects, and he isn't the type to blindly accept a course of action Wanda would take. I mean, he liked and respected her, but he has a spotty record of agreeing with her. She liked that — she didn't surround herself with 'yes' men. But he'll lean on me to get up to speed for the next two days and I *am* a fan of time travel projects. I'll make a good case for it."

Drake and Harrison looked at each other.

"Better do it fast," Drake said. "We have less than four days to stop the operation."

Monday, December 22nd, 2036 - 7:00 PM - Doctor Emily Pritchard's office, Centers for Disease Control, Atlanta GA

McKnight entered Doctor Pritchard's office. She turned from her computer and motioned for him to sit.

"What can I do for you, Colonel?"

"Thanks for seeing me, Doctor. I know you found we were uncontaminated and we're grateful, believe me, but I wanted to know what you found."

"It's all in my report," she said. "I'm sure your leadership will copy you on the report."

"Yes, ma'am, I'm sure they will," he said. "But it's going to be a few days before it filters down to my level, and we have a critical deadline in three days. I need as much knowledge as I can get about our situation."

Pritchard leaned back in her chair, reached back and removed an elastic band from her hair, allowing her dreadlocks to expand across her shoulders. She sighed and nodded.

"What can I tell you?"

"For starters, what killed everyone? Was it a biological agent? If so, was it naturally occurring or was it an attack?"

"Oh, definitely a bio agent," she said. "A nasty one. A strain of botulinum. It was deadly, highly contagious and man-made. It depended on several factors, including weather and temperature, but we believe it swept across the earth in three to four months. It was the worst scenario because it was very contagious in the initial stages, and the symptoms took several days to surface."

"So, a person might catch the bug and infect dozens of others before having any symptoms?"

"Yes," she said. "And it killed everyone who caught it. Nasty stuff."

"Wow. *Scary* stuff."

"You bet, Colonel. Anything else I can tell you?"

"Yes, ma'am. As you might guess, I'm very interested in the time frames here. Do you have any idea when the plague happened?"

"No, but I know how old it is."

"Pardon me?"

"I'm aware of what you do, Colonel, but I don't know what era of history you were in when you found this. I presume it's from the future since we're still here."

"Of course, Doctor. How old was the virus you found?"

"Based on the samples you provided, I'd say the virus swept across the area where you found it ten to twelve years before. Does that help?"

"Yes, ma'am, it does." McKnight fidgeted in his seat. "Do we know where the toxin came from?"

"Unfortunately, we do," Pritchard said. "Based on the residual genetic markers, it's ours. We developed the toxin here."

"Here? You mean at the CDC?"

"Yes, about eight months ago."

McKnight calculated the date interval in his head.

2086 minus ten to twelve years. The plague was in 2074 to 2076.

"We're sure it came from here?" McKnight said. "They released it from here?"

"We don't know who released it or from w*here. We* developed it here as B-870919. But there are additional markers in the toxin we don't recognize. In layperson's terms, someone else refined the toxin."

"Refined it?"

"Yes. When we develop a toxin, we program it to mutate and become less virulent as it spreads. In biological warfare, you try not to develop a bug that kills you as well as the enemy. Someone else made it a planet killer."

"Do we know who developed… What was it… B-870919?"

"Yes, her name is Susan Walker. She reported to me."

McKnight perked up. "You said 'worked'. She's not here anymore?"

"No," Pritchard. "She disappeared two weeks ago."

McKnight sat up in his chair.

If the FBI is still tracking the Jihadi, maybe we can stop it at the source. Or maybe we can stop her before she leaves.

"Excuse me, Doctor, but you're sure it was a couple of weeks ago? Not *one* week ago? What date was it?"

Pritchard shrugged and pulled out her calendar and flipped back a few pages.

"Yes," she said. "It was over two weeks ago. The last day she showed up for work was Friday, November 28th. She didn't come to work the following Monday. We sent someone to look for her on Tuesday, but her apartment was empty. We opened a case with the FBI because it's a national security issue. We always do when something unusual happens with one of our employees."

Not enough time to go back and intercept her. We have to find out where she went.

"Was Miss Walker a good employee?"

"Mostly," she said. "Susan was an outstanding employee until a few months ago."

"Oh?" McKnight said. "What happened to her? Family issues or something?"

Pritchard hesitated, then shrugged.

"Well, I guess it doesn't matter now."

She leaned back and looked as if she was searching for the right words.

"Susan isn't a pretty girl. She didn't have many boyfriends, and she got involved with a young man here at the lab. He wasn't as kind as he should have been. They dated a few times, and she was very interested, but he wasn't. Anyway, he dumped her, and she was out for a few days. She was depressed, and I felt sorry for her. Anyway, she perked up a few days before she disappeared. I thought maybe she found someone else, but I don't know for sure."

"I see. Thank you for your time, Doctor, and for sharing the details with me right away. You've been more than helpful."

"I'm glad to hear it, Colonel."

McKnight stood. "Now, I have to get my team back to D.C.. Let me get to it."

Pritchard slapped a hand to her forehead. "Dammit. I knew I forgot something. Your Doctor Wu? She said to call her when you're ready to come home and you can do a… what did she call it?… A non-jump, or something like that?"

"Ah," he said, then laughed. "A non-time jump. That's great. We can take off right away. Thanks again for all the information, Doctor Pritchard."

"It's my pleasure, Colonel," she said. "Now, I don't want to see you and your people in my lab again."

McKnight grinned. "Believe me, Doctor. As much as we like you, we don't want to come back. Have a great day."

CHAPTER TWENTY-THREE

Monday, December 22nd, 2036 - 11:00 PM - McKnight Apartment, Alexandria, Virginia

McKnight pulled into his apartment parking lot and switched off his truck.

He didn't expect Megan to be all smiles and joy when he arrived.

Kathy briefed him after Megan called the office, looking for him when he didn't get home as planned. She admitted Megan dragged the details out of her - that he was in a CDC isolation chamber being checked for a dangerous pathogen he may have encountered.

McKnight called Megan from Atlanta to let her know he was okay and coming home, but she didn't sound very excited.

Time to get it over with.

He got out of his truck and walked up the stairs to the apartment. Before he could put his key in the door, it opened.

Megan stood in the doorway, dressed in a short flowery dress with a smile on her face. Her strawberry blonde hair cascaded down around her shoulders and her blue eyes sparkled. She never looked so beautiful to him. As he stepped across the threshold, she threw herself into his arms.

"I'm so glad you're safe," she said. "I was afraid for you."

"Thanks. It's good to be home. I missed you."

He pulled her closer and kicked the door shut behind him with his foot.

She pulled his face down to hers and kissed him. It was a kiss that signaled love and joy.

When the kiss ended, she buried her face in his chest.

"Are you okay?" he said.

She pulled away from him. "Yes, of course. Are you hungry? Would you like something to drink?"

"No," he said. "Well, yes. I hadn't thought about it. I guess I'm hungry and thirsty."

"Good. We have some of my famous beef stew and cornbread. How about a Blue Moon?"

He told her it sounded perfect, because it did.

"Let me go grab a shower," he said. "It's been a long day."

"Sure. That'll give me enough time to heat it up."

"Good. Thanks, Babe."

"No problem. I love you, Marc."

He entered the bedroom and stripped off his clothes. He slipped into the shower and scrubbed himself down, then switched the temperature to cool and let it shock his body. After toweling off, he slipped into a pair of sweatpants and a long-sleeved t-shirt.

When he returned to the kitchen, the table was set, and a steaming bowl of stew and a Blue Moon beer were in his place. Megan was sitting next to his chair.

The aroma of the stew drew him forward. He sat in his chair, and she reached over and stroked his hair. She pushed an errant strand off his forehead and back into place.

"I'm so glad you're home."

"Me, too."

"Were you in danger? Kathy was afraid that you were."

"For a while we thought we might be. That's why she sent us to Georgia, just to make sure. It was a precaution. An unnecessary one, thank God. We were never in danger."

"Good. I was worried there for a while."

"Yes," he said, and turned toward her. "I'm sorry you had to go through that."

"It's okay. I'm getting used to it. It's what you do."

That's not true. She isn't used to it.

"When I talked to you earlier," he said, "you didn't sound as happy as you do now."

She paused, then said, "Yes, and I'm sorry about that. I was just worried, that's all. You mean so much to me." She stroked his hair again.

"And you to me," he said. "I should talk to Kathy about sharing details. Some of them aren't necessary and just make things seem worse."

"No, I'm glad she shares those details. What you do is dangerous, Marc, I know. But I also know it's important and needs to be done. And everything about you makes you the right person to do it. Your training, your compassion, your sense of right and wrong, your love of country… everything. I have to learn to trust you and accept all the aspects of your job."

He started to speak, but she held up her hand.

"I finally know what I want to say, so don't interrupt me. I admit I was angry with you, but I've thought about it and I think I was being selfish. I was angry because of how that situation made me feel, and I was mad at you for making me worry."

He started to speak again, but she touched her forefinger to his lips.

"Shhh," she said. "What I realized was it's not you creating the danger. The danger is there, and somebody has to confront it while doing something for the greater good. And I know who you are. Someone has to do the hard thing, so you do it so someone else doesn't have to. It's who you are, and it's part of what makes you the man I love."

"So I decided I can worry and fret about it… or I can push it aside and embrace the things that make you who you are. And I'm so glad you chose me to be by your side. I know it was hard for you to make a commitment. You've always been cautious about relationships. But we're here together now, and I can't wait to see what's next for us."

McKnight couldn't speak. If he tried, he knew his voice would break, and he couldn't countenance that.

He nodded at her, and she smiled.

If I ever did a right thing, it was committing to this woman.

He kissed her, and they embraced there at the dinner table.

When the kiss ended, they rested their foreheads together for a long moment.

McKnight pulled away and lifted his spoon.

"How are the wedding plans coming?" he said.

She laughed.

"Very well," she said. "Would you like to hear the latest?"

"Yes," he said, and dug into the stew.

"I engaged the pastor from my church in Gainesville to perform the ceremony."

"What ceremony?" he said through the stew.

"Shut up," she said, and he smiled. "We're still working on the date. He's given me several and we can match them up with when you can take leave."

"Okay," he said. "What else?"

"And Kathy agreed to be my wedding coordinator."

"*My* Kathy? I mean, Kathy Wu?"

"Yes. *Your* Kathy." She laughed again.

Megan got up, walked across the room, and returned with her bridal book. She opened it and began sharing what she and Kathy had arranged.

He finished his stew and let the music of her voice caress his heart and mind.

I must have done something right, dear Lord, to be so blessed.

Tuesday, December 23rd, 2036 - 9:30 AM - Telegraph Road Lab, Alexandria, Virginia

McKnight walked to the team lab from his office. Drake was in the office today and asked to meet him and Kathy Wu there. He spotted

Kathy in the break area. She was sitting at the table with her usual cup of tea. He strode over to her.

"Good morning, Marc," she said.

"Same to you. Any idea why General Drake asked us to be here?"

"None. You?"

"Nope. But I hope it's about canceling the Kosar kidnapping."

"Me, too. Oh, look, he's here."

McKnight turned to see General Drake across the lab. He walked over, and McKnight came to attention and saluted.

Drake returned the salute and said, "As you were, Colonel. Let's sit, shall we?"

Once they settled around the table, he spoke again.

"Kathy, I want you to plan the mission to abort the Kosar kidnapping. I was thinking Marc should be on point and maybe take one other resource. What are your thoughts about that?"

"That's great news, General," Kathy said. "It's already planned. Two resources are what I planned for. I thought they should be the Colonel and Major Tyler. So he approved the mission?"

"Not yet. But I can't imagine it won't be. What could be the argument against it?"

He paused for a second. "Scratch that last statement. This *is* Washington. Anything's possible."

Drake smiled without mirth. "I want to be ready to go when we get the approval. Time is short."

"Yes, sir," she said. "How's President Taylor? Did she have a stroke? That's what I heard."

Drake's mood turned somber.

"She's resting quietly. They suspect it was a mini-stroke. She's always exercised and eaten right. She has a strong constitution, so I'm hopeful."

"Do you think she'll recover?"

"It's hard to say. She gets the best health care in the world. They got her to Walter Reed quickly, so she has a good chance to survive, maybe recover fully. We're waiting to hear."

"That's good," McKnight said. "What have you heard about the Vice President?"

"He's a good guy," Drake said. "The President picked him because he's smart and honest, and to deliver his home state of Georgia in the election, which he did."

Drake's phone rang. While he dug it out of his pocket, he said, "But he's no fan of time travel. He was against its use and the President's mistake in using it supports his point."

He looked at the caller ID. "This is Detweiler. Hopefully, it's our approval."

Drake put the phone to his ear. "Drake here."

He listened for a moment, then stood and gestured for McKnight and Kathy to wait. He walked away to have a private conversation.

McKnight and Kathy watched his face from their vantage point.

He doesn't look happy. There's a problem.

"Uh-oh," Kathy said.

"Mm-hmm," McKnight said in agreement.

"Marc, what if he doesn't approve the mission? That would be a disaster."

"We'll figure out something. Don't worry."

After five minutes, Drake disconnected the call and returned to where they were sitting.

His face was a mask of concentration. He sat and drummed his fingers on the table for a few seconds.

"This changes nothing," he said. "It isn't approved yet, but it will be soon. The Vice President wants to meet with Doctor Astalos and me this afternoon to discuss the merits of the mission before he approves it."

"Then he *will* approve it?" McKnight said.

"We don't know yet, but at least he didn't say no. Detweiler thinks he's hesitant to approve a mission to fix a problem caused by a poor decision. He doesn't want to compound the problem. We need to convince him that can't happen since the mission is to prevent the original mistake."

He looked back at Kathy. "Go back over the mission plans again and look for anything that might catch the attention of someone determined to cancel it. It's true Vice President Crumpton isn't a fan of time travel projects, but he's smart and he's fair. He'll see the light on this."

Drake stood, and they stood with him.

"Kathy, get started as soon as you can."

"Yes, sir," she said, and walked out the lab door toward her office.

Drake caught McKnight's eyes and held them for a moment.

"Marc, do you have a few minutes? I'd like to get your thoughts on something."

"Of course, General."

"Come walk me to my car," he said.

CHAPTER TWENTY-FOUR

Tuesday, December 23rd, 2036 - 10:00 AM - Telegraph Road Parking Lot, Alexandria, Virginia

McKnight and Drake walked in silence out to his car.

I wonder what he wants to say that he doesn't want overheard.

Drake said, "Frankly, I'm worried."

"Yes, sir?"

"Like I said, Vice President Crumpton is a good guy, but politics at this level is unpredictable. He's President for the next few days, and this may be his only chance to do something Presidential, and he'll want to do the right thing."

"That should be okay then, right, sir?"

"It's hard to tell. In politics, it isn't about what is right, but what the public perceives as right. When it gets out, the opposition party will scream bloody murder about President Taylor's blunder, and Crumpton might want to run in 2040 against President Harrison. This is a real presidential decision and a career-ender if it's wrong. I'm confident he will approve it, but I'm aware of the game and the chance he might not risk it."

"Wouldn't the public think reversing the kidnapping is a good idea?"

"It would, but maybe not the urgency. The public doesn't understand the window of opportunity we have, and some people in Congress will try to make political points and argue for a few days."

"I see. Congress will argue prudence and delay."

"Correct. Most politicians are cowards. They remain neutral until they figure out which way the wind is blowing. Then they take a stand and say they always felt that way."

McKnight shook his head. "I don't understand that way of thinking."

"Yes, I know. Anyway, I mention that as a pretext to what I'm saying next. If Vice President Crumpton decides not to approve the mission, I'm thinking about ordering it, anyway. That's the other reason I wanted Kathy to recheck the planning. If I ordered it, would you execute the mission?"

He's placing his career in my hands. If I refuse, he'll be dishonored, and the problem doesn't get fixed. His career and influence would be over, even if we fix the problem another way.

"I can't let you do that, General," he said. "They'll roast you without thinking twice."

Drake didn't respond and McKnight continued, "What if I disobey your order to scrub the mission and go fix the problem? Then we can both sleep at night."

Drake paused for a second and nodded.

"Okay. I think we do it together, Marc. We both know what's at stake. Two careers are not worth ten billion lives, even if they don't exist yet."

"Yes, sir."

"So we're fellow conspirators, then."

"Looks that way, sir. But I have more faith. I don't think the Vice President can decide otherwise. Even if there's a political firestorm about his decision, history will prove him right. Maybe not in the short-term, but time has a way of providing a clearer lens to view events."

Drake laughed. "Thanks."

"For what, sir?"

"You just gave me a good approach for the Vice President, and a significant point to make. In the end, posterity will perceive him as decisive and bold, and it'll be the right thing to do at the same time. I'll share that with Doctor Astalos on the way over, and I'm sure he'll add ideas to the approach."

"I hope the Vice President sees it your way and we don't have to disobey a direct order from the Oval Office."

"That would be nice, wouldn't it?"

"Yes, sir."

"Okay, I have to get going here. Do me a favor?"

"Anything, sir."

"When you go back inside, ask Doctor Astalos to call me. I want to get on this right away."

"When are you meeting, sir?"

"Our appointment is at thirteen hundred this afternoon."

McKnight looked at his watch. "Yes, you'd better get going, sir. I'll go see Doctor Astalos right now."

"Good, and Marc?"

"Yes, sir?"

"Thanks for the support. I want you to know I regret some decisions I've made in my career, but selecting you to lead this team was not one of them. You always work to do the right thing, and I appreciate that."

"Thank you, sir. I'm very glad to be here. You'd better get going, sir."

"Right," Drake said.

McKnight came to attention and saluted. Drake returned it, got in his car and drove away.

Now to find Doctor Astalos.

CHAPTER TWENTY-FIVE

Tuesday, December 23rd, 2036 - 1:00 PM - McKnight's office, Telegraph Road, Alexandria, Virginia

McKnight sat at his desk, working on his detailed report from the verification trip to 2086. He found it agonizing to find the right words to express the details so future readers would understand what transpired.

Preserving an accurate picture of the history of time was the most challenging aspect of his job.

When a time traveler goes into the past and makes a change, it's like a person in the present who makes a choice — a fork in the road for his future. Making that decision in the past is different. It creates an alternate path that wasn't there before and cuts off the original path. This creates a change wave that travels forward through time.

As the change wave catches up to the present, those who traveled on the mission are the only ones who remember both the old and the new history. The new history path will be what everyone else remembers. Therefore, the responsibility for recording and preserving history falls on the time travelers. The actual history of what happened during the mission — good or bad — becomes a report filed in the National Archive. The more detailed the report, the better future readers will understand what happened and why.

Something must record and share the reports of each mission conducted by the HERO Team with everyone else. It's difficult to do. Frequently, the story the 'non-traveler' remembers from his own personal history is at odds to the history in the reports, and he must learn to trust the reports over his memory.

Each time traveler must develop the habit of documenting what happened on their mission upon their return and communicating to the rest of the team what happened and, sometimes, even why we conducted the mission.

It's always a time-consuming and exhausting task to document the mission.

McKnight's desk phone rang, breaking his concentration. He picked it up. "McKnight."

"Colonel McKnight?" It was the new receptionist.

"Yes, Suzie?"

"Doctor Astalos is here to see you."

Doctor Astalos? McKnight looked at his watch. *He's supposed to be with General Drake and the Vice President right now.*

"Suzie, are you sure? Doctor Astalos is supposed to be at the White House."

"Oh," she said. "Not him. The *other* one. The one from Finland."

Robby? He's here?

"I'll be right out." McKnight stood and walked out of his office.

As he headed for the reception area, he thought about the strange case of Robert and Robby Astalos. In truth, they were the same man. Credit for the invention of time travel belonged to both men, but it was Robert, and he's the first to admit he stumbled upon it.

Back in 2025, Robert Astalos was in his office at MIT working on a warp drive idea for interstellar travel. Through a strange accident, he executed the first time travel event by jumping twenty-five years into the past. He landed in his same office, right in front of his younger self.

He had no way to return to the present, so he convinced his younger self who he was, and they worked together in secret to determine how the accident occurred and perfect the science of time travel. When the two men reached the year 2025, they traveled back to the year 2000 again, but this time on purpose. They needed more eyes on the warp drive problem, so they traveled back to enlist his younger self again to help.

When they landed this time, there were others present and their secret was out. The college called the federal government, which swooped in, classified their work, and turned it into a military project. They brought Drake and McKnight on to manage the time travel project, and the rest was history.

As the three men worked together, the 'name thing' grew complicated. To make it easier, the oldest went by Robert, the next by Rob, and the youngest by Robby.

Robert lived through the period from 2000 to 2025 three times. Rob did it twice, and Robby once.

A couple of years ago, a training accident merged Rob's consciousness into Robert's body.

McKnight's thoughts came back to the present as he entered the reception area. There was Robby, complete with three suitcases, a briefcase, and his laptop.

"Robby! It's great to see you. I thought you were still in Finland?"

"I was. I completed my work there and now I'm back in the U.S.. Do you have an office I can use for a few days?"

"Sure. I heard you'll be working with Tyler on his new mysterious project."

"That's correct. Congratulations on your promotion, by the way."

"Thanks," McKnight said. "Come along and we'll find you a place to sit."

"Thanks, Marc. Do you think we get the team together for a few minutes? I have a mission innovation to share with you all."

"Yes, we can. I don't think Tyler is here — I guess you know that — but everyone else is here."

"Cool," Robby said. "Let's find a place to put my stuff and we can start."

In fifteen minutes, McKnight invited everyone to the big conference room and Robby connected his phone to the overhead display interface cable. Kathy Wu, Trevor George, Mitch Wheeler, and Karen Hatcher filed into the room. After greeting Robby and catching up for a few minutes, they seated themselves around the table.

Robby stood at the head of the table, smiling.

"I can't tell you guys how great it is to see you again. While I was in Finland on sabbatical and doing research, I couldn't stop thinking about the technology ideas you guys mentioned over the last few months. Robert and I discussed it and decided this was something you needed." He held up a device that was so small, the team could barely see it. It was the size of a pea.

"What's the hardest part of your job?" he asked.

"The mission paperwork," McKnight said without hesitation.

All but Kathy nodded.

"I agree," she said. "I know it's hard, but it's the only way we can keep up with how each mission affects reality. There's no substitute for it."

"That's right," Robby said, and held up the device. "But this will make it easier."

"We're all ears, Doc," Wheeler said.

"Me, too," Hatcher said.

"Tell us what it does," Wheeler added.

"Okay," Robby said. He tapped his phone and a set of bullet points appeared on the screen. "Here we go."

"This device — we call it 'the pea' — is both a computer and a storage device. It has a custom set of programs that interface with the data storage. It's official name is the 'mission implant'."

"Meaning it's implanted in our body somewhere?" McKnight said.

"Right. It'll be implanted in your left thigh so you don't lose it. Unless maybe you lose your leg, but then you have bigger problems."

Everyone laughed.

"But does it have to be implanted?" Kathy asked. "It feels very much like Big Brother is watching you."

"I get it," Robby said. "I do. But it's just a library of information. It does nothing but carry mission history information through the mission, so it doesn't change. It's a resource for the traveler. In effect, you can use your phone to pull up any mission information and even the history of all our missions. If someone makes a history modification while you are time-traveling and your world gets turned upside down, you can use it to reconfirm what your mission is. It doesn't carry any bio or neurological information about you, other than whose leg it's in. It's nothing to worry about. There is no additional memory to run new programs. It's a single purpose app."

"I'll table my objections for now. If it saves a lot of time, that would help our situation."

"And it will," Robby said. "Our history of missions and reports are kept on and backed up from the HERO mainframe at DLA Headquarters. There's two apps for your phone, one for missions, and one that leadership uses for briefing and debriefing. Kathy and Trevor will use it to load the history into your pea before you travel and unload it to the mainframe when you return. Everyone uses the mission app to dictate their report and add it to the mission record before it's uploaded to the mainframe."

"Wow," McKnight said. "No more typing of reports?"

"For the most part," Robby said. "You dictate the report and then edit it by typing into your phone or comm pad. The dictation software is a customized AI application and converts your oral report into a mission report. If you leave out any of the key fields — date, time, purpose of the mission, and so forth, the application will prompt you for it. In a short time, you'll learn how to give your oral report and all the right data so you don't have to fill in details afterward."

Hatcher raised her hand. "Doc? Could you run through a typical use of the pea for a mission?"

"Sure," Robby said, "and I'll send out a link to the user manuals for the two phone apps. Here's what we do."

He changed the visual on the screen.

"First, Kathy plans the mission. She uploads that plan to the mission record in the mainframe. Then, right before you travel, she downloads the total mission history of the team into your pea. Next, you do your time travel mission. When you get back, Kathy first uploads the history of the Team to the mainframe from your pea. Then you use the app to make your mission report. Dictate what happened, then check to confirm the report is correct. Or turn it on to record the meeting while you brief someone else and it will pull out and capture the data it needs. Anyway, once the report is complete, you upload it to the mainframe, and it's attached to the history."

"What happens when more than one person travels at a time?" Trevor asked.

"The mission database manager software is smart enough to figure that out. It will integrate the reports of two different missions, based on the timestamps and actual dates of events. If we assign more than one person to a mission, Kathy notes that in the mission plan, and the software knows the mission isn't complete until all team members have submitted their personal report."

"Can I get some time with you to get checked out on the app?" Kathy asked.

"Yes, ma'am," Robby said. "Right after this session."

"Are there any restrictions for how close you must be to the pea for the apps to work?" Hatcher asked.

"No practical limits. You can access your pea with the app from anywhere on Earth, as long as the satellites are working. If there are no satellites, you can prox the data within ten feet of the pea. By the way, Colonel McKnight and Major Tyler will also have the brief/debrief software on their phones so they can update the history and upload mission data. Any more questions?"

"I have one more," Wheeler said. "Can I upload or download the mission history *during* the mission? Like when I'm still in the past?"

"You can always see the existing mission reports," Robby said. "But you can't upload your finished report from another time. You *can* send updates to your beacon and it will forward it to the time Engine, which then sends it to the mainframe as a partial report. It isn't complete until you return and make your report. We're still working to implement this part, but it'll be ready in a couple of weeks."

"Okay, I'm sold," Kathy said. "This will save us a lot of time after each mission. Thank you."

McKnight nodded. "That sounds great. Thank you."

Everyone applauded the innovation.

"When do we get our peas implanted and get the apps?" Wheeler asked.

"Today. I have the surgeon in the small conference room, ready to insert the peas in your thighs as soon as we can get down there."

Wheeler swallowed hard. "Today?"

Hatcher punched him in the arm. "You are such a wimp."

CHAPTER TWENTY-SIX

Tuesday, December 23rd, 2036 - 2:34 PM EST - Telegraph Road, Alexandria Virginia

McKnight heard the PA announcement while he was in the lab.

"Colonel McKnight, please call the receptionist. Colonel McKnight."

He pulled out his phone and speed-dialed the front desk.

"Front Desk. Sergeant Draper here. How may I help you?"

"Sergeant, this is Colonel McKnight. You just paged me?"

"Yes, sir," Draper said. "There's a Special Agent-in-Charge David Ritter here to see you, sir. He's in the reception area."

"Thank you, Sergeant. Sign him in and I'll be right there."

McKnight disconnected the call.

I wonder why he's here? He could have just called. Regardless, I know he'll want to see Trevor.

McKnight called Trevor and asked him to meet him at the front desk. He found him in the hall on the way to the reception area.

"What's up?" Trevor asked.

"Ritter, your buddy from the FBI. He's here," McKnight said.

"He is? How come?"

"No idea. Let's ask him."

Ritter wore a navy blue suit with a gold tie. His hair was dark brown and slicked back. He wore black glasses and a magnificent tan. There was a white visitor ID tag clipped to his suit's breast pocket, along with his SAC badge for government buildings. He carried a black leather briefcase.

McKnight and Trevor walked toward him.

"Thanks for seeing me, Colonel. Congratulations on your promotion, by the way. Hi, Trevor, it's nice to see you."

Trevor stopped short.

"Dave, why so formal? What's up?"

Ritter looked at McKnight. "Can we talk in private, Colonel?"

"Excuse me?" Trevor said.

Ritter waved his hand at Trevor. "No, with both of you," he said. "But let's do it in private."

McKnight glanced at Trevor, then back at Ritter.

"Sure, Special Agent. Follow me."

McKnight led Ritter and Trevor to a small conference room. They closed the door behind them and sat.

"What's this all about, Dave?" Trevor asked.

"Trevor, I allowed you to join us because of our extensive history together and because I trust you. But my questions are for Colonel McKnight."

Trevor stared at Ritter for a moment. "Okay," he said.

"What can I do for you, Special Agent Ritter?" McKnight said.

"Do you have a Lieutenant Karen Hatcher on your team?"

"No, but I have a Captain Karen Hatcher. She just got promoted. What about her?"

"How's her performance? Is she a good soldier?"

"Yes, of course," McKnight said.

"What's up, Dave?" Trevor asked. "It sounds like you suspect Hatcher of something."

Ritter ignored the question. "Do you trust her?" he said, and stared at McKnight.

McKnight stared back at him. "With my life," he said.

Ritter nodded and opened his briefcase, extracted two eight by ten photographs and handed them to McKnight. One picture showed a naked man sitting on a toilet, dead. Blood trickled from his nose and the corner of his mouth. The second showed the bodies of two men lying in a hallway.

McKnight pointed at Trevor with the photos. "May I?" he said.

"Yes, of course," Ritter said, and McKnight shared them with Trevor.

"What do these photos have to do with Captain Hatcher?" McKnight asked.

Ritter pointed at the bathroom picture.

"That's a ladies' room in the Las Vegas airport. They found Captain Hatcher's fingerprints in the stall."

"I'm sure lots of people use those restrooms," McKnight said.

"Yes, I know," Ritter said. "And *this* one..." Ritter pointed at the other photo. "... is from a hotel in Rachel, Nevada. These gentlemen were detectives from the Las Vegas police department. They were investigating the other murder and followed the trail to a hotel room. Captain Hatcher's fingerprints were all over the room." Ritter let his words sink in.

"So, I have three dead men, two of them cops, and your Captain Hatcher's fingerprints at both crime scenes. What conclusions must I make, given the evidence? They took the first picture on December twelfth, the second on December twentieth. So, where was Captain Hatcher on those dates? Was she in Las Vegas? If so, what was she doing there?"

"She was here working," McKnight said. "I can confirm that by the duty roster, but I don't need to. I was here. So was Trevor. There are several people who can swear she was here."

Ritter nodded. "I'm sure you'll agree with me... right, Trevor? That's powerful evidence—"

"*Circumstantial* evidence," Trevor said.

Ritter waved his hand at Trevor. "I'll grant you that," he said, "but I'm sure you'll agree I can't call it coincidence. I have to ask questions about this. Is Captain Hatcher here today?"

McKnight nodded.

"May I speak to her?" Ritter asked.

"Does she need a lawyer present?"

"If she asks for one. But it's better if she answers the questions. If she hasn't done anything and has nothing to hide, why shouldn't she talk to me?"

Trevor rolled his eyes. "Dave, you can't be serious. If I were her lawyer, I'd tell you to buzz off. Sounds like a trap to me, and I know you're one of the *good* guys."

Ritter shrugged. "What I'm trying *not* to do is arrest her and take her downtown for questioning. You know you'd have to arrest her if you were me."

Trevor turned to McKnight. "He's got a point."

"I'll explain the situation to her and see if she wants a lawyer present, Special Agent Ritter," McKnight said. "If she does, you might have to arrest her. Give me about ten minutes. Why don't you and Trevor get some coffee?"

"We can do that," Trevor said. "Come on, Dave."

Ritter looked skeptical. Then he shrugged and followed Trevor out of the conference room.

McKnight walked to Hatcher's office and explained what was going on.

"What do you think, Captain?" he asked. "Do you want to talk to him or call your lawyer?"

"You don't believe I did this, do you, sir?"

"Not for an instant."

Hatcher thought for a few seconds.

"I'll talk to him, sir," she said. "I have nothing to hide. Let's go."

"Okay, Captain. But don't forget — you can tell him when you were in Nevada, but you can't tell him anything that will confirm or acknowledge the existence of the facility. That's still top secret, and he doesn't have proper clearance to know about it."

"Yes, sir."

They walked to the conference room and waited for Ritter and Trevor to return.

After introductions, Ritter got down to business.

"Thank you, Captain Hatcher, for agreeing to talk to me," he said. "Just tell me the truth about everything you can." He placed a recorder on the table. "I'll be recording our conversation if that's okay with you."

"Yes, it's fine," she said. "Can I see the pictures you showed the Colonel?"

"Yes, you can, but not yet. Have you been to Nevada in the last two weeks?"

"Yes, sir."

"You have? When were you there?"

"A little less than four days ago, sir. On the nineteenth of this month."

"Are you sure about that?"

"The date? Yes, sir. I was there from 1:15 PM Pacific time to about 3:15 PM. I was on an assignment."

"Where did you go in Nevada, Captain?"

Hatcher glanced at McKnight. "I can't say, sir."

"You *can't* say? What does that mean? You're choosing not to say, or you cannot say?"

"Both, sir. I can't say, so I'm choosing not to."

"Okay. I noticed you looked at the Colonel before you answered." Ritter turned to McKnight. "Can *you* help me out, Colonel? Do you know where she was?"

"Yes, sir, I do, but I can't say either. Her mission was classified and so was her location."

"She was on a time travel mission?"

"I can't say, sir," McKnight said, and looked Ritter in the eyes. "I'm truly sorry, Special Agent Ritter, and I understand the situation this puts you in. But we can't say."

Ritter shook his head and looked at Trevor, who was busy studying his fingernails.

"Trevor, I suppose you can't say, either?"

"No, Dave. I'm sorry, but I can't. But let's get back to the murders, shall we? Captain Hatcher told us she was in Nevada for two hours on December nineteenth, from 1:15 to 3:15 PM. When were the murders committed?"

"The first was on December twelfth at around 11:00 PM. Murders two and three occurred at 6:30 AM Pacific time on December twentieth."

"Okay," Trevor said. "Captain Hatcher, were you in Nevada on the twelfth or the twentieth?"

"No, sir, I wasn't. I was here with witnesses during those two times."

"Can you prove it, Captain?" Ritter asked.

"Yes, sir, I can, but I'm not sure I'm allowed." She turned to McKnight, who nodded. "Our time Engine keeps a log of who travels and when. That record will show all my travels. I'd have to edit the destinations, but the jump times are there."

"Good," Ritter said. "When can I see the records? Or are they classified, too?"

"I'm sorry, sir," she said.

McKnight leaned forward. "Special Agent Ritter, I can review the records and confirm what the Captain said. And I will ask General Drake for an exception so I can provide you with a redacted copy of the log. Would that be good enough?"

"Probably not, but I'll accept the redacted version for now if you can get them approved *and* Trevor reviews and certifies them."

"That's fair," McKnight said. "And if the General doesn't approve, I will at least review the logs with Trevor so he can certify my statement."

"Thanks," Ritter said, and leaned back in his chair. He didn't speak again for ten seconds.

"Of course, you know," he said, "I'm aware of what you do. If you have a time Engine, the times don't matter — you can still go there from another time."

"It's not as easy as you might think," McKnight said. "We can only travel to a time within a week of the present day, or twenty-five years away—"

"Or a multiple of twenty-five years," Hatcher added.

"Right, but more than a few days from now is irrelevant," McKnight said, and turned back to Ritter. "For example, to be in Nevada on the twelfth, she would have to travel after December fifth and before December nineteenth. To be there on the nineteenth, she would have to travel after December twelfth and before December twenty-sixth. That last interval is a time overlap for murders two and three, but the Engine log will tell us. We have two Engines here at this facility and a couple others in the D.C. area. I'll check the log files for all of them and let you know."

Ritter sat still for a moment.

"Captain Hatcher," he said. "How do *you* explain your fingerprints being at these crime scenes?"

"I can't explain it, sir. I mean, I've heard of people spoofing fingerprints with prosthetics on their fingertips, but I can't imagine why they would do that. What is there to gain, except maybe to throw off an investigation? But why *my* fingerprints? No, sir, I don't have a clue."

Ritter nodded. "Let me show you the photos." He handed them to Hatcher.

She looked at them, then up at Ritter. "Yes, sir. A lot of Army Rangers can do this level of damage. I'm no exception. But it wasn't me, sir."

"Let me show you another picture," Ritter said. He reached back into his briefcase, pulled out another image, and handed it to Hatcher.

She looked at it. Her eyes flared, and she handed it to McKnight.

The picture appeared to be from a security camera. It showed an image of a woman McKnight would swear was Hatcher.

"This is from December twelfth in the Las Vegas Airport?" he asked, as he handed the photo to Trevor.

Ritter nodded.

Hatcher looked at Ritter, then McKnight.

"I don't know what to say, sir. It sure looks like me. If I didn't know better, I'd think it was me. But it wasn't. I haven't been there in years. I flew there to go to the Grand Canyon when I was a teenager. Somewhere around 2024, I think."

"To me, this person looks older than you, Captain," Trevor said. "But it's hard to tell from this shot."

Ritter nodded again. He looked at McKnight and Trevor. "If you two will stay with me for a few minutes, we can let Captain Hatcher get back to work."

"Thank you, sir," Hatcher said. She rose and saluted McKnight. He returned it and she left the room.

Ritter shook his head.

"What?" Trevor asked.

"I've interviewed a lot of subjects over the years. So have you, Trevor."

Trevor nodded and said, "Yep."

"Your Captain Hatcher... unless I'm losing my touch, she's innocent, or the best damned liar I ever met."

Trevor smiled. "You're not losing your touch. I don't think Hatcher knows how to lie."

Ritter looked at McKnight. "I'm baffled by this. Until we figure this thing out, can you put Hatcher on the bench? Not let her travel? I'd hate for her to disappear, for whatever reason."

"For how long?"

"A month. Maybe more."

McKnight shook his head. "Sorry, I can't do that. I have too few resources as it is. But I'll do this — she'll be the last one I send out and, if I *do* send her out, I'll keep you posted on where and when, as long as it isn't classified. A lot of our missions are, so I'm not promising much, but I can at least let you know *when* she travels. Is that acceptable?"

"No," Ritter said, but he smiled without humor. "But it'll have to do. I have no idea what to put in my report. My District SAC will scream bloody murder and insist I come back down here and arrest her."

"Would it help if I get General Drake to call him?" McKnight said.

"Maybe, if Drake will make it clear that you guys are cooperating and will help wherever you can. The fingerprints are circumstantial evidence only. They don't prove Captain Hatcher killed anyone, but they're mighty suspicious."

"I understand, Special Agent Ritter. Give me your SAC's number. I'll call General Drake and ask him to contact him."

"I appreciate that. Thanks."

Ritter wrote the name and number on his card and handed it to McKnight.

"I have a mission to execute," McKnight said. "But I'll call the General and review the logs right away. Look for Trevor to call you with the results before the end of the day."

"Thanks," Ritter said, and Trevor escorted him out.

McKnight leaned back and stared at the ceiling.

What next?

CHAPTER TWENTY-SEVEN

Tuesday, December 23rd, 2036 - 4:05 PM - McKnight's office, Telegraph Road, Alexandria, Virginia

McKnight sat at his desk and tried not to rub the fresh wound on his left thigh. The surgeon did a good job installing the pea, but it itched like crazy.

He chuckled. The surgeon warned him not to exercise that leg for a while. Stay off your feet he said.

Sure. Right before a mission.

He turned around in his chair and set his feet up on the credenza. He clicked the wall remote to turn it from opaque to transparent.

Robby told him the mission management app was up and running. He helped Kathy load everyone's pea with the mission database. McKnight pulled out his phone and brought up the mission management app. After a few taps, he found all the previous missions.

He accessed one of his early test missions and read through the brief report. The report took a long time to type; he remembered. He found an update button and added a test update. It worked perfectly.

This app is going to save me an enormous amount of time. Robby, you rock!

He pulled up the mission list and scanned it. There were more than a hundred missions on the list, including the original testing missions. He took part in most of them.

Have we done so much in the last two years? It seems longer than that.

A knock on the door behind him jarred him out of his reverie.

He kicked off the credenza to spin back around, and a twinge of pain from the pea incision was his reward. *Dammit! Wish I hadn't done that.*

"Come in," he said.

The door opened. Drake and Robert Astalos stood there. McKnight came to attention and saluted. *Ouch! Don't move so fast.*

"Hi, Marc," Astalos said, and turned to Drake. "I understand Robby's here, so I'll see you later." He waved at McKnight and walked down the hall.

Drake entered the office. "As you were," he said. "Are you alright?"

"Yes, sir. Why?"

"You seemed unsteady when you got up just now."

"Oh, no, I'm fine, sir. We all had new technology implanted today, so I'm still recovering."

"Ah," Drake said. "Robby's pea."

"You knew about that?"

"Robert briefed me on the way back from the White House. He and Robby worked on it for a while. What do you think?"

"I'll know more after we do field tests, but it looks promising."

"Good," Drake said. For a few moments, the General stared at the desk between him and McKnight.

Uncomfortable with the silence, McKnight said, "How was your meeting with the Vice President, sir?"

"I'll let you be the judge of that, Marc. In short, Vice President Crumpton approved our mission to abort the Kosar kidnapping, but with conditions. As you know, he isn't a fan and doesn't want us to make decisions without his input."

"His input? Excuse me, sir, but what does that mean?"

Drake nodded. "Years ago, we fought that way in the Mideast. Our rules of engagement were to protect ourselves, but don't take any offensive action without orders, and wait for the orders from the Oval Office."

"Sounds like a disaster to me, sir," McKnight said.

Drake looked at him and paused. "Disaster? Yeah, that's an appropriate description of it."

"What would we do? Send a request back from wherever we are and someone will relay it to the President's office for a decision?"

"Something like that. It'd be a pain in the ass, wouldn't it?"

"Yes, sir. Isn't there a way around that? What if we need a split-second decision? It seems like he wants us to fail."

Drake considered this, and shrugged. "That might be part of it, but I think he's being cautious. Too much, I think."

"Yes, sir."

"Given time, he'll understand, but Wade Harrison will be President in a month, and I'm sure he'll reverse the requirement. In the meantime, it's our... well, *your* cross to bear."

"Thank you, sir." McKnight managed a feeble smile.

This is going to suck.

"Well, it's better than you think," Drake said. "After the Vice President dropped this bomb on me, he trotted out an option that'll make things better. He's given us an agent to represent him."

"An agent? What does that mean? A politician who sits here in the office and approves everything we do."

"Nope. The agent will travel with each mission. For now, we can only run one mission at a time."

McKnight opened his mouth to speak, but Drake held up his hand.

"Remember," he said. "This is for the next month, then Harrison is President."

McKnight shut his mouth, but his mind flashed back to the Atlanta project where Senator Lodge insisted they take his agent along on a mission. Drake had enough leverage to make Lodge back down, but this time, it was the acting President pushing an agent on them.

"I disapprove, sir," McKnight said, "but given the choice of taking an inexperienced agent along or disobeying a direct order from the Vice President, I think I choose the agent."

Drake nodded again.

"Yes, that was my thought as well."

"Okay, so we have to get moving on the Kosar mission. When do I get to meet this agent person? Soon, I hope?"

Drake rose from his chair. "How about now? He's waiting in the reception area."

McKnight stood in response. "He is?"

"Yes."

The light dawned on McKnight. Drake knew he would be unhappy about taking along an agent, and he delivered the bad news the best way he could — by letting him know it could be a lot worse.

Drake turned and left the office. McKnight bounded around his desk to catch up. Another twinge of pain in his left thigh.

"Who is he?" McKnight asked. "Don't I get to see his personnel file or anything?"

"They classified his file above your level. But he is free to share with you what he will."

"Geez, who is this guy, sir?"

"Well, Detweiler advised he is the Vice President's favorite CIA guy."

"Is he a field agent?"

"I suspect he has experience in the field. Most do. I'm sure he'll be fine."

Drake stopped and examined his watch. "Damn, I've got a conference call, and it's already started." He looked at McKnight. "You've got this. He's in the reception area. His name is Smalls, Arthur Smalls."

"Arthur Smalls," McKnight repeated.

"Right. Go welcome him to the team and get Kathy to brief him on the beacon, the pea, and how we operate around here."

"Yes, sir." McKnight saluted the General. Drake returned it and walked away without a word.

McKnight stood still for a moment.

Damn, this just keeps getting better and better.

"Smalls. Arthur Smalls," he mumbled, and walked to the reception area.

A half-dozen men and women were in the reception area.

Hatcher and Wheeler's interviewees.

One of these people must be Smalls.

One man dressed in civilian clothes stood away from the others. He stood six feet tall and bore himself like an officer. McKnight walked toward him and said, "Agent Smalls?"

A voice came from over his shoulder. "Here, sir."

McKnight stopped and turned. A man rose from a chair and picked up a briefcase. He was a black man dressed in a three-piece dark gray suit. He was only five foot eight and 170 pounds. A stylish haircut, a trim moustache, and gold-rimmed glasses completed the look.

This is my CIA agent? He looks like an accountant!

The man walked over to McKnight and extended his hand.

McKnight took it and smiled. "Marcus McKnight," he said.

The man didn't smile back. "Pleased to meet you, Colonel. Arthur Smalls."

McKnight gestured toward the hallway. "This way, Smalls."

Smalls strode through the door and half-turned as McKnight caught up with him. "Colonel, I know my presence here might be a burden to you. It wasn't my plan either."

"I'm sure it'll work out fine," McKnight said. "We're pretty easy to work with."

Smalls shrugged. "I was supposed to be off with my family for Christmas, but..." He sighed. "Duty calls."

"I sympathize, Smalls. I was hoping for a few days off myself. Here's my office. Come on in, and let's chat for a minute."

He pointed Smalls to a chair in front of his desk and walked around it to sit.

Smalls sat erect in the chair. McKnight leaned back in his.

"So, Mr. Smalls, we have an imminent mission and need to get moving. What are your orders?"

Smalls leaned forward. "For the next month, I'm to provide executive oversight to your team. I report to Vice President Crumpton, dotted line to you, and my orders are to go along on your time travel missions and keep you aware of the Vice President's guidelines."

"Guidelines? Are they different from the HERO Team's official charter from Congress?"

"I haven't studied them yet, sir. That's my reading assignment for tonight. But I know the Vice President, as the acting President, has oversight and must, from time to time, issue executive orders to control the excesses of the team."

Control the excesses? McKnight felt his temper rise close to the surface.

He responded with as even a tone as he could manage. "I wasn't aware of any activity that might be excessive. Could you give me an example?"

Smalls didn't waver. "The Vice President's words, not mine," he said. "The jury on time travel is still out with me. I know that changing history is risky and can be dangerous. I don't yet understand the need to change history."

"At least we agree on the risky and dangerous part," McKnight said. "Our original charter was one of verification of events — historic research. Most people are fine with that. The problem arises from external forces that use time modification to advance agendas. Our charter has grown to play an aggressive role in *preserving* history."

"Like snatching George Kosar," Smalls said.

McKnight shrugged. "When you check out the records — which I'm sure you'll do, right? — I think you'll find our entire team was against that solution and lobbied against it. But we follow orders."

"I was not aware of that," Smalls said. "I didn't get much of a briefing, but I'll remedy that tonight."

"Good. I have something that will help. Stand by a moment."

McKnight picked up his desk phone and called Kathy. "Could you come here for a minute?" he said.

A moment later, she appeared at the door.

"Hi, Kathy," he said.

Smalls rose from his seat and waited to be introduced.

He has manners. That's a good sign.

"Smalls," McKnight said, "this is Doctor Kathy Wu. She is our mission planner and all-around organizer of the Team."

Smalls took her extended hand and said, "Charmed, Doctor. I'm pleased to meet you."

"Likewise," Kathy said.

"Smalls, we have a mission app that accesses an implant we call 'the pea'. It contains the mission records for everything we've ever done. Kathy can fix you up with the app for your phone and get the implant installed for you."

"Implant?"

"Yes," Kathy said. "It goes in your left thigh."

"Everyone on the Team has the implant," McKnight said. "Nobody travels without it. I think it will help you accomplish your mission. At minimum, it gives you a convenient place to record and store your notes and observations. Kathy, do you have time now to set Mr. Smalls up? He'll be going with me on the mission tomorrow."

"Yes, of course. Mr. Smalls, what's your background? Ever been in the military?"

"Yes," he said. "I was in the Navy."

Her eyes flickered at McKnight. "And what was your specialty? Do you have a college degree?"

"Yes, of course," he said. "I have a degree in accounting and my Masters is in business management."

Accounting? Oh, my God! He really is an accountant.

"Good," Kathy said. "We should get along just fine. Come, follow me and I'll get you fixed up."

"Sure," he said, and turned to McKnight. "Thanks for your time, sir. When is the mission scheduled for?"

"Tomorrow morning at 10:00 AM sharp. Please be here by 7:30 AM and meet with me. We'll cover the mission and I'll answer questions you have from your research tonight. Any questions for now?"

"Quite a few," Smalls said, "but I don't want to waste your time. I expect the mission records will answer most of them during my research tonight."

"Very good. I'll see you tomorrow, then."

"Yes, sir, and Colonel?"

"Yes?"

"I assure you, I come here with an open mind. I'm under orders, but I have a mind of my own and, I believe, a pretty good sense of fairness and moral direction. And I know politics can get in the way."

"We agree there for sure, Smalls. See you in the morning."

Smalls walked past Kathy and down the hall. She paused long enough to mouth her thoughts to McKnight — *What the hell?*

McKnight shrugged, and she followed Smalls down the hall.

Well... this will be fun.

He rolled his eyes and chose to leave the office and go get a good night's sleep.

CHAPTER TWENTY-EIGHT

Wednesday, December 24th, 2036 - 7:00 AM EST, HERO Team Lab, Telegraph Road, Alexandria, Virginia

McKnight pulled his F-150 truck into the parking lot at the Telegraph Road office. He headed for his usual parking spot and backed the vehicle into the space.

Overnight, he became both irritated with Smalls, and resigned to the fact the man would be in his hair for the next month. Add that to having to work on Christmas Eve, and his mood was less than cheerful.

He went straight to the lab. Trevor and Kathy were early risers and would be here already. He wanted Kathy's opinion of Smalls. He trusted her judgement of people better than anyone's, except for General Drake.

And Drake wasn't concerned about Smalls. What does he know I don't?

As expected, he found Kathy and Trevor hovering over the time Engine. They cross-checked each other as they configured it. Besides being mission planner, Kathy developed a keen interest in the Engine.

McKnight didn't know anyone who possessed more curiosity about the world and everything technical than Trevor. His background in cold case investigations gave him analytical skills that transferred to finding technical problems and working out a solution.

They greeted McKnight as he came in the loading dock door. He waved and walked to the coffee machine. Kathy was a tea drinker, but Trevor made it his mission to have coffee ready in the mornings for anyone who wanted it.

With a couple of sips in his system, McKnight's mood improved. He walked to where Kathy stood. Trevor came to join them.

"So," McKnight said. "What do you think of Mr. Smalls?"

Kathy faced him with her hands on her hips. "Who *is* that guy?"

"Inquiring minds want to know," Trevor added with a smile.

McKnight took another sip of coffee. *Better now.* "What do you mean?"

"What's he doing here?" Kathy said. "And how come he gets to go on a time travel mission and we've never met him before? Has he been traveling elsewhere?"

"What? Did he say he's traveled before?"

Kathy shook her head. "Quite the contrary. I'm sure he's never traveled before. You misunderstand my question. Trevor and I never get to travel, but this guy waltzes in and gets to go on his first day at work."

"He doesn't work here. He'll be here for a month."

Trevor and Kathy looked at each other.

"Do you not see that makes it even worse?" Trevor said. Kathy nodded.

"Oh," McKnight said. "Did he say he works here?"

"Well, to be honest," Kathy said, "that isn't exactly what he said. He said he'd be here working for the time being. I assumed he's a new member of the team, but I'm not sure what he brings to the table, you know?"

"Yes, I do."

McKnight exhaled deeply and crossed his arms with the coffee cup still in his hand. He leaned against the Engine console. "What he brings to the table is permission to execute time missions... for now."

"What?" Trevor and Kathy said in unison.

I need to get in front of this before it causes a problem.

"Okay, let's not get wrapped around the axle here. You're aware that the President has to give an executive order to allow us to perform a short lead time mission, right?"

"Yes, but the President is in the hospital." Kathy said.

"Right. The Vice President is calling the shots, and he isn't a fan of time travel. He doesn't understand how our mission is inherently defensive."

"Uh-Oh," Trevor said. "I see where this is going."

Kathy glanced at Trevor, then looked back at McKnight.

"So the Vice President sent Smalls here to be his man on the scene?"

"Something like that, and he'll be with us until Wade Harrison becomes President next month. What I want to know is, Kathy… What do you think about him? You spent a couple of hours with him last night, right?"

"Yes, I did. Okay, I understand now."

"And?"

"I found him to be charming and very polite, but not the warmest person I've ever met. I asked him if he preferred to be called by his first name, and he said Smalls would do. He's also very precise. I got the impression he wasn't wild about being here, either. I think he's curious about time travel and excited to get to do it, but it's Christmas Eve and he was hoping to be with family. How's Megan, by the way?"

McKnight winced. "Unhappy. The only consolation is we'll be back in a half hour and can take the rest of the week off."

"As long as it goes well," she said.

"Right. To that point, tell me about your briefing with him."

"Sure. Smalls now has the pea implanted by the surgeon, he has the beacon app on his phone so he can send status messages, and he knows what to expect when he travels."

"Okay."

"But is he ready to lead a time travel mission? No. But he has enough information to travel with supervision and how to use the beacon to get home if there's a problem. As long as we're with him when he travels, he should be fine."

"Good. Or as good as it could be."

McKnight's phone pinged, and he pulled it out.

"This is a text from the front desk. Smalls is here." He looked at his watch. "Right on time."

"I'll go get him in," Trevor said. "You guys can continue your discussion." He turned and left the lab.

"What else can you say about Smalls, Kathy?"

"Well, do you remember he said his background was in accounting and business management?"

McKnight rolled his eyes. "How could I forget? Of all the people at his disposal, why would the Vice President send him?"

"Right. But I think there's more he isn't telling us. He isn't built like an accountant, is he?"

McKnight thought for a second. "No, he isn't."

"He works out to stay in shape. When the surgeon implanted the pea, I got a look at his thighs. They are huge."

"Okay."

"Now, it might be nothing. But there's something about him. A calm or a peace. Call it inner strength, I don't know. But I don't think he rattles easily."

"Well, that much is good. We'll see. Let's hope he doesn't get tested enough for us to find out."

"Yes," she said and smiled. "Here he is, now."

McKnight turned to see Trevor and Smalls enter the lab. Smalls was carrying a small gym bag.

Smalls gave McKnight a nod and said, "Good morning."

"Good morning, Smalls," McKnight said. He pointed to the kitchen area. "Help yourself to some coffee, courtesy of Trevor here."

"Thanks," he said to Trevor. "Don't mind if I do."

Smalls got coffee, took a few sips, and walked to the console.

"Are we ready to go?" he said.

"Close," Kathy said.

"Smalls, do you have questions for me after your briefing with Kathy?" McKnight said.

"Nothing much. I'm wondering about the kneeling during travel and the landing. Could you explain why we kneel during the jump?"

"Sure. Nobody knows why, but when you land, you lose your balance and fall backward. Ever get pushed by a bully when you were a kid? That's what it feels like."

"Well, I know that feeling," Smalls said. "I was little for my age as a kid."

McKnight nodded.

"If you stand during travel, you will fall down when you land. We kneel because you can control your balance and stay in that position when you land. Did Kathy tell you about the stars?"

Smalls glanced at her. "No, she didn't. She mentioned some people get nauseated during travel."

"That's true. Seeing stars is no big deal. It doesn't affect your travel. That's why she left it out. During the travel itself, you'll feel like you're falling backward, and you'll see what looks like stars flying past. The sensation lasts varying amounts of time."

"Stars? I wonder why?"

"Doctor Astalos has some theories. One theory is that our planet is hurtling through space, and during time travel, we are jumping to the earth in a different place in space."

"Through the vacuum of space? I think I need a spacesuit."

McKnight grinned, and Kathy giggled into her hand.

"We haven't experienced any issues with that. Maybe the time bubble protects us, or maybe it contains enough air to get you through it, or maybe both. There's still a lot we don't know about the travel."

"I see," Smalls said. "So jumping through time is not for sissies."

McKnight nodded. "Correct. But we've never had an accident with travel. No one's ever been hurt."

"Good," Smalls said.

"Anything else?"

"Well, yes. I feel compelled to reiterate that, during the mission, I'm charged with oversight, and any decisions to act that might affect history must have my approval. I'm asking that you discuss any such actions with me before executing them. Are we on the same page?"

McKnight felt his temper rising within his chest. He pushed it back down with considerable effort.

"Yes, we are," he said. "And I want to remind you that you've never done this before and there are dangers. I must insist that you obey direct commands from me related to the time travel itself. I'd hate to explain to the Vice President how you got killed because you didn't follow my commands."

Smalls' eyes widened. A look McKnight interpreted as anger flashed across his face, but it faded as he replaced it with a slight smile. His lips drew a tight line across his face.

"Noted. I agree," he said. "And what else?"

"That's clear, don't you think?" McKnight said.

Then Kathy was there, standing between them.

"Gentlemen," she said. "Trevor and I brought in breakfast for us all." She pointed to the break area where Trevor was putting out coffee, orange juice, and egg and sausage sandwiches. "Let's eat, shall we?"

She slipped an arm into theirs and pulled the two men along to the table. Kathy sat between them and urged them to dig in.

McKnight reflected again on how intuitive and skillful Kathy was with people and chastised himself for almost losing his temper.

Smalls piled a couple of sausage biscuits on his plate and poured a large glass of orange juice for himself. He poured another and handed it to Kathy, and she passed it on to McKnight.

McKnight went to the coffee machine and poured another cup for Smalls and himself. He also poured boiling water over a tea bag for Kathy. He carried the drinks back to the table.

Smalls attacked his sausage biscuit with gusto and hummed a tune as he ate.

McKnight chuckled under his breath.

Any man who loves sausage biscuits this much can't be bad.

CHAPTER TWENTY-NINE

Wednesday, December 24th, 2036 - 7:02 AM PST - Nevada Desert near Rachel

The Operative woke and looked at her watch.

I slept for two days.

She inspected the cave. Everything appeared as before. No intrusion by animal or man.

She rebuilt her fire to take the chill off the early morning. Outside the cave, the desert was heating up, but the sun hadn't yet made an impact in the canyon.

She checked the log file of the locator again for a sign of Rachel Patterson.

Still no signal.

She cooked a modest meal to take in protein and carbs, then packed up her gear to begin the long drive to Washington. She checked her money.

I need to sell another diamond in the first big town I come to.

She loaded up the Jeep and headed through the desert back to the highway. She pondered the biggest question.

North or South?

Should she go south through the town of Rachel and then break east? This was the shorter route and shorter was her preference. But there might be a large law enforcement presence based in Rachel.

North up to Ely and then to Salt Lake City was the safer, but longer route.

The Operative tuned her phone to the police radio band again.

There was a lot of chatter on the police band. Most of it concerned a run-in between the police and the military in the desert. It was easy to understand. The police searched the area around the Iceberg and set off dozens of alarms. The Army guys told the police to leave the area, and the police demanded access to search for the murderer of two detectives in Rachel.

I killed them both.

But the exchanges didn't answer her question.

Is the town full of cops? Would I run a gauntlet of police cruisers just to save time?

She reached the highway and looked both ways. Her tactical mind was screaming at her.

Turn right. Go north. Avoid confrontation. You won't lose that much time.

She turned left… south. Her instincts railed against this choice, but she would save time if possible.

I can stop short of town and sneak forward to recon. I don't have to push my way through.

When she reached the northern edge of town, she could see police car lights in the distance. She turned off onto a dirt road and parked in a brushy area under some gnarled trees.

She engaged the mission suit and walked across a couple of dusty fields until she came in behind a building.

Careful to keep the building between her and the rest of town, she peeked around the edge. When she did, she realized she was hiding behind the town bar and grill.

The hotel stood fifty meters away across a sandy dirt parking lot. Ten police cars sat in front of it.

She pulled back from the edge and slid down to a sitting position.

This way is a terrible choice.

A police car took off, going north with its lights on.

They must have found something. I hope it wasn't my cave.

She looked down at her mission suit. It had taken on the color of the building. She gave thanks to late twenty-first century technology. If the cop looked in his rearview mirror, she'd be hard to see.

She decided to retreat to her desert hideout and leave the area by driving north instead. But she didn't feel comfortable walking in the open across the fields if that cop came back soon.

After fifteen minutes of waiting, she decided she had waited long enough. She stood.

As she rose, she heard voices. A glance to the left revealed an open window. She paused, hoping to gather more intel.

A male voice said, "Thanks for calling... yeah."

A raspy woman's voice said, "What was that all about?"

"They're looking for guides for the desert."

"Who?"

"Who do you think? The cops."

"Are you going to do it?"

"I dunno," he said. "Seems like a lot of trouble to me."

"That's a lot to ask citizens to do. You might get shot or something, just for volunteerin'."

"Ha," he said. "They ain't looking for volunteers, they're offering 1500 bucks a day per man."

"$1500 a day! You just git yourself over there and sign up with them. You know the desert as good as anyone does, and better than most."

"I dunno. It's gonna be pretty hot out there today."

"Harry, listen to what you're saying," she said. "How often do you get a chance to make 1500 bucks in a day? Never! Think of what you could buy. Go sign up to be a guide."

"Well, now that you put it that way, I guess it does make some sense. Okay. I'll go over there after lunch."

"You will not!" she said. "You get over there right now and ask what you can do to help."

The Operative heard a chair creak, and the man said, "Alright, alright… I'm going."

She heard the man shuffle across a wooden floor and moved so she could peek around the building's corner. An old man in shabby clothes made his way across the parking lot to the hotel.

It's time to leave.

She looked up the north road.

Nothing.

She ran across the fields, keeping the building between herself and the motel. When she reached her car, she felt heavy fatigue set in.

Why am I so tired?

She was certain she knew why. Gathering her strength for a big push, she jumped in the Jeep, started it, and hurried up the road to the north. It occurred to her she might meet the patrol car coming back from the north, but it was her only option.

She didn't see him on the way. She made it back to her cave without incident. It was noon.

I'll start again tomorrow after a rest. I could use more rest, anyway.

CHAPTER THIRTY

Wednesday, December 24th, 2036 - 10:00 AM EST, HERO Team Lab, Telegraph Road, Alexandria, Virginia

Kathy and Trevor approached the console. She carried her checklist.

It's time to get the show on the road.

McKnight and Smalls approached and stood next to the console.

"Before I forget," McKnight said to Trevor, "Please don't forget to send off that report to Dave Ritter."

"Will do."

"Dave Ritter?" Kathy said. "The FBI guy? What's that all about?"

"Don't worry about it," McKnight said. "Trevor knows what to do."

She regarded him suspiciously, then shrugged. "Whatever you say, boss."

She handed their beacons to them and they slipped them over their heads. She also gave them two small satchels with survival rations, nausea medication, and sleep bulbs, just in case they stayed longer than expected.

"Easy trip," she said. "Go to Hungary in 1986, then jump back home a few minutes later. We're setting you down in the woods near the lake, about fifty yards from where the SEALS landed."

"Understood and agreed," McKnight said.

Kathy nodded and looked at Smalls. "You won't need your beacon until you're ready to come back. Don't let it get away. You can't get home without it unless you're in someone else's bubble."

McKnight turned and went to the platform.

Smalls' brow wrinkled as he frowned.

Kathy smiled at him. "Stick close to the Colonel. He'll make sure you get back in one piece."

"Oh, I'm sure of that." He looked over his shoulder at McKnight.

She reached out and touched his hand. "Smalls, you got this. Simple mission. Go there. Find Major Tyler and the SEALS, tell them to abort the kidnapping, then come back."

The frown disappeared, and he chuckled. "Thanks, Kathy." He turned and followed McKnight to the platform.

McKnight knelt facing the console, and Smalls did the same.

Trevor stood by her to operate the Engine's controls.

"Okay, time to rock-and-roll," he said. "By the book... Travelers? Do you have your beacons?"

McKnight pulled his beacon out of his shirt and showed it to them. Smalls watched him and mimicked the action.

"The travelers indicate they have their beacons," Trevor said.

Kathy marked the checklist.

"This mission is to abort the George Kosar kidnapping," Trevor said. "The destination is Friday, December 19th, 1986, at 4:05 PM. The location is the shoreline of Lake Balaton in Hungary. Travelers, are you ready?"

Both men nodded.

"Travelers indicate—"

"Hold!" Kathy said. "We have an indicator that doesn't show green."

"Where?"

"Here," she said, and pointed to a button on the console. The button was bright yellow.

Trevor glared at it. "What's that for?"

"I don't know. I've never seen that button be anything but green before. Trevor, please get Robby from his office."

McKnight stood. "What's the holdup?"

"Bad indicator light," she said. "Hang tight for a minute. We're getting Robby to look."

McKnight saw Trevor at Robby's office, sticking his head inside.

"We don't have time for this," he said.

"Better safe than sorry," Smalls said.

McKnight ignored his comment and watched Robby make his way to the Engine with Trevor. He and Smalls stood and approached the console.

"What's the issue, Kathy?" Robby asked.

She pointed at the console. "We have a yellow light on one indicator." When she looked for it, all lights were green across the console. "What? It was yellow, just now."

"Which one?" Robby asked.

"I'm not sure now." She pointed at a cluster of indicator lights. "It was one of these three. I'm not sure which one," she said.

"Are we on or off?" McKnight asked.

Kathy looked to Robby for support.

"Are you sure the light was yellow?" he asked.

"Of course I am," she said. "But it's green now."

"I saw it, too," Trevor said.

Robby checked each of the lights. One cover was loose. He tightened it and said, "Maybe it was just the light. Check it again."

"Looks okay now."

"Great!" McKnight said. "Let's get going."

"Okay," she said. "Trevor, resume the countdown."

"Yes, ma'am. Travelers, please assume the travel position again and we'll continue."

McKnight and Smalls knelt on the platform again.

"I think I'll stay and watch," Robby said.

"Travelers, are you ready?" Trevor said.

Both men nodded.

"Travelers indicate ready." Kathy marked her checklist.

Trevor plugged in the trigger, picked it up, and flipped up the safety cover. "Trigger armed and ready,"

"Check," Kathy said. She glanced again at the console. The button was holding green.

"Starting countdown." Trevor held up the trigger. "Five…"

Kathy heard the low hum of the Engine. In a moment, it would work hard. It would transport two men four days off the anniversary of the target date. The power requirement to time-jump would go up as the jump time tracked further from the target date.

"Four… Three…"

Kathy glanced again at the console. She thought she saw the button flicker from green to yellow and back. She stared at it.

"Two… One… Zero!" Trevor called as he pressed the trigger.

The volume of the Engine hum spiked up. The time bubble formed around McKnight and Smalls. Tiny sparkles appeared within the bubble and spun around. They lit up like stars. A windstorm inside the bubble whipped McKnight's and Smalls' clothes about them.

Robby leaned over to Kathy and said, "I wish I was going along."

She looked at him and nodded. The volume of the Engine was spiking up, and the brilliant light of the bubble made it difficult to see the men within.

Any second now…

She looked at the console and found the button. Before her eyes, it turned yellow and didn't change back to green.

"Robby!" she called, but it was too late.

The bubble bulged out to twice its normal size and disappeared with a bang.

The room was dim by comparison.

"Robby!" she said again. "The button!"

Robby and Trevor stared at the console. All the travel status lights were off except for one. It was yellow and blinking.

Wednesday, December 24th, 2036 - 4:05 PM Hungary time; 10:05 AM EST, Hungary

McKnight watched for the stars. He looked forward to seeing them whenever he jumped across time.

This time, it was different. The stars were there, but near the end of the jump, they jogged violently to the side. Before he had time to guess what it might be, they were on the ground.

Smalls fell backward. McKnight felt the tug, but he didn't lose his balance.

He stood and reached out a hand to help Smalls to his feet.

Smalls waved him off and groaned. "Oh, my God," he said. "I feel sick."

McKnight knelt next to him and unzipped his satchel. "Here," he said. "Remember? You have a nausea med in your pouch."

He pulled out a small packet and handed it to Smalls.

Smalls tore off the top of the packet and poured the white powder on his tongue.

After swallowing, he said, "Sorry, I didn't think I'd be a person who got sick during travel."

"It happens to the best of us. My former X.O. has the same problem, but it's a minor issue. You feel better already, right?"

Smalls laid on the ground for a second. "Yes, I do, as a matter of fact." He pulled himself to his feet.

"Good," McKnight said. "Let me send off an arrival status message."

He brought up the status message app and selected the quick message named Arrival. "There, done. Now, first thing when you land, you turn around 360 degrees, just to ensure there's no threat nearby."

"Sounds smart. Check for threats and survey the terrain."

"Correct," McKnight said. He executed his turn, and Smalls did the same.

"Are we in the right place, Colonel?"

"Yes, I think so." McKnight engaged the compass app on his phone. "There's no Wi-Fi or broadband here, but the phones still work." He pointed east to a path. "That path should lead us to the Lake."

He turned to the north and pointed in that direction. "The SEALS landed over there. Let's go see if we can find them before they take Kosar captive."

They hadn't walked fifty feet when a time bubble formed around them and started spinning.

McKnight turned to Smalls. "What did you do?" he asked.

"Me?" Smalls said. "Nothing. I'm just walking."

The bubble bulged and went out with a bang.

They found themselves back where they landed. Both fell to the ground.

McKnight bounded up. "What the hell?"

"Oh, God," Smalls said. He unzipped his satchel and pulled out another packet of nausea meds. He looked wretched.

"What did you do?" he asked Smalls. "Did you click your beacon?"

"No, but even if I did, it shouldn't affect both of us, right? Hey, I'm the new guy here. I only do what I'm told."

McKnight considered this.

"You're right," he said. "And we didn't go home. If we click our beacon, we should go home and this isn't it." Glancing around, he said, "It looks like where we originally landed."

Smalls stood, and McKnight sent the arrival status message.

"Looks the same to me," Smalls said. He looked east and north. "Yep." He turned back to McKnight. "What do you think caused that?"

McKnight shook his head. "No idea."

"Aren't you supposed to be the expert?"

McKnight glared at Smalls. "Experienced, yes. Expert? Who knows? It must be a glitch. I'm at a complete loss to explain it."

Smalls chuckled. "Well, we'll never know, will we?"

McKnight set his hands on his hips.

"We have a mission to execute. Let's get to it."

"I'm with you on that. Let's go."

McKnight pointed down the path, and they started walking.

After twenty feet, the time bubbles formed around them again.

"Dammit!" McKnight said.

In a moment, they sprawled on the ground in the landing spot.

McKnight leapt to his feet and looked around. Smalls was digging in his satchel for another nausea med packet.

McKnight set the arrival status message and dragged Smalls to his feet. "Let's try to get out of this area. Let's run out."

"Shall we split up?" Smalls asked.

"No!" he snapped, then toned down his response. "Sorry, no. Do you want to be stuck here by yourself?"

"Not my first choice, no," Smalls said. "Which way?"

"Toward the lake." He jogged, motioning for Smalls to join him. Smalls caught up to him, and they set a strong pace at five miles per hour.

In minutes, they can smell the lake and see the edge of the woods.

"I think it's working," McKnight said. "We're almost—"

The bubbles formed again, bulged, and they were back on the ground, back where they landed.

McKnight jumped up and helped Smalls to his feet as he fished another med out of his satchel. Smalls swallowed the med and said, "How many doses do we get standard in our kit?"

McKnight shook his head. "Not enough to do this all day." He fired off the arrival message.

"We're stuck," Smalls said.

"Yes, I think so. I don't know why, but we are. I think we have no choice but to abort. We'll go back to our time and try again."

"Okay." Smalls pulled out his beacon and held it up. "So we just squeeze this thing?"

"Yes, but let's make sure we do it together. This is so weird. I'm afraid to do otherwise — I don't want us to get separated. So, on three, okay?"

"Right. Together," Small said. "Wait! Is that one, two, three, go? Or one, two, go on three?"

"Argh," McKnight said. "We'll say one, two, three, go and we click on go, okay?"

"Okay."

Together they counted and squeezed their beacons.

The time bubbles formed, and after a few seconds, bulged out.

And they were back at the same landing place, sprawled on the ground.

"Crap," Smalls said.

McKnight didn't get up this time.

"What do we do now?" Small asked.

McKnight sent the arrival status message, then put his hands back behind his head and looked at the sky.

"Colonel, did you—"

"Yes, I heard you. I'm thinking. There are more things we can try, but I don't think they'll help. I think we're stuck until Kathy, Robby, and Trevor figure out what happened to us."

"I'm listening."

"I hope they figure it out soon. I'm not wild about spending the rest of my life reliving these last few minutes."

"Me, neither," Smalls said.

At least he's not panicking. Come on, Robby, get us out of here.

"In the meantime," McKnight said, "I'll keep on sending the status arrival messages out, every time we jump. And I'll send an SOS. Maybe it'll get their attention."

CHAPTER THIRTY-ONE

Wednesday, December 24th, 2036 - 12:46 PM EST, HERO Team Lab, Telegraph Road, Alexandria, Virginia

Kathy checked her watch.

They should be back by now.

She looked at the break area where Trevor was working at the table with his laptop.

It's so sweet he likes to be near me. He could be in his office where it's comfortable, but he's out here.

She sat across from him and waited for him to look up.

When he did, he said, "You're worried about that status button that went yellow."

"Yes." She smiled at him.

"And you're worried they haven't come back yet."

"Yes."

"Me, too. Have you tried to send them a message through the beacon?"

"I was thinking about it."

"Let's see. What were they supposed to do? Take a walk, find Winnie and the SEALS, and tell them to come back without Kosar, right?"

"Yes."

"And how much time would that take?"

Kathy wrinkled her nose. "Let's see... five minutes to land and get acclimated... they're a half mile from the shoreline, so call that eight minutes. Ten minutes to convince Tyler to abort the mission. Eight minutes back to the landing point... and they don't have to do that.

Add in five more minutes to prepare to jump… I make that thirty-six minutes." She checked her watch. "It's been at least two-and-a-half hours."

Trevor pushed his laptop aside and folded his hands on the table. "So they could have completed their mission four or five times now."

"Yes."

He rose, and she did, too.

"Let's get Robby to take a look," he said. "Why don't you ask him and I'll look at the Engine?"

"Good idea." She turned and trotted to Robby's office.

Wednesday, December 24th, 2036 - 1:05 PM EST, HERO Team Lab, Telegraph Road, Alexandria, Virginia

Robby wasn't in his office. The receptionist said she saw him leave earlier with his gym bag.

Kathy texted a message to him:

<<< *Robby, I'm worried about the Colonel and Smalls. They should have returned hours ago. I checked with the Iceberg — Kosar is there. So they didn't get to Tyler.* >>>

When she returned to the lab, she found Trevor pouring over the travel logs in the Engine.

"Any luck?" he asked.

"No, I texted him. Hopefully, we'll hear from him in a few minutes."

"Good. I think I've found something. Look at this."

"Hey, have you been trying to reach me?"

Robby's back.

Trevor waved him over and explained the situation.

"What did you find?" Robby said.

"Look here. The status log looks weird. Look at all the arrival messages. There should only be one, right?"

"Yes, how many are there?"

Trevor counted them. "About thirty."

"Exactly thirty," Kathy said. "And look here. Their arrival time shows almost the same time in every entry. The messages' log time here — that is, when we received the message — is later each time. They're spaced at about ten minutes apart. What does that mean?"

"Wait a second," Robby said. With a pen, he calculated the time between each of the arrival times and added them together. Then he counted the number of messages again and divided it into the sum. "Well, would you look at that?" he said.

The answer was 600 seconds.

"What does that prove?" Trevor said.

"I don't think it proves anything," Robby said. "But it suggests Marc sent those messages after landing in 1986 almost exactly every ten minutes."

"You mean like a loop?" Kathy said.

"Yes, that's what it sounds like."

They were all silent for five seconds. Kathy knew they were all thinking the same thing.

How long could that go on? Is it a temporary thing or are they stuck forever?

Trevor recovered first. "Kathy, I think you should notify General Drake."

"I do, too." She stepped away from the console to text Drake.

"What else do we see?" Robby said. "Are there any other messages in the log — other than arrival messages?"

"Let's see," Trevor said, and scrolled down through the messages. He sorted the messages by the time the Engine received them.

"Ah, there is one unique message type. An update message. It says... oh, damn..."

"What?" Kathy said, returning to the console.

"It's from McKnight. They believe they're stuck in some kind of time loop. They've tried to move out of the area, but they still got pulled back to the landing place and time after about ten minutes."

"Not good," Trevor said. "Ask them if they've tried to click the beacon and return."

Robby created a status message and sent it out. Then he 'tailed' the log so they could see each message as it came in.

After three minutes, a new message came to the log.

"Rats!" Robby said. "Yes, they've tried clicking the beacon. When they do, they go back to where they landed."

"Can they try to go somewhere else?"

Kathy shook her head. "No, I only programmed their beacons to bring them home. They can't jump to any other place."

The three looked at each other.

"If we don't come up with something, they'll be there forever," Robby said.

"How long can they last?" Kathy said. She was close to tears.

"They have rations, but... not long," Trevor said. "Three days without water. If they find a source of water, close to a month without food."

"Can we go after them?" Kathy asked.

"I don't think we dare," Robby said. "We might get caught in the same loop. And if we don't, we might not land in the same place where they are."

"Can we try to send them some food and water?" Kathy said.

"Yes, we can try that, but don't forget... they have their satchel, which contains some rations and water. They won't starve or die of thirst today. Let's think about what we can do right now and we'll worry about the rest when the time comes."

Kathy's mind raced forward.

We need to set them at ease if we can.

"Robby, please send them a message. Tell them not to worry, we're on it."

Wednesday, December 24th, 2036 - 5:23 PM EST, HERO Team Lab, Telegraph Road, Alexandria, Virginia

After four hours of deliberation, they didn't have any ideas to try.

Trevor watched for messages on the console, while Kathy and Robby brainstormed possibilities and ideas.

"Hey," Trevor said. "Here's a message from Smalls."

"What does it say?" Kathy said.

"He says the loop reminds him of an eddy in white water. It's a phenomenon where river water rushes over rocks and flows back under itself, creating an endless churning of water. They attribute most drowning accidents in whitewater rafting to eddies."

"I don't know how that applies here," she said. "They aren't in water. Time doesn't flow back under itself. I don't see how—"

"He says he got caught in one once. He barely made it out alive."

"No," she said. "Let's not go down a rabbit hole. We need a real life solution."

"Hold on," Robby said. "Don't discount this idea so fast. Trevor, send him a message back. Ask him how he got out of the eddy."

"Okay," Trevor said. He typed the message and sent it.

Fifteen minutes went by before he got a response.

"Here we go. Smalls says it's counter-intuitive. When you're underwater, you want to swim to the surface. In an eddy, when you swim to the surface, the current catches you and pulls you down under again. The trick is to do the opposite — dive and you can swim out underneath it."

Trevor and Robby pointed at each other.

"What did I just miss?" Kathy asked.

"What if," Robby said, "we get them to jump to another time? Maybe that will bypass the eddy."

"But their beacons are only programmed to bring them home. How can they jump elsewhere?"

"Well, what resources do we have?" Trevor asked. "We can send messages back and forth. Isn't that all we can do?"

"It isn't," Robby said. "Robert and I set up the beacon firmware to accept updates. I think I can write some code to reconfigure the beacon."

"You can?" Kathy said. "How long will that take?"

"A few hours. Send me a copy of the beacons' programming so I can see exactly how they're programmed. I don't want to make any assumptions about it. My goal is to reconfigure the beacons to add another jump location... say, eight hours ahead. If that works, then they can squeeze the beacon again and come home."

"What about the mission?" Kathy asked. "Could we jump them backwards to earlier and still get the mission done?"

"No, I don't think we dare. If there is a problem with that ten minutes of history and we jump back before it... they might fall right back into the eddy. Better to go forward, I think."

Trevor looked at Robby. "How long to configure the beacon?"

"Not long," Robby said, "once they get the update."

"How does it work?" Trevor asked.

"Once I write and test the code, we send the updated configuration through the beacon to their phones attached to a status message. Then they can install it on the beacon and run it. That's easy, just a couple of steps. It may take a few hours to write and test it, though. We can't afford a mistake. We only get one shot."

"Let's do it," Trevor said. "I'll send them a status to explain what we're doing. You go write code. Kathy, how do I send him the beacon programming?"

"I'll do it," she said. "Easier to do it myself than to explain it."

"I'm on the code," Robby said, and dashed toward his office.

Kathy logged in at the console. She went to the active beacon list, captured the configuration of both beacons, and emailed them to Robby.

She handed control of the Engine back to Trevor so he could alert McKnight and Smalls about what to expect.

He was almost through composing the message when her phone rang.

Oh, my gosh, it's Megan. It's Christmas Eve, and she's probably looking for Marc.

She answered the phone.

"Hello, Megan, how are you?"

"I'm fine, Kathy, but I'm looking for Marc. He said he had something to do this morning, but he'd be back for lunch. But I haven't seen him and he's not answering his phone. Do you know where he is?"

"I do, Megan. He's on a mission and he's stuck. He's not hurt, but he can't get back yet. We're working on getting him back now."

When she spoke again, Megan's voice had an angry edge to it. "I was afraid of that. He *promised* me we'd spend tonight together, just the two of us. And work got in the way *again*."

Kathy shook her head. "Megan, listen to me. That's not what happened at all. Marc had no control over it. What happened isn't precedented — it's never, ever happened before. Marc didn't choose to be late. There was a glitch. It's not his fault."

Megan paused. Kathy could feel her fear coming through the phone.

"Is he okay?" she asked.

"Yes, as far as we know. He's texting us and he isn't injured."

"Will he get home tonight?" she asked.

"I'm sorry, Megan, but I can't promise that. We're in unfamiliar territory here."

A long pause. When Megan spoke, her voice was husky and soft. "Is there a chance he won't come back? I mean, not be able to come back?"

"It's too early to make a judgement about that, Megan. I'm sorry. We still have options to explore, so we're not thinking that at all..."

"Yet," Megan said. "Yet, you mean."

"Believe me, Megan. If we were out of options, I would tell you."

Megan sniffed on the other end of the line.

Kathy's heart broke for her.

"Hang in there, Megan. We're doing everything we can to get him back. There are still many reasons to hope and you know there's no one better than Robby or Robert to get the problem solved."

Megan sniffed again. "I know you're right," she said. "Should I come down there?"

"No, stay home, where Marc can find you when he gets back. He can receive messages, so I'll send one to let him know you're worried."

"Please do," she said. "Call me if you get any news. I know I won't be able to sleep until he gets back."

"I will, Megan. Try to get some rest, but I promise I will call you with any news I get."

"Thank you, Kathy. I appreciate it… and you."

"We're on it, Megan. Good night."

"Good night."

Kathy disconnected the call and looked across the lab at Robby Astalos' office.

Prayers to you, Robby. Marc and Smalls are depending on you.

CHAPTER THIRTY-TWO

Thursday, December 25th, 2036 - 4:38 AM EST, HERO Team Lab, Telegraph Road, Alexandria, Virginia

Kathy and Trevor slept with their heads down on the break area table.

Robby came out of his office and walked to the Engine Console.

Kathy heard him moving and jumped up. She whacked Trevor on the arm and ran over to the Console. Trevor stumbled to the kitchen area to get coffee started.

"Did you get the code finished and tested?" she said.

Robby nodded. "Yes, finally. I had a couple of bugs to shake out, but they're fixed now."

"Good. How do they install it?"

"All they have to do is save the software to their phone and execute a five command sequence to install and run it. Do they have the skills to do that?"

"The Colonel does. I don't know about Smalls."

Robby glanced at her, and she shrugged.

"Okay, it is what it is," he said, and held up a thumb drive. "There are two files on this drive. The one labeled 'INST' is the instructions. The second one, labeled 'CODE', is the code for the beacon. I'll send them a message about that and then I'll send the two files, okay?"

"Sure," Kathy said. "I'll get you a cup of coffee and me some tea."

"Good idea, but it looks like Trevor beat you to it."

She turned to see Trevor approaching with two steaming cups.

Robby pulled a chair over to the Console and started typing. When he finished, he sipped some coffee and watched the display for messages.

After a few minutes, Kathy said, "How long has it been since you sent the message?"

Robby glanced at his watch. "At least ten minutes."

"I was afraid of that," she said.

"What do you mean?" Robby asked.

"There have been times when I sent a question and they never got it. I believe the messages to them disappear when the eddy jumps them back."

"So you think—"

"That everything resets when they loop? Yes. If they don't get the message during each loop, it's gone for the next loop."

"That's not good," Trevor said. "So they have to receive and read the message, download the software, install it, and run it. All within 600 seconds. If they don't finish, they have to start over, including receiving the software."

Kathy touched Robby's arm. "Do you think they forget everything, each time they jump? Oh, scratch that — What am I thinking? We always remember stuff when we travel."

"Right," Robby said. "If we can get the software to them early in the ten-minute interval, they can take a swing at downloading and executing the code. If they don't get it done in the 600-second interval, they can try again and do it faster each time as they gain experience with it. Our job is to make sure it's there at the start of each interval."

"How do we do that?" Trevor asked.

"Easy," Robby said. "I'll create a loop that keeps sending the instructions and software every five seconds. Let me do that now." Robby started coding the loop while Trevor and Kathy waited.

Kathy heard a familiar voice behind her. She and Trevor turned to see General Drake approaching.

"How are our tourists?" Drake asked.

"Hanging in there, sir," she said. "We're trying to get their beacons reprogrammed so we can get them out of this loop."

"How long have they been stuck?" he asked.

"A little over eighteen hours, sir."

Drake looked up over their heads and blinked. "That makes about a hundred loops. How are they holding up?"

"They're okay, sir, but I'm sure they're getting frustrated."

Drake grunted agreement.

Kathy raised her forefinger to get his attention.

"Sir, we are six days after the anniversary of the kidnapping. We're running out of our time window to stop it before it happens. Do you want us to send Hatcher or Wheeler? If not, we can't prevent the kidnapping after today."

"Negative," he said. "No, not while we have people stuck out there. Priority is to get them back first. Then, we analyze the problem and make sure it doesn't happen again."

Kathy started to speak, but he held up his hand. "I'm not willing to risk anyone else until we get our people back safe."

She inclined her head. "I understand, sir."

"All set," Robby said. "Kicking off the looped message now." He pressed the return key and entries showed up in the log every five seconds.

"Okay," Kathy said. "Now it's up to Colonel McKnight and Smalls to understand and reprogram the beacons."

Thursday, December 25th, 2036 - 6:20 AM EST - Telegraph Road Lab, Alexandria, Virginia

Kathy was worried and looked for Robby. She found him leaning back in a chair with his feet up on the Engine Console. His eyes were closed.

"Are you thinking or sleeping?" she asked.

Robby opened his eyes and smiled at her.

"Mostly thinking."

She nodded. "I'm getting worried. It's been two hours since we started sending the code. Do you think they got it?"

"Oh, I'm sure of it. We're sending it every five seconds. But it takes a few minutes to digest. I don't believe they could receive it, understand what to do, download the code, *and* install it in ten minutes until after the twentieth time or so."

"Really?"

"Really. Remember, Colonel McKnight doesn't do programming much, if at all, and we don't know about Mr. Smalls. But after about twenty cycles, memorization will kick in. They'll figure out what they need to do and will get better at it every time they try it. And they only have to get it right once."

"So you're not worried?"

"Well, not just yet," Robby said. "There'll be time for that later. I was thinking about something else. This time eddy is interesting. I wonder if it could be useful somehow."

Kathy shook her head. "It's hard for me to see that. All I see is danger. For all we know, they might starve to death because they can't find any food in the ten minutes before the next jump."

"Yes, I thought of that. But that's not a danger yet. They have rations in their satchels. They're okay for now."

"I hope so," she said, and turned away. She walked a few steps away, stopped, and turned.

"Robby, I think I might have an idea."

She walked back to him, smiling.

"What?" he said. The look on her face spoke volumes. "What's your idea?"

She held up a finger and looked up.

Robby followed her gaze up, then looked back at her.

"Oh," she said, and giggled into her hand. "You're going to love this."

Friday, December 19th, 2036 - 4:05 PM Hungary time; 10:05 AM EST, Hungary

Somewhere around the fiftieth loop, Smalls started setting a timer on his watch to calculate when they would jump again. After tracking it three times, they learned the loop was 600 seconds long. There was no explanation for that length, it was just what it was. The jump undid anything they did after 600 seconds.

"How many times have we looped?" Smalls asked.

"I lost count at about seventy," McKnight said. "Probably a few hundred by now."

"It's about time for the next jump."

"Yup."

They landed again in the same place. As many times as they looped, no scuff marks could be seen from previous landings.

McKnight activated the arrival message, and Smalls reset his timer.

Their phones started pinging every five seconds.

"It's a message from Robby," McKnight said.

"I'm getting one, too. They want to try something."

"Yes, they sent it to both of us. Let's see... two files... one is instructions..."

"And the other is code." Smalls rolled his eyes. "I failed typing in school."

"Well, better remember what you can. This is our ticket out."

They fell silent and read the instructions.

I can do this, but can he?

He looked at Smalls, who was busy reading the instructions.

Smalls' timer pinged, and they jumped again.

When they landed, sent the status message, and set the timer, the messages started arriving again. They started reading the instructions again. McKnight started the installation and got halfway through it, and Smalls just started the installation before his timer pinged. Smalls cursed, and they jumped again.

Over the next seven loops, they got further into the installation process each time. They improved, but they were losing their patience.

On the ninth try, McKnight finished his installation. "How much time left?" he said.

"Thirty seconds," Smalls said. "Did you finish?"

"Yes. Where are you in the process?"

"About three more steps." Smalls looked at McKnight.

McKnight looked down at his phone. All he had to do was push the 'Execute Code' button. He looked back at Smalls, who was furiously tapping his phone to finish the installation.

Smalls looked up at McKnight. "Go," he said. "Get out of here. I'll have this in a couple more tries."

Smalls' timer went off. "Go!" he said again.

"No," McKnight said, and they jumped.

They landed back in the original spot. McKnight sent the arrival status, and Smalls started his timer. They both opened their phones and began the installation again. They typed in the commands as fast as they could.

McKnight finished slightly earlier than the last time. He was approaching his maximum speed for the installation. He looked at Smalls. "Done," he said. "How much longer for you?"

"Four more steps," Smalls said. "Go on, I got this."

"Not on your life," McKnight said.

He dashed over to Smalls and embraced him.

"What are you doing?" Smalls said, and squirmed in McKnight's arms.

McKnight grinned and said, "Click the Execute Button."

His phone picked up the audible command and executed the code. A time bubble formed, and they jumped.

When they landed, they were in the same landing place, but it was dark.

"What happened?" Smalls said. "Are we out?"

"Looks like it." He sent the arrival status message, and Smalls reset his timer. "I guess we'll know in a few minutes."

"Yup." McKnight looked off to the north. "I don't see any sign of the SEALS. I guess they executed their mission and now they're gone."

Smalls moved to stand beside him. "Why'd you grab me like that? I was almost finished with the programming. How d'you know it would work — both of us on a single beacon?"

"It made sense. We do it all the time — jump more than one person with one beacon."

"Seems risky."

"Not at all. We've done it dozens of times. It wasn't a high-risk guess. I knew it would work."

Smalls' timer went off. They braced for another jump.

But none came.

McKnight smiled and Smalls frowned, then smiled back at him.

First time the guy's relaxed, I think.

"Looks like you did it, Colonel. Thanks."

"You're welcome."

Smalls looked to the east. He took a deep breath.

"Smell the lake?" he said. "Let's walk down to the lakeshore."

"Why?"

"Our mission was there. I just want to see the place."

"Don't you want to go home?"

"I do, but let's take a minute or two."

McKnight shrugged. "Okay. Let's go."

It took twenty minutes to hike down to the shore.

"What's that over there?" Smalls whispered.

A small rowboat sat on the shore. Two small boys leaned against it. They were sound asleep.

McKnight shrugged. "If I remember correctly, it's Kosar's kids. Tyler said Kosar told them to stay with the boat."

"That's what I thought. Hang on a second."

Smalls approached the boys and the rowboat while McKnight stood back.

"Sziasztok fiúk," he said. The boys woke and leaped to their feet. They clung to each other in fear of this stranger.

"Ne félj," Smalls said. "Apád hamarosan otthon lesz. Menj haza és aludj most."

The boys looked at each other, then ran away in the night.

Smalls returned to McKnight.

"You're full of surprises," McKnight said. "You speak Hungarian?"

"A little."

"Where did you learn Hungarian?"

"I picked up a little over the years. I'm not very good at it."

I forgot he's CIA. Maybe from an earlier assignment?

"What did you say?"

"I told them to go home and their father would be back soon."

"Is that why you wanted to come here?"

"Pretty much," Smalls said. "They're little kids. No sense in them staying here all night when there's no need."

Nice. There's more to this guy than I thought.

"By the way," Smalls said. "Why didn't you jump out of the loop without me? I would have gotten it done."

"Yeah, I know. But we don't leave anyone behind if we have a choice."

"I see. Thanks."

"We wouldn't even leave a pain-in-the-ass CIA guy."

Smalls turned to McKnight and found him grinning from ear to ear.

Smalls chuckled. "Well, I don't see any more mission decisions here to fight about, do you?"

"No, sir, I don't. Let's get our asses home."

"Oh, I'm with you."

The two men squeezed their beacons and the time bubbles formed.

CHAPTER THIRTY-THREE

<u>Thursday, December 25th, 2036 - 6:35 AM PST - Nevada Desert near Rachel</u>

After failing to get on the road the previous day, the Operative was determined to make progress today.

She built a fire, cooked a meal that would sustain her strength all day, and packed up her gear. The sleep reduced her weakness, but the use of the shield took a toll on her stamina.

As she walked out of the box canyon, she checked the log file of the locator for Rachel Patterson. There was no sign of her.

Failure is discouraging.

She stowed the locator in her pack. It was time to get on with her plan.

She uncovered the Jeep and drove toward the highway. Her thoughts already turned to what she must do when she reached Virginia. She didn't know how to program the time Engine, so she needed help. She would get it from a team member, and she needed to figure out how to motivate them to help her.

Which one?

Tonight in Salt Lake City, she would pull up the HERO Team files and decide who to get to help. It was a short list, but she didn't remember who was on it. The trick was to decide who to use and what levers she could push to get their cooperation.

She reached Nevada Highway 375 and didn't pause before turning right and heading north. Salt Lake City was 419 miles away. She had 400 miles to go.

Her plan was to travel first to Warm Springs, Nevada, and throw off potential pursuers before heading north on US Highway 6 to Ely. She knew what to do.

When she reached the intersection at Warm Springs, she cursed under her breath. She needed a small, populated area, but Warm Springs was nothing more than a couple of old, dilapidated buildings.

Ha. A strong breeze would blow down the entire town.

She drew out her phone and consulted the map application. The small town of Tonopah was fifty miles west on Highway 6. She decided it was worth it to detour for the sake of throwing off pursuers. Just in case, she checked the satellite option on the program and found what she was looking for. She turned left and headed west.

When she reached Tonopah, she turned south on US Highway 95 and drove a quarter mile to her destination on the right. It was a big box store, with a lot of shoppers who left their cars unattended. She parked on the edge of the lot and waited for the right person to arrive. It didn't take long.

A late model SUV pulled into the lot and parked. A young mother with two small children got out and walked to the store.

I can't imagine living a life like that.

Nonetheless, something deep in her soul stirred. She couldn't identify it — she just knew it was there.

She shook off the feeling.

As soon as they were inside, the Operative drove to their vehicle. She had the door open in two minutes. Five minutes later, she was back on Highway 6 in a new vehicle on the way to Warm Springs.

With any luck, her pursuers would track her to Tonopah, and believe she was headed for Carson City, Nevada or Bakersfield, California. By that time, she would be east of the Mississippi River.

The Operative almost missed Warm Springs as she passed through it and by the highway back to Rachel. She checked her watch — she was making good time.

Now she had 120 miles to go on Highway 6. At Ely, she would catch US Highway 93 to drive through the Western Rockies to Wendover, Utah. From there, she'd take Interstate 80 along the south shore of the Great Salt Lake and stop in Salt Lake City.

Who must I influence to help me get back to 2086?

Friday, December 26th, 2036 - 5:32 AM EST, HERO Team Lab, Telegraph Road, Alexandria, Virginia

Kathy sat at her desk, calculating when it would be too later to try again to abort the Kosar kidnapping. Trevor slept on a cot in the lab.

She did the math three times. They were already past the largest time interval from the anniversary they ever tried to time-jump. That one was pretty dicey. The power cables heated to where a support beam melted and the cable fell onto the concrete floor and indelibly scorched it.

She shook her head. If asked, she couldn't recommend they attempt the jump. She would recommend option two — return Kosar to his own time *after* the kidnapping.

A text message came in on her phone. She picked it up from her desk and saw it was from the Engine. *An incoming time-jump.*

She dashed from behind her desk to the lab at a dead run.

Trevor stood behind the console when she got to the lab. Two bubbles appeared. They were so close together they merged into one. Two figures knelt in the middle of the spinning light.

It's them!

She ran to the platform, being careful not to get too close.

When the bubble surged, the light flared as well, making shadows dance on the walls. It dissipated, leaving two men sprawled on the floor.

At first, she thought they were crying out in pain. Then she understood...

They're laughing.

She and Trevor ran to help them up.

"Oh, am I glad to be home," McKnight said. "What time is it? I mean… what day is it?"

"Yeah," Smalls said. "What day is it?"

"Friday, the 26th," Kathy said.

McKnight and Smalls exchanged a look.

"Yes, you missed Christmas."

McKnight rolled his eyes. "Damn. What about the kidnapping? What's the status?"

"It was a no-go. The General wouldn't let anyone time-jump until we got you back safe."

"But it's not too late to try again, is it?"

"No, it isn't too late. But it's so close that I'm concerned about damage to the Engine. I think the potential danger outweighs the benefits. We're on to option two with Mr. Kosar. Here, let me scan your implants to get the mission data."

McKnight and Smalls stood before her, while her phone extracted the mission data from their peas and uploaded it to the mainframe.

"Is Robby here?" McKnight asked.

"No, Trevor sent him home late last night. He was dead on his feet and we'll need him here awake and productive for the next phase."

"Okay. Do we have anything to eat here?"

"Just MREs," Trevor said.

"Yuck," Smalls said. "I'm headed for the Waffle House. Want to join me, Colonel?"

"No, he doesn't," Kathy said. "He's going home to his wife, who is worried sick about him."

McKnight grinned. "Thanks, Smalls, but another time."

"No problem. Trevor? Kathy? Would either of you like to go?"

"I'm in," Trevor said.

"I'm in, too," Kathy said. "I'm famished and I could use a good cup of tea."

McKnight bowed at them. "Enjoy. I have a date with a beautiful woman, and I'm out of here." He turned and walked out the loading dock door.

"Well, I guess it's just us, Smalls," Trevor said. "You can tell me about being caught in a time eddy."

Smalls grinned. "It's a short story. But I have to tell it a few hundred times so you'll get the full effect."

"You know what, Smalls?" Kathy said. "We have an idea about how we could use the time eddy for our benefit. I'll like to know what you think."

"Sure thing, Kathy, but let's do it over scrambled eggs and raisin toast. I'm starving."

Friday, December 26th, 2036 - 6:45 AM EST, McKnight Apartment, Alexandria, Virginia

McKnight unlocked the door to his apartment and opened it as quietly as he could. He hoped Megan was asleep.

He tiptoed in, set his briefcase down, and stopped to listen. There was no sound. He walked through the dining room and into the kitchen. Then he saw her.

She was asleep on the couch, her cell phone clutched in her hand.

He walked to her and surveyed the room. The TEV was on with the sound muted. A documentary was playing. He picked up the remote and turned it off. He knelt next to her.

She's such a pretty sleeper. I hate to wake her.

He pulled a blanket from the linen closet and spread it over her. He smiled at her sleeping form and slipped into the kitchen.

We must have quiet food, right?

He opened the refrigerator and found a plastic bowl of fruit and a SlimFast. He sat at the table and made quick work of the fruit. The SlimFast was dispatched in one gulp.

I'd better slow down. Let that settle.

He returned to the couch and knelt again. He caressed the back of her hand and she stirred. She opened her eyes and blinked.

They're so blue.

"You're home," she said.

"Yes, baby. I'm sorry it took so long."

She raised up and threw her arms around his neck. "You're safe. From what Kathy told me, I was afraid for you."

"What did she say?"

She pulled back so their faces were two inches apart.

"She said you were stuck in time and they couldn't get you home."

"That's right. But they figured it out. I'm here and I'm safe."

"Thank God. I was so worried." She paused. "Oh, Marc…" She sniffed.

"What?"

"We missed Christmas together."

"I'm here now. Let's just pretend it got delayed and we'll do Christmas today."

"Okay. Oh, Marc, can't you send someone else on missions like this? Do you always have to take the dangerous ones yourself?"

He smiled.

"I can't send anyone on a mission I wouldn't take myself. You know that. Besides, this one was supposed to be a cakewalk. Nobody expected danger. We discovered a new phenomenon — a time eddy."

"A time eddy? What's that?"

"Think of it as a time whirlpool. It keeps you spinning around one time. We lived through the same ten minutes a few hundred times. It would have been boring if we weren't worried about getting out."

"Well, what keeps that from happening next time?"

"Good question. There were some unusual signals and error indications on our Engine before the event. I suspect Robby has already re-programmed the jump software to watch for those signals and stop a jump before it happens. I doubt it'll ever happen again unless we do it on purpose."

She sat up on the couch. "Promise?"

"Yes, unless something unexpected happens."

She pouted. "That's not very encouraging."

McKnight nodded. "I know. We're a lot like test pilots. Of course, we test everything before we try it, but things we don't expect sometimes happen."

She rose from the couch and brushed at her clothes with her hands. "I must be a mess. I stayed up, hoping Kathy would call and let me know you were safe."

He stood and embraced her. "If it's any consolation, she demanded I go home within thirty seconds of our return. She was looking out for you."

"That's good. Have you had anything to eat?"

"Some fruit and one our your SlimFasts."

"Do you want more? Are you still hungry?"

"I think I'm okay for a while. I need some sleep."

"Okay, you get undressed, and I'll run a hot shower for you. Then you can sleep."

"Okay, thanks."

"When do you have to go back?"

He looked away from her as he answered.

"I need to check in later today to see what the next step is."

"Okay, sleep. Then eat a late lunch. Then check in. But then you're mine until you have to leave. Tell General Drake I said you can't go before tomorrow morning."

McKnight smiled.

"I'm sure he'll take it under advisement. At any rate, I don't see us traveling again until Robby convinces him it's okay and the eddy won't happen again. Maybe tomorrow. More likely the day after that."

"Good," she said. "Then we'll have Christmas Eve tonight and tomorrow morning we'd do Christmas. Then we'll see what we shall see. Until then, you're mine."

"There are worse things…" he said, and he wrapped his arms around her and tried to kiss her.

She squirmed away and shook a finger in his face. "Bath first. You stink."

CHAPTER THIRTY-FOUR

<u>Friday, December 26th, 2036 - 11:34 PM CST - Lincoln, NE</u>

The Operative drove the SUV into the parking lot for the StarLite Motel in Lincoln, Nebraska.

She chose a room on the back side of the motel.

She was so tired, she could hardly move.

Regardless, it was a productive day.

Earlier, when she woke in Salt Lake City, she ate in a diner and went shopping.

She visited a pawn shop and sold two diamonds for cash. She bought a radar detector for the car.

From the pawnshop, she went to an outdoor living superstore. There, she bought a one-man tent, cooking supplies, an all-weather tarpaulin, winter weather clothes, and a large duffel bag. She stuffed everything but the tarp in the duffel bag and set the radar detector on the dashboard.

She felt a little fatigue but fueled the SUV and started the trip from Salt Lake City to Lincoln. It was over 800 miles. She stopped for fuel three times and maintained an average of better than seventy-five miles per hour. She slowed for major cities and radar beeps, but blew through the intermediate states like a tornado.

Now, after midnight, she needed sleep. But she had one more task to complete.

She sat on the bed and pulled up the HERO Team files to validate her assumptions. Memory was one of her strong suites, but she wanted to review her analysis of the HERO Team. Then she summarized the thoughts that formed her decision.

Who would she target to help her travel back to 2086? The candidates are Kathy Wu, Robert Astalos, Marc McKnight, Karen Hatcher, and Mitch Wheeler.

Marc McKnight?

Major Patterson captured McKnight and tried to condition him. She failed. He proved himself to be mentally tough, and his military training was a tremendous strength.

Not a suitable candidate.

Doctor Robert Astalos?

Doctor Astalos was the expert in time engineering. As such, he might bring into play some unknown Engine capability to disrupt her plan. Also, Astalos was ancient and might not survive the pressure she used to coerce him.

He is the candidate of last resort.

Karen Hatcher?

Rachel's team kidnapped and brainwashed Karen Hatcher, but she shook off that conditioning at a critical point and captured Rachel.

She's not a suitable candidate.

Mitch Wheeler was military and loyal to McKnight and Hatcher.

Not a suitable candidate.

The Operative sighed.

That leaves Kathy Wu. She's the weakest one. She's young enough to take the pressure, but inexperienced with terroristic situations.

She's the best candidate. She is the weakest.

The Operative put a mental check next to Kathy's file. She would be the target.

I need a line of attack.

The most obvious approach was to threaten harm to her friend Trevor George. But given George's background as a police detective, he was a poor choice as a hostage.

Kathy was the weakest candidate, and that was the most important factor.

She put away her phone and laid on the bed. Her energy and strength depleted, sleep took her.

There was one boy named 761. He was handsome, but 638 saw a meanness in him that others didn't have. Taller than everyone, he crippled more than one boy in combat, after which she did not see them again.

The other boys were rough and assertive, but respectful toward 638. She was smarter, tougher, and better at almost everything. She had beaten most of them in physical training and in the martial arts ring.

But 761 was different. He treated 638 with disdain and implied that besting her in combat would be easy and not worthy of his time.

761 found 439 insufferable. He spoke rudely to her and make her uncomfortable. But sometimes, 638 would catch him looking at 439 differently. She was experienced enough to recognize the look — desire and longing.

One evening, 638 got extra duty in class because she showed promise in physics. She didn't complete the work until early in the morning.

She wasn't around to help 439 when she needed it. On that evening, 761 decided that 439 would play with him, even if she didn't want to. He seized her and other boys held her down. When he was finished with her, 439 was bruised, battered, and exhausted. When 638 returned from class, she learned what happened. She realized 439 would not survive the fight with 761 the next day.

Early the next day, she intercepted 761 on his way to the showers. She asked him to play with her. He was wary, but she was convincing. He followed her behind the barracks, and she pulled off her shirt, exposing herself to him. His hunger for her exceeded his better judgement. When he reached out to touch her, she attacked.

When the fight ended, he was in worse shape than 439. As a symbolic gesture, her final blow was a hard kick to the groin.

While 761 laid on the ground in pain, an Uncle approached and picked up her shirt.

"Cover yourself," he said.

She did as she was told.

"Why did you do that?"

638 feared for her safety, but her anger bubbled up. "He deserved it."

"I see. And how did this help your mission?"

When she didn't reply, he slapped her with the back of his hand so hard she cried out.

Others heard the sounds of battle and came running toward them.

"If you decide to punish someone," the Uncle said, "do it with purpose. You defeated him here, where no one could see. Why didn't you do it in front of the others? That would help your mission. It would make them fear and respect you."

She hung her head. "I did not think first."

"Now you know what to do. Think, then act."

He pointed at 761 on the ground. To another uncle, he said, "This one is in no shape to fight today. Let everyone know the truth — 638 humiliated him in battle."

The Uncle cupped her face with both hands and lifted it to make eye contact.

"Do you know what to do next time, girl?"

"Yes, Uncle."

"Good. Stand tall and make them fear you."

Friday, December 26th, 2036 - 2:55 PM EST, The big conference room at Telegraph Road, Alexandria, Virginia

Time for the Kosar planning meeting.

McKnight picked up his coffee cup and headed for the big conference room.

When he checked in with General Drake earlier, he learned he wouldn't get time off yet. Drake ordered him and Smalls to return Kosar to 1986 as soon as possible to minimize the impact of the kidnapping.

I should have guessed that would happen.

And Megan was not happy. He had relationship repair to do when he returned.

As he entered the room, he noted Smalls, Kathy, and Trevor were already there. He filled his coffee cup from the service along the wall and sat at the head of the table.

"Okay," he said. "Let's get started. Kathy? Do we have permission from the President's Office to proceed with another mission?"

"No," she said. "He delegated the decision to the CIA agent on staff, Mr. Smalls."

McKnight turned to Smalls.

"Do you approve of a mission?"

Smalls leaned forward at the table. "I agree we need a mission. No question about that. Before I approve, I need to know what I'm approving. Shall we proceed to that phase of the meeting? Then we can talk about approval."

"Fair enough," McKnight said. "Kathy, what are you thinking so far?"

"I think it's pretty well mapped out. Here's the gist. The travelers are Colonel McKnight and Mr. Smalls. Since we can't erase his memory, we need to provide him with an excuse for disappearing for several days. Maybe he gets drunk for four days? Or maybe he eats rotten food and hallucinates for a few days before he recovers? Anyway, you guys meet with him at the Iceberg, and scare the crap out of him. Tell him we can reach out and touch him whenever we want, so he better not mess with us. Then you put him under, take him back to 1986, and drop him off. When you come back, we check history to see if it's made a difference."

"Do we tell him who we are? I mean, US vs. Russians or somebody else?" Trevor said.

"We should tell him as little as possible," Kathy said. "We want to get across two ideas — don't mess with the United States or we'll come back for you... and don't tell anyone where you've been, because they won't believe you."

"I like that idea," McKnight said. "Simple."

Nods around the table, but Smalls shook his head.

"May I suggest something?" he said.

"Sure," Kathy said.

Smalls rose and paced the floor behind his chair. "People might not buy the four-day drunk, especially if it's out of character for the man. What about today's Kosar? Does he drink?"

"He's a teetotaler," Kathy said. "I thought the three-day drunk might look like the reason he doesn't drink today. But you interest me. What's your idea?"

Smalls gestured with his hands. "What if we plant the story that some local thugs kidnapped him to milk his family for ransom money, but they're amateurs, right? They find out his family has no money so, rather than kill him and risk a murder charge, they drug him and release him. That will at least jive a bit with what happened to him."

"Ah," McKnight said. "I like it. And the story is consistent with what the kids remember and what he'll remember."

"Correct," Smalls said, "And if it doesn't work, we can still grab him in our time and drop him in the Iceberg."

"Good idea, Mr. Smalls," Kathy said. "Have you considered a career in time travel mission planning?"

The corners of Smalls' mouth turned up slightly. "I already have a job."

"Well, come see me if you get fired," Kathy said.

Even Smalls chuckled.

"Does this mean you approve the mission?" McKnight asked.

"Yes," Smalls said. "When do we go?"

"Tomorrow morning," McKnight said.

"Why not today?" Kathy asked.

"Because I want to call Sheila Souther, my old friend who runs the Iceberg. I want her to know we're coming and why. That'll minimize their confusion and compensate for the lack of orders on their side. Kathy, I need a copy of the VP's delegation and Mr. Smalls' signature on the mission. And some release papers that tell them we are taking custody and responsibility for the prisoner."

"No problem," Kathy said. "Shall we plan the jump for oh-eight hundred hours tomorrow?"

"No, make it eleven hundred hours. They're on Pacific time."

"Okay. We'll meet in the lab at ten-thirty hours tomorrow for implant programming and pre-mission details. Have a great day, all!"

Everyone filed out and went to their offices.

McKnight sat at his desk and thought about the approach he would use with Sheila Souther. When Kathy brought by the paperwork, he called her.

Sheila was upbeat and understood the need to return Kosar to his time. She also mentioned she had two new guests — two ISIS fighters from Iraq. She was all business until he mentioned Smalls would come with him.

When he told her, she said, "Really? Arthur Smalls is coming with you?"

When he said yes, she grew more animated and friendly. "Sure, no problem," she said.

How does she know Smalls? I'll have to ask him about that.

CHAPTER THIRTY-FIVE

Saturday, December 27th, 2036 - 7:01 AM CST - Lincoln NE

When her watch chimed, the Operative awoke with a start.

She dreamed of sleeping in a hammock on an island resort. The dream was a signal, her mind needed rest.

She left the bed and started the shower. When she slipped into the warm, comforting stream, she stood still for a few minutes, letting the water wash over her body. She poured liquid soap into a washcloth and washed herself. Then she turned up the heat as hot as she could stand it. After a few seconds, she turned the faucet control to cold and let it run for thirty seconds.

She turned off the shower and shivered. She patted herself dry with a pair of towels and opted for winter clothing instead of her mission jumpsuit.

The shower helped, but it wasn't enough. She felt the fatigue of the previous two days in her bones. She planned to drive again today, but she wasn't up to it. Still, she needed to get there as soon as possible.

She turned on the TEV to get the local weather.

The third item on the newscast was about her. On the screen was a grainy security camera photo. She assumed it was from the Las Vegas airport. The news reported on the woman wanted for three murders in Nevada. They described the woman as tall with long dark hair and thirty years old. Armed and dangerous. The authorities believed the woman was on her way to California.

She checked the listing for the TEV channel. It was local.

If they think I'm in California, why are they putting a watch on a local channel in Nebraska?

This seemed inconsistent.

Maybe she didn't fool her pursuers? Maybe she did, and they were being thorough.

The newscast was the tipping point. She was tired, and now the local authorities might be watching for her. She decided not to travel today. Rest and recuperate.

She sat on the bed and let her thoughts wander. Without thinking, she pulled her backpack across the bed and pulled out the locator. She checked the log file again. There was no sign of Rachel Patterson.

Why do I keep checking?

She knew the answer. She never failed before, and this was unfamiliar territory. She needed a way to complete her mission.

This isn't logical. She's gone. Live with it.

She stowed the locator and laid back on the bed. The overall fatigue was too strong.

I'll rest today and tackle it again tomorrow.

She pulled the med pack from her backpack and selected the restorative drug. She drew out a half dose and slipped the needle under her skin. The drug felt cool and reassuring as it rushed through her bloodstream.

She called the front desk.

"Hi, this is Mary Smith in room 201?... Yes... I won't be checking out as planned today... That's right... I plan to check out tomorrow morning.... Yes.... Thank you. Bye."

She ended the call and laid on the bed.

I'll sleep today and go again tomorrow.

She felt drowsy. The drug was working now, making her sleep and repairing damaged cells.

It's not a waste of time to check the locator. It's diligence.

She closed her eyes and let sleep take her.

439 was never the same after 761 attacked her. She no longer marveled at the world around her. She spoke to no one but 638, and then only rarely. The energy that kept her moving was no longer there. She was a shadow of her former self.

638 remembered the last time she saw her. They were sent for a ten-mile run and 439 faltered near the six-mile mark.

She slowed, dropped to one knee, and told 638 to leave her. But 638 refused.

"I can't do this anymore," she said. "638, leave me or they'll wash you out, too."

"We can make it together," 638 said. She pulled 439 to her feet and dragged her forward.

An Aunt approached. "What's wrong here?"

"I'm too tired to do this. Let me lay here and die," 439 said.

The Aunt looked at 638. "Go about your business, I'm here."

"No, I want to help."

"It's not your mission. Go about your business."

When 638 didn't show any signs of compliance, the Aunt drew a weapon and shot 439 between the eyes. The impact of the bullet drove her body backward into the ditch beside the running trail.

638 gasped, and the Aunt pointed the weapon at her.

"Go. About. Your. Business."

638 stared at the lump of flesh that had been her only friend. The transition from life to lifelessness was complete.

She turned and ran after the rest of the boys and girls. She passed the others and soon led the pack.

An Uncle fell in step with her. "Are you okay?"

"Why wouldn't I be, Uncle?"

"One of your teammates is dead. What do you think about that?"

"It's not my business, sir. It's not my mission."

"Are you sure? I thought you two were friends."

"No," she said. "Friendships make you weak. I have no time for weakness. It impedes an Operative's ability to achieve their mission. My mission is more important than anything."

CHAPTER THIRTY-SIX

Saturday, December 27th, 2036 - 08:00 AM PST - The Iceberg Detention Facility, Rachel, Nevada

As they fell through the field of stars, McKnight wondered why they saw them, even on a jump that didn't involve time travel.

They landed in the receiving area of the Iceberg. This time, Smalls didn't fall backward.

He's mastered the art of keeping his balance.

Smalls reached into his pack for the anti-nausea meds.

Through the spinning light in the time bubble, they could see Major Souther waiting for them.

As soon as the bubble dissipated, Souther approached them. "Welcome back to the Iceberg, gentlemen."

"Thanks, Sheila," McKnight said.

"It's good to see you, Marc. And it's good to see you again, Agent Smalls."

Smalls tossed back his meds, then smiled at her. "The pleasure is all mine, Major."

Souther smiled at him.

Sounds like they know each other well. I'll have to find out about that.

"Mr. Kosar is aware he has visitors coming in this morning," Souther said. "Shall we go see him?"

"Absolutely," McKnight said as they started walking. "How's his mood?"

"Confused. He doesn't know why he's here and, as you're no doubt aware, he thinks the year is 1986. He was pretty vocal when he first got here, but now he doesn't say much. I'm sure he's trying to figure out how to break out. He isn't combative because he doesn't want to jeopardize his conditions here, but he's also reluctant to give any information."

"I think he'll talk to us," McKnight said. "We're going to offer him a way out. That won't put you guys out of business, will it?"

"Heavens, no. Our two terrorists are singing like birds, trying to curry favor with the guards. Out in public, they talk tough and kill us whenever they can, but once they see they're not getting out? They aren't the tough ISIS leaders they think they are. They're scared shitless and give up anybody they can to ingratiate themselves to us. We'll get tons of intel from them."

"I like the sound of that," Smalls said.

"Me, too," McKnight said.

Souther stopped in front of a cell. "Well, here we are." She pointed at a stretcher leaning against the wall. "That's for you guys."

"Thanks," McKnight said.

She stepped to the comm station on the wall and held down the talk button.

"Mr. Kosar, are you there?"

An accented voice came from the speaker. "Yes, I am here and ready to receive visitors."

She released the talk button. "Okay, he's all yours. Remember, he thinks it's 1986." She pressed the door release.

Both men nodded and stepped through the heavy steel door. It closed behind them.

Kosar stood in the middle of the room. He was average height and in his mid-thirties. His hair was brown and his eyes were blue. He wore eyeglasses.

"Hello, I am George Kosar," he said in English. "May I ask who you are?"

McKnight paused. He'd rather not say, but he was wearing his combat uniform with his name on the left breast pocket.

I can't believe I was so stupid to wear my own ACU.

His mind leapt back to this morning. He chose his combat uniform to establish himself as an authority figure.

"I'm Colonel McKnight," he said.

"And you?" Kosar said to Smalls.

"Joe Smith," Smalls said without hesitation.

"Mr. Smith and Colonel McKnight, what can I do for you?"

"We're here to find out if you want to go home," McKnight said. "Would you?"

A flash of interest flew across the man's face. He hid it as fast as it showed up.

"Yes."

"What would you be willing to do to be released?"

"Anything. I just want to go back to my family. I'll do anything you ask."

"Well, it's not that we want you to do something."

"Correct," Smalls said, "it's that we want you to *not* do something."

Kosar looked between the two men. "I don't understand," he said.

"We heard you want to overthrow the United States government. We don't want you to do that."

Kosar looked shocked. "I would never consider doing such a thing. Why would I do that? I live in Hungary. I'm just a poor man trying to support my family."

Smalls and McKnight looked at each other.

Under his breath, Smalls said, "Maybe we have the wrong man?"

"You do," Kosar said. "I have never considered taking any action about the U.S.. Everyone I know wants to live there, not bring it down."

McKnight glanced at Smalls. "But what if he's lying? He might double-cross us as soon as he gets back home."

"No, I would never do that. And I would never assist someone who wanted to hurt the United States."

"Maybe," Smalls said. "But how do we know?"

Kosar looked back and forth between them.

"Believe me," he said. "Please. I swear by all that is Holy I will never attack America. I will allow no one else to do so if I can prevent it."

Smalls turned to McKnight. "What do you think?"

McKnight looked conflicted. "If we let him go, we can always come back for him."

"Yes, yes," Kosar said. "You can trust me to keep my word. I will do as I have sworn."

Now the threat.

"Very well," McKnight said. "We will take you home, but we will watch you. If we even suspect you have plans to attack us, we'll bring you back here and there will be no release. You will be here until you die."

Kosar looked at them both and nodded. "I agree to your terms. I want to go home."

"Very well," McKnight said. "We have provided you with a winter coat and boots."

Kosar looked puzzled.

"Check in your wardrobe, please. Bring them over here. Remember, it is still winter. You don't want to catch a cold, do you?"

"No, I don't," Kosar said. He opened the wardrobe. There, along with several orange prisoner jumpsuits, was a coat, a muffler, and a pair of boots. He looked surprised, then pulled the coat and muffler off their hangers and picked up the boots.

"Put the boots on," Smalls said, "then sit on the sofa and roll up your sleeve."

Kosar did as instructed, as Smalls drew a small syringe from his satchel.

"This is a sedative. You cannot know where you are now or how we transport you home. When you awaken, you will be back home in Hungary."

Kosar nodded.

Smalls administered the sedative. "Don't be afraid. You'll be home before you know it." He helped Kosar slip on the coat and muffler.

McKnight spoke again. "If you tell anyone where you have been, they won't believe you. If I were you, I'd tell them someone thought you were rich and kidnapped you. They let you go when they realized you don't have any money. Do you understand?"

"Yes," Kosar said. His eyes were glassy, and he nodded his head once, and jerked it back up to look at McKnight.

"Thank you, Colonel," he said, then fell back onto the sofa.

Smalls pressed his index and middle fingers to the man's throat. "Pulse slow but strong. Let's go."

Saturday, December 27th, 1986 - 5:35 PM - Lake Balaton, Hungary

They landed in Hungary with Kosar lying on the stretcher. McKnight stood and rotated to check for threats or witnesses. Smalls dug in his pack for the anti-nausea meds.

The woods off the shoreline of Lake Balaton were quiet. A light, icy breeze whispered in the trees. The sun was setting in the west. It would be cold tonight.

They set down the stretcher with Kosar asleep on it.

McKnight rubbed his hands together, then stuck them in his pockets. "You don't think there's a chance he'll freeze to death, do you?"

"No, the forecast is for near freezing, and he'll be awake five minutes after I give him the stimulant. He'll wake up and walk around a few minutes before he's clear-headed enough to think straight. Then he'll realize where he is and find his way home."

"Good," McKnight said. "I hope our plan works."

"Yes, me too."

"I know he's a bad actor, but I'd hate for a guy to be locked up for what he hasn't done yet."

Smalls stood next to him, looking down at the unconscious man. "But he will do those things again. He's the worst enemy the United States can have... the one who becomes a citizen and uses his American rights to tear down the system. I could've left the guy in the Iceberg and slept just fine at night."

"Well, he hasn't attacked us," McKnight said. "Not yet. Something happened to him in the old timeline that made him our enemy. Maybe he won't attack, now. At least, we've warned him. I hope he'll heed that warning."

"Me, too."

"By the way, I've been meaning to ask you..."

"Yeah?"

"I noticed you and Sheila knew each other from before."

"Really?"

"Yes. How do you two know each other? I'm curious."

Smalls looked McKnight in the eye.

"I noticed the same thing. Seems like you know her, too."

McKnight shrugged. "We dated a few times after the Academy. But then we both got assignments elsewhere. The relationship didn't develop far enough to keep it going over long distance."

"I see," Smalls said as he slipped a syringe needle between Kosar's index and second finger.

"Okay, time to go," he said.

"And you?" McKnight said, struggling to keep irritation from his voice.

"Me? I consulted on the Iceberg construction, and I'm the one who brought her the other two prisoners."

"The terrorists? You're a field agent?"

"Yes."

"I thought you were an accountant for the CIA."

"No. I have a master's degree in Accounting."

"Well, I'll be... Sorry if I haven't given you enough credit. I'm embarrassed."

"Don't be," Smalls said. "I've found that things go smoother if people don't know much about me."

"Did you... Were you faking your problems with programming the beacons? Were you screwing around with me?"

"Oh, no," Smalls said. "I *did* fail typing in school."

McKnight laughed.

The two men knelt, squeezed their beacons, and the time bubble pulled them backward through the familiar field of stars.

Saturday, December 27th, 2036, 11:50 AM EST, Telegraph Road Lab, Alexandria, Virginia

Smalls and McKnight landed back in the lab. The mission took less than an hour.

When the time bubble dissipated, Kathy dashed onto the platform.

"Are you both alright?" she asked.

The two men glanced at each other and nodded. They slipped off their heavy coats and tossed them onto a chair near the platform.

She pointed her phone at their thighs and extracted the latest data from their implants. "Okay, I've uploaded the data to the Mainframe. You guys need to separate and add your personal notes to the mission report."

"Yes, ma'am." Smalls said.

McKnight gave a thumbs-up.

The two men walked to different areas of the massive lab to sit and dictate their report with the implant app.

When he finished, McKnight walked back over to Kathy. "So, what do we know so far?"

"What do you mean?" she asked.

"I mean, did it work? Did returning Kosar to his time put history back where it should be?"

Smalls walked over to join them. "Yes, do we have anything new?"

"We don't know anything yet," she said. "Remember that, when they grabbed Kosar, it took about thirty hours for the change wave to roll to 2086. We should have a complete picture then."

Of course I knew that. How could I forget?

"I apologize," McKnight said. "I knew that. I guess my mind jumped into high gear and I'm a little stressed. Sorry."

"Me, too," Small said. "The colonel and I have been going full speed today, working hard to fix this."

"Not a problem," Kathy said. "Look, you guys. Go home. Spend time with your families. I'm scheduling a briefing for tomorrow night at 5:00 PM. Don't come around here until then. Can I send Hatcher and Wheeler to 2086 to check on the future and return for the meeting? Is that okay with you, Colonel McKnight? Mr. Smalls?"

McKnight nodded. "Good idea. Smalls?"

"Yes, of course. As long as that's all they do… Strict observation of history is okay with me."

"Good," she said. "I'm also having Robby compare the current time frequency to the frequency from *before* we grabbed Kosar. Comparing it to the last few days doesn't tell us much. Now that we've tried to put things back where they were, there should be fewer discrepancies between the current frequency and before the kidnapping. After we look at that, we should know if we need to take action."

"Sounds good," McKnight said. Smalls nodded.

The two men left the building for home.

CHAPTER THIRTY-SEVEN

Saturday, December 27th, 2036 - 8:30 PM EST - Tyler and Sarah's apartment, Alexandria, Virginia

McKnight and Tyler sat on the back deck of Tyler's apartment. They were nursing Jack Daniels on the rocks and relaxing after a splendid dinner.

"Thanks for inviting us over," McKnight said. "That was a meal to die for."

"Sarah's a superb cook. One of her many talents."

"You're a lucky man, Winnie. I always knew you guys were a good match."

"Well, amen to that," Tyler said.

The two men clinked their glasses together.

"And speaking of matches, Marc, that's why we invited you and Megan over for dinner. We wanted to help celebrate your engagement and marriage. When's the big date?"

"Soon, I think. Megan is a whiz at planning, and we'd like to get it done. I can tell you it'll be in Gainesville, Georgia."

"Makes sense. She grew up there and her parents still live there. All her girlfriends are there. And I went to high school there at Riverside Academy. "

"Yes, she told me that. My sister Janie and Mom will fly down and I'm hoping the entire team can be there."

"Oh, we'll be there. Gramma and Pops have already offered to pay the entire team's airfare."

"Really?" McKnight said. "I didn't know that."

"They can afford it. And they spare no expense with the family. They want it to be perfect for Megan. And you."

"That's really nice. Please thank them for me."

McKnight's thoughts flew back to when he first met Tyler's grandparents. His friendship with Tyler's grandmother started on the same day as his first mission on the HERO Team.

Tyler touched McKnight's arm and looked back over his shoulder into the apartment. McKnight looked, too. Megan and Sarah were on the sofa, looking at Megan's bridal planning book.

"Well, they should be busy for a while. They don't need us."

"Yup," McKnight said. "I think we're on our own."

"Can I bring up a little work stuff?"

"Sure, Winnie. What's up?"

"I talked to General Drake, and he suggested I read you in on where we are."

"Sure, I'd like that."

"Good," Tyler said. "What do you know so far, Marc?"

"Not a lot. I know you're supposed to go back to 1761 and help teach Francis Marion's troops how to fight — tactics, strategy. The purpose is to break them out of the European mold, where two armies stand fifty yards apart in formation and systematically butcher each other. The only people fighting effectively in 1761 were the Indians, so it became known as the Indian style of fighting."

"Yeah, that was the original mission."

"The original mission?" McKnight said. "Has the mission changed?"

"Expanded is a better word. The new direction is to meet Washington in 1775 and teach all the Revolutionary forces to fight 'Indian-style'."

"Interesting," McKnight said. "And what's happened so far? Or am I allowed to ask?"

Tyler laughed.

"General Drake told me to let you know all the details going forward."

"Really? Why?"

"Because, pretty soon, you'll be heading out to meet the big man himself."

"What? Colonel Marion?"

"No, General Washington."

McKnight blinked twice.

"General Drake and I have been working on that mission," he said. "I didn't know who else knew about it."

"Yup, I'm going to lay the groundwork. Help the troops get up to speed and, all the while, edifying my mentor — you — to Marion and Washington, and telling them they'll meet you some day."

"What? Are you kidding?"

"You're lucky," Tyler said. "I do all the work and you show up and take the credit."

"But I—"

"Just kidding, Marc," Tyler said, and laughed again. "Man, you gotta loosen up a little. I'll be a general in the Continental Army way before you get there."

"It would be well deserved."

Tyler waved off the compliment. "Relax. I'm just having fun with you. Anyway, here's where we are. I've met Marion. I like him. He grew up wanting to be in the King's army and now he's there. But he's also a country boy like you. He wants to move up through the officer ranks, but the British Army thinks all colonists are country bumpkins. That frustrates Marion. He also thinks the fifty yard battle line slaughter is silly. Today, of course, we know he's right. So he's torn between following the army way of kissing ass and moving up in the ranks or fighting his own way and being successful. He doesn't have enough confidence in himself yet, but he's getting there."

"Interesting," McKnight said. "How did you get his attention?"

"I went back with a couple of troopers and we pretended to be civilians. We volunteered to fight in his company. We distinguished ourselves in battle. He came by to thank us, and we asked why the entire company wasn't fighting our way. That intrigued him and it started a dialogue. He understood the value of jungle warfare. We helped him teach his troops how to fight."

"Against who?"

"The Indians. And the French. It's 1761, remember? The French and Indian War?"

McKnight rolled his eyes.

Of course.

"Sounds like it's going well," he said.

"Yeah, but… it's turning into a long-term project. I didn't expect that. I'm still excited about it, but it will change our lives."

"I think I see. It's not a consulting job. Out on Monday morning. 'See you later, honey'. Jump to 1761 for four days, then back to 2036 for a long weekend."

"Exactly. It's 1761 there now. The war with the British doesn't start for another fifteen years. So I need face-time with the principal actors so they don't forget me when it's time to train the troops for the fight with the English."

"Makes sense," McKnight said. "Makes it hard to take part in any other missions."

"It does. I'm okay with that. This one will be all-consuming, I suspect."

"That it will. What does Sarah say about it?"

"That was the surprise. I've discussed with Sarah and General Drake. I think we've found a solution."

"And what's that?"

"Sarah's going with me. Well, at least part of the time."

"She what?"

"She wants to be with me. If I'm going to spend a lot of time in the past, she wants to be there, too."

"Are you sure about that?" McKnight said. "It was a hard time to live in."

"Yeah, but most of it will be peaceful. The French and Indian War will be over in 1763 — that's two years from now. Then there'll be peace in the Colonies until 1775. That's twelve years."

"I see."

"If we want to raise kids — and we do — I don't want to be the absentee father. You know, gone all the time? So it makes sense. But we'll return to the present periodically, for months at a time."

"Wow. I'm still trying to wrap my head around this," McKnight said.

"Really? I think it's great. Think about it. Remember how we used to talk about military history at the Academy? Now we get to be part of it. I met Francis Marion, one of the inspirations for the Regiment. And think of who we might get to meet. Maybe Robert Rogers. I'll spend the rest of my thirties and most of my forties studying history up close. How cool is that?"

"I didn't see it that way. Sounds inviting. So, what did General Drake say about Sarah going?"

"He didn't like it much at first. After he thought about it for a while, he agreed it was a good thing. You know, most men in the Continental Army were just fighting for their families. They never dreamed about the country we could become. It'll help my credibility with Marion and others if they know I have a family."

"But won't Sarah need some training on how to live in those times? Does she understand what she'll give up to go back there?"

"Yes, on the training. But she's more excited about it than me. She's looking at it as the ultimate adventure."

"I see," McKnight said. "That's great. But what about health care and disease and unsanitary conditions? They won't have lots of stuff we take for granted, like modern medicine, wonder drugs, and stuff. Isn't it an enormous risk?"

"Not as much as you might think. We'll still come back to the present as needed. If anyone gets sick, we jump back here and get it taken care of. We'll have the inoculations that screen us from the major diseases of the period. And there's an entire program for training spouses to accompany a soldier into a dangerous environment. Sarah's already started it. She's having a ball."

From behind them, they heard Megan whoop and yell something indiscernible. Both men turned and looked through the window. Megan was standing in front of Sarah with arms crossed and the wedding book on the floor.

"Hmm," Tyler said. "I think it's safe to assume Sarah has mentioned her intentions to Megan."

"You think?" McKnight said and then laughed.

Megan came to the door.

"Marc, did you hear this? What Sarah and Winnie are planning to do?"

"I think Tyler may have mentioned it."

She turned to Tyler. "Are you crazy?"

"Absolutely," he said, and winked at McKnight.

She looked back and forth between them.

"You guys are useless," she said, and went back inside. She sat next to Sarah on the sofa.

McKnight and Tyler looked at each other and laughed. It might have been nervous laughter. Or maybe the effects of the Jack Daniels.

McKnight tossed back the remaining whiskey in his glass and set it on the table with a loud clink.

"So... how will you know when you've accomplished your mission?"

Tyler nodded, swallowed the rest of the brown liquid from his shot glass, and banged his glass on the table, too.

"Good question. My short-term goal is to teach Marion's Raiders how to carry out jungle warfare. Attack and withdraw tactics."

"And the long-term goal?"

"Teach the concepts to the entire Continental Army. That's the goal."

"And the stretch goal?"

"Easy," Tyler said with a gleam and sparkle in his eyes. "Introduce you to George Washington in the winter of 1787 with enough credibility that he'll listen to you. I have twenty-five years to do it. We'll find out if I was successful in six weeks, when you go to 1787 to find him."

Sunday, December 28th, 2036 - 6:34 AM PST - Lincoln NE

The Operative woke up refreshed and hungry from the regenerative drug. She felt better than two days ago.

Time to get on with it. Indianapolis, then Washington, then home to 2086.

She showered, packed her gear, and drove to a diner down the street. She wolfed down a meal packed with carbs and protein. When she finished, she got in the SUV and checked the local police band.

No one was looking for her vehicle in this town. She programmed the vehicle's navigation program for the shortest route to Indianapolis. It was 643 miles. It would require ten hours to get there.

Do I have everything I need? Do I need to buy anything?

She couldn't think of anything, so she backed the vehicle out of the parking space.

The locator pinged. It took a moment to realize where the sound came from. She pulled the locator from her backpack and checked the log file. There it was.

<<< 20361227:19:35 - Subject Not Found >>>
<<< 20361227:23:35 - Subject Not Found >>>
<<< 20361228:03:35 - Subject Not Found >>>
<<< 20361228:07:35 - Finding >>>

A finding?

She shifted to forward and pulled back into the space. She searched for Rachel Patterson again.

It's true!

There was a finding. She adjusted the screen. There was no doubt.

Whatever happened… wherever she had been… Rachel was now back in Nevada. She stretched the map with her fingers.

She's back in the Iceberg?

She turned off the locator and restarted it. A new search got the same result. Either the locator was malfunctioning, or Rachel was back in the Iceberg.

Could the machine be broken? Again, she doubted it.

No, you must trust your equipment. If you can't do that, you're operating in the dark.

The Operative turned off the vehicle's engine and sat in thought.

What do I do now?

She was halfway to DC. It was as far back to Rachel as it was to DC.

She felt the pull of her last decision and her discipline to remain on course.

Is it possible I can salvage the mission?

There was really no decision necessary. The essence of an Operative was reliability, reputation, and agreements. If you took a mission, you completed it or died trying. If she wasn't sick and tired, she wouldn't have considered the idea of going home without meeting her objective.

I've never failed to complete a mission. Failure is not an option. I'm not leaving 2036 without Rachel Patterson.

She would go back to Nevada. She drafted and sent a short status note for Number Three.

> <<< *638: Still in pursuit of objective. Will report*
> *when more intel is available.* >>>

She started the vehicle, backed out, and drove to the on-ramp for Interstate 70 toward Salt Lake City and Rachel, Nevada.

CHAPTER THIRTY-EIGHT

Sunday, December 28th, 2036 - 5:50 PM - Telegraph Road Lab, Alexandria, Virginia

McKnight parked his truck in the usual spot and let himself into the building. He walked down the hall to the large conference room.

Kathy, Trevor, and Smalls were seated around the table.

"Where's everyone else?" he asked.

"Oh," Kathy said. "Robby is still working on the time frequency comparison report. He said he'd have it ready by…" she checked her watch. "Fifteen minutes from now. Hatcher and Wheeler got back from 2086 about an hour ago. They're in Hatcher's office preparing their report for you."

"Okay. I'll see if they're ready for the meeting."

McKnight strode to their shared office and knocked on the door before pushing it open. Both officers leaped to attention and saluted.

"As you were. Are you about ready for the meeting?"

"Yes, sir," they said in unison.

"Okay, come on to the conference room when you're ready."

"Yes, sir, we're coming now," Wheeler said. They followed McKnight back to the conference room.

McKnight sat at the head of the table. The two Captains found seats together across from him.

He turned to Kathy. "Doctor Wu, what do you have for me and Mr. Smalls now? Has the wave of changes from our activities affected us yet?"

"Indeed, they have. I want to keep the briefing as short as possible. It's New Year's Eve and everyone has a family. So let's focus on what our next steps should be."

Nods around the table.

"As I mentioned, Robby is working on the comparisons of the timeline frequencies, so he will go last. So, now I will turn the floor over to... Captain Hatcher? Or Captain Wheeler? Who's going to brief us?"

"I am," Hatcher said. She walked around the table to the lectern.

"Colonel, you probably have some vague memories of our new present. I'll try to sort them out for you."

"Thanks, Captain."

"You're welcome, sir." To the group, she said, "The executive summary is that our efforts were mostly successful. There are still some problems."

"First, there's still a civil war brewing in 2086 between the Hamiltons and the Devotees. For Mr. Smalls' sake, I'll recap a little."

"In 2086, there is a large section of the American population that leans toward a democratic monarchy, with the two grandsons of George Kosar in the royal position. They call themselves the Devotees. The Hamiltons are the constitutionalists that favor keeping the country as a democratic republic. A substantial number of Devotees have made their way into the US government and so there is disagreement about who runs the country." She pointed at Smalls. "Make sense, sir?"

"Yes, I've got it. Thanks."

"Good," Hatcher said. "The update today is that fighting has broken out. When the Devotees first started taking control, many Hamilton sympathizers retreated across the Mississippi River. The country is divided into three parts. The Devotees control the United States east of the Mississippi and the states of California, Oregon, and parts of Nevada, and the Hamiltons control the states in between. A little more than half of the nation's military personnel left their assignments, took their weapons and equipment with them, and reformed in the Hamilton zone. From a strategic point of view, the two sides are at equal strength. For example, the President in 2086 sided with the Hamiltons and the Vice President sided with the Devotees. It was like that all across the country."

"I see," McKnight said. "What's going on right now?"

"Good segue, sir. At present, a large band of Hamiltons have pushed across the Mississippi there at St. Louis and have established a beachhead in East St. Louis. Everywhere else, the opposing factions are shaking their fists at each other over neutral zones."

"What about my daughter Colleen?"

"There's a change there, sir, and it's good news," Hatcher said. "In this new timeline, she escaped west with Rick Alarcon and Doctor Wu to Kansas City, where they're part of the Hamilton leadership. Previously, she waited too long and time-jumped with Major Tyler after being wounded. I dare say she is better off in this new timeline."

"That's good news," McKnight said. "Please continue."

"There's another circumstance that's causing people in 2086 great concern. There is a pandemic breakout in the Mideast. The internal conflict in America increases the harm the pandemic can do when it reaches our shores. And it will. The virus is very contagious and doesn't show symptoms until days after exposure."

"Does this mean our efforts didn't prevent the pandemic? We just delayed it?"

"Yes, sir, it does." She pointed at Wheeler. "Captain Wheeler and I confirmed Rachel and Stagne are back in the Iceberg. In this timeline, they behaved badly, just like last time. And so they still ended up in our custody. I recommend you interview Rachel about the pandemic. I know she was working on measures to prevent it from coming to America, but apparently she failed."

"Okay, I'll plan on that."

"There is one additional thing we learned about the pandemic we didn't know before. You'll remember that an Islamist seduced the virologist who developed the toxin and the Iranian scientists did gain of function research to develop it to weapon strength. Anyway, in this timeline, he was vocal and took credit for it."

"Who was or is he?"

"It was Osama al-Zawahiri, sir. He's the son of Ayman al-Zawahiri, the top Al Qaeda guy for years. And he is still very much alive."

The guy who killed Dad!

McKnight didn't hear the next few lines from Hatcher. His memory leaped back to that day when the principal came to his third-grade classroom and pulled him from class. They walked back to his office, where his mother told him terrorists killed his father in Paris. And now, twenty-five years later, the same man seduced a young woman and convinced her to commit treason.

He forced himself back to Hatcher's briefing.

"… So that's the gist of it," Hatcher said. "Are there questions?"

"Yes," McKnight said. "We hoped we frightened Kosar enough that he'd stay away from the United States. Looks like things didn't change much. He didn't stay away. Did anything happen differently in his life?"

Kathy spoke. "We can't identify everything that happened. Day-to-day things, for example. But we know a few things."

"Like what?"

"We noticed Kosar had one son fewer than before. Robby and I pieced together some things. We think we know why Kosar hated the United States in general… and you, Colonel, in particular."

"Me? Why?"

Smalls leaned over and whispered to McKnight, "I was afraid of this."

McKnight turned to him and said, "What? Why?"

Continuing in a low voice, Smalls said, "Kosar is pretty bright. He learned from the SEALS team it was the Americans who grabbed him. And he learned your name when we interviewed him."

McKnight sighed and looked at the floor. When he raised his gaze back to Smalls, the man spoke gently.

"Your ACU. You wore your combat uniform to the interview. He read your name on the breast pocket."

McKnight nodded. "I realized that when we talked to him. It was a bad mistake. You were smart enough to wear civvies."

Small shrugged. "We all make mistakes."

McKnight nodded and looked at Kathy.

"Okay, so he identified me. Smalls and I were the ones who let him go. He should have been okay with us. What did I do?"

Kathy leaned forward and clasped her hands together on the table.

"When Kosar returned to 1986, he found his youngest son ill from exposure. He and his older brother stayed outside in the December elements all night, waiting for him until you and Smalls told them to go home. That son died from pneumonia—"

"And he blames me."

In my attempt to scare him, I created a mortal enemy for our country.

"He should have blamed himself, Marc," Kathy said. "He told them to stay with the boat and wait for him. None of this is your fault. You and Smalls sent them home. Regardless, Kosar has followed approximately the same path he did before all this."

"With one notable exception," Robby said from the doorway. "Sorry I'm late." He took a seat next to Kathy.

"What was the exception?" McKnight asked.

"In examining the Time Frequency log now and comparing it to the pre-kidnapping log, there was change activity in June 2011. There were occasional events after that until January 5th, 2012—"

"The day they killed my father in Paris," McKnight said.

"Yes, I'm sorry," Robby said. "There was a spike on that day."

"Meaning…?"

"There's reliable intel that Kosar funded the attack on your father," Kathy said. "It's not one hundred percent, but strong."

"So he took his anger out on my father?"

"No," Robby said. "On your son."

Kathy nodded. "Kosar didn't know he was time-traveled. He thought he met you in 1986. Then he heard of Colonel McKnight through Al Qaeda and just assumed — after twenty-six years — that Colonel McKnight was your son."

"Do we know this for certain?" McKnight asked.

Kathy looked at Robby. "Some of it is conjecture, but one message intercepted during surveillance of the Paris cell made little sense until now. Al-Zawahiri mentioned he would avenge his friend from Hungary while in Paris."

"That's right," Robby said. "We aren't positive, but it all fits together."

McKnight felt wretched.

Did I cause my father's death, too?

"Wait a second," Smalls said. "Not to drag this out and increase the Colonel's distress, but wasn't his father assassinated in the previous history? Before Kosar ever met the Colonel?"

"Yes," Kathy said. "Thanks for bringing that up. It's true."

"Right," Robby said. "We're pretty sure that al-Zawahiri didn't know who the Colonel's father was. In the former timeline, another member of the cell killed Colonel John McKnight. To *that* man, he was a hated American. Someone in their cell noticed this American frequented this cafe and liked to sit outside. They wanted to show the world they were still relevant. Remember this was three months after they stormed the American Embassy in Benghazi. Al Qaeda feared they were losing the world's attention."

McKnight looked around the room.

I don't like this attention to my personal life. It's not good for the team to see me going through personal loss.

"In the new timeline, Kosar must have communicated his desire for revenge to al-Zawahiri, who learned who the targeted American was and decided to gain favor with his benefactor."

"Let's move on to other things," McKnight said. "What should our course of action be next?"

"Of course, Colonel. The next step is to talk to Rachel and see what she was doing to stop the Pandemic from 2086. Maybe there's something we can do in this time period to stop it. Like it or not, she has intel we could use. It's worth a try, anyway."

"Excuse me, Kathy," Wheeler said. "But am I the only one who sees a chance to do great things here?"

"No, you're not, Captain," Kathy said. "But I thought I'd bring it up with General Drake. I didn't want him to think the idea came from the Colonel."

"What idea?" McKnight asked.

What do they see I don't?

"Go ahead, Captain," Kathy said, "now that you've piqued the Colonel's interest."

Wheeler looked uncomfortable now, but he pressed forward.

"Yes, ma'am," he said, then turned to McKnight.

"Colonel, we know al-Zawahiri seduced the virologist and got the virus for Al Qaeda. We also know the American military has been looking for this guy since we took out bin Laden. Thanks to your father, we now know where he was on a specific date in history. And we're coming up on the twenty-fifth anniversary of that event in six days."

Wheeler looked around the room. "Don't you guys see? We can take out the number one Al Qaeda guy, prevent the pandemic fifty years in the future, and save the Colonel's father from assassination, all at the same time!"

CHAPTER THIRTY-NINE

Monday, December 29th, 2036 - 7:00 AM MST - Salt Lake City, Utah

The Operative woke up in Salt Lake City. Though she was tired, she was invigorated to be back in the hunt. Today, she would drive to Ely, Nevada.

She could make it to Rachel today, but she didn't want to arrive there tired. If there were still police in the area, she wanted to be strong enough to deal with them.

No, she would go to Ely, get a good night's sleep, and arrive fresh in Rachel tomorrow.

At a local paint store, she bought a large tarpaulin and some brown and beige paint. She took them back to her hotel and painted the tarp. As she finished the job, she hung them over the top of the SUV and admired her work. The tarp would provide excellent camouflage for the vehicle in the desert.

She rested in her hotel while the paint dried in the sun and wind of Salt Lake City. When it was dry, she folded it and stowed it in the SUV.

She checked the locator again. It still showed Rachel Patterson was in Nevada. She smiled at the prospect of finding Rachel and going back home.

Her phone pinged. She expected it to be the response from Number Three. It was.

>   <<< *003: Where have you been? Why haven't you reported in?* >>>

She didn't know how to respond. She almost had Rachel, and then she was gone.

She doesn't want an explanation. She wants results.

The Operative responded to the real question:

>   <<< *638: Locator malfunction. Estimate mission completion in three days.* >>>

She didn't wait for a response. She didn't expect one. With renewed motivation, she pulled out of the motel parking lot and headed west on Interstate 80.

Tuesday, December 30th, 2036 - 8:05 AM PST - Rachel, Nevada

As she approached the town of Rachel, she remembered seeing activity in the distance from her canyon hideout. She decided to check her hideouts in case she needed to lie low again. It shouldn't take long to check.

She wasn't sure she could find the turnoff coming from this direction. It took a couple of wrong turns to find the right road.

They must have found them — they've been here for a week.

She was glad she picked up water and food before leaving Salt Lake City. Now she might need them.

When she arrived at her first desert hiding place, she got the answer to her question. It was obvious the police found this camp. There were footprints in the sand everywhere.

Okay, they found it. What does that tell me?

They scoured the campsite for clues and fingerprints. They could tie the campsite owner to the killings. But they couldn't lead anyone to her — in this time period, she wasn't born yet.

She doubted she left many clues.

She moved on to check her canyon hideout. There was one set of tracks there — the ones she made a few days before.

They haven't found this one. I can still use it.

She pulled out her phone, connected to the satellite, and tapped into the police band. She learned the police found a few guides and were looking for more.

She decided to recon the town.

I'll need to be more careful this time.

She drove back to the highway, and turned left toward Rachel.

A mile north of town, she passed a deep ditch on the right side. She braked, turned around and drove back to inspect it. It was just what she needed.

The ditch was about ten feet deep. It was wide enough for an SUV, and became shallower two hundred yards west of the road. It was perfect. She left the highway and drove to the end of the ditch. She directed the SUV into the ditch and drove back toward the road. Fifty feet from the road, she stopped and pulled out her gear. She dragged out the painted tarp and threw it over the SUV. Then she scouted the surrounding area for tumbleweeds and bracken to position around it. In ten minutes, she made the SUV invisible from the road. She stepped back and admired her work.

Let them try to find that without standing right on top of it.

She engaged her mission suit and began the mile-long hike into town, walking a route about a quarter mile from the road. She intended to get close enough to observe the police presence, if any.

A shallow ditch twenty yards behind an old barn was the first sign of town. Like most of the buildings here, the barn featured a rusted tin roof and weather-beaten wooden walls.

Okay, be more cautious now.

She glanced at the highway. There was no traffic.

As she moved around the barn, she heard voices. They came from the other side of the barn.

She circled it on the desert side and flash-glanced around the corner. Back out of sight, she processed what she saw. Two men stood there with their backs to the barn, sharing information. One was bald, and the other wore a blue work shirt.

If I go inside the barn near the front door, I'll be closer and able to hear better. Maybe I can learn something.

She backtracked and entered the barn through a back door. It was dark inside, but she could see well enough to creep to the front door. Peering through a crack in the old wood, she could see them standing ten feet away.

"What's all the hubbub, Ed?" Baldy said.

"You haven't heard?" Ed said. "A woman staying at the hotel shot two deputies from Vegas dead last Saturday. I mean *dead*!"

"You don't say? Who was she?"

"Don't know," Ed said. "All I know is they say she was a looker."

"You don't say?" Baldy asked.

Baldy shook his head. "How'd it happen?"

"Them big city cops came to the hotel looking for her. According to Rusty over at the restaurant, one of them was bigger'n six foot four. They say the woman was five foot two."

The Operative smiled at his exaggeration.

"No!" Baldy said.

"That's right. She beat the shit outa both of 'em, then shot them while they lay busted up on the floor."

"You don't say? Then what happened?"

"Well, I think she hightailed it outa here, but the cops think she's still here. I don't know why... staying around here seems stupid to me. Wuz me, I'd a-hauled ass outa here and been in California by now."

"Me, too. Hey, do you think it has anything to do with that, you know, that thing in the desert?"

"What?" Ed said.

"You know what I mean, Ed. Don't play dumb. That Army thing in the desert."

"Oh, *that*... Could be. Who knows? But town looks like a cop convention. They are everywhere. Hey, look at this."

The Operative looked through the door crack. Ed was pointing toward the highway.

She moved closer to the open door and saw the Las Vegas police cruiser turn off the highway into Baldy's driveway.

Time to go!

She tiptoed to the back of the barn and glanced toward the front door.

The cruiser stopped where the two men stood, and two officers got out.

"Sorry to bother you folks," one of them said. "We're searching the area for a murder suspect and I was told that Ed Smith was a competent guide for the desert. Are either of you Ed?"

They'll search the barn.

As quietly as she could, she stepped through the back door. Keeping the barn between herself and the men, she sprinted to the ditch and dropped her pack. She tore it open and pulled out the shield.

She could hear sounds coming from the barn now.

After tossing some dirt on her pack, she strapped on the shield and laid on the ground.

Don't use the shield if you can help it.

She watched the barn's back door. It moved an inch, and she engaged the shield. She drew in a breath and held it.

Don't move.

A police officer stepped through the door and stood, scanning the desert horizon. For a long minute, he didn't move at all. Then he disappeared back through the door.

The Operative switched off the shield and let out her breath. A short wave of nausea passed through her, and she willed herself to remain still and not vomit. She kept it down.

Brief exposure has less impact.

After a few minutes, she heard the cruiser rolling on the gravel driveway, then speeding away on the highway.

She looked toward the barn, then back toward the desert.

That was too close.

She stowed the shield in her pack and walked back into the desert. When she reached the SUV, she was exhausted. She stowed the tarp, backed out of the ditch, and got back on the highway, heading north.

The shield sapped a lot of her strength. When she reached the dirt road that led to her hiding places, she headed for her first hiding place. As she drove, she considered the situation and tried to decide on her approach. A solution wouldn't come.

Maybe I'm too tired to think.

When she reached her first hiding place, she got out of the vehicle and looked at the footprints the cops made there. They were unlikely to return without a reason, and she couldn't think of one.

She opened the back of the SUV to unload it. Exhaustion threatened to overwhelm her. She stopped, climbed into the vehicle, and fell asleep.

After two hours, she woke up. Still tired and nauseated, she climbed out of the vehicle and looked around. She scanned the desert horizon in all directions and looked at the mountains in the distance. Then she looked at the footprints in the surrounding sand.

I need to lie low until they stop looking for me. Or at least a couple of days.

I need proper rest and I don't feel safe enough here. I can't get back into the Iceberg until they stop looking. And when I do, I need to be well rested and strong.

She knew what she needed to do. She checked the campsite again for new clues she may have left. Then she climbed into the SUV, started it, and headed for her canyon hideout.

All the mountain foothills looked alike in the gathering gloom. But she persisted and found her box canyon after exploring three others.

She covered the vehicle with her improvised camouflage and hiked into the canyon with her supplies. It was getting darker, and she used a flashlight to check out her cave. She gathered firewood and set up camp. She ate a modest dinner of rations and rebuilt the barrier to the cave.

Satisfied with her camp setup, the Operative checked the locator to confirm Rachel was in the Iceberg.

Yes, she's still there.

Relieved, she wondered if she somehow misused the device before when she lost Rachel.

Let it go, you can't solve that question.

She pulled the drug package from her pack and gave herself another injection of the restorative drug. She planned to sleep for two days again, then check to see if the police were still looking for her.

Before she drifted off to sleep, she stared at her pack against the cave wall, knowing the personal shield was inside.

I don't want to use it again, but I have to get back in the Iceberg. There's no way to avoid it.

She worried about the damage the shield caused to her body. She tried to push it out of her mind so she could sleep. The drug won out, and she slipped into restful unconsciousness.

When she awoke, *there were no Uncles and Aunts in the camp.*

The students were left without a mission. 638 led them through their daily physical training. She took charge of the mess hall and organized others to prepare meals for everyone.

The Uncles and Aunts didn't show up the next day, so 638 took charge again and repeated what she did the previous day.

She worried about the students. They needed a mission and it wasn't good for them to be idle.

On the third day, a senior Uncle came to the camp with other people 638 didn't recognize. She met him at the gate and asked what she could do to help.

The Uncle wanted to address the camp.

638 called the students together and, within thirty minutes, the Uncle was standing on the barracks' front porch with 600 teenagers before him.

He said the training camp was closed and they would interview each student to determine where they should go next. The interviews would begin the next day, starting with the camp leaders.

638 assumed she would be in this group. It surprised her to learn she was the subject of the first interview.

The man who interviewed her never introduced himself. He asked her questions about her fitness. He seems impressed with her command of the classroom skills. She learned the project would position her to perform special tasks for her country, and they would pay her well for it. This made her happy, but more important to 638 was the knowledge that she was an Operative and she would always have a mission.

She took pride in knowing she successfully completed her training.

At the end of the interview, the man pulled out a gold medallion on a chain. He asked her to relax and listen to the sound of his voice. He swung the medallion before her eyes and spoke softly to her. She felt herself growing warm and relaxed.

She jumped to her feet when she realized she had been sleeping. The man was gone. She walked out of the building and an Aunt directed her to a car.

She had never ridden in a car.

She never saw the camp again.

CHAPTER FORTY

Thursday, January 1st, 2037 - 8:05 AM PST - Cave in Nevada desert

She regained consciousness. Light from the sun bounced off the opposite canyon wall and illuminated the cave. She pushed herself up from the sleeping bag and blinked.

What woke me?

She checked her phone and understood. She had been asleep for thirty-two hours. It was hunger. She rose from her sleeping bag and stretched. Her body complained about the exertion after a long rest.

She rummaged through her supplies and found wafers and water. They weren't much, but they took the edge off her hunger.

With phone in hand, she left her campsite and tuned to the police radio. She listened to their transmissions for thirty minutes.

The authorities sounded busy, but they couldn't keep the hint of despair out of their voices. They thought they found the suspect yesterday, but it was a false alarm. One officer complained that everyone on the team responded when they got the lead.

She smiled.

No one is turning up information, so everyone jumps at any hint of a clue. The hunt will be over soon.

She switched to the locator and checked for Rachel Patterson. The device still showed a powerful signal from twenty miles away. She nodded.

Still in the Iceberg.

She stretched again and returned to her campsite. She rebuilt the fire and cooked a more nutritious meal to satisfy the chorus her stomach was singing.

We'll see tomorrow. If the hunt is over, I'll add a stimulant to help me manage the attack on the Iceberg.

She pulled out the drug pack again and gave herself a half-dose to start a final night of recuperative sleep.

She felt better. The hunt was nearly over, and she could fulfill her mission.

CHAPTER FORTY-ONE

Wednesday, January 2nd, 2012 - 10:00 AM - Telegraph Road Conference Room, Alexandria, Virginia

McKnight walked to the big conference room at Telegraph Road. He was a little nervous because this briefing covered the first mission planned with Hatcher instead of Tyler.

Not that he didn't have confidence in Hatcher. He missed being able to bounce the mission details off Tyler. And he still wasn't comfortable with the added mission goal of saving his father. It was all approved, but it still bothered him.

He wanted with all his heart to save his father's life. He dreamed about it since the first time he did a time jump. But the idea was against the principles of non-interference that he hammered into the team. What would change by saving one life twenty-five years ago?

It would change him. No question about it.

How would it feel to grow up with two parents instead of one? How would he be different with a father figure in his life? Would he still be the man who could lead a team like this? Or the man Megan could love?

And what if the team failed to accomplish the mission for reasons outside their control? He would second-guess his decision to let someone else plan and lead the mission.

He pushed all this emotion and unnecessary thoughts to the back of his mind.

Get your head clear. Hatcher has this one. Just do your oversight thing. Make sure the mission is tight.

He entered the conference room. The five members of the mission team sat at the table, Hatcher and Wheeler to the right and Smalls, Lagunas and Cutty to the left. Trevor and Kathy sat at the end of the table.

"Good morning," he said.

The military part of the team rose and came to attention.

"As you were," he said. "Please be seated. Let me get some coffee."

He went to the coffee service and poured a cup, then moved to his seat at the head of the table.

"Okay, Captain Hatcher, let's hear it."

"Yes, sir," she said, and touched a button on her phone.

The screen behind McKnight lit up, and he turned to face it.

A list of the team and the objectives were on the screen.

Hatcher rose and walked to the display.

"As you can see, sir, these are the priorities of the mission as approved by General Drake and Vice President Crumpton. Mr. Smalls has been briefed and approved the plan as well."

McKnight looked at Smalls, who nodded in agreement.

"Priority one is the assassination of Osama al-Zawahiri," Hatcher said. "Priority two is to deliver the 'do not touch' message to Al Qaeda and Kosar. We must meet these two objectives at all costs. Priority three is to prevent the murder of Colonel John McKnight. This objective is a 'nice to have' and it is to be achieved if we meet the other objectives and the risk to the team is moderate." She looked around the room. "Is everyone clear on that?" Then she looked at McKnight.

"Yes," he said. "Please proceed."

She advanced the presentation to the next slide. It now showed a street map of a small section of Paris. Hatcher pointed at the most prominent street.

"This street here is the Avenue des Ternes. It's a congested route on the west side of Paris, near the perimeter highway. It runs east to west." She pointed to a small park on the north side of the street. "And here is the Au Petit Marguery Bistro. This is where Colonel John McKnight will have lunch tomorrow... in 2012, that is."

"Lieutenant Cutty is on point for priority one, killing al-Zawahiri. Lieutenant Lagunas is his backup. Captain Wheeler, Mr. Smalls, and I will take out the cell and deliver the message... priority two. Lieutenant Lagunas will be at the cafe to confirm al-Zawahiri's death, or cause it if necessary. She will look after the safety of Colonel McKnight, if possible. Questions about the priorities and who is on point, sir?"

"None yet," McKnight said. "Please proceed."

"Yes, sir. The plan is pretty simple. History tells us al-Zawahiri approached the cafe from the west on a motorbike at moderate speed. It was a sunny day, and Colonel McKnight was having lunch in the bistro's outside seating. Al-Zawahiri tossed a bomb into the seating area and sped off on the bike. The bistro was crowded that day. The bomb killed Colonel McKnight and four other people, and wounded five others."

McKnight felt himself becoming impatient. He wanted to ask Hatcher to get to the point, but restrained himself.

She needs to present all the details and I need to hear them.

"History also tells us where the cell was located," Hatcher said. "Hindsight is always twenty-twenty. The French didn't know where the group's cell was, or that there would be an attack. They learned it all in the investigation's course. But since it is history, we know where the cell was located and al-Zawahiri's probable route to the bistro."

She glanced at Kathy. "I ran the plan by Kathy. As the official mission planner for the team, I felt compelled to do that."

"That's fine," McKnight said. "Good thinking."

"Thank you, sir. Everyone already knows what their job is. So here's what will happen. We'll jump tomorrow morning at 4:30 AM. That puts us in Paris at 10:30 AM. That gives us time to work out any kinks in the plan. Lieutenant Cutty will jump in on top of a building about two blocks away. He'll set up in a vacant apartment with an overlook of the bistro's outdoor seating. When al-Zawahiri gets close to the cafe, Lieutenant Cutty will take him out. The French will identify the body and won't care much who did it."

"Lieutenant Lagunas will jump in on the roof of the bistro and position herself in the cafe's outside seating area as a customer. She'll sit where she has a view of the oncoming traffic. If Lieutenant Cutty doesn't take al-Zawahiri out, her priority is to kill him. After that, she will do what she can to protect Colonel McKnight."

"Understood, Captain," McKnight said. "Go on. What about the rest of the team?"

"Yes, sir. We will jump in onto a rooftop about a mile away, near the cell's apartment. Al-Zawahiri starts from there. We'll alert Cutty and Lagunas when he leaves the place. We expect the rest of the cell — current estimate is four targets — to be waiting for an observer to signal that the operation is complete. When they get the signal, they'll bug out. Our job is to take out the cell and leave a warning for Al Qaeda, either a note left with a single survivor or a transmission to Al Jazeera. That's the plan, sir."

McKnight nodded. "Okay, a few questions…"

"Yes, sir?"

He looked at the new members of the team. "Don't read anything into this." He turned back to Hatcher. "Why are the new guys assigned to the black ops work, and the experienced time travelers are performing the assault, which is more of a Ranger assignment?"

Hatcher nodded. "Great question, sir. Lieutenant Cutty distinguished himself in the Mideast as a sniper."

McKnight looked at Cutty.

"That's right, sir," Cutty said. "I hunted a lot as a kid, and my dad taught me how to 'aim small, miss small'. I can do the job, sir."

McKnight nodded and turned to Lagunas. "Lieutenant?"

"Yes, sir?" she said.

"So did you shoot someone as a teenager, too?"

Lagunas smiled and said, "No, sir. In Iran. I was on a team with a covert mission. We got ambushed, and the firefight turned into a hand-to-hand event."

"How many casualties?"

"Our squad lost four people, sir. Good friends of mine, and they were five feet away from me, when it happened."

"Sorry to hear that," McKnight said. "That was my primary concern. Shooting someone at thirty yards with a semi-automatic is a lot different from doing it with a pistol at three yards, right?"

"Yes, sir," Lagunas said. "I've done both and I agree."

"She's also a better shot with a pistol than any of us, sir," Hatcher said. "She's more than capable to take out al-Zawahiri with a handgun when he gets close."

"Understood."

McKnight looked at Smalls. "You've chosen to be on the assault team?"

Smalls looked surprised at the statement. "I have a little training in that area. I'll be fine."

"And you've approved the details of the mission?"

"Captain Hatcher has done a thorough job planning this, Colonel. She considered the possibilities, ran the options, consulted with each team member — not to mention Kathy."

McKnight turned to Kathy. "How much of this plan is yours?"

Kathy grinned at him.

"I made one contribution," she said. "I suggested that Lieutenant Lagunas wear a dress."

CHAPTER FORTY-TWO

Friday, January 2nd, 2037 - 8:23 PM PST - Outside Iceberg near Rachel Nevada

When the Operative woke again, she was feeling much better.

After eating, she left the cave. It was night in the desert, and the sky was full of stars.

She tuned to the police band and listened. In thirty minutes, she heard the town's deputy say that all of their guests were gone, and it was good to be back to normal. A little later, she heard the sheriff say he was tired; it was the end of his shift, and he was going home.

The search is over.

She hiked out of the box canyon and drove to the Extraterrestrial Highway. She stopped fifty yards short of the highway to monitor the traffic. After thirty minutes and no vehicles passed her position, she decided it was worth the gamble to recon the Iceberg.

The Operative drove to her now familiar stopping place and hiked to the base of the hill.

She pulled the infrared goggles from her pack and looked at the hill. A few minutes of observation told her the lasers were still operating in the same patterns and frequency. Nothing had changed.

She retrieved the locator from her pack and confirmed Rachel Patterson was still in the Iceberg.

She dreaded using the personal shield again. She felt a memory of nausea touch her gut. It reminded her of what was to come when she used the shield again. She shrugged it off and focused on the next step.

She would attempt the intrusion before dawn the next day. With luck, it would be the last time she had to use the shield.

A few hours' sleep, then down the rabbit hole.

She returned to the SUV and drove back to the cave.

638 opened her eyes. She was in a light green room. She was lying in a bed. There were machines with blinking lights and beeping sounds behind her.

The door opened.

439 came into the room. 638 knew it couldn't be her, but the resemblance was stunning.

She was older now. No longer a teenaged girl, but a full grown woman. But the sparkling eyes and shining blonde hair gave proof to who she was. If 638 had any doubt, it vanished when the woman smiled.

"Hello, 638," she said.

"439? How could it be you? You're alive?"

"Yes, as alive as you."

"What are you doing here?" 638 asked her.

"I've come to fetch you," 439 said. "It's time to go."

"Where are we going?"

"To a place of release. A place of freedom."

638 paused. "I can't."

"Why not?" 439 said, her smile as wide as ever.

"I've done terrible things. I deserve chains and darkness, not release or freedom."

439 nodded. "Don't we all?" she said. "But there's still time. Come on."

638 attempted to rise, but she felt a pressure on her shoulders. Her eyes focused on the face of a woman whose hands gripped her shoulders. She wore medical scrubs and a look of genuine concern.

439 turned and walked out of the room.

"Let me go," 638 said to the woman. "It's 439."

The woman's mouth moved, but nothing came out. The pressure released, and 638 rose from the bed and walked to the door.

Saturday, January 3rd, 2037 - 4:22 AM PST - The Iceberg Detention Center near Rachel Nevada

The Operative returned to the hill, ready to attack the Iceberg.

She hiked from her car to the base of the hill with her gear. When she reached the position, she laid her burden on the ground and donned the infrared goggles. The security lasers were visible and operating as before. In thirty minutes, the morning watch would come out of the portal and allow her access.

She moved to the outside edge of the lights and paused, waiting for the right time to run up the hill. She donned the combat uniform.

Secure the shield and my mission jumpsuit low in the pack so they won't shift and affect my balance.

She slipped the pack on and pulled the straps tight.

With two minutes to go, she injected the stimulant and discarded the syringe. Her face flushed with heat, and all her senses went into overdrive. She brought her donor's image to mind, took a runner's start posture, and watched the lasers as she waited for the window to open.

When it did, she barely perceived the event. Her body was running of its own accord, the benefit of years of training. She felt like she was flying over the ground. As the slope increased, she blew into it as if she were wind itself.

It wasn't long before she felt the burn of the effort. She was making excellent progress, but her lungs and muscles burned. Her eyes darted back and forth, looking for the air vent that signaled the end of her run. For each step in the sandy slope, she felt herself slide back as the sand gave beneath her feet.

When the stimulant's rush subsided, she ran on willpower alone. She had no perception of time and space. There was only her and the hill.

Finally, she saw the air vent ahead of her. She wasn't sure how far it was, but the sight of it renewed her will and energy enough to carry her past the vent.

She collapsed just beyond it, gasping for air. The laser pattern changed.

As her breathing returned to normal, her thought processes returned.

Even with the stimulant, I just made it. The shield is sapping away my stamina and strength.

She wanted to rest, but she didn't dare wait long. She struggled to her feet and trudged up to the hill's crest. Kneeling, then crawling, she approached the far edge of the hill. She could see two sets of teams on the slope below, none of them closer than fifty yards from her.

With two minutes to go, she swallowed hard, slipped on the shield, and activated it. It's faint hum was louder in her ears somehow. She crept down the slope to the portal.

Two men were standing next to the portal, smoking cigarettes. She crouched near it, nausea roaring in her ears.

The portal opened, and the men threw down their cigarettes and jumped to attention.

The major! A surprise inspection?

Two staff members followed her through the portal opening. The Operative peered into the hole, struggling to see if anyone else was coming.

The major dressed down the guards for smoking and being inattentive. The staff members took notes beside her.

The Operative saw her chance and took it. As quietly as she could, she slipped past them and down into the Iceberg.

She turned off the shield, slipped it into her backpack, and searched for a restroom. Then she dug the ID she stole out of her pocket and put it on.

She waited in the restroom until the nausea passed. She felt weak and tired, but at least the shield use was behind her. Now she would find a place to rest before breaking Rachel out of her cell.

Thursday, January 3rd, 2012 - 4:00 AM - Telegraph Road Lab, Alexandria, Virginia

Hatcher watched the four other members of the mission team prepare for their time jump. Everyone seemed calm and cool, but she felt the undercurrent of stress and resolve.

Bottom line: This is a combat mission and there's always a danger of not coming back, so you lean on your training and trust your teammates.

Kathy and Trevor were in the break area, discussing the jump in low voices. Kathy would operate the Engine for the jump.

One thing seemed amiss. She picked up her gear bag and walked over to where they were packing gear. Lagunas wore her combat uniform. The rest of the team wore period costumes as French Police.

"Lieutenant, didn't I hear something about you wearing a dress?"

"Yes, ma'am, I am. I was just going to change. I wanted to get my gear squared away first."

"Good. Snap to it, we're leaving in five."

Lagunas left the group and entered the ladies' locker room.

Hatcher checked on Smalls. To her, he was still somewhat of an enigma. He said little, but everything he said was spot on.

He might be CIA, but he knows his way around combat gear, especially weapons.

She watched him disassemble his weapon, clean it, and reassemble it. She didn't think she could do it any faster.

He's had combat experience.

She walked over to him.

"Why do I think you've done this before?"

Smalls gave her a shy smile.

What's he not telling us?

She nodded at him and looked for Wheeler. She found him helping Cutty with his gear.

Lagunas came out of the locker room. The transformation was jolting. She was wearing a close fitting black dress of stylish length. Her makeup was flawlessly applied, achieving a look that was flattering and not overdone. Her jet black hair was perfectly styled around her shoulders, and her handbag was small but functional. She picked up her gear bag and carried it to the edge of the Engine's platform.

Hatcher and the rest of the team followed her.

"Okay," Hatcher said. "Questions? Are we ready?"

Wheeler raised his hand and said, "Hey, I have a question."

Uh-oh. Why do I think this won't end well?

"Go ahead, Wheeler," she said.

"Okay," he said, and turned to Lagunas.

"Hey, Lieutenant, what's this all about? You have a date later today or something?"

Hatcher rolled her eyes.

Good, Wheeler. Very P.C.

Lagunas smiled at him. "Permission to speak frankly, sir?"

"Of course," Wheeler said.

Lagunas smiled at him again. "Thanks for the compliment, sir," she said. "Now, please blow it out your ass."

Wheeler laughed out loud. Cutty smiled with sparkling eyes.

I'm gonna like this girl.

"Well, Wheeler," Hatcher said. "Looks like Daisy here is gonna fit in just fine."

"I think so, too. Welcome to the team, Daisy."

"Daze," Lagunas said.

"What?" Hatcher asked.

"Days?" Wheeler said. "Like Thursday? What does that mean?"

Lagunas shook her head. "No, not D-A-Y-S. *Daze*, like D-A-Z-E. Call me Daze."

Hatcher nodded.

"I like it," Wheeler said. "Daze, it is."

"Okay, enough foreplay," Hatcher said with a tiny smile. "Kathy, are you ready to send us to the City of Lights?"

Kathy and Trevor jumped up from their seats. "Sure thing. Is everyone ready?"

There were nods all around.

"Yep," Hatcher said. "Let's go."

CHAPTER FORTY-THREE

Tuesday, January 3rd, 2012 - 1:02 PM - Au Petit Marguery Bistro, Paris France

Colonel John McKnight walked down the Avenue des Ternes on his way to lunch. He carried the Wall Street Journal in his left hand.

It's amazing how quickly you can fall back into a work routine after Christmas with the family.

This was his fourth day back in Paris. While he loved his work and the City of Lights, he would rather be home in Oregon with his wife Madeleine and his kids, Marc and Janie.

But he loved his favorite cafe in Paris, the bistro Au Petit Marguery. He liked to sit outside under the sky and soak up the atmosphere that was Paris. There was a saying about Paris: "If there is any art or passion in your soul, it will awaken in Paris." He believed this with all his heart.

Paris inspired him to write.

He checked the sky. There were clouds, but it was a nice day. Despite being winter, the cafe would still let you sit outside unless the weather was bad. Just ahead, he saw the cafe and he could already smell the bread, coffee, and wine.

The waiter recognized him as a regular and took him to the outside seating. The man smiled and positioned McKnight next to a space heater, which issued heat and the low roar of gas blowing and igniting.

He looked around before he sat. No matter what your job was, American military personnel survived in a foreign country by knowing what was happening around you. He saw nothing that looked like a threat, so he sat and relaxed. He opened his paper and looked for news from the United States.

The waiter returned and spoke in accented English. "The usual, Monsieur?"

"Oui," McKnight said. "Merci."

The waiter bowed and left the table.

Tuesday, January 3rd, 2012 - 1:03 PM - Islamic Cell Safe House, Paris France

Osama al-Zawahiri stood next to his motorbike and closed his eyes. He relaxed by taking deep breaths. He prayed to Allah for the redemption of his soul.

Today, he would execute a different type of mission. He would kill a man for Allah's benefactor.

The Hungarian Kosar, a friend of Islam, gave a large sum of money to the Brotherhood of Paris and asked for a favor. The Supreme Mullah in Paris tapped al-Zawahiri to fulfill his promise to kill the son of a man who wronged Kosar. It would be an honor to send an infidel dog to Allah for judgement.

He checked his bomb for the fifth time. Once he armed it, a pressure switch was activated. As long as he pressed the switch, it would not blow up. Once he released the switch, he had eight seconds before it detonated. It was the perfect tool for the job.

He slipped the device into his satchel.

He turned and looked up at the second-floor window where the rest of his cell waited for their observer to report the death of the infidel dog McKnight. He raised his hands in prayer and made a quick bow toward the window to honor their trust. Then he bowed to the east.

He climbed onto his bike, cranked it, and sped away to the west side of Paris.

Tuesday, January 3rd, 2012 - 1:04 PM - Islamic Cell Safe House, Paris France

From the alley next to the Cell apartment, Hatcher, Smalls and Wheeler watched al-Zawahiri get on his bike and leave.

"It would have been so easy to take him out right there," Wheeler whispered.

Hatcher pointed at a woman with three children playing across the street. "I can see the headlines now. 'French Police shoot unarmed student.' Better to stick to the plan."

"Yeah, but I hate to let the opportunity go." He shrugged and said, "C'est la vie."

Hatcher smiled and whispered into her comm. "Team one to team two. Acknowledge."

The ear bud crackled, and she heard Ed and Daze check in.

"ACK. The bird is on the wing. Copy?"

"Copy that," Daze said.

"Copy that," Ed said. "Eyes are up and expecting company."

Hatcher looked at Smalls and Wheeler. "Okay," she said. "Let's roll."

The target apartment was on the second floor. They left the alley as a group and tried their best to look French. The police uniforms helped. The street was a low traffic route in a residential area of the city.

They entered the building and crept up the stairs. The banisters were ornate wood sculptures, and the steps were hardwood, but they had seen better days. Decades of use had worn the steps and the bannister.

They paused at the top of the stairs on the second floor. Hatcher and Wheeler confirmed the apartment number with each other. Smalls remained focused down the staircase, covering their rear.

Hatcher observed Smalls as he looked around, checking angles and their escape route.

He knows his tactics. I need to ask where he learned them.

She took several deep breaths to calm herself.

In five minutes, they would storm the apartment and ruin the Cell's day.

Tuesday, January 3rd, 2012 - 1:05 PM - Au Petit Marguery Bistro, Paris France

McKnight looked up from his paper at the sound of her voice.

The young woman in the black dress talked to the waiter and pointed at the outside seating. The man led her to an empty table about fifteen feet from McKnight. She sat and ordered coffee.

Her light brown skin glowed in the sun, and her dress fit just right to attract a man's attention.

McKnight sighed and returned to his paper.

I love Paris.

He finished the article he was reading and stole another glance at the young woman. She was looking down the Avenue.

What is she? Not French with that coloring. Spanish? Close, but not right. American Southwest? Maybe.

She turned back toward him, and their eyes met. She smiled. He sensed intelligence and purpose. And… recognition, maybe?

McKnight broke off eye contact and went back to his paper. Had he met her before? He reminded himself how much he missed his wife and pushed away that train of thought.

Still, he had trouble focusing, because the woman seemed incongruous somehow.

He decided he would keep an eye on her and smiled to himself.

Not so hard to do.

Tuesday, January 3rd, 2012, 2012 - 1:10:23 PM - Islamic Cell Safe House, Paris France

The time came to storm the apartment.

Wheeler slid the camera gooseneck under the door and confirmed three individuals in the room. Hatcher made eye contact with Wheeler and knew they were thinking the same thing. The police records they reviewed showed five individuals living in the apartment. Subtracting al-Zawahiri, there was one individual unaccounted for.

We have to proceed. We'll sort it out later.

She would show them her fingers and count down from five to zero. Then Wheeler would hit the door and the firefight would begin.

But she didn't get the chance.

They heard a noise behind them. Someone was coming up the staircase. A man appeared at the mid-story landing and turned toward the landing where they crouched.

The man was of Mideastern descent. He had an armload of groceries, a stick of celery in his mouth, and his cellphone in his other hand.

When he saw them, he froze, his eyes wide with surprise. The celery stick fell from his mouth. He dropped the groceries and cried out as he ran back down the stairs.

Smalls launched himself over the banister and landed on the man below. He tried to get up, but Smalls knocked him out with a single punch, and ran back up the stairs.

Hatcher heard excited sounds from inside the apartment.

"Go!" she said to Wheeler.

Wheeler threw his weight against the door, and it gave way at his thrust.

The first thing that appeared was an AK47 gun barrel. Wheeler grabbed it with his gloved hand and pushed it up. It stitched holes across the stairwell ceiling.

Wheeler pushed his way in and tore the weapon from the man's grasp, then clubbed him with it. The man went down like a dead weight.

Hatcher and Smalls pushed in and killed the other two men with one shot to the chest. They fell where they stood.

She turned back to Smalls and made eye contact. He nodded and went downstairs.

Hatcher and Wheeler searched the dead men for intel.

Smalls returned carrying the man he subdued by the collar. He released the man, who fell to the floor, crawled into a corner, and cowered there. Hatcher handed the intel she gathered to Wheeler and approached the man.

He pushed himself back into the corner as if he could hide there.

Hatcher grabbed him by the lapels of his shirt and drew him close to her face.

"Do you speak English?" she said.

The man stared blankly at her.

She drew out her pistol and shoved it under his chin, pushing his head back.

"If you don't speak English, I have no use for you and will kill you now."

The man's eyes widened with fear. "I speak English fluently."

"Well done," she said. "I knew we could find common ground. I want you to deliver a message. Can you do that?"

The man nodded.

"The message is for George Kosar. Say his name."

"George Kosar."

"Very good. Here is the message, and I want you to give it to him and your leadership. Do you understand?"

"Oui. Yes."

"Tell Kosar to leave McKnight and his family alone. If he dares to try this again, remember that we found him once before. We can do it again, no matter where he is. But next time, there will be no forgiveness. We will kill him, his family, and anyone who helps him. If Al Qaeda helps him, we will castrate you and send you to Paradise without balls."

She paused for effect. "Did you get that?"

Sweat glistened on the man's face. "I'm not sure I can remember all that," he said. "Mercy."

She shook her head. "No mercy for you when you attack this man or his family."

She reached into a pocket and pulled out a piece of paper. "Here, I've written it down for you." She stuffed the paper in the breast pocket of his shirt.

Hatcher hauled the man to his feet.

"Deliver my message. Remember, all who help George Kosar will die. Now, go!"

The man backed out the apartment door. Then he turned and ran down the stairs.

"Hatcher," Wheeler said, "you warm my heart with this overflowing of love for your fellow man."

"Shut up." She looked around. "Let's get out of here."

As Wheeler and Smalls walked through the apartment door, she pulled out the burner phone she purchased earlier.

Now to call 911.

She dialed '17' on the keypad and pressed the call button.

When the dispatcher came on the line, she said, "Il y a eu une fusillade." She put the burner phone on the table and walked out the door.

They headed back for the alley. Once in position, Hatcher poised to order the return time jump.

"Nicely done," Smalls said. "Best case, Al Qaeda will tell Kosar to buzz off. At least they'll think twice before doing him another favor."

"Thanks," she said. "You did pretty well yourself. Tell me the truth. You're not an accountant, are you? What did you do before you joined the CIA?"

He told her.

She and Wheeler laughed out loud.

Then she gave the order for the return jump.

CHAPTER FORTY-FOUR

Tuesday, January 3rd, 2012 - 1:11:55 PM - near Au Petit Marguery Bistro, Paris France

Cutty sat in the furnished apartment, staring out the window at the oncoming traffic. His sniper's rifle was propped up on a table, set back three yards from the window so no one could see the barrel or the muzzle flash.

Kathy was right about the apartment. It was vacant, except for a few sticks of furniture. How she could learn about places in the past was a mystery to him. But he picked the door lock with ease and set up inside to shoot and kill al-Zawahiri.

Avenue des Ternes was a one-way street with five lanes of traffic coming toward him. The bistro's outdoor seating area was just below him and to the right.

Cutty felt at home behind his rifle. Paris was not a war zone, but the situation didn't feel much different from Baghdad or Ramadi.

No, I won't have any trouble taking out this bastard.

He took his finger off the trigger, and pointed the rifle to see the assassin's target through the scope. He found Captain McKnight near the entrance, reading a paper. Two tables away from him, he could see Daze.

Gotta hand it to her. She looks cool as a cucumber.

Cutty turned his scope back up to watch the street and replaced his finger on the trigger. He received the heads-up from Captain Hatcher. The bird is on the wing, she said.

The target is on his way.

Cutty estimated the man was thirty seconds away now. He focused on the side street where they expected al-Zawahiri to turn onto Avenue des Ternes.

After twenty seconds, he expelled the breath he didn't know he was holding.

There he is. Range is one half mile.

He wanted the man within one hundred yards when he fired — just on the other side of the cafe. He took a shallow breath.

What's this? He swung the scope back down to the bistro. *Crap!*

While Cutty watched, a delivery van pulled up and stopped in front of the cafe. A man jumped out and ran inside. It wasn't a big truck, but just big enough for the target to be behind it before he entered the optimal range.

He swung back to the bike rider. He disappeared behind the low-hanging trees along the way.

There he is.

The biker rode in the second lane from the curb.

As long as he stays in that lane, I have a clear shot. Ten seconds.

Cutty saw the biker reach back and pull something from his satchel. He watched as the man glanced back and forth between the object and the road.

He's arming the device. Five seconds.

Cutty put the crosshairs of the scope square between the man's eyes and held his breath.

He's an experienced bike rider. Constant speed, no wobble.

Cutty squeezed the trigger and knew his shot didn't hit the man dead center. Even as he pulled the trigger, a car in the next lane swerved toward him and the rider responded.

He saw the target lose control of the bike and fall off it, landing hard on the pavement behind the delivery truck.

Damn. At least I know I hit him. He's off the bike and on the pavement.

With practiced speed, he dismantled his rifle and put it in the case.

I've got to get down there in case Daze needs help.

Tuesday, January 3rd, 2012 - 1:11:55 PM - Au Petit Marguery Bistro, Paris France

McKnight heard the screeching of tires. On the street, a motor bike crashed into the back of a delivery van.

He dropped his paper and stood to get a better look. Out of the corner of his eye, he saw movement. He turned and saw the young woman striding toward him. She was carrying a pistol down by her side.

His heart jumped into his throat. *She's here to kill me.*

But as soon as they made eye contact, she shouted, "Get down!"

She pivoted and strode toward the street.

McKnight dropped and laid on the brick patio.

Idiot. I let my guard down. I got comfortable.

"Descendre!" she cried.

She's warning the others.

She walked to the edge of the seating area, defined by a low brick wall. She stood facing the street in standard shooting stance, holding the weapon with both hands.

Who is she aiming at?

Tuesday, January 3rd, 2012 - 1:12:31 PM - Au Petit Marguery Bistro, Paris France

The impact of his body on the pavement stunned al-Zawahiri. When he regained cognizant thought, he remembered where he was and why he was here.

The bomb!

He struggled to his feet and searched for the device. He heard screams and saw people running.

There!

Its momentum carried it over to the curb. Al-Zawahiri staggered towards it and wondered why he was having trouble with his balance. He felt warm liquid trickling down the right side of his face. He touched his temple, then inspected his hand. Blood dripped from his fingers.

A deep cut ran across the right side of his head from the temple to the back of his head. Deep enough that he correctly guessed his skull was compromised.

Someone has shot me!

He reached the curb and picked up the bomb.

So today is the day I meet Allah. And I will bring him the soul of an infidel American. It will be a great day.

His vision darkened. He turned to search the crowd for his target and drew back his right arm to throw the device.

There, in front of him, stood a woman with a pistol pointed at him. Their eyes met, and he hesitated.

Allah, don't let me die at the hand of a woman.

He drew back further to throw, and the woman's gun exploded twice. Both rounds struck him in the chest and drove him backward into the street.

He didn't feel the impact when his body landed on the pavement. A gray fog clouded his mind.

I have something I must do.

He tried to rise, but his body wouldn't respond. He turned his head to the side and saw... something.

What is it?

Then he recognized it and knew he should be much further away.

Tuesday, January 3rd, 2012 - 1:12:35 PM - Au Petit Marguery Bistro, Paris France

McKnight heard the dual reports of the woman's weapon, but he couldn't see who she shot at.

She ran back to him. He tried to rise, but she threw herself on top of him.

"Stay down, it's not over."

She looked around at the other people. Some were fidgeting on the ground, others were rising.

"Non! Descendre! Ce n'est pas fini."

The other patrons stayed down.

She's protecting us.

"Who are you?" he asked.

Somewhere close, a bomb detonated with ear-shattering force. The windows of the bistro disintegrated. Trees along the avenue were charred and broken. The blast shredded the umbrellas over the tables. Smoke and glass were everywhere. The delivery truck was in flames. His right bicep stung like fire.

He glanced toward the source of the blast. Black smoke and the crackling of fire permeated the area, but he could see the low brick wall that surrounded the outdoor eating area. The wall and the woman's command to get down saved him and many others today.

The woman got up and pushed her weapon down into her pocket. Then she helped him to his feet.

"Are you okay, Colonel?" she asked.

"I'm fine. Who are you?"

"Oh, you're bleeding," she said, pulling his arm closer to examine it.

"Who are you?" he repeated.

"Just part of your protection detail, sir," she said, and let go of his arm. "You should get that looked at, but you'll live."

"My protection detail...?"

"Yes, sir. Respectfully, sir, please stop talking and listen to me. Vary your schedule. Don't create any patterns. You've made a mistake by coming here every Thursday. The enemy noticed and came after you."

"But why were they after me?"

"Not sure, sir. Maybe they're trying to stop you from doing your job, or maybe you're just a target of convenience. No matter what, though, becoming more unpredictable will increase your chances of making it home alive. And that's a good thing."

"I don't have a protection detail," McKnight said.

"Then I couldn't be on it then, could I?" she said, and smiled. She backed away and saluted. "Keep your head down, sir."

She turned and trotted away, back up the Avenue.

John McKnight looked around at the devastation. He heard the sirens of the Parisian emergency vehicles. His waiter sat on the patio floor with a wounded leg. He helped him up into a chair.

"Are you all right, Monsieur?" the man asked.

"Yes, I am, Gaspard. Your leg is injured, but it doesn't look bad. Can I do something for you?"

"Ach, non!" With effort, the man managed a smile and said, "I have received graver wounds from the chef in the kitchen."

McKnight smiled and patted the man on his shoulder.

I've been lucky today.

He looked around the scene again. Almost everything in the area was destroyed.

If that young woman hadn't acted...

He looked down the avenue in the direction she left.

He thought of his wife and kids, and of going back home after his tour.

I won't make those mistakes again.

CHAPTER FORTY-FIVE

Saturday, January 3rd, 2037 - 7:10 AM EST - Telegraph Road Lab, Alexandria, Virginia

McKnight sat with Kathy and Trevor in the break area. Coffee cooled in front of them as they chatted. The conversation was social and friendly, but the underlying mood was tense. Everyone knew the consequences of a failed mission. If al-Zawahiri was dead and the message delivered, but his father was killed, there would be no subsequent mission.

McKnight supported the decision as a leader and a soldier, but the little boy inside him wanted to save his dad.

When he was a kid back in Oregon, he asked his mother why his father had to be gone. In her faith, she always said the same thing — God needed a good soldier up in Heaven, so he selected Dad over all the other good men in the Army. That helped, but it didn't fill the emptiness he felt when he saw his friends interacting with their dads.

Mom would remind him that his father's absence made him self-reliant. In his heart, he knew it was true, but it was also why he had trouble committing to close relationships.

Megan helped him realize his fear of personal loss caused him to keep others distant.

McKnight reached for his coffee cup and hesitated.

Is my eyesight going?

Everything seemed less colorful, and there was a gold haze in the air. He looked up. Kathy was staring at him.

"What?" he said.

"Marc, you're glowing."

"I am?"

"Yes, you are. Remember? That means you're affected by some change in the past. I hope that's a good thing."

A rush of conflicting memories flashed through his mind. His father attending and not attending his high school graduation. Playing football games with his father gone and his father coaching the team. He tried to identify which memories were real, but the harder he tried, the more memories came.

He looked at Kathy again. She was studying his face.

Then Trevor spoke.

"I feel static electricity."

McKnight felt it, too. They jumped out of their seats and approached the Engine platform. Wheeler, Hatcher, and Smalls arrived first.

After the travel bubble dissipated, Hatcher approached McKnight and saluted.

"Report, Captain."

"We won't know everything until Cutty and Lagunas get back, but objective two is accomplished. We took out the cell except for one guy, and he has the message for Al Qaeda and Kosar."

"Understood," McKnight said. "As you were."

"Yes, sir." Hatcher saluted again and stood with the others to wait for Cutty and Lagunas.

It didn't take long.

Two minutes later, Cutty arrived with his gear.

McKnight was the first on the platform.

Cutty looked distraught.

"I'm sorry, sir. The target swerved on his bike right as I pulled the trigger. He went down behind cover — I had no shot or any clear sighting of him. I think he's dead, but I can't confirm it."

"At ease, Lieutenant," McKnight said. "We'll do the readout after Lagunas returns. Ah, there she is now."

Another time bubble formed. When it bulged and dissipated, Lagunas stood and moved to McKnight. The smile she wore encouraged him.

"Objectives one and three accomplished, sir. Al-Zawahiri is dead and your father survived the attack. He got a scratch from shrapnel in the blast, but otherwise he is unhurt."

"So he was alive when you left him?"

"Yes, sir. Very much so. And he looks like you, sir. We're all looking forward to meeting him."

"What?"

"You have your father's eyes, sir," she said.

"All right, everyone," Kathy called out. "We need to get the readout from your implant and you need to record your personal report. Let's do that and then meet in the large conference room for the readout." She looked around. "Okay, let's start with you, Daze."

"Yes, ma'am." Lagunas saluted McKnight and walked over to Kathy for the implant reading.

McKnight saw another memory pass through his mind. This time, his father was with him at his college graduation. Next, he saw his father talking to him before he left for his first tour in the Mideast.

Why do I have this feeling of dread?

He watched as the five members of the mission team lined up for Kathy to read their implants. When they were all completed, they headed for the conference room.

McKnight walked over to Kathy.

"Do you think we stopped the plague?" he asked.

"I don't know," she said. "It should take a while for the change wave to get here. Why don't you check on Rachel, if she's still here? Better yet, why don't you go see her? That's the best way to find out."

"You're right," he said. "Do me a favor and call Major Souther at the Iceberg and confirm Rachel is back. If she isn't, then we have bigger problems. But if she is, let her know I'll be coming to see Rachel."

"Sure, Marc, I can do that." She turned and headed for her office.

"Thanks, Kathy," he said to her back.

His phone pinged, and he looked at it.

A text from Megan.

He read it and said, "Call Megan."

His speed dial called her, and seconds later she was on the line.

"Hey, Babe. You pinged me?"

"Yes, I did," she said. "Is your mission over?"

"It is. We have to do the paperwork to wrap it up."

"That's good." She paused. "Janie called again."

"She did?"

"Yes. She wants you to call her as soon as possible."

"Okay. Do you know why?"

"She didn't say, and I didn't ask. She seemed a little upset."

"Okay, I'll call her right away. If it's anything critical, I'll call you back and let you know."

When he disconnected the call, another memory surfaced. It explained the dread he felt.

Colon cancer.

More memories without Dad now, but they were different. They were adult memories.

He walked over to a corner of the lab, dialed Janie, and she answered on the third ring.

"Hi, Marc," she said.

"Hey, Janie. What's up? Are you okay?"

"Yes, I'm fine. Mom called me."

"She did?"

"Yes, she did. She wanted to let me know it was okay that we didn't make the memorial service. I guess you'll get a call from her, too."

"Dad died from colon cancer."

"I know. I was there, remember? Anyway, she knew I would lose this role if I came home. And you're in the middle of a big investigation. But all of her friends were there to comfort her. Then again, I'll bet they asked her a million times why we weren't there."

Another memory almost slipped past him.

"He died this past summer."

"*Yes.* What's up with you? You act like you just found out about it. You were there, for goodness' sake."

McKnight felt numb.

I was there.

"Yes, of course," he said. "I just got back from a mission. You know how stressful that can be. I was just confused, that's all."

"Well, shake it off. I just wanted to warn you that you'll get a call from Mom. She must be feeling lonely. Is there any chance you can get out to see her soon?"

"Not now, but I'll work out something as soon as I can."

"Okay, glad to hear it. It'll be a few weeks before I can get there. Oh, gotta run, I'm having breakfast with my agent and she has some questions for me."

"Sure thing, Sis. Have a good day."

"I will. Bye," she said, and hung up before he could speak.

McKnight stood there, looking at the phone.

After all we went through, I still lost Dad. I didn't even get to say goodbye.

Even as he thought it, he knew it wasn't true. He was there in Oregon by Dad's side when he passed.

It never occurred to me that something else might happen to him.

He looked over his shoulder for the team. They had already left the area.

Good.

He needed to get control over his emotions before he talked to the team again. He crossed his arms and leaned against the wall, fighting back the tears that threatened to come.

How can I tell them, after all they went through today?

He sighed. He'd tell them the truth. It was always the best course. He pushed himself off the wall and headed for the conference room. He'd reassure them and get back on track.

The briefing went smoothly. The team went over the mission and their reports. Everyone's performance was top notch.

After adjournment, he went back to his office, sat, and put his feet up on the credenza. He used the remote to turn the wall's status to transparent and stared out the window.

One thing said at the meeting stuck with him.

Who said it? Smalls, I think. He said at least I have some fresh memories I didn't have before. That was something, wasn't it?

McKnight took comfort in this and let the new memories flood his mind. He wondered how he would ever explain to Megan how this felt.

There was a knock at his door. He didn't want to answer it, but couldn't think of a good excuse not to. He kicked off the credenza and slipped his legs under the desk.

"Come," he said.

Cutty stuck his head in the door. "Do you have a minute, sir?"

"Sure. Sit down."

"I'd rather stand, sir," he said as he came to attention. He executed the most perfect salute McKnight had ever seen.

"Very well. At ease, then."

Cutty snapped to position and stood shock still.

"What's on your mind, Lieutenant? Speak up."

"Thank you, sir. I'd like another chance to show you what I can do."

"I don't know that it's needed," McKnight said. "Why do *you* think it's needed?"

"I missed the target, sir. I can't say it any plainer than that. I mean, I hit him, but he got back up and posed a threat to Lieutenant Lagunas."

"I see," McKnight said. He came around to the front of the desk and leaned against it.

"So you believe you failed?"

"Yes, sir."

"What did Captain Hatcher say?"

"She told me it was okay, sir. But I know she was trying to make me feel better."

"You don't know Captain Hatcher very well yet, do you?"

"Well, no, sir. I—"

"I can tell you without a doubt that, if you screwed the pooch, she'd be the first person to explain it to you—"

"Yes, sir, but—"

"I'm not finished, Lieutenant. Can I finish my sentence, please?"

"Yes, sir!" Cutty said. His face grew red. "Sorry, sir."

"Did you notice I was in the readout with you, soldier?"

"Yes, sir."

"Who was primary for the target?"

"Me, sir."

"Correct. And who was secondary?"

"Lieutenant Lagunas, sir."

"Correct again. And why do we have a primary and a secondary?"

"Sir?"

"Don't disappoint me, Cutty. Spit it out."

"We have a primary to take out the target. The secondary comes into play if the primary doesn't perform as expected."

McKnight paused. *Am I taking out my disappointment on this poor lieutenant?*

"Close. We have a secondary in case something or someone prevents the primary from performing as expected. In this case, we had the video from your scope, didn't we?"

"Yes, sir."

"And Captain Hatcher played it at our meeting. You had the crosshairs on the target and he jogged left when you pulled the trigger.

No way you could have predicted or expected that. And Lagunas reported he had blood streaming down the side of his face. That didn't come from road rash. You didn't miss him. Am I right?"

"I guess so, sir."

"You *guess so*?"

"I'm sorry, sir. Of course, you're right. I just… I just wanted my first mission here to be perfect."

McKnight chuckled. "Well, Lieutenant, if I ever experience a perfect mission, you'll be the first to know."

"Yes, sir."

"Lieutenant, are you familiar with Field Marshal Helmuth von Moltke?"

Cutty looked perplexed. "No, sir."

"He lived in the 1800s and is credited with the following quote. He said, 'No plan of operations extends with certainty beyond the first encounter with the enemy's main strength.' Today, we say something like 'No battle plan survives first contact with the enemy.' You followed the plan, Lieutenant, but we can't control the world. Things happen outside our control. That's why we adapt, improvise and overcome."

"Yes, sir."

"The bottom line is, you follow the plans, but always keep an eye out for that one thing we didn't plan for and be ready to respond to it. Make sense?"

"Yes, sir."

"Good. If there's nothing else on your mind, you're dismissed."

Cutty snapped to attention and saluted. When McKnight returned it, he turned to leave.

"And, Lieutenant Cutty…?"

"Yes, sir?"

"Don't worry. You'll get more chances here to prove yourself than you'll want, and not all of them will be about performance with your weapons."

"Yes, sir," Cutty said, and closed the door behind him.

McKnight turned back to the credenza and the trees outside.

His phone pinged again. It was a message from Kathy.

> <<< *Wu: Talked to Souther. Rachel is in custody at*
> *Iceberg. When do you want to see her?* >>>

So at least we didn't screw it up worse. Going to see her is the logical next step.

He needed to confirm with Rachel that the virus was not as big a danger as it was on the previous timeline. But he didn't want to see her. He needed answers, and he didn't have time to play mind games with her.

Wait a minute. I'm looking at this wrong.

He sent an answer to Kathy.

> <<< *McK: Thanks, Kathy. I'll take it from here. I'll*
> *schedule it.* >>>

He sent a text to Hatcher.

> <<< *McK: Hatcher, come see me when you have a*
> *minute.* >>>

That should do it. Rachel fears Hatcher and Hatcher won't put up with any crap from her.

CHAPTER FORTY-SIX

Saturday, January 3rd, 2037 - 10:12 AM EST - McKnight's office, Telegraph Road, Alexandria, Virginia

Someone knocked on McKnight's office door.

"Come," he said.

Hatcher entered the room, came to attention, and saluted. "You wanted to see me, sir?"

Still seated, McKnight returned the salute and said, "As you were, Captain." He pointed at one of the guest chairs.

Hatcher sat and leaned back in the chair.

"I want you to go to the Iceberg and talk to Rachel Patterson."

"Sir?"

"Since she is back at the Iceberg, we know the plague hasn't wiped out the future population. What we need to know now is whether it's even on her radar before we captured her."

"I see. She tried to stop it by killing the CDC scientist who developed the virus, and now we've tried to stop it by taking out the terrorist who romanced her and secured the virus for the Iranians. So we need to confirm with her that, in 2086, it isn't an oncoming threat."

"Exactly."

"Permission to speak freely, sir?"

"Of course."

"Thank you. Why me, sir? We know she doesn't like me. It hasn't been long since I popped her one. I doubt she's forgotten that."

"I daresay she hasn't," he said. "Let me share my logic in picking you for this. First, you and I are the ones who know her best. While the quality of our relationships isn't good, we're familiar enough to know how to dance with her."

"Yes, sir, I agree with that."

"Second, her thoughts about me are…. unstable. The last two times I saw her, she wanted or tried to kill me. She gets emotional and somewhat incoherent around me. I think I would have a lot of problems getting her to focus."

"That's true, too, sir," Hatcher said. "But she's probably still pissed at me."

"Granted. But you've known her longer and she will still remember all the times she worked on you during your captivity. And there's always the aspect of her thinking she might still control you."

"She has no power over me, sir," Hatcher said. "I believe I've proved that beyond any doubt."

"I know that, Captain." McKnight looked her in the eye. "There's no question in my mind. But *she* might think there's a chance of getting to you, and that's why you're a better fit to go talk to her. Remember how bright she is. She might show her anger, but then logic will kick in and she'll want to be on your side. Use that."

"Yes, sir. Okay. Then, should I just ask her about the plague and see what she says?"

"Yes, I think so. Mention we know about a plague from the Mideast in her time and ask her if it's a concern?"

"Yes, sir. When should I go? Today?"

"Yes, the sooner the better."

"Yes, sir. Should I fly out?"

"I don't see why. Do a non-time jump to the Iceberg. Let them know you're coming, and get permission to jump right into her cell."

"Yes, sir." Hatcher rose to leave.

"And, Captain?"

"Yes, sir?"

"You told me she has cancer. I don't know if she's been told. Find out from Major Souther. If you think it will help in the interview, use it. I don't know if it will help, but it might. Use your best judgment. Understood?"

"Yes, sir." Hatcher saluted and left the room.

McKnight turned around in his chair and put his feet up on the credenza. With the remote, he turned the wall setting to transparent. When the wall changed, the outside world streamed in. Sunlight. Blue sky. The woods behind the Telegraph Road office.

If Rachel thinks the plague is not important or doesn't know about it, then we've done our job. It's a good way to finish out the project and start a new year.

Saturday, January 3rd, 2037 - 2:45 PM PST - Iceberg Detention Center, Rachel, Nevada

The Operative slipped down the staircase to the detention level. There was no one near to witness her intrusion, but the combat uniform she wore made her appear to be just another GI, doing their job.

She approached Rachel's cell.

Over the last eight hours, she dealt with traffic around Rachel's cell. She needed five minutes alone with Rachel's guard to get access, but traffic prevented it.

The traffic subsided during the last twenty minutes, and she made her move.

The last two times I walked by, her guard looked me up and down.

It was something she could use.

The man smiled as she approached him with a pen in hand and her clipboard.

She smiled back. When she got close, she spoke. "Hi. I need to see your prisoner."

He stiffened, and said, "I'm sorry, ma'am, but no one is allowed to see her." The rifle he held before him moved to block her.

"Oh, they'll make an exception for me. Here are my orders."

She handed him the clipboard. He let go of the rifle to take it. When he did, she drew and pressed her weapon to his neck so fast he had no time to react.

She moved close enough to him to whisper in his ear. "Move a hair and I'll kill you. Nod once if you understand."

The soldier glared at her for an instant, but the look on her face convinced him. His expression turned to fear, and he nodded once.

"Good." She grasped his rifle with her other hand. "Let go of it."

He did, and she leaned it against the wall.

"Now, open the door."

The guard hesitated.

She pushed the pistol harder against his neck. "Don't try me, soldier. I'm not a patient person."

"Okay," he said with a gasp. "Let me key in the code on the console."

"Tell me the code."

"033053," he said, and she watched him type it in.

"Careful. Your next actions could be your last if you screw around with me."

He nodded. He pressed the return key, and the door hissed open.

She pushed the weapon harder against his neck. "Go inside."

She reached back for his weapon and the pressure of the weapon on his neck lessened. The soldier whirled and swung his fist at her. She ducked, then slammed her weapon into his groin. He doubled over and she hit him in the face with the pistol with all her strength. He went down. She grabbed his collar and drug him into the cell.

"You!"

The Operative turned in the voice's direction.

Rachel stood there, her fists clenched by her sides.

"I'll be with you in a minute, Major," the Operative said. She inspected the damage caused by the pistol butt. The soldier's nose bled and both eye sockets were bruised and turning purple.

He'll have a concussion at least. Maybe brain damage.

She searched the soldier's belt and pockets.

He's a guard. He must have restraints.

She rolled him over and found what she needed. Handcuffs. She pulled his arms up behind him and cuffed him. Then she stood and turned toward Rachel. She did a quick assessment of the prisoner before her.

Major Rachel Patterson, Federal Time Services. Ambulatory. Bandage over nose.

Rachel stared at her. Her face was a mask of anger, but it turned to confusion, then curiosity. She moved behind the sofa.

She's placing an obstacle between us.

"Major Patterson," the Operative said.

"You aren't Hatcher," Rachel said.

Why would she say that?

"No."

"Who are you?"

"I'm known as 638. I've been engaged to find and return you to 2086."

"By whom? Where is Number Four?"

"He's in a cell down the hall. He's irrelevant. My engagement only applies to you."

Rachel looked thoughtful. "Who engaged you?"

"Someone who wants you. I'm authorized to find and return you to your benefactor."

"My benefactor? Wow. It's nice to have friends." Rachel stayed behind the sofa. "How do I know I'll live through the first meeting with this... benefactor?"

I did not consider that.

"I don't know. I am only charged with getting you back to 2086 safely."

"Safely? That sounds better than this..." Rachel spread her arms to indicate the cell.

The Operative said nothing.

Rachel came out from behind the sofa.

"You're an Operative, aren't you?"

638 stared at Rachel, but said nothing.

Rachel smiled. "I'll take that as a yes." Her smile got bigger. "If anyone can get me out of here, it's you."

The Operative pointed at her. "Are you injured, Major? Can you travel?"

"I'm more than healthy," Rachel said. "You resemble someone I know. A Lieutenant Hatcher from the HERO Team. Do you know who she is?"

"I have the records for the Federal Time Services team and its predecessor, the HERO Team. Hatcher was a member of the HERO Team."

"*Is* a member now, 638. In this time, she *is* a member of the HERO Team. Remember that."

The Operative didn't respond. There was no need to.

Rachel nodded. "You look like her. Or maybe her in ten years. Were you aware of that?"

"I am, now."

Could she be my donor?

"And what about you, 638? How is your health? What are your assets and what are your plans?"

Damaged. I should say damaged.

"I am... less than optimal," she said. "The personal shield damaged my biological state, but I am capable of fulfilling my mission. I can take you back to 2086."

"The personal shield? They gave you one to use? I used it once before. It's not safe. How much have you used it?"

"Quite a bit, but not more than necessary."

What's that? Static electricity?

The Operative looked down. The hair on her arm was standing up.

"Someone is jumping in," Rachel said. She moved to stand by the Operative.

The static electricity emanated from across the room. A time bubble formed.

The Operative drew her sidearm and pointed it at the bubble.

CHAPTER FORTY-SEVEN

Hatcher sat at her desk, making notes for the mission. She wanted to ensure she knew her talking points before she interviewed Rachel Patterson.

Oh, almost forgot to call Major Souther.

She looked up the number and called it.

"Major Souther, how can I help you?" said a familiar voice.

"Major, this is Karen Hatcher from Colonel McKnight's team? We met a few days ago?"

"Of course, Captain. What can I do for you?"

"Thanks, ma'am. I need to interview Rachel Patterson today. Can we work that into the schedule?"

"I think so. What time would you like to see her?"

Hatcher glanced at her watch.

I have a briefing for another mission at oh-sixteen-hundred.

"How about 5:45 PM my time? That would be 2:45 your time?"

"I have a planning meeting at two," Souther said. "But it should be over by then. I'm presuming that you're going to 'jump' in?"

"Yes, ma'am."

"Do you want to meet me at reception?"

"No, if it's all the same to you, ma'am, I'd like to jump into her cell. She doesn't like me, but she has reason to fear me. I'm hoping to use that as an advantage. You know, hoping she'll give up more before she catches her breath?"

"I see." Souther paused. "I'd like to be there, too."

"I get that, ma'am."

Hatcher let Souther think about it.

"You're not planning any violence against her?" Souther asked.

"No, ma'am. Not at all. I just want to catch her off guard."

"Okay, Hatcher. I'm going to trust you on this. I'll let the duty guard know you're coming, and I'll meet you there as soon as I finish my meeting. You have the coordinates you need?"

"Yes, ma'am, I do. One more thing… Does Rachel know she has cancer?"

"Yes, she does."

"How did she take it?"

"Well, she wasn't happy about it, but she isn't crying about it, either. She'll get good care from us and we'll whip it if we can."

"Okay, very good. Thank you, Major," Hatcher said, and ended the call.

She spent the next two hours thinking about her approach to Rachel, then she called Kathy to get the jump set up.

At the appointed time, she went to the lab. Kathy had everything ready. After the usual checklist, beacon setup, and countdown, the globe of spinning light formed around her and she was on her way to the Iceberg.

She fell through the field of stars and, with an effort, held her body in the kneeling position.

The globe formed, and she sensed the room outside the time bubble. She thought she could see two figures.

Am I seeing an illusion? Rachel should be alone.

Reminding herself that no visual distortions had happened before, she drew the logical conclusion.

Souther must be here already.

As the bubble became more defined, she could identify which figure was Rachel. The other figure was too tall to be Souther and her hair was dark.

The bubble surged to twice its size and disappeared. Hatcher felt the familiar tug backward, but maintained her kneeling position. When the tug stopped, she stood.

A woman stood there, pointing a weapon at her. It was like looking into a mirror.

"Don't move," the woman said.

"I'm unarmed," Hatcher said.

"Ha!" Rachel said. "She's never unarmed."

"Unless I jump into a detention center."

"Don't talk unless I ask you a question," the Doppelganger said. "Who are you?"

"I would ask you the same question. You're the one who's not supposed to be here."

The woman hesitated, then her face flushed red.

"Understand and be aware of your situation, clone. What's your number?" the woman said..

"My number? You mean my service number?" Hatcher asked.

Rachel smiled. "Now I get it." She turned toward the woman.

"This is Captain Karen Hatcher from the HERO Team. She is most likely your donor."

The woman glanced at Rachel for an instance, then poked the air toward Hatcher with her weapon. "I said, don't move."

Hatcher didn't understand.

Donor?

"If you want to get us out of here," Rachel pointed at Hatcher, "her time beacon is our best option. I recommend you kill her and let's get out of here."

She called me a clone. Does she think I'm a clone of her?

"Who are you?" Hatcher asked.

"She's an Operative from 2086, Captain," Rachel said. "You don't know who you're messing with."

"A what?" Hatcher said.

"I am 638," the woman said. "I am here to bring Major Patterson home. I have no orders that relate to you."

"What is an Operative?" Hatcher said.

Rachel stepped toward the woman. "We're wasting time here. Kill her, take her beacon, and we're out of here."

"Silence," the woman said, and glanced at Rachel, but her attention remained fixed on Hatcher.

"Have you given blood for a project, Captain?" the Operative asked.

"What?"

"When was the last time you gave blood or a skin sample?"

"I don't know what you're talking about," Hatcher said.

"Kill her!" Rachel hissed. "They'll get it from her posthumously."

"Silence!" the woman said, and gave Rachel a withering look.

Hatcher understood.

Rachel's trying to take control.

The woman motioned to Hatcher. "Lie down on the floor face down. Put your hands behind your back."

Hatcher didn't move. She was figuring it out.

"I'm your donor. They cloned you from me."

The woman nodded. "I believe that to be an accurate statement."

"If you kill me before I donate blood, and believe me, I haven't — you don't exist."

"I'm aware of that fact. I'm not opposed to trading nonexistence for completing my mission. Lie on the floor, or I *will* kill you. Please have no illusions about that."

"What's your name? 638? Look, 638 or whatever your name is... I won't lie down and let you kill me like an injured horse. If you plan to kill me, you'll have to take me straight on. I plan to die in battle."

The woman smiled.

"You *are* my donor. I no longer have any doubt." She turned to Rachel. "Major Patterson, what is your plan? I have my beacon to return us to 2086. Why do we need hers? What happens next?"

Rachel took a step toward the woman.

"Easy," she said. "We press her beacon to do a recall. It takes us back to home base, which for Hatcher is the lab at Telegraph Road in Virginia. From there, I can program their Engine to take us back to 2086."

"What about my beacon?" the woman said. "Won't it take us back to 2086?"

"Yes," Rachel said. "But I need to go first to the HERO lab to finish *my* mission."

"And what is that mission?"

Rachel paused, then said, "I'm not authorized to tell you, but it's critical we go there first." She paused again. "Please."

"Unacceptable," the Operative said. "It is contrary to my mission."

"I want to go there first," Rachel said. "If we don't, I won't cooperate with the benefactor, and that will render your mission meaningless and therefore a waste of time and money."

"I don't think your benefactor would be amused," 638 said.

"I don't care. I'd rather die than pass up the chance to complete my mission."

"I expect that death *will be* your fate if you don't cooperate."

Rachel nodded. "I understand that. It's your choice."

The Operative glanced at Rachel, then back at Hatcher. "Major Patterson, I will follow your lead on this unless or until it endangers my mission, but beware. I reserve the right to override your desires. Is that clear?"

"Yes," Rachel said. "It won't affect your mission."

"Very well. Back to her beacon. Do I have to kill her to get it? Is it an implant?"

Hatcher moved her hand to her neck.

The Operative waved her weapon at Hatcher. "Careful, Captain."

"I'm trying to show you my beacon." Hatcher said.

The Operative nodded. "Slowly."

Hatcher pulled on the chain at her neck. The beacon flopped out of her uniform blouse and hung between her breasts.

"You see?" Rachel said, pointing at Hatcher.

"I do. Captain Hatcher, I have no reason to kill you. I need your beacon for Major Patterson and myself. If you resist, I will kill you, and Major Patterson will have your beacon, anyway. If I kill you, I won't exist. My mission is paramount. If I fail, I am nothing and no longer valuable. So it's to our mutual advantage for you to give me the beacon."

I don't have a choice. But I feel a... sense of honor coming from her.

Hatcher laid on the floor and put her hands behind her back.

"Major Patterson," the Operative said, "please confirm the guard is still unconscious and remove the handcuffs. Here..." She pulled the key from her pocket and tossed it to Rachel.

She approached Hatcher warily and pressed her weapon's muzzle against Hatcher's ear.

"Please don't move."

Rachel returned with the handcuffs.

"Is he still alive?" the Operative said.

"Yes, he is. And still unconscious."

"Good. Put the handcuffs on Captain Hatcher."

Rachel jerked Hatcher's hands closer together and applied the handcuffs.

"Gently," the Operative said. "This is my donor, and you must respect her. Now, take the beacon."

Rachel grasped the chain and slipped it over Hatcher's head and pulled it to her chest.

A loud ding sounded. Souther's voice came through the intercom.

"Major Patterson, I can see you through the monitor. Lay down your weapon. We are coming in. Do not resist or we'll use deadly force. Do not resist!"

"We have to go now," Rachel said, and pulled the Operative toward the center of the room. She pressed the beacon twice and dragged the Operative down into a kneeling position with her. The time bubble formed, and the air inside lit up and spun.

Hatcher turned her face toward the two women.

"Rachel!" she called out.

Rachel turned toward her.

"What about the plague from the Mideast?" she yelled.

The door hissed open and a soldier in battle dress rolled in and came up to one knee, training his weapon on the bubble. A second soldier entered before he stopped moving.

"Don't shoot!" Hatcher yelled. "Don't shoot!"

She looked back at the bubble.

Rachel was staring at her.

"What plague?" Rachel asked.

The roaring of the brilliant lights in the bubble nearly drowned out her voice.

"What plague?" Rachel yelled.

The bubble bulged to twice its size, and the two women disappeared.

Souther entered and ran with the soldiers to Hatcher.

"Call the Colonel," Hatcher said. "Get these things off me. Call him now. Try to warn him."

It's already too late.

CHAPTER FORTY-EIGHT

Saturday, January 3rd, 2037 - 6:04 PM EST - McKnight's Office, Telegraph Road, Alexandria, Virginia

McKnight was in his office, talking to Megan on the phone.

"Hi, babe. I was just thinking about you. Thought I'd call. I won't be much longer."

"Who all is there?" she asked.

"Just me, Trevor, and Kathy. I'm waiting for Hatcher to get back from an interview, and Trevor and Kathy are here to support. Well, Kathy is. Trevor is just here because she is."

Megan laughed. "They're quite a pair, aren't they?"

"They are. They're such a great team here in the office. It's nice they also have a good thing going together. Office relationships aren't so easy to do, but they pull it off."

"Where's everyone else?"

"Gone for the weekend. I think Wheeler and Smalls went for a beer."

"Or two."

"Or two." McKnight laughed.

His phone dinged, and he checked for the reason.

"Oh, gotta go. Hatcher is arriving. See you in a little while. I'll call when I leave the office."

"Love you."

"You, too."

He disconnected the call, slipped his phone into his pocket, and left his office.

He ran into Kathy and Trevor in the hall, and together they walked to the lab. McKnight pressed his access disk against the lock and heard the click as it disengaged.

The time globe formed, and they could see two forms inside. They hurried to the platform.

Kathy turned to McKnight. "Hatcher wasn't supposed to bring Rachel back here, was she?"

"No, she wasn't. Something's not right."

The time bubble bulged and dissipated, leaving the room darker by comparison.

It was Hatcher and Rachel. And Hatcher was pointing a weapon at them.

McKnight, Trevor, and Kathy started forward.

"That's close enough," Hatcher said.

What the hell? Did Rachel get control of Hatcher again?

"Don't try to stop us," Rachel said. "We're just here to use the Engine."

She stopped and smiled. "We'll be out of your way in a few minutes." Then she busied herself with programming the Engine.

Kathy leaned toward McKnight. "She looks older."

He glanced at her. "What?"

"Hatcher," she said. "She looks older to me. Years older."

McKnight looked back at Hatcher. Kathy was right.

Has she somehow been gone for ten years? How could that be, with the twenty-five-year limit on time travel?

"Captain Hatcher, report."

Hatcher's face wore no expression. She looked at him as if she was seeing him for the first time. The weapon in her hand didn't waver.

"You're Colonel McKnight, Doctor Wu, and Trevor George," she said.

If she's Hatcher, she's lost it. Why is she helping Rachel escape?

Almost as if she heard his thoughts, the woman responded.

"I am not your Captain Hatcher. She is alive and waiting at the place they call the Iceberg."

What the hell?

"Is she injured?" McKnight asked.

"She was uninjured when we left her."

"Who are you?" Kathy asked. "How come you look like Hatcher?"

The woman shrugged.

"What's your name?" Trevor said.

"Irrelevant," she said. "It would mean nothing to you in this time period."

"Try me," he said.

Rachel looked up from the console. "She is 638, Trevor. She's an Operative."

"Operative? What does that mean?"

The Operative threw a menacing look at Rachel.

"She is a clone of Hatcher. That's why she looks so much like her. Operatives are problem solvers for the wealthy and connected people in my time. They are expensive, but they—"

"Major Patterson!" the Operative said. "Stop talking about me. It's... inappropriate."

Rachel paused.

Rachel's afraid of her. She's not in charge.

McKnight looked again at the Operative.

This woman is in charge. She's allowing Rachel to do whatever she plans to do.

Rachel glanced back at the console. "All done. I programmed it to return us to 2086."

Kathy spoke up again. "You shouldn't do this. You won't get the results you want."

The Operative looked at Kathy, then at Rachel. "What does she mean?"

"Nothing," Rachel said. "She's just trying to trick us."

The Operative looked skeptical, but she let it go. The gun she held never wavered. Every few seconds she switched her aim between McKnight, Kathy, and Trevor.

Rachel placed both hands on the console and leaned forward.

"Marc?" she said, and waited for him to focus on her.

"Come with us. Come with *me*."

McKnight shook his head. "I'm good right here, thanks."

"We can begin again. That Southern princess of yours doesn't deserve you. On the other hand, I appreciate you and what you know how to do and what you'll become. Come with me and we'll chart new history."

McKnight shook his head again. "Sorry, Rachel, but we're not a good match."

"Time to go," the Operative said.

Rachel looked at her. "No! He's mine. He's reluctant because he doesn't know you."

The Operative looked at McKnight, then back at Rachel.

"No, it's clear he doesn't want to. It's time to go."

Rachel stared at the Operative with an expression of disbelief. She looked at McKnight and her face reflected sadness.

"We could have been great together," Rachel said.

As McKnight watched, her face contorted with rage.

She tugged at the Operative's arm. "Kill him."

The Operative shook her head. "There's no logical reason to do so. Killing him would affect the future, would it not? My engagement is to retrieve you and return you to your benefactor. Time to go."

"I'm not leaving until he is dead. Kill him."

"No. It's time to retreat."

Rachel looked back and forth between McKnight and the Operative. She grabbed at the Operative's gun hand. McKnight and Trevor sprang forward.

The Operative elbowed Rachel in the face, square on the bandage on her nose. She was stunned and swayed where she stood. The

Operative shrugged off her grasp and pointed the weapon at McKnight and Trevor again.

They stopped in their tracks.

She motioned with the pistol for them to retreat. Then she turned to Rachel and said, "Major Patterson, it's time to go. If you delay any longer, I will engage my beacon and drag you back to your benefactor."

Rachel recovered enough from the blow to understand she lost that battle.

"Okay, we'll go," she said. "But let's travel with *this* Engine. I want to go back to FTS — to *my* lab — first. I want to get some things."

She plugged in the Engine trigger and beckoned the Operative to follow her to the platform.

McKnight, Trevor, and Kathy backed away.

The Operative joined Rachel on the Engine platform, the weapon in her hand never wavering, still pointing at McKnight, Trevor, and Kathy.

Rachel pressed the Engine trigger and the time bubble formed around them. She tossed the trigger onto the console. The air inside the bubble ignited and spun. Their hair flew in all directions at once as the light and spinning air intensified.

We can't let them get away.

McKnight ran through the options in his head. He decided to pursue them.

Rachel touched the Operative's hand. She motioned they should kneel for the jump. Together, they knelt, but the Operative never lowered her weapon.

The bubble bulged, and the two women were gone with a bang.

McKnight turned and sprinted for the weapons locker. Over his shoulder, he called out, "Kathy, get the Engine ready to send me to the same location."

Kathy took three steps after him and said, "Marc, where are you going?"

"What? I'm going after them, of course."

"And you need a weapon because…?"

"Are you kidding? They're going to the FTS Lab… Rachel's lab… where her team is. I'm not jumping into that place without a weapon."

"How do you know where they went?"

"She told us. She…" he stopped, looking at her face.

Kathy was smiling at him.

"Okay, what is it about this that I don't know?"

"That's the right question," Kathy said. "After your adventure with the time eddy, Doctor Astalos and I were trying to think of something useful to do with it. We came up with the idea that we could change the jump software so that unauthorized users could not use it. So, if you engage the normal jump program and program it to go wherever, it will ignore the programming and send you—"

"To the time eddy? That's brilliant. So how do we get them back?"

"Well, sending them to the time eddy was my idea. But Mr. Smalls had a better idea."

"Smalls?" McKnight asked. "What did he suggest?"

Kathy giggled into her hand. "It was brilliant, really. I wish I had thought of it myself. *I* came up with the idea to neutralize any beacon within ten feet of the one they carried. But his idea was perfect. But then again, I didn't know what he knew. So it was only natural that he was the one to—"

"Kathy!" McKnight said. "Tell me the story later. Where did they go?"

"So Mr. Smalls thought of his friend Major Souther, and we called her, and she liked the idea, so that's where they are. Now we need to call to make sure she has them."

"You mean, they're—?"

"Yes. Our friends just jumped into Cell 20 at the Iceberg."

Saturday, January 3rd, 2037 - 3:14 PM PST - Control Room, Iceberg Detention Center, Rachel Nevada

Hatcher and Souther hurried to the Control Room as soon as they freed Hatcher from the guard's handcuffs. As they arrived, an alarm went off.

"What's that?" Souther said.

"It's the alarm provided by Doctor Wu, ma'am," the duty officer said. "We hooked it into our alarm system. It means someone is time-jumping into Cell 20 as you arranged."

"Damn. Was she right or what?"

"What?" Hatcher said.

"Your Doctor Wu put in an emergency capture system in case an unauthorized person got control of your Engine. We got the alarm and countermeasures installed a couple of days ago. If a bad guy uses your Engine, all the programming is ignored, and they get sent here — no passing Go, and no $200. Into a cell. Brilliant."

"Sounds like Kathy," Hatcher said. "What now?"

"Ma'am," the duty officer said. "Looks like we have two women arriving."

"Put cell 20 on the monitor, Lieutenant."

The duty officer turned a dial to select the cell and flipped a switch to activate the monitor. They saw the Operative and Rachel looking around and speaking. The audio feed was turned off.

"Looks like our runaways, Hatcher."

"Yes, ma'am, it does. And they don't look happy."

"What do we do next, you asked, Hatcher? Great question." Souther turned to the duty officer. "Let's give them a nice nap. Lieutenant, turn on the gas."

"Yes, ma'am."

"Hatcher, you're with me. We're going down to Cell 20 and see how they're doing."

Before they could leave the room, the outside phone line rang. The duty officer listened for a second and turned to Souther.

"Major, it's Doctor Wu for you."

Souther returned to the console and took the phone.

"Doctor Wu?" she said.

A pause.

"Yes, we have them. We are sedating them now and.... Sure, we will... Give Colonel McKnight my regards."

She glanced at Hatcher.

"Yes, and tell him Captain Hatcher doesn't have a beacon and needs a ride home. Unless you want her to take a plane from Las Vegas... Yes... Thanks. Goodbye."

"Someone will come for you soon, Captain," Souther said. "Let's go check on our girls."

Saturday, January 3rd, 2037 - 3:15 PM PST - Cell 20, Iceberg Detention Center, Rachel, Nevada

After the field of stars, the Operative and Rachel landed in Cell 20. The Operative was the first to understand.

"What went wrong?" she said.

"What do you mean?" Rachel asked.

The Operative pointed outward. The bubble bulged and dissipated.

"No!" Rachel said. "They tricked me."

"Is this your cell?"

"No, it isn't, but it's identical. We're in the Iceberg in a different cell."

"What do we do now? Will my beacon still work?"

"Yes!" Rachel said, and moved close to her. "Try it now!"

The Operative pulled out her beacon and squeezed it. Nothing happened.

"Let me do it," Rachel said. She grabbed the beacon and squeezed it multiple times.

"Damn it. They disabled it somehow." Rachel looked for something to throw, but there was nothing in the cell but the Operative and herself. She screamed with rage.

"Not helpful. We should have used my beacon from your cell. We'd be in 2086 and on our way."

"Shut up!" Rachel said.

The Operative felt weak. But it didn't feel like the weariness she felt after using the shield.

She looked around and sniffed the air. She detected air moving in the cell that hadn't been there before. "We're being gassed."

She looked at Rachel, but her vision grew blurred and dim. Rachel was moving around.

No, staggering around was more accurate.

Her vision worsened. She had a sense of falling. She remembered nothing after that.

Saturday, January 3rd, 2037 - 6:30 PM EST - McKnight's Office, Telegraph Road, Alexandria, Virginia

McKnight went back to his office and called Major Souther at the Iceberg. It took a minute to locate her and patch him through to her phone outside Cell 20.

"Major, do you have our two fugitives? How are they doing?"

"Hello, Colonel. Yes, we have them. They're right here in Cell 20, fast asleep."

"Are they okay?"

"As far as we know, yes, they're fine," Souther said.

"Good. What's the next step?"

"We separate them and give them both a thorough medical checkup. Then we'll interview them."

"Thanks. What do you know about the one who calls herself 638? Who is she?"

"No clue at this point. But I reviewed the security video feed. She severely injured one of my people, and she fits the description of a fugitive from Las Vegas who killed a man at the airport and two deputy sheriffs in Rachel, Nevada. Chances are, she's the same person. The circumstantial evidence is piling up. And I want to find out how she defeated our security and broke in. That can't happen again. The local authorities will want her, but we still have questions for her. What do you say?"

McKnight thought for a second. In all the excitement, he forgot about the visit from Agent David Ritter.

If 638 is a clone of Hatcher, it explains why Hatcher's fingerprints showed up in Nevada at the scene of three murders.

"I think we need to keep it quiet and sit on her for now. Her prints are the same as Hatcher's, so the FBI came here, looking for answers."

"Oh, no."

"Yeah. It's all good, though. We'll work with the FBI on this one to get Hatcher cleared. They'll want to interview her."

"Sure, we can arrange that. Not here, though. Too many people already know about my little place in the desert. Maybe we can jump her to your facility for the interview?"

"I don't see why we can't do that. Works for me. Here's the bottom line... She's a time traveler and dangerous. If we put her in local custody, we'll never get to ask her any more questions. More to the point, if she can get in and out of your place, I doubt any civilian jail is going to hold her for long. It's better you hang onto her there. You know how talented she is and won't underestimate her."

"Yes, I thought you might say that. Okay. We'll add her to our guest list for now. You'll report it to General Drake and get him to square it with my command chain?"

"Absolutely. Consider it done."

"Very good. Now, how are we going to get Captain Hatcher back to you? She says she's here without a beacon."

"Easy. Can I meet you two in your reception area in ten minutes?"

"Sounds like a plan, Colonel. See you then."

CHAPTER FORTY-NINE

After the time bubble dissipated, McKnight stood and walked toward Souther and Hatcher. The two women came to attention and saluted him. He returned it and said, "As you were."

"It's nice to see you again, Colonel," Souther said.

"The feeling is mutual, Sheila. It's good to see you, too. Thanks for all you've done for us."

"No problem, sir. And I'll reach out next week with Rachel and 638's conditions. We know Rachel has cancer, but it's treatable. I'm curious about the other. What do you know about her?"

"Not much," he said. "She's an operative from the future. I'm looking forward to asking her questions."

"I'll bet you are."

"And thanks for taking care of Hatcher. She's one of my best."

"I can see why. Well, I have work to do unless you have more questions?"

"Nope. We're all done. Thanks, Sheila."

Souther nodded and walked away.

"Hatcher, are you ready to go home?"

"Yes, sir," Hatcher said.

McKnight led her back to the center of the reception area and she knelt beside him to be inside his bubble. He pressed the beacon and they fell through the field of stars.

When they arrived at Telegraph Road, McKnight took Hatcher to his office. They sat at his conference table and he asked for her report.

"I lost my beacon, sir," she said. "It shouldn't have happened."

"How did you lose it?"

"I was unarmed when I jumped into Rachel's cell. The Operative had a weapon trained on me from the moment I arrived. I was too far away to attack. I should have had a weapon."

"While jumping into a detention center? No, it was a good decision. You didn't have the benefit of knowing the future to guide your actions. I'm okay with that and it turned out okay. What about the plague? Did you ask her?"

"Not directly, sir. I never got control of the conversation. But I yelled it out to her as she was jumping out. She asked me 'what plague' two times. The second time, she had mild panic in her voice... like there was something I knew that she didn't. No, I don't think she knows anything about a plague from the Mideast."

"I hope you're right," he said. "For the record, I believe you are, and that's something to celebrate. I think we can put this plague issue to rest. I'll do a follow-up interview later, but I believe we're in the clear."

"Glad to hear it, sir. I'm sure the rest of the team will agree."

"Okay," he said as he stood. "You're dismissed, Captain. I have to get home to my wife-to-be. It's late on Saturday and I've worked half the weekend."

Hatcher came to attention and saluted. "Very good, sir. Good night."

Thursday, January 15th, 2037 - 2:24 PM EST - McKnight's office, Telegraph Road, Alexandria, Virginia

McKnight sat in his office, reading about George Washington. In a few days, the Team would embark on his most important mission and he wanted to know everything he could about the man's history.

His desk phone pinged, and he checked it.

It's General Drake.

He picked up the phone. "Hello, General, it's nice to hear from you."

"Good afternoon, Marc," Drake said. "How are the wedding plans coming?"

"Almost complete, sir," he said. "Megan is wrapping up a few details. We're nearly there."

"That's great. Good to hear. I have my invitation and I'll be there for the ceremony."

"Thank you, sir. Megan will be delighted to hear it. What can I do for you, sir?"

"First," he said, "Congratulations on wrapping up the 2086 plague issue. From what I understand, it looks like we've stopped it from happening."

"Yes, sir. As far as we can tell. There may be variables we don't know about or can't control, but we've addressed and mitigated the risks we know about."

"And you have Rachel Patterson and the operative in custody. That's a bonus."

"Yes, sir."

"Is it true they both have cancerous tumors?"

"Yes, sir."

"What's the prognosis for the two women? Are they in trouble?"

"Yes, sir, they are. Rachel's tumor was small and operable. They've already removed it and she is responding to treatment. The operative, not so much."

"And?" Drake said.

"And her condition is terminal, sir. Like Hatcher, she was a skilled fighting machine, but the cancer is widespread and she's not going to make it. They give her three months, max."

"What can we do for her?"

"We're already doing all we can. We're keeping her comfortable. I'm talking to Rachel about the state of cancer treatment and research in the future. I want permission to take the operative to 2087 and see what they can do for her."

"A gracious thing to do. Do you have any roadblocks I can help move?"

"Maybe, sir. There's hesitation up the line because she killed three people we know about in our time. She'll stand trial in Nevada for murder if she survived. They're already trying to get her pulled out of the Iceberg and into a local cancer center."

"I see. And what do you think?"

"She probably deserves death, sir," McKnight said. "But I'd rather see her healed and then stand trial. But I guess I'd feel differently if those killed were from my family. As it is, the Operative is who they trained her to be. She didn't choose this life. According to Rachel, they trained these Operatives from birth to hold their mission more important than anything else, including human life. But mentally and physically, she's the same as Hatcher and you know how strong *her* moral code is. So I feel sympathy for her, but I'm angry with her for what she's done."

"I see. It's a moral dilemma if I've ever seen one. But it sounds like you've thought it through. For the record, I'm ambivalent about it myself. I'll talk to General Flynn and we'll see what we can work out."

"Yes, sir. Thank you, sir."

"Marc, I do have some bad news. Because of a couple of snafus, I'm pulling Ed Cutty and Daisy Lagunas from your team and moving them to Major Tyler's team. I'm sorry, but he has an immediate need for two more experienced resources. Cutty and Lagunas are the closest we have to that, without taking Hatcher and Wheeler from you."

"But, sir—"

"I know, Marc. I know." Drake paused. McKnight sensed Drake was making a hard choice. "Major Tyler's mission needs them early next week. The good news is that, while you're losing those two, you keep the headcount, plus a headcount for a new X.O.."

"So I lose two officers, but I now have headcount for three resources?"

"Correct. Losing Major Tyler from your team hurt, but now you have permission to select a new X.O. and two new officers. I've heard there are a couple of people vying for the X.O. job."

"Really? Who's that, sir?"

"I think we'll wait on that. I've heard, but I don't know anything concrete. We'll both find out soon, I guess."

"Permission to speak freely, sir?"

"Of course."

"This is unlike you, sir," McKnight said. "Being so mysterious. What's going on, if I may ask?"

"Enlightenment and change, Marc. I'll see you later. Thanks for understanding about Cutty and Lagunas. You'll have a full complement of teammates soon."

"Yes, sir. I hope so."

"Well, I have another meeting. I'll be in touch soon. Have a great day."

"Yes, sir," McKnight said. "Goodbye."

He disconnected the phone.

Well, at least I get to keep the headcount. And added one as well, somehow. I wonder who he's thinking about?

Monday, January 19th, 2037 - 4:15 PM EST - McKnight's Office, Telegraph Road, Alexandria, Virginia

McKnight sat in his office at the end of a long day.

Tomorrow, Wade Harrison would become the new President of the United States. Harrison supported the HERO Team and the work they were doing. With the change of leadership, McKnight would again be the decision maker for his team's missions. That was a relief.

McKnight expected to meet with Arthur Smalls today for the final report on his team oversight. Though Smalls had been a pain in the beginning, McKnight had to admit the man was competent and resourceful. Smalls was an asset to the team while he was here, and McKnight would be sorry to see him go.

He's probably got several good assignment opportunities coming up.

A knock at his door interrupted his thoughts.

"Come," he said.

It was Smalls.

"Good afternoon, Colonel," he said.

"Good afternoon. Have a seat if you like."

Smalls sat in one of the guest chairs.

"I presume you're here for a final readout, Smalls," McKnight said. "It's been instructive and informative to have you here."

"I'll take that as a compliment, Colonel," Smalls said. "My assignment ends at noon tomorrow and I wanted to circle back to give you my report."

"Very good, sir. Well, let's get started. How'd we do? I know Vice President Crumpton was not a big fan of time travel."

"No, he's not, sir. And he still isn't, but his bias will be history as of tomorrow."

"Bias?"

"Yes, sir. I admit I was skeptical about the time travel capability. I was convinced it was a colossal opportunity to screw things up, but I tried to keep an open mind. You and your team's commitment to keeping history in line impressed me. Even when President Taylor ordered you to change history, you argued against it, but then followed orders and then helped fix the resulting disaster."

"Thank you, Smalls. I'm glad you saw it that way. We started as a research organization, but once we found bad actors out there, we turned into a repair team and, occasionally, time cops."

"It's a shame that it's necessary. You and the rest of the team are doing excellent work here."

"You held up your end. Your contribution to Kathy's time trap idea was genius and a significant improvement over the original solution."

"Thank you, sir."

"No problem. So, what's next for you, Smalls? Another exotic assignment in some foreign country, keeping America safe from her enemies?"

Smalls laughed. "I have options. Over the years, most of my assignments have been in the armpits of the world. I was always trying to get someone out of a country, or keep them *in* it and away from America. Regardless, they were all less fun than this assignment."

McKnight paused.

What does that mean? Does he want to work with us?

"Are you suggesting something, or am I reading too much into that statement?"

"Colonel, while I've worked with you, I've seen some things I haven't seen in a while. I admire your integrity. I know that, if you say you'll do something, you'll move heaven and earth if necessary to get it done. And you struggle to do the right thing instead of the easy thing. There isn't much of that here in Washington."

"Well, thanks for that, Smalls. It's much appreciated."

"It's also in the way you treat your team. Wheeler tells me you don't ask anyone to do something you wouldn't do yourself."

McKnight shook his head. "Except talk to Rachel."

Smalls laughed again. "That was a strategic delegation. You would've talked to her if necessary."

McKnight shrugged. "You're probably right, but I do have a superior team who pick up the slack."

"Yes, a team you personally trained. I have to tell you this is what I've been looking for. I'd like to be considered for a role on your team."

"Seriously?"

"Yes, sir. A long tenure at the CIA makes you a cynical S.O.B.. I'd like to do work that's more honest and I can see the results of the work. You and your team make a difference. I want to be part of it."

He is *serious.*

"I'm honored, Smalls," McKnight said. "Do you have any idea what you'd like to do? I should probably ask what other qualifications you have, other than being a spook?"

"I heard through scuttlebutt you were looking for a new X.O., sir. I have experience there. But I do have one potentially disqualifying event in my history and I'd like to get it out on the table."

"What's that, Smalls?"

"There's no easy way to say it, so I guess I'll just throw it out there. Before I was a CIA guy, I spent ten years in the Marines and then two years on SEAL Team Four."

"You were a Navy SEAL? My God, man, what were you thinking?"

Smalls stopped talking and blinked.

McKnight laughed. "Sorry, Smalls. I couldn't resist. Hatcher told me about your 'dirty' secret and it's safe with me."

Smalls gave a timid smile.

"All kidding aside, we have huge respect for the SEALS teams. That experience carries considerable weight. You'd be an asset to our team."

"Thank you, sir."

"Hatcher also told me she sparred with you in PT and you nearly beat her in martial arts. That's impressive — I've only beaten her once, and it was on my best day. Between that and your brains, you'd be a handy man to have around. Can you deal with me being your commanding officer? That's a bit of a switch, I know."

"It's okay with me, Colonel. You treat your team with respect. That's all I need. Well, that and interesting assignments."

McKnight nodded. "Well, *that* I'm pretty sure I can promise. The job is yours — *if* you want it and *if* the CIA will let you take it."

Smalls rose and saluted. "Thank you, sir. I'm confident I can get it done. I look forward to being on the team."

McKnight rose and returned the salute. "Thanks for coming by, Smalls."

"Yes, sir." Smalls turned on his heel and left the office.

McKnight sat again.

Well, I didn't see that coming. Things are looking up.

CHAPTER FIFTY

January 23rd, 2037 - 2:45 PM EST - McKnight's office, Telegraph Road, Alexandria, Virginia

McKnight opened the door to his office and found the desk phone ringing. He set his notepad on the desk and sat as he answered it.

"Colonel McKnight. May I help you?"

"Marc, it's Sheila Souther. How are you?"

"Hi, Sheila. I'm just fine," he said. "How are you?"

"Good. I hear you're getting married soon. Congratulations."

"Thanks. Tomorrow as a matter of fact. So, what can I do for you?"

"Could you please add Captain Hatcher to the call? It concerns her, too."

"Sure thing. Stand by for a second."

McKnight added Hatcher to the call.

"Sheila, you there?"

"Yes, sir."

"Hatcher?"

"Yes, sir."

"The wonders of modern telecommunications. You have us both now, Sheila. What's going on?"

"Thanks, Colonel. First, the last time we talked, you asked us to look into the cause of the cancer Rachel and the Operative both have."

"Yes, and we thought the personal shield they used may have caused it?"

"Yes, sir. Rachel is convinced it was the shield. She thought it had a flaw that exposed the user to radiation, and she was right. And the other woman... 638? She admits to using the shield a lot. She used it multiple times to penetrate my facility."

McKnight thought she sounded irritated.

"Did your guys check out the shield?"

"Yes, they did. The power supply leaks an unidentified radiation. They're afraid to test it much because they can't identify the radiation type and they don't want to risk exposing anyone to a confirmed carcinogen. They're not even sure lead shielding stops it."

"Wow," McKnight said. "And it's terminal for 638? How much time does she have?"

"A month, give or take a week."

"That bad?" he said. "I'm sorry she's dying. I want to find out more about her... where she came from and how she tracked Rachel to Nevada."

"Me, too," Hatcher said.

"Well, you can ask her. That's my second reason for calling. She asked to speak to you."

"When?" McKnight said. "I'm getting married tomorrow. I can't get out there for at least a week, and—"

"Not you, Marc," Souther said. "Sorry, I should have been more specific. She wants to talk to Captain Hatcher."

"Me?" Hatcher said.

"Yes, Captain. I suggest sooner rather than later. She's losing more and more strength every day."

"Yes, ma'am," Hatcher said. "How about Monday? The Colonel can't be there, but I can."

"Sounds perfect. Let's do it around oh-nine-hundred, my time. Does that work for you?"

"Yes, ma'am."

"And I have a question for you, Captain. How come this Operative looks like you? I'd swear you two are related."

"It's true—sort of," Hatcher said. "If 638 is to be believed, they cloned her from my blood. We should get that tested. Should be easy to find out, right? Take a blood sample of us both and compare them? I'm pretty sure it's true. She's a direct copy of me, for all intents and purposes. Except her environment and belief systems differ from mine."

"Good idea," McKnight said. "Can we do that, Sheila? When Hatcher comes out there, can your doctor check Hatcher and do the comparison? Doctor Wu and Doctor Astalos would kill me if we neglected to do this. And it may have other ramifications. For example, we know there's an issue when two people with the same DNA time-jump to the same place at the same time."

"Okay," Sheila said. "So, Hatcher, I'll expect you at 9:00 AM on Monday morning."

"Yes, ma'am. I'll be there."

"Hatcher," McKnight said, "Stay on the line for a minute."

"I'll talk to you later, Marc," Sheila said. "See you Monday, Hatcher." Then she disconnected the call.

"Still there, Hatcher?"

"Yes, sir."

"Okay. When I get back in town, I want an update on your visit. I want to know what you learned."

"Yes, sir."

"And we'll see you tomorrow?"

"I wouldn't miss it, sir. See you then."

Saturday, January 24th, 2037 - 5:48 PM EST - Lakewood Baptist Church, Gainesville, Georgia

"And here's to the new President of the United States, Wade Harrison!" Tyler said, and raised his champagne glass.

The HERO Team, General Drake, Arthur Smalls, and Doctor Astalos all shouted, "Here, here!"

It was unusual to see the entire team in their dress uniforms and smiling. McKnight couldn't remember the last time he saw it.

"I might add that," Drake said, "yesterday morning, an executive order removed the restrictions imposed by the previous administration. The order restores the ability of the team to operate independently and autonomously. Congratulations, Colonel McKnight, and thank you, Major Smalls, for making the last few weeks easier than they might have been."

Smalls raised his glass and smiled. While he was not yet officially a member of the HERO Team, the Marine Corps reinstated him as a major. He would soon report to McKnight as his executive officer.

Tyler had returned from his latest mission to 1762. Things were progressing as expected. He gained Francis Marion's confidence and was commissioned as a Major in the North Carolina Regulars.

Tyler, Cutty, and Lagunas impressed Marion with their leadership and performance in the French and Indian War. They were exceeding their goals for integrating with the Colonists and hoped their tactics would come to the attention of General George Washington once the War for Independence started. But that was years in the future from 1762.

Kathy Wu stuck her head in the door. "Hatcher? Wheeler? We're ready for you guys."

Hatcher and Wheeler set their glasses down on the linen-covered high-top table, saluted the General, and left the room.

Cutty, Lagunas, and Smalls made eye contact with each other.

"Well," Smalls said, "I guess we should go, too. Good luck, everyone." The three saluted the General and left the room.

Drake turned to McKnight. "And now we come to it. We said everything that needed to be said last night. Today's mission will be the hardest you've ever undertaken, but also the most rewarding. Once you've begun it, then we'll get moving on the Washington mission. Good luck, Colonel."

Astalos raised his glass with the General. "It's about time, too," he said. The two turned and left the room.

McKnight and Tyler stood alone in the room.

"We've come a long way together, Marc. Thanks for letting me help with this."

"No one was more qualified, Winnie. Salud!"

They raised their glasses in a last toast. As they sipped from their glasses, Kathy stuck her head back in the room and spoke with her lowest, most doomsday voice. "It's time."

Tyler extended his hand to McKnight and said, "Good luck, Marc. I'll see you on the other side."

McKnight followed him out of the pastor's ready room into the sanctuary of the Lakewood Baptist Church in Gainesville, Georgia.

Senior Pastor Emeritus Tom Smiley met them outside the door. He whispered in McKnight's ear. "Take care of Megan, Marc. She's one of my favorites." He embraced both men with a bear hug, then joined the congregation.

Tyler said, "So, who's performing the ceremony?"

"Tom's son Tyler. He became senior pastor when Tom retired, years ago. Megan knows him better than Tom."

McKnight and Tyler joined Senior Pastor Tyler Smiley at the altar. Wheeler, Hatcher, and Trevor stood with them there. Three of Megan's long-time friends stood on the other side of the altar.

McKnight scanned the room for familiar faces. He didn't know many people in Gainesville. His mother and Janie were in the front row, and several of his West Point classmates were in attendance.

On Megan's side, he saw Megan's grandmother, Merrie McAllister Tyler. He made eye contact with her, and she waved and blew him a kiss. Merrie was a kindred spirit to McKnight. Their family swore that Megan was the spitting image of Merrie when she was the same age.

The wedding march began, and McKnight focused on the end of the main aisle. There stood Megan and her father. She was so beautiful, he could hardly breathe.

He gave his soon-to-be wife the biggest smile he owned.

"Who knew?" Tyler said under his breath. "My cousin cleans up pretty good, doesn't she?"

Wheeler, standing on the other side of Tyler, chuckled.

McKnight had to agree.

The wedding march music began. As Megan and her father moved down the aisle toward him, a sense of rightness and relief overcame McKnight. All his fears about commitment and lost opportunities disappeared, leaving only the vision before him. His friend, his lover, and his soulmate.

For the first time in his life, he didn't second-guess his decision.

With all his heart and mind, he knew Megan was the one he was waiting for. He thanked God for sending her to him.

CHAPTER FIFTY-ONE

Friday, January 30th, 2037 - 7:30 AM EST - McKnight's office, Telegraph Road, Alexandria, Virginia

Hatcher waited with a folder in her hand near the building entrance.

When McKnight arrived at the office, she saluted and fell in step with him.

He looks rested. Good.

"Good morning, sir. Welcome back."

"Thanks, Captain. What's on your mind this morning?" He opened his office door and set his backpack on the floor next to it.

She waved the folder in his direction. "I have a report for you from my meeting with the Operative. You said you wanted to hear about it when you got back."

"Yes, I do. Have a seat, Captain. Give me a minute here."

"Thank you, sir."

McKnight pulled some items out of his backpack and laid them on his desk, then leaned back in his chair.

"Okay, what do you have for me?" he said.

She pushed the folder across the desk to him.

"I'll give a verbal summary, sir, and you can read the report at your convenience. Rachel called 638 an Operative, and on reflection, that's the best way to describe her and what she did. She has no name, only the number 638. She had no parents other than her trainers. These people trained her to do black ops from birth. Learning to fight, kill, disrupt, create intrigue where there is none — that's what she learned as a child."

"According to her, the project was called the Operations Management Team, or OMT, and she and her peers were called Operatives. They rented them out to the highest bidder to perform favors. They paid them to kill political enemies, perform dirty tricks, set up blackmail opportunities, etcetera. Any kind of dirty trick you can think of, someone trained them to do it."

"Wow, are you kidding?"

"I wish I was," Hatcher said. "She was better than most. She outlived almost all of her peers. After we grabbed Number Four and Rachel, she was engaged by Number Three to—"

"Number Three?" McKnight said.

"Yes, sir. Number Three was Number Four's boss, according to 638. It sounds like something from a low budget Hollywood spy movie, but that's what 638 called her. Number Three wanted Rachel back to do some deal, and didn't care about Number Four. So Number Three engaged 638 to bring Rachel back."

"That's almost absurd."

"Yes, sir, I know. You can't make this stuff up. If we hadn't dealt with those folks before, I wouldn't have believed it."

"What else did she say? Does she know the other members of the Deep State?"

"She doesn't, but she knows how we can find out."

"How's that?"

"The Operations Management Team were the brokers for the Operatives. Their offices are out in Reston, or at least they will be in 2087. Their computers are there as well. If we can get into their client database, we'll know who their customers are. We know Number Three and Number Four will be on the list. I'll bet we can figure out the rest."

"Your point is, there's opportunity here to find the rest of the Deep State people and stop their interference with our political system," McKnight said. "Okay, what else?"

Hatcher paused.

How do I talk about this?

"Spit it out, Captain," McKnight said. "What is it?"

"It's just that... she used me as a model for all her work."

"Huh?"

"They lied to her, sir. They told her I was some top-notch Black Ops person, and I was someone to look up to. *Me*, of all people. They made up an entire history of my Black Ops. Assassinations, revenge killings, kidnappings, you name it. They put me up as an example of the very best. They encouraged her to think of me when things got tough. They even suggested she use my image as motivation and encouragement, something to remind herself of who she was. She *killed* people because it's what she thought I would do."

"I see what you mean. You feel responsible for all the—"

"No, sir, I don't. But I'm angry they told her these lies and urged her to live up to them. These people manipulated her all her life. As a result, she's done terrible things. Now she's dying, and she's learned her entire life was based on a lie."

"Is that why she wanted to see you?"

"In part, sir," Hatcher said.

"What's the rest of it?"

"It's a little hard to explain, sir. But I believe she felt a connection with me. Maybe it's the common DNA, or maybe that we look alike. I don't know. Maybe she thought since I shared her DNA, I could be the one person who would understand her. So she wanted to tell me her story. And she did. I sat with her for three hours... until she ran out of energy. She's tough, but cancer is tougher."

"You think she wanted to confess to you?"

"Maybe at some level. Or maybe to sort out what's real and what isn't. She told me about her only friend. Another Operative."

"That's interesting. What did she say?"

Hatcher paused.

How do I explain this? She was introverted, like me.

"Captain, are you still with me?"

"Yes, sir. I'm not sure how to talk about this."

"Okay, take your time. If it's important to you..."

"It is, sir."

Wheeler said the Colonel is introverted. Maybe he'll get it.

"Her friend had a different personality. Unlike 638 and me, she was vibrant and outgoing and funny. It reminded me of... well, of my friendship with Wheeler. You know what that is. So I related to her on that point."

"Does she want you to contact the friend?"

"No, sir. Their trainers saw her friend's emotional qualities as weaknesses. When they were teenagers, an instructor killed her in training."

"No kidding? That's..."

"Brutal. There's no other way to describe it, sir. Brutal. 638 never forgot it and she never considered friendship again. Can you imagine that? These people exposed her to so much evil, and she was totally alone. No moral compass, no guiding principles except dedication to mission."

She paused.

I don't know where else to go with this story. We should act.

"Sir, isn't there something we can do? It's too late for her, but can't we stop the OMT somehow? Who knows how many Operatives are still active?"

McKnight thought for a moment.

"I understand your argument, Captain," he said. "A business that trains people to do black ops for the political class? It shouldn't exist."

"Yes, sir. No one should live that life. OMT treated them like animal predators because of the circumstance of their birth... because they were clones. But they're living, feeling, and cognizant people who should have rights."

"Another reason why cloning was banned," he said.

"Yes, sir. And if that isn't enough, I have another scary thought about this."

"What's that, Captain?"

"They sent an Operative to retrieve Rachel, and she came close to succeeding. These people are serious political weapons. The deep state in 2087 is still functioning. It's only a matter of time before they realize they can use Operatives against us in our time. I'm surprised it hasn't happened already. If we don't put a stop to these people, we could end up with a bunch of people like 638 in our time, actively working to shape history to their agenda."

McKnight sat still for a moment, then nodded. "I see your point, Captain. We've fought this battle twice now. If we don't stop them, we'll have to fight it over and over again. I'll talk to General Drake and see what he has to say. Maybe there's something we can do."

"Thank you, sir."

McKnight's desk phone rang.

"Hello..." he said into the phone. Hatcher stood and started to leave, but McKnight shook his head and motioned for her to stay.

"Yes, Sheila, hold on. I'll put you on speaker. Stand by."

He pressed a button and turned the speaker so that Hatcher could hear better.

"Can you hear us, Sheila? It's pretty early out there, isn't it? I have Hatcher right here with me."

"Yes, I can hear you, and yes, it's early. Hello, Captain. I'm glad I found you both. I just got a call from the infirmary at the Detention Center. They advised me the woman we know as 638 has died. I thought you'd like to know."

Hatcher looked at McKnight and leaned back in her chair. Her eyes glistened, but her face was like stone.

And so it ends. No resolution, no redemption.

"Thank you for letting us know," McKnight said. "Was she in any pain?"

"No, I don't think so. But..."

Hatcher leaned forward in her chair. "What, Major?"

"It's a little unusual," Souther said. "She was comatose, but she tried to get out of bed."

"Really?" Hatcher said.

"Yes. The nurse restrained her, then she laid back and passed on."

"Did she say anything?"

"She did. The nurse thought she was delirious. She said 'Let me go. It's 439.' The nurse thought she meant the time."

"439? You're sure?" Hatcher asked.

"Yes. She wrote it down. Do you think it means anything?"

Hatcher looked over McKnight's shoulder and through the transparent wall behind him. She saw the woods and the morning sky, and fluffy clouds with pink accents from the rising sun.

"Perhaps," she said, and smiled.

CHAPTER FIFTY-TWO

Sunday, February 2nd, 2087 - 10:00 AM EST - 31st St NW, Georgetown, DC

Laura Rand prepared for the day's work. As the President's advisor, she had many responsibilities.

Rand was known to some as Number Three, and her position enabled her to influence the resources at the President's fingertips. Today, she would help the President understand how it was in his best interests to accept a visit from Joe Kosar, the grandson of George Kosar, the legendary financier and leader of the Open World Order movement.

All the pieces were in place. Except one.

Her phone pinged. It was a message from the Operative.

> <<< *638: I have Major Rachel Patterson in my possession. I'm bringing her to you.* >>>

"Well, it's about damn time," Rand said aloud. She typed her response.

> <<< *003: Bring her to the office where we first met.*
> *Now.* >>>

She called for her assistant. "Bob, have the car brought around. I want to go to the Law Enforcement Center. And let them know I'm coming."

Bob nodded and carried her briefcase outside.

She gathered her purse and coffee and walked out her front door. Waiting for her was a long black limousine and a suburban lead car that carried her security detail. Bob stood by the limo with the back door open. She entered, and Bob followed. She sat on the bench seat on the left side. Bob rode opposite her in one of the folding seats by the door. He laid his data pad across his knees and prepared to take notes.

While the two drivers discussed the destination and the route, she stared out the window. Her stylish Georgetown home filled her view.

Excellent. With Rachel in my pocket, a deal with Kosar is all but assured.

The driver returned, slipped the limo into gear, and followed the Suburban out of her gated compound onto N Street. Rand relaxed as they drove through the dense residential neighborhood to 30th Street.

When they reached 30th Street, they obeyed the stop sign before turning. Rand looked out to the right. There on the corner stood the Operative and Rachel Patterson. Rachel was bound and gagged.

Rand called out to her driver. "Stop, stop. Check those two."

The driver spoke into his radio and shifted into 'Park'. The Suburban erupted with the security team armed with machine pistols. They surrounded the Operative and Rachel. Rand slid across to the right side so she could see better.

After talking to the Operative, the security chief approached the limo. Rand rolled the window down two inches.

"What?" Rand said.

"She, the tall one," he pointed at the Operative, "says she has a package for you. She isn't armed."

Rand frowned. "Bring her over here."

The security chief attempted to take the Operative by the arm, but she shrugged it off and stepped forward, dragging a stumbling and incoherent Rachel with her.

"What are you doing here?" Rand said. "You're supposed to meet me at the Law Enforcement Center."

The Operative shook her head. "I couldn't trust anyone. Someone hit the OMT last night. They destroyed all of OMT's records. I didn't dare use the regular channels. Everyone I know there is dead or gone."

"How did you find me?"

"I'm resourceful. Do you still want Major Patterson? Or shall I take her back to 2037?"

Rand looked at Rachel. She was leaning on the Operative, and her head lolled back and forth. Rand pointed at Rachel. "What's wrong with her?"

"I applied a sedative to ensure she was compliant."

"I see. What do you want, 638? I'm busy and I have a meeting to get to."

The Operative looked distressed. "Oh, I'm terribly sorry, ma'am. All I wanted was a few minutes of your time. But we'll just go to a hotel and you can let me know when you have time to meet with us. It's no problem at all." Then she cast her eyes down, like a maid waiting for her mistress to pick out shoes for the ball.

Rand stared at her for a moment. "I'm uncomfortable with this impromptu meeting, 638, and I don't appreciate your attitude. Why shouldn't I just take Rachel from you right now?"

The security chief stepped back and pointed his weapon at the Operative.

The Operative shrugged. "You could do that. I'm unarmed. I'm at your mercy." She paused. "But know something about Rachel first, before you decide."

"And what is that?"

Rand was becoming impatient.

"Rachel has ingested a poison, which will kill her in two hours without the antidote. I can give her the antidote, but I won't be able to if I'm not here with her."

Rand sighed heavily. "I grow weary of this game. And why wouldn't I have my team kill you and take the antidote instead of playing this little cat-and-mouse game with you?"

"Yes, that would work if I had it with me. But I don't. We have another stop to make."

Rand stared at the Operative, her anger growing.

The Operative smiled. "Look, Number Three, I just want a few minutes of your time. You promised me a big reward if I delivered Rachel, which I have. I just want to get paid, and I have additional information you might find useful. Maybe more useful than Rachel here."

"More useful? What is this? Are you trying to change the deal?"

"No, ma'am. I told you. I just want to get paid and disappear."

The Operative paused and looked both ways. She leaned toward the limo window and lowered her voice.

"You're not my only benefactor, Number Three. I know things about many people here in Washington. I have information to trade for additional reward. I want to retire and disappear."

Rand considered what the Operative said. *The information she has might be valuable. If it's not, I can always have her killed afterward. But bringing her into the car is risky.*

She looked at the security chief. The Operative was tall, but the chief was armed, six inches taller, and outweighed the Operative by seventy-five pounds. She took the risk.

"Get in," Rand said, and pointed to the security chief. "You, too, Charlie."

Rand unlocked the door and slid back across the bench seat. Rachel and the Operative got in and sat beside her. The chief took the right jump seat, facing the bench. Rand ordered the driver to proceed.

The security chief pointed his weapon at the Operative.

"Can we do without the cannon, Ms. Rand? I'm just here to talk business. I have no reason to hurt you. You're my benefactor."

"Sorry, 638," Rand said. "I take my security seriously."

"I appreciate that. However, I'm going to reveal information to you that some people would kill me for sharing with you. I'm taking an enormous risk in doing so, and I'd appreciate a gesture of good faith. For example, I know about Number Four's penchant for sex drugs. And I know his supplier."

Rand laughed and dismissed her with a wave. "Who cares? He's no longer a factor. Washington has forgotten him already. He's old news."

"Of course he is. And what about the person Number Two has watching your every move?"

Rand paused and stared at the Operative. *I knew about Number Four's addiction, but this is new. Could it be true?*

"Tell me what you know," she said.

The Operative looked at the security chief. "Could you *please* stop pointing that at me? You're making me nervous."

The chief glanced at Rand, and she shrugged. He pulled the weapon back toward his chest with the barrel pointed skyward.

"Thank you," the Operative said, then pointed at Rand's assistant Bob.

"Bob here is your man. Number Two threatened his sister to get his cooperation. He's done a good job — Number Two knows everything you do, including your little boyfriend in Alexandria."

Rand's eyes opened wide and turned to Bob.

Bob pointed at the Operative. "I haven't told anyone. She's lying."

Rand waved her hand at the chief, who turned his weapon toward Bob.

Bob shook his head and began to cry. "I haven't told anyone."

"Shut up. I'll deal with you later," Rand said. She turned back to the Operative.

"So you *do* have information worth trading. What do you want?"

The Operative nodded. "I want ten million dollars in diamonds and twenty-four hours to disappear. And I want to be left alone. The rest of the information I have will be more than worth my price."

"Holding up your benefactor for money is not what an Operative does."

"The OMT is out of business. There's no future for me here. I want to get lost with enough assets to be comfortable. You'll never see me again."

"I see."

Rand thought about the deal. *This isn't right. It doesn't pass the smell test. Something's wrong.*

She glanced from Bob to Charlie to the Operative and finally to Rachel.

She grabbed Rachel by the chin and turned her face back and forth. *Is this really Rachel?*

The skin on Rachel's face felt loose. Rand pinched her cheek and pulled. She peeled off a layer of skin to reveal an Asian face.

A skin mask!

"This isn't Rachel," she said with a gasp.

The Operative kicked and slammed the security chief's weapon hand against the hard plexiglass of the cabin partition. The bones in his hand broke with a loud pop. He winced at the pain, then reached for the Operative. Her second kick drove the cartilage in his nose back into his head. He lost consciousness.

Rachel's bonds came loose. "Hi," she said brightly, then looked at the floor of the cabin. "Oh, is this your briefcase? Let me see." She leaned forward.

Rand reached forward to prevent the woman from touching it, but the Operative grabbed her hand.

An aura of brilliant light surrounded the Operative, then expanded to cover Rand, her briefcase, and the woman between them.

Rand felt herself lurch forward out of her seat as the driver slammed on the limousine's brakes. A member of her security team pulled at the door handle.

Then she fell backward through a field of stars.

CHAPTER FIFTY-THREE

Friday, February 2nd, 2087 - 10:45 AM EST - Telegraph Road, HERO Team Lab

The new vintage Time Engine turned on by itself. Travelers were returning. McKnight and General Drake stood behind Wheeler and Trevor at the Engine console.

Three white silhouettes appeared on the platform.

"They look like they're sitting down," Wheeler said.

The silhouettes became people, and they dropped onto the platform when the aura dissipated. It was Hatcher, an older woman, and Kathy Wu.

"There you go, Trevor," Wheeler said. "She's fine."

"Yeah, but my nerves are shot."

Hatcher helped Kathy to her feet. Then the older woman.

"You'll pay for this, 638," the woman said.

"I'm not your Operative, Ms. Rand," Hatcher said, and peeled off the makeup that faked a scar on her cheek and added ten years to her appearance.

McKnight and Drake stepped over to the platform. Hatcher saluted them, and McKnight asked for her report.

"Yes, sir," she said. "Meet Ms. Laura Rand, the President's most influential political advisor. In 2087, that is. She's also known as Number Three, the person responsible for sending the Operative 638 after Rachel Patterson, and the deaths of at least three people."

"How dare you treat me like this?" Rand said.

"Oh, I think your treatment is a good deal more reasonable than your intentions," Drake said. He turned to McKnight. "Is that all of them?"

"Yes, sir, it is. The records in the OMT's headquarters identified the conspirators. We now have them all in custody, either in the Iceberg or on their way there."

Rand searched from face to face, looking for a friend. There was none to be found. Hatcher pulled her arms back and slipped handcuffs around her wrists.

Trevor and Wheeler joined the group on the platform.

Kathy slipped her arm around Trevor's waist, her face flush with excitement. "That was outstanding! I got to go on a mission and be part of it."

"Yup."

"You didn't want me to go, did you?"

"Not really, but I can't tell you what to do."

She put her arms around his neck and pulled him down to kiss him.

"That's why I love you so much, Trevor George. You get me." She released him. "I hope I get to do another mission." She darted away before he could speak.

"Well," Wheeler said. "Maybe you didn't have any say."

Trevor tried to frown, but chuckled instead. "I might as well tell her not to breathe."

McKnight motioned for Wheeler to come forward.

"Captain Wheeler," McKnight said. "Please escort Ms. Rand to her new accommodations in the Iceberg. Tell Major Souther that Rand is our last contribution to her little underground hotel."

"With pleasure, sir."

Wheeler took Rand by the arm and led her away.

Hatcher approached McKnight. "A minute, sir?"

"Yes, Captain, what can I do for you?"

"I just wanted to thank you, sir, for making it possible for 638's life to count for something. I think there was a good heart in there somewhere."

"It was the right thing to do, anyway. The war between the future and the present is over. It's good to know Rachel and her associates were a radical faction within the government, and not the whole thing."

"We know that, sir? How?"

"Easy. General Drake and I time-jumped with President Harrison to see President Nelson in 2087. They had a nice long talk."

"You did?"

"President Nelson had his suspicions, but no proof. We gave him what he needed to clean house. President Harrison promised we would bring them here, keep them alive and comfortable, but out of government forever."

"And President Harrison's staff let him time travel? I'll bet that was an interesting discussion."

"It was a short discussion. He *is* the President, after all."

"I see. Um...."

"Yes, Captain?"

"I was just wondering, sir. How will he explain all these top government people going missing?"

"The public story is they were all on a plane, flying to a secret peace conference in Norway. The plane went down in the North Atlantic. No survivors. Very sad."

"Would the people believe that?"

"Maybe. Maybe not," McKnight said. "But they probably *would* believe they were all on a plane to a tropical island for a weekend of sex and drugs. *Big* scandal. That's the confidential story leaked to the conspiracy theory websites."

Hatcher laughed. "Yes, they might believe that. What's next, sir?"

"If we can manage it, a couple of days off."

"That would be great, sir. And then?"

McKnight paused and smiled.

"1787, Captain. The President has ordered us to risk screwing up our history to save our country from the politicians. If that's possible."

"Sounds like a worthy endeavor, Colonel. May I request to be included in this project, sir?"

"I wouldn't have it any other way, Captain."

The End

A Note from The Author:

Dear Reader:

I hope you enjoyed reading Time Plague as much as I enjoyed writing it. I have to tell you, I really fell in love with these characters since I started this series.

Sometimes I get asked if I have a favorite character. I like all of them for their variety, but I do have favorites and they change over time. Originally, it was Marc McKnight. To me, he's a lot like the Ranger Aragorn from The Lord of the Rings.

As the series progressed, I've gravitated toward Karen Hatcher. She's hard as steel and as close to Wonder Woman as they come. But there's this compassionate side that sneaks out front once in a while.

From the first book in the series, I've gotten notes from folks asking about the characters and telling me which are their favorites. I love feedback from readers. Tell me what you liked, what you loved, and even what you hated. I'd love to hear from you. You can write to me at kim@authorKimMegahee.com and visit me on the web at the address below.

Finally, I need a favor. If you're so inclined, I'd love it if you would post a review of Time Plague. Loved it, hated it. Whatever — I'd just like to hear your feedback. Reviews can be tough to come by these days, and you, the reader, have the power to make or break a book. If you have the time, please post an honest review of this book. Here's a link to my author page, along with all my books on Amazon here: https://www.amazon.com/~/e/B086N5Y73J

Thank you so much for reading Time Plague and for spending time with me.

Cheers and regards,
Kim Megahee
Website: www.AuthorKimMegahee.com

Coming Soon...

Marc McKnight meets Virginia citizen George Washington in 1787.

ABOUT THE AUTHOR

Kim Megahee is a writer, musician, and computer consultant. He retired from an IT consulting career in 2017 to focus on his writing career and performing live music.

Kim lives in Gainesville, Georgia with his soulmate wife Martha and Leo, the incredibly smart, but stubborn red-headed toy poodle.